PRAISE FOR KE

"Readers coming in cold to this thriller won't have to worry about missing the series' previous books: It reads just fine as a standalone plot, its wintry twists and turns paced adroitly and warmed up with a touch of romance."

—*The Oregonian* on *A Merciful Secret*

"Elliot delivers a fast-paced, tense thriller that plays up the small-town atmosphere and survivalist mentality, contrasting it against an increasingly connected world. The romantic angle is subtle, with the established relationship between Mercy and Truman slowly and satisfyingly maturing as they solve the mystery."

—*Publishers Weekly* on *A Merciful Secret*

"Each Mercy Kilpatrick mystery improves on the last . . . In this third installment, the whodunit, a tale that blends a hint of the paranormal with some all-too-human ghastliness, is engaging, but the real power comes from watching Mercy evolve as an individual."

—*RT Book Reviews* on *A Merciful Secret*

"In the debut of her new Mercy Kilpatrick series, Elliot crafts an eerily fascinating small town. An air of menace is palpable throughout the story, and the characters hide a wealth of secrets and twisted loyalties."

—*Romantic Times Book Reviews* on *A Merciful Death*

"In Elliot's latest gripping novel the mystery and suspense are top-notch, and the romance embedded within will quench love story junkies' thirst, too. The author's eye for detail makes this one play out more like a movie rather than a book. It can easily be read as a standalone but is obviously much better if the prior three are digested first."

—*Romantic Times Book Reviews* on *Targeted*

"Elliot's latest addition to her thrilling, edge-of-your-seat series Bone Secrets will scare the crap out of you, yet allow you to swoon over the building romantic setting, which provides quite the picturesque backdrop. Her novel contains thrills, chills, snow, and . . . hey, you never know! The surprises and cliffhangers are satisfying, yet edgy enough to keep you feverishly flipping the pages."

—*Romantic Times Book Reviews* on *Known*

"Elliot's best work to date. The author's talent is evident in the characters' wit and smart dialogue . . . One wouldn't necessarily think a psychological thriller and romance would mesh together well, but Elliot knows what she's doing when she turns readers' minds inside out and then softens the blow with an unforgettable love story."

—*Romantic Times Book Reviews* on *Vanished* (Top Pick)

"Kendra Elliot does it again! Filled with twists, turns, and spine-tingling details, *Alone* is an impressive addition to the Bone Secrets series."

—Laura Griffin, *New York Times* bestselling author

"Elliot once again proves to be a genius in the genre with her third heart-pounding novel in the Bone Secrets collection. The author knows romance and suspense, reeling readers in instantaneously and wowing them with an extremely surprising finish . . . Elliot's best by a mile!"

—*Romantic Times Book Reviews* on *Buried* (Top Pick)

"Make room on your keeper shelf! *Hidden* has it all: intricate plotting, engaging characters, a truly twisted villain. I can't wait to see what Kendra Elliot dishes up next!"

—Karen Rose, *New York Times* bestselling author

A MERCIFUL FATE

ALSO BY KENDRA ELLIOT

MERCY KILPATRICK NOVELS
A Merciful Death
A Merciful Truth
A Merciful Secret
A Merciful Silence

BONE SECRETS NOVELS
Hidden
Chilled
Buried
Alone
Known

BONE SECRETS NOVELLAS
Veiled

CALLAHAN & MCLANE NOVELS
PART OF THE BONE SECRETS WORLD
Vanished
Bridged
Spiraled
Targeted

ROGUE RIVER NOVELLAS

On Her Father's Grave (Rogue River)
Her Grave Secrets (Rogue River)
Dead in Her Tracks (Rogue Winter)
Death and Her Devotion (Rogue Vows)
Truth Be Told (Rogue Justice)

WIDOW'S ISLAND NOVELLAS

Close to the Bone

A MERCIFUL FATE

KENDRA ELLIOT

Montlake Romance

This is a work of fiction. Names, characters, organizations, places, events, and incidents are either products of the author's imagination or are used fictitiously.

Text copyright © 2019 by Oceanfront Press Company
All rights reserved.

No part of this book may be reproduced, or stored in a retrieval system, or transmitted in any form or by any means, electronic, mechanical, photocopying, recording, or otherwise, without express written permission of the publisher.

Published by Montlake Romance, Seattle

www.apub.com

Amazon, the Amazon logo, and Montlake Romance are trademarks of Amazon.com, Inc., or its affiliates.

ISBN-13: 9781503903302
ISBN-10: 1503903303

Cover design by Eileen Carey

Printed in the United States of America

For my girls

ONE

Shep had left him behind.

Ollie didn't worry as he hiked through the woods. Even if he had no idea where Shep was, no doubt Shep knew exactly where Ollie was. The dog had bolted out of the old truck's cab when the teenager had opened the passenger door, and then he'd dashed from tree to tree, sniffing the air, his entire body quivering in excitement.

Shep needed his wild dog time in the forest.

Ollie needed it too.

His years of living alone in the woods had made the real world loud and crowded.

Or is this forest the real world?

He rested a hand against the distinctive red bark of a ponderosa pine, looked up through its branches at the perfect blue sky, and inhaled deeply. Dust, pine, and earth. Nothing was more real than this very moment.

The warm day in May was cooler in the woods and hills, and his heart felt lighter and his senses more focused in the quiet. He could think clearly out here. He sent a mental note of thanks to Christian

Lake, who'd suggested that Ollie hike his property to get away from town.

Hundreds of acres to roam. No one around.

Christian had been the first to hire him, giving Ollie a job in his sporting goods warehouse. Solid physical work that made Ollie feel good at the end of the day. After Ollie had driving lessons and passed his license test, he'd also been hired at a Chevy dealership. He moved, washed, and detailed cars. Or did whatever was needed.

He loved the smooth feeling of a car's shiny paint under his fingertips, and the excitement when he drove a car (ever so briefly) with three miles on the odometer. The smell of tires and oil had grown almost as addicting as the smell of the forest.

Between the two jobs, his tutor, and online classes, Ollie's days were full.

But every week Ollie made time to explore Christian's woods. It reset his soul. Brought him back in balance.

"Shep!" he shouted.

Ollie listened for the familiar sounds of Shep tearing through the scrubby underbrush.

Silence.

"Shep!"

There he is. Shep wasn't a big dog, but when he ran, he stomped and plowed headfirst through whatever was in his way, making plenty of noise. Ollie turned west, following the sounds of Shep's approach through the woods.

"Here, boy!"

The dog appeared, his eyes bright and excited, one of his floppy ears inside out. He slid to a stop in front of his master, dropped a stick, and looked expectantly at Ollie.

"Good boy." Ollie rubbed his dog's head and straightened the ear, scouting his surroundings for a good place to play a boisterous game of fetch. They'd have to move. He couldn't throw the stick more than ten feet in this part of the woods.

Giving the dog's ears a scratch, Ollie picked up the stick. "Let's go . . ."

The bark felt wrong to his fingers. Ollie stared at the stick in his hand, eyeing the shallow grooves and smoothed ridges. One end was slightly pointed; the other end was slightly bulbous.

Bone.

He blew out a breath and gave a short laugh. *It's from an animal, of course.*

Photos of bones from an old magazine flashed in his head. He'd read his grandfather's small stack of *National Geographic* magazines dozens of times, memorizing the fascinating images. Ollie's education had been . . . limited . . . sporadic. But he clearly remembered one photo of a skeleton in Africa.

What if it's human?

He waved the bone in the direction Shep had appeared from. "Let's go, Shep. Where'd you find this?"

The dog bounded off and Ollie followed. *As if he understood what I said.*

He scrambled after Shep, who appeared to be on a mission. The dog never looked back. A few minutes later, Shep vanished through the open front door of a cabin with a collapsing roof. It was tucked among several tall pines. Ollie stopped and stared. No paths or driveways led to the pine needle–covered cabin. The stillness and lack of upkeep indicated it was empty, but Ollie wanted to make sure.

"Hello, the house!"

Shep appeared in the doorway, his tail wagging in an invitation for Ollie to join him.

"What did you find, boy?" Ollie moved closer, judging the stability of the roof.

A sharp pang lanced his chest as he thought of the cabin where he'd lived alone for two years after his grandfather had died. Where he'd read old books and played card games alone every night because there was no electricity. Where he'd brought Truman after rescuing him from men who'd wanted to kill him and where he'd then nursed the police chief back to health.

After he'd agreed with Truman that he needed to attend school and rejoin society, Truman had taken Ollie to pack up his belongings. The cabin he'd built with his grandfather was smaller than his new bedroom in Truman's home. It'd felt claustrophobic, and the small room of belongings seemed cheap and shabby. Truman had noticed his hesitation over packing up his grandfather's battered books. "The value isn't in the books' condition, Ollie. The value is in the memories they awaken in your heart and mind."

Truman had been right. Every time Ollie touched the books, he remembered them in his grandfather's rough hands and heard his low voice as he read to Ollie each evening.

Ollie suspected this cabin's roof wouldn't fully collapse anytime soon, so he tentatively stepped through the doorway. The door had been bashed in at one point. The wood frame was splintered and broken where the lock would have been. The floor was dirt. *What a piece of crap.* The whole thing appeared speedily thrown together. Plywood walls, studs too far apart. A large hole in the roof allowed in sunlight that worked its way down through the trees and lit the interior. Water damage streaked and stained every wall, but the interior was currently dry. It smelled of decay, mold, and old dirt.

Shep whined and padded to the far corner. He halted and looked over his shoulder at Ollie, who stepped closer. Ollie squatted and studied the items in the corner.

The bones were intertwined with scraps of dirty and stained fabric. Rotting Nike tennis shoes. The man had lain down and never gotten up.

In place of the right eye socket, the skull had a giant rough hole.

Ollie automatically looked up and spotted the bullet hole in the wall of the cabin.

At the height of a man's head.

◆ ◆ ◆

Eagle's Nest police chief Truman Daly hated the crumbling cabin on sight. Dread stirred in his stomach and expanded as he stepped inside.

Molding odors slapped him in the face and threatened to set loose buried memories.

Focus.

He squatted next to some rotting lengths of fabric on the floor, eyed the long zippers, and realized they'd once been sleeping bags. The stuffing hadn't decomposed; it'd just flattened and turned brown, making Truman wonder what sort of hardy fibers had insulated the bags. Besides the sleeping bags and the remains, there was little else in the cabin. A few rusted food cans that had lost their labels. Two plastic gallon jugs of water—still full. A rusted can opener. A bag of plastic spoons, forks, and knives.

They didn't plan to stay long.

"There's a ring of rocks outside that could have been a firepit," said Deschutes County detective Evan Bolton, standing behind Truman.

"Let's see," Truman said, grabbing the excuse to get out of the cabin.

Outside, Ollie, Christian Lake, and two Deschutes County deputies waited.

Ollie had called Truman as he hiked back toward Christian's home, unable to get cell service at the body's location. After hearing Ollie's description of the remains, Truman had notified the Deschutes County Sheriff's Office and requested a detective. Everyone had arrived

5

at Christian Lake's rugged forest mansion at nearly the same time, ready to hike to the location. Christian had insisted on accompanying the group, emphasizing that the land was his.

When they'd arrived at the shack, Christian had shaken his head. "I had no idea this existed. I've never been out this way."

Detective Bolton had raised a brow at him, and Christian had stared back. "Do you have any idea how much untouched land is out here?" the millionaire had asked.

Christian had been silent since, quietly listening and observing, staying out of the way. Truman wondered what was going on in Christian's head, considering one of his employees had been murdered on his property about four months ago. Truman liked Christian; the sporting goods store owner and Truman's fiancée, Mercy, went way back.

"Over here," Bolton indicated, and Truman followed him to the far side of the shack. Next to the ring of large stones were a few rusting tin cans showing through the layers of pine needles and dirt.

"Why do I get the impression they weren't used to roughing it?" Truman murmured.

"Agreed," said Bolton. "Cans, plasticware, sleeping bags. Weekend getaway, I guess."

"Wasn't a fun weekend for the guy inside," added Truman.

"Are you sure it was a male?" Bolton's brown gaze met Truman's. "There's no wallet."

"Not completely. I'm no bone expert. But there were a few things I spotted . . . The shoes were men's . . . The belt looked male—"

"Neither of those rule out female."

"True." Truman took a deep breath and went back inside the cabin, breathing lightly through his mouth, telling himself that the scents of this cabin and those of the one he'd been chained up in two months ago were distinctly different.

No shit or piss odors. No constant smell of rain that I can't drink.

His heart pounded in his ears, he closed his eyes, and he was back in the past. Chains. Cuffs. Beat to hell. A broken arm. After months of not needing it, Truman immediately launched a silent anxiety mantra.

Name one thing you can see.

The fucking gigantic hole in the roof.

Name two things you can hear.

Bolton talking to Ollie. Shep's panting.

Name three things you can smell.

Dirt, rot, dust.

Truman opened his eyes. *I'm not in that prison.* He sucked in a deep breath and concentrated on the crime scene before him.

He and Bolton silently stood next to the pile of bones. Some connective tissues were still attached, and Truman spotted little gnaw marks here and there. "All the tiny hand bones are gone," Truman pointed out. "Vermin, probably." He didn't want to touch the old Nikes; they weren't empty.

"Damned scavengers."

"The skull doesn't look feminine," Truman stated.

Bolton waited, looking at him expectantly.

"See those big ridges above the eye sockets? And how the forehead slopes back? I think that means it was a man. Mercy and I have talked about the differences before."

"Sounds more like a Neanderthal."

Truman snorted. "Maybe he was."

Someone had believed the man should die. One of the eye sockets had been destroyed—probably the bullet entrance—and there was a large hole in the back of the skull. Truman imagined that was the exit wound, but he could be wrong. Had the man been shot in the face or from the back?

The medical examiner would know how to tell.

The bullet hole in the wall gave Truman the creeps. It was at his eye level, and he could see directly through it.

"Hey, Truman, are you about done?" Ollie asked, standing just outside the door. He'd refused to enter the shack when they'd returned. "Something bad happened in there," he'd repeated several times to Truman. "I saw enough."

"Give me a few more minutes." Technically the murder case was Bolton's since it'd happened outside the Eagle's Nest city limits. But Truman had a vested interest. It had been found by Ollie, Truman's . . . *What is Ollie to me? A ward? A friend?* Truman shook his head. He'd asked himself the question a dozen times over the last two months since Ollie had saved his life in the woods. *What do you call the person who saved you from dying multiple times?* To him there was no word to describe the bond he felt with the teenage orphan.

Anyway, Ollie had found the remains; therefore, Truman was interested.

No weapons were in the shack. No personal items. And clearly a lot of time had gone by since the death, because most of the bones were bare and the fabrics had nearly disintegrated. Possibly decades had passed.

"Look here," said Bolton.

Truman turned at Bolton's sharp tone. He had lifted part of a sleeping bag with a stick in his gloved hand. The rotted fabric fell into tiny pieces, but the filling stayed intact. Truman spotted what had caught Bolton's eye. There were several small, flat bags under the sleeping bag's remains. They looked heavy duty, made out of a vinyl that hadn't decomposed.

Bolton slid one out with his foot. It wasn't much bigger than his shoe and had one zippered side.

Truman could make out the faded logo. A big number one.

Below the logo it read First Interstate Bank.

Bank money . . . or money on its way to a bank.

Curiosity got the better of Bolton and he unzipped it. "Empty." He checked the others. "All empty."

Truman glanced back at the remains in the corner. "We may have found the motive."

"And I might have to hand over this case." Bolton sighed. "If this is related to a bank robbery, it belongs to the FBI."

TWO

FBI special agent Mercy Kilpatrick hid her excitement as she headed toward the meeting room. She'd never landed a notorious case before.

A nearly thirty-year-old armored car robbery. A murdered driver. Multiple missing suspects. And now a dead body who might be one of those suspects.

Fascinating.

In the Portland FBI office this case would have gone to the violent crimes department, but here in Bend's tiny office, everyone did a little of everything. She'd studied all the photos that Deschutes County had sent over from the cabin. A few minutes of investigating had pointed her toward the most likely source of the money bags. The more she dug, the bigger the situation got, and the more questions she had. Adrenaline buzzed in her veins.

But first she needed to update her coworkers.

"Someone looks excited," said Special Agent Eddie Peterson as she entered the meeting room. He'd followed her lead by moving to the small Bend office from Portland. The young urban agent had discovered a love for the outdoors.

"I thought I was hiding it," Mercy confessed as she set her notes on the table.

"You are. But your eyes give you away."

"Did Jeff tell you to meet him here?"

"Yep. I suspect he wants me to give you a hand."

Mercy should have figured that. If this case was what she believed it was, more than one agent would be needed to work it.

Their boss, Jeff Garrison, entered with Darby Cowan and Melissa. Jeff was Mercy's age, tall, and the most competent supervisor she'd ever had. Darby was an amazing data analyst and always dressed in practical clothing that suggested she was minutes away from taking a fifteen-mile hike. Mercy suspected the older woman worked only to support her outdoor pursuits of camping, skiing, and kayaking. The office manager, Melissa, was a little younger, cheerful and chatty, and wore a smile every single day. Everyone took a seat and looked at Mercy expectantly.

"You've all heard that empty money bags were found with remains in a shack about an hour out of town," she started.

Everyone nodded.

"From my preliminary investigating, I believe those bags are from the armored car robbery near Portland's downtown First Interstate Bank nearly thirty years ago."

Jeff already knew this fact, but Melissa and Eddie leaned forward in their seats.

"The Gamble-Helmet Heist?" Eddie stumbled over the words. "That was one of the biggest robberies in the Pacific Northwest. Everyone has theories about what happened to the thieves and money. It's second only to the D. B. Cooper case."

"Cooper was the guy who hijacked a passenger jet and then jumped out with a bunch of money and was never seen again, right?" asked Darby. "I know about that one, but why haven't I heard of this Gamble-Helmet case?"

11

"I remember when the Gamble-Helmet group robbed the armored car," said Melissa. "I was just a kid, but it was all over the news for weeks. Wasn't one of the drivers murdered?"

"Yes," answered Mercy. "Five men robbed the truck, and the one who shot the driver was caught. Shane Gamble. He's currently in the Two Rivers prison in Umatilla. The other four men vanished along with the money. Nearly two million dollars."

"My brothers used to search in the woods for the Gamble-Helmet money when we went hiking," Melissa added. "They were convinced it'd been buried somewhere in the forest."

"The escape vehicle was last seen headed east along I-84 toward the gorge. We were lucky that Gamble was caught at the scene and gave the names of the other men; otherwise we might have never found out who did it. These are the only pictures from the robbery." Mercy turned her laptop around for everyone to see.

"They're all wearing freaking motorcycle helmets," muttered Eddie.

"Hence the Gamble-Helmet name for the heist," said Darby as she made notes. "Why wear helmets? Wouldn't the limited vision and hearing put them at a disadvantage? There has to be an easier way to hide an identity."

"The armored truck had stopped for a scheduled pickup, and the thieves immediately moved in, catching the first man off guard as he opened his door and dousing the driver with pepper spray," said Mercy. "Presumably the helmets were to protect them from the pepper spray—it travels."

"I don't know if that's brilliant or stupidly risky," said Darby.

"The whole operation was risky," said Mercy. "Four men swarmed into the truck, shoved what they could in their own bags, and ran to a waiting car with a driver. The first guard drew his weapon as Shane Gamble exited the truck, but Gamble fired first. The guard's return shot brought Gamble down, the escape vehicle left without him, and he was caught at the scene." Mercy took a deep breath. "The guard died before the police arrived. Gamble healed, went to trial, and was convicted."

"And the other four drove off into the sunset with a lot of cash," finished Jeff. "Like Eddie said, this robbery is *almost* as big of a legend as D. B. Cooper's airplane jump. That means lots of media interest."

Everyone groaned.

"All media calls go to me," stated Jeff, looking at Melissa. "No one needs to know which agents are working the case or how it's proceeding."

Melissa nodded. "My phone is going to ring nonstop. Since the day it occurred, everyone has speculated on what happened to the other four thieves."

"I suspect the body in the woods will turn out to be one of them. With Gamble in prison, that leaves three more to find," Eddie stated.

"And money. A lot of money to find," added Mercy.

"Two million doesn't go very far when divided between three or four people," argued Eddie. "It's got to be long gone. It's been nearly thirty years."

"Maybe only one of them ended up with the money, and there could be more bodies," suggested Mercy. "I'm getting ahead of myself. I'm waiting on final confirmation that these are some of the missing bags from the robbery, and if so, I plan to interview Shane Gamble first thing tomorrow morning."

"The Two Rivers Correctional Institution is over two hundred miles away," said Jeff.

"I figure it'll take me three and a half hours—maybe less."

"No speeding tickets on company vehicles."

"Of course not."

"Eddie will be working with you," said Jeff. "Divide up the load and stay away from the media. We'll keep Deschutes County in the loop about the body since it's their jurisdiction. Have you been in touch with the original lead FBI agent on the robbery case?"

"Art Juergen," answered Mercy. "He retired last year, and they're getting me his current contact information. He's a good guy. I worked with him for a few years. A lot of agents worked the case thirty years ago, but Portland's ASAC says Juergen knew it inside and out. He'd told the ASAC that he regretted not solving it before he retired."

"And one year later we have a hot lead," said Eddie. "This could make Juergen's day. I'll dig up background on the guys Gamble named as his associates." Eddie looked at a piece of paper Mercy had shoved across the table. "Ellis Mull, Nathan May, and Trevor Whipple."

"What's the name of the fifth person?" asked Darby.

"No one knows the full name of the getaway driver," said Melissa. "I remember angry wives and girlfriends would turn in their significant other to get the men investigated and humiliated. What a waste of investigator time."

"Melissa is right," said Mercy. "From what I've read, no one knows who the fifth person is. Shane Gamble claimed Trevor Whipple brought the fifth man into the plan at the last minute to drive the car, and called him Jerry. Gamble didn't know anything else about him."

"Hopefully that's not Jerry up in the cabin," said Eddie. "I think we can determine if it's Mull, May, or Whipple, but figuring out if it was the unknown driver will be a challenge."

"The body could be a random hunter," Darby pointed out. "Let's get that final confirmation on the bank bags before we jump to conclusions."

Mercy met Eddie's gaze. Her gut told her the dead body was part of the Gamble-Helmet Heist, and based on the smug smile on Eddie's face, he suspected it too.

◆ ◆ ◆

Not again.

This was the fourth car in two weeks.

14

Sandy Foster tuned out the words of the furious man with her behind the Eagle's Nest bed-and-breakfast. She didn't blame him as they stared at the glass on the pavement. She'd be pissed too if someone had broken her car window. From the way he spoke, he seemed to believe that the two-year-old Honda was a rare, valuable car.

It was a nice car, but she saw a dozen of them every day.

"I'll get the police over here," she promised her customer. "And I know the owner of the auto glass repair shop in Bend. He'll have someone here this afternoon." *I hope.*

Her relationship with the auto glass shop owner had formed out of necessity, and she wondered if he had a "break ten, get one free" program. Her lips twisted at the thought.

"This isn't funny," the customer snapped.

"I'm not laughing," she assured him. "Believe me, this makes me furious. I want a safe place for my visitors to park. Incidents like this don't make anyone feel safe."

"At least nothing was stolen," he muttered. He crossed his arms, and his mouth sagged in a frown.

"Let me buy you dinner at the town diner tonight," Sandy offered. Her breakfast buffet was included in the price of a room; otherwise she would have offered that. Instead the cost of his and his wife's dinner would come directly out of her cash.

"It wasn't your fault," he admitted.

It was the nicest thing he'd said in the last five minutes. "I want to do something to make it up to you. Were you driving anywhere this afternoon?"

He sighed. "Just to dinner in Bend a bit later."

"I bet it will be repaired by then," she said, forcing herself to sound cheerful.

"I hope so. We've been looking forward to trying the seafood place in the Old Mill District." He gave her a sideways look.

15

Shit. "They have fantastic food. I'll pick up the dinner tab for you."

He brightened. "That'd be great. I'll go tell my wife." He took off toward the back door of her bed-and-breakfast.

Sandy sighed and closed her eyes for a long moment. The seafood restaurant would cost five times as much as a meal at the diner. If her customer decided to push the boundaries and order lobster and multiple bottles of wine, it could be much more.

I wouldn't put it past him.

She slid her phone out of her back pocket to call the Eagle's Nest Police Department and her auto glass contact. Regret jabbed her in the chest. She adored her bed-and-breakfast. It was the result of years of backbreaking labor. She wanted the best experience for her customers and paid attention to every detail. Fine linens on the beds, updated huge bathrooms, spotlessly clean floors, and a breakfast buffet that made clients rave. She never took a day off; the old restored home was the pride of her heart.

I love what I do, but if this damage keeps up, I'll be broke.

Then what?

"This is happening too often," Truman said as he wrote in his notebook. As soon as the department had received a call from Sandy, he knew what she would report.

More vandalism to customer vehicles at her bed-and-breakfast.

Beside him Sandy ran a hand through her long red hair in frustration. "Tell me about it. This isn't good for business. I can read the future online reviews now: 'Great place, amazing food, but expect to get your tires slashed or car windows broken.'"

"People wouldn't write that in a review," said Truman. "This has nothing to do with the quality of your business."

"You'd be surprised what people will complain about. I've received a one-star review because I don't provide shuttle service from Portland—give me a break! It's over three hours away. In another one-star, a woman complained because her husband lost his coat while skiing! It didn't even happen at my place."

"A rational person reading that review will see how ridiculous that is."

"Some people only look at the number of stars." Sandy glared at the broken window.

"How about installing cameras? You could find some inexpensive ones these days."

"How about you catch who is doing this?" Sandy suggested with a quirk of an eyebrow. The tall B&B owner was a force to be reckoned with. The fortysomething woman took no crap from anyone, but she was a natural in the hospitality field. She'd moved to town a decade before him, and he'd heard she'd been married at some point, but her passion was running her business. Truman still appreciated the time she'd backed him up in a domestic dispute with her rolling pin. He'd had no doubt she would use it if needed.

"I'll do my best. You know we don't have the manpower or budget to run patrols at night. An officer on call is the best I can do."

"I know." Sandy lowered her gaze. "It's tight everywhere. That's why I need this damage stopped. I haven't had a profit since Christmas, and I can't afford to lose a single customer. Any more of this and I'll be frying eggs and hash browns at the restaurant down the street."

"You're too important to this town for that . . . although you'd improve the diner's breakfast tenfold." Truman felt bad for the hard-working woman. "Your B&B brings in customers for other local businesses. We're all dependent on each other. I'll ask around and see if someone has some cameras they'd loan for a while," he lied. "I'll help set them up."

After I order them from Amazon.

17

"I hope they don't move the vandalism to the house," Sandy said, looking up at the stately Queen Anne home. "I put a lot of work into restoring it, and my insurance deductible is huge."

"You said no one has heard the glass breaking or seen people near the cars?"

"I asked all the guests. I can't even tell you when this one happened. The owner didn't come out to his car until lunchtime. It could have happened anytime in the last twenty-four hours."

"I suspect nighttime."

"I agree." Her dark brows came together, and she frowned at the broken window of the Honda sedan.

"What is it?" Truman asked. The look on her face was thoughtful.

She shook her head and smiled at him. "It's nothing. I'm trying to imagine what kind of person from around here does this. Teenagers, I expect?"

"That's a solid guess. I'll file a report—another report—and find some cameras for you. Until then, warn your guests not to leave things in their car." He paused. "Nothing was stolen this time either, right?"

"Right. Someone simply enjoys causing damage."

Truman slipped his notebook in his pocket. "Be careful, Sandy."

"Don't worry. I'm always on my toes," she said grimly. "Later, Chief."

THREE

Truman inhaled deeply as he stepped inside the Eagle's Nest station.

Lucas's mom has been here.

The smell of her pulled pork nearly made him weep with hunger. He hung up his cowboy hat and turned to see his office manager, Lucas, and his mom walking out of the small room used for meetings. She had a grocery bag in one hand, but Truman could tell it was empty. She must have just dropped off dinner.

And for once I'm here before the other guys.

Too many times he'd been out on a call when Bree Ingram dropped off food, and he'd come back to find a tiny plate of cold leftovers that survived only because Lucas had saved it for him. Bree's pulled pork was Truman's favorite, but he also liked her pasta salad, fried chicken, and berry pie.

"Evening, Chief," Bree said with a smile. "I made a little extra pork, so I brought it by. Goes to waste in my house." Bree Ingram had Lucas's big smile, but that was the only physical attribute the widow shared with her son. She was tiny, especially when she stood next to linebacker-size Lucas. With her dark coloring and peppy attitude, she reminded him of a happy lab puppy.

Lucas was a Saint Bernard, a gentle giant.

"Thanks, Bree. We always appreciate your extra food." Truman swallowed back a curse as all three of his officers emerged from the small room with paper plates loaded with pulled pork and fresh rolls. *So much for being first.* He glared at Samuel. The officer wasn't even working today. No doubt one of the other officers had given him a heads-up. Samuel was a bachelor, unlike his other two officers, and was always happy to eat food someone else had made.

The three officers greeted Truman with their mouths full.

"You outdid yourself this time, Bree," Royce Gibson told her. "You ever going to share the recipe with my wife?"

Bree laughed. "I did months ago."

Royce took another bite, chewing thoughtfully. "It doesn't taste like this at all."

"Hmmm. Maybe I left something out of the recipe I gave her. I'll get in touch."

Lucas squeezed his mother's shoulders, and she gently slapped at his hand as she smiled up at him.

Looks like Lucas knows Bree doesn't share her exact recipes.

"You working with Ollie tonight?" Truman asked. Bree tutored the teenager a few times a week as he worked toward his GED. Bree was an English teacher at the high school but spent her little spare time tutoring.

"Not tonight," she answered. "He's coming along really well. It's like his brain is a sponge. I don't think I've ever had a student who *wants* to learn with such enthusiasm."

Truman agreed. Ollie was thirsty for knowledge.

Lucas walked his mother to the door as she said goodbye to the men. Once she was gone he turned to Truman with suppressed excitement. "You gonna tell us about the remains Ollie found?"

Truman hadn't told anyone what had happened that morning. "How'd you hear about that?"

"Ben told me."

"I heard about it at the feed store at lunch," Ben said with a full mouth. "Not sure how it got started there."

Truman scanned his four men—his work family. Ben was the oldest, with decades of police work under his belt. Samuel was a solid ex-military man who now lived and breathed law enforcement. Royce was young and rather naive, and barely kept up. And Lucas was Lucas. One of a kind.

All trustworthy, good men.

But damned gossips, each one of them.

"I think we all know the feed store is a front where the men in this town go to gossip," said Truman.

"It's a news source," Ben corrected him. "Our own little local newsroom."

"It's gossip. And it's often wrong."

"Ollie didn't find a body this morning?" Samuel asked with a confident look in his eye.

Clearly they knew the story was true and were deliberately ignoring the point of his lecture.

He gave in.

"Ollie found remains in the northern section of Christian Lake's property. Looks like they've been there for years. Maybe decades," admitted Truman, keeping silent about the bullet hole and the money bags.

The men immediately turned to Ben, Truman forgotten. "Remember anyone who went missing over the years?" Royce eagerly asked the older officer, who stored most of Eagle's Nest's history in his brain.

Ben swallowed before answering. The seventysomething-year-old looked pleased to be recognized for his longtime-resident expertise. "Well now . . . old Don Ward vanished one day in the 1980s. Don't know what happened. He lived alone, and one day his mailman went up to the house because his mailbox was overflowing. Never heard a word about what happened to him. Simply gone." Ben looked at Truman. "Were the remains male?"

"Don't know for sure. Odds look good." *How much of this will be repeated at the feed store tomorrow?*

"If it's female, it could be Harriet Zimmerman. College girl that disappeared while hiking on her summer break . . . I think that was somewhere in the nineties." Ben rubbed his chin. "Those are the unsolved disappearances I can remember off the top of my head. There're more. I'll look into it."

"This case is Deschutes County's," Truman pointed out, keeping the FBI's involvement to himself. That fact would come out soon enough, and he didn't want to answer a dozen questions about why the FBI had been brought in so quickly. A phone call from Mercy after lunch had caught him up on the emerging details of Ollie's discovery.

She believed it was related to the infamous Gamble-Helmet Heist.

"We've got our own problems to focus on. Another car at Sandy's had a window bashed in today. I want everyone driving by her B&B whenever they have a spare moment. Maybe park across the street for a few minutes. Let our presence be seen."

Scowls filled all four men's faces. "Asshole," muttered Samuel. "I don't like that someone's targeting her. I'll stop by a few times each shift."

Sandy would roll her eyes at the testosterone that'd suddenly filled the station.

Her recent issues had struck a chord with his men. You didn't mess around with one of their residents. Especially a single woman. "I'll find her some security cameras," added Truman, glad he'd redirected his men's focus. They didn't need to worry about remains in the woods.

But he struggled to contain his own curiosity.

Has Ollie discovered the answer to a decades-old robbery?

◆ ◆ ◆

That evening, Mercy parked and admired the new structure in the woods.

Four months ago, Mercy's secret cabin had burned to the ground. The hidden location had been where she found peace of mind as she stocked supplies for an uncertain future, compelled by a survivalist upbringing that had taught her to prepare for the end of the world. If society collapsed, she'd be ready.

For years the cabin had been her dirty little secret. She'd been raised by preppers, and though she'd angrily left home at eighteen, she couldn't shake her deep-rooted need for a safe place. One with a good defense and years of fuel, food, and medical supplies. When she worked for the FBI in Portland, she'd spent her weekends and vacations improving her safety net in the Cascade foothills near Bend, telling no one where she went. Now her new coworkers believed she had a little cabin getaway for skiing.

She didn't correct their assumption.

The destruction of her years of work on the cabin had dismayed her until Truman urged her to rebuild. The new cabin wasn't finished yet. The inside was bare, but the contractor had completed most of the basic structure. It had solid walls and a fireproof metal roof. The image of flames destroying the old roof was still fresh in her head. She wanted brick walls, but the cost was beyond her at the moment. *Someday.* She and Truman would try their hands at amateur masonry in the future.

Finishing the interior was up to her and Truman. The goal date for completion was the end of summer. Three months had sounded

23

doable to her until she landed the Gamble-Helmet case. Her evenings and weekends were no longer her own and wouldn't be until the case was solved or, if her research produced no leads, downgraded to a back burner. She knew Jeff would give her at least a month to run full tilt at the case.

She was determined to make the most of it.

Tonight's trip to the cabin was to work on her shopping list for the new structure, knowing she might not be back for a few weeks.

Infrared floodlights. Night vision goggles. A few infrared break beams for the long driveway to warn her of visitors.

The photovoltaic solar power system had been ordered, along with a new gun safe. A bigger one.

She also needed to buy the basics. Beds, chairs, a table, kitchen supplies.

Getting out of her truck, she noticed Truman had arrived first and parked around back, closer to her big storage barn. Thankfully, the barn's contents had been spared during the fire. It held her years' worth of stocked food, medical supplies, tools, fuel, and batteries, and a backup generator. The knowledge that her reserves and larder were safe had kept her from completely falling apart as her cabin went up in flames.

She went up the steps and opened the front door. A heavenly scent greeted her, and her jaw dropped open as she stared at the scene inside.

A plywood board was balanced on sawhorses and set for dinner for two, complete with lighted candles and paper plates. Two large bags from her favorite Italian restaurant sat at one end of the table.

Her mouth watered.

The sight of the man unpacking the bags also made her mouth water and her heart swell with happiness. Truman brought excitement, laughter, and love to her everyday life. Things she had rarely experienced before she moved to Bend.

24

He grinned at her with a smugly pleased expression. Surprising Mercy wasn't easy.

"Hungry?" he asked.

"I didn't eat dinner."

"I figured that would happen." He spread his arms to indicate the makeshift table. "I thought I'd arrange a little surprise."

"You got food from Marta's?"

"Where else?"

The tiny Italian restaurant had yet to be discovered by the tourists, and Mercy hoped it'd stay that way. It was cozy and quiet, with impeccable service and food. Marta, the Italian owner, would talk to her customers and pour more wine. If you hadn't ordered wine with your meal, she'd wink and pour you a small glass "for just a taste."

Which always inspired Mercy to buy the exact bottle from Marta's tiny Italian food market next door.

Marta knew how to drive sales.

"Sit," he ordered.

She sat on a stool that was too high for the makeshift table. She didn't care. They could sit on the ground and she'd be happy with Truman. Currently the home had plywood subfloors and open framing, but part of Mercy loved the empty, bare look; it promised that something fabulous was coming.

Fabulous and practical.

Truman leaned over and poured red wine into the plastic cup by her paper plate. Mercy spotted the Italian label and knew Marta had recommended the wine. She sighed and buried her nose in her cup. The fragrance was deep and bold, with hints of plum and smoke.

"Italy," she mumbled into the wine.

"What?" asked Truman.

"I want to visit Italy. How does a honeymoon in Italy sound?"

A grin filled his face, and the sensation of butterflies fluttered up her spine.

Or maybe it's the wine.

She took a sip of her wine as she studied his face. So familiar and dear to her. A smile to stop traffic. Eyes that crinkled in happiness. Several scars that testified to his love of law enforcement. Her attraction to him was more than skin deep. She was in love with the person he was. He was a natural leader and easily commanded respect. His people turned to him, followed him, admired him. His natural sense of honor was a magnet for her.

No. It's not the wine.

He gets me.

He understood how her mind worked, and they fit together like a couple of complicated puzzle pieces. She'd been painfully aware of her missing puzzle piece when he'd been taken away, chained by men planning to kill him, and then rescued, thanks to Ollie. The two weeks when no one knew his fate had been the worst of her life. When he'd been returned to her, she'd known she couldn't waste any more time.

He'd been of the same mind-set and proposed.

"I'll try Italy." He dished spaghetti carbonara onto their plates. "Especially if the food is half as good as Marta makes."

"We can ask Marta for travel suggestions," she stated, pleased with her honeymoon idea.

Traveling abroad had never been an option for her. What would she do if society collapsed while she was in another country? No resources. No preparation. No escape. She'd be dependent on the kindness of others. Mercy waited for the knot to start in her stomach.

It didn't come.

She hid her shock with another sip of wine. *Am I getting soft?*

Truman reached across the table and took her hand, giving a knee-melting smile.

No. Something else has shifted to the top of my priorities.

"What's Kaylie up to tonight?" he asked as he ran his thumb over the ring on her fourth finger.

He'd picked out the engagement ring. It was a platinum band encircled with diamonds in a channel setting. "I knew a big solitaire wouldn't be practical," he'd told her when he slipped it on her finger. "I saw this and I knew it was right. With this setting the diamonds can't get caught on anything . . . even while chopping wood."

He gets me.

"Kaylie is at Pearl's, working on a gluten-free lemon bar recipe for the café." Mercy's seventeen-year-old niece had lived with her since her father died last fall. Levi's dying wish had been for Mercy to take in his daughter. The teenager didn't need much supervision. She managed a coffeehouse, went to school full-time, and got great grades.

Taking in Kaylie had been one of the scariest decisions of her life. It'd felt as if she had stepped off a sky-high ledge into an unknown world, but now she wondered how she'd lived without the girl.

I didn't know I had a Kaylie-shaped hole in my heart.

"Kaylie's hair is no longer pink," Mercy added as she took a bite of the carbonara. Her niece had surprised her with the cotton candy color a month ago. It'd been cute. But Kaylie had quickly tired of it and didn't like the brown roots that had started to appear.

"Blue?" guessed Truman. "Or striped?"

"Normal. It's as dark as mine now."

He exhaled in relief. "That's good."

Mercy grinned. "Old-fashioned? Too crazy for you?"

"She looked like an anime character."

Mercy laughed and nearly spilled her wine.

"And what's on your agenda for tomorrow?" he asked over the rim of his plastic cup.

She perked up. "The bank confirmed the money bags are from the Gamble-Helmet Heist. And I have the go-ahead to visit Shane Gamble at the Two Rivers prison tomorrow."

"What are your thoughts on the remains?" Truman asked. "Did the medical examiner get to them yet?"

"Yes. They spent the afternoon removing the remains, and Dr. Lockhart was going to start an examination tonight. The woman never takes time off."

"Same could be said for you."

"Only when I'm deep in a case."

"I guess this means your weekends are booked for a while?"

Mercy sighed. "I know. The two of us are supposed to be working on the interior of this place . . . We'll get it done at some point. It'll have to wait awhile."

A grin filled his face.

"What?" she asked.

"You're not the same person I met last fall. Back then, if the cabin had been in the half-completed state it is now, you'd be climbing the walls with anxiety because your safety net wasn't perfect."

"You're right," she agreed. "I had a similar thought earlier, but nearly all my supplies are still intact, so it'd be rough living but doable. I can temporarily live with that for now. Especially with this case to distract me."

His lips twisted.

"Jealous?" she asked with a grin. "It's an amazing case, isn't it?"

"It is. Considering there have been no leads for decades, and the robbery is practically modern folklore. It's like a buried treasure hunt, and Ollie found the first clue."

"Is Ollie okay after his morning?" she asked with a small wince. She'd nearly forgotten the teen had made the grisly discovery.

"He's okay. I spent some time with him and he was very quiet, but I could tell he was processing it. He's dealt with death before."

"He's been through a lot," sympathized Mercy.

They silently ate for a few moments until he glanced up and caught her staring at him. Longing shone in his eyes, an appetite and craving that had nothing to do with food, and she struggled to find her breath.

How does he do that to me?

"You know," he said, his voice low and tempting, "this place hasn't been christened yet."

Mercy blinked. "People do that to homes?"

Patience filled his features. "That's not what I meant." His brown gaze held hers.

"Ohhh," she breathed as heat flashed through her.

"Dessert." His smile was sinful, and energy pulsed between them. She melted. "Yes. Dessert."

FOUR

The guard who escorted her into the Two Rivers prison warned her that Gamble liked to toy with people. "He'll say whatever he can to get under your skin," the guard stated as they waited for clearance at a third set of electronic doors. "It's how he entertains himself. I swear he must sit around for hours thinking up ways to bug everyone." The guard looked at her. "Show no fear."

"Not a problem," Mercy promised.

"They say he's some sort of genius," the guard went on. "Scored a 130 on an IQ test a long time ago."

"Isn't that nearly Mensa level?" Mercy hadn't seen a mention of an IQ score when she reviewed Gamble's file.

"Dunno. But he acts like he's smarter than everyone here. His social status in prison is unusual. He can get anyone to do anything for him, but he doesn't run around with a flock of followers. He keeps to himself." A buzzer sounded, and the door slid open.

"Does he create problems?" Mercy asked.

The guard blew out a breath. "Yes and no. He's never at the center of a problem, whether it's a fight or missing items. Evidence always points at someone else, but those of us who know him are positive he masterminded things that got other inmates in trouble. It makes me believe the IQ score. He reminds me of a lazy genius—getting everyone else to do his dirty work while he sits by and enjoys watching the repercussions that never involve him. It's like he's Teflon coated or something."

"He has help from higher up in the prison system?" she questioned.

"Oh, hells no. We all know better than to let him get in our heads." The guard's tone left room for doubt. "It's amazing that he can be the nicest, most personable guy and can carry on a friendly conversation about the latest basketball game. But then I'll see him study a group, and I just *know* a different part of his brain has taken over. It's like he's two people." He leaned closer to Mercy. "You know he killed an inmate, right?"

That piece of information *had* been in Gamble's records. It'd happened during his first year of prison, when he was still at the Oregon State Correctional Institution, and the act had guaranteed he'd die an inmate.

That murder was foremost in Mercy's thoughts as she took a seat across from Gamble.

He didn't look like a killer. He looked like the next-door neighbor who was happy to loan you his tools. He was tall, with long arms and salt-and-pepper hair. If they hadn't been sitting in a prison, Mercy could have seen him as a typical dad cheering on his teenager at the high school football game. He spoke slowly and deliberately while keeping his facial muscles and shoulders relaxed. Only his eyes indicated that his mind was working at top speed; his gaze was fierce.

Shane Gamble's gaze lingered on her left hand. "You married?"

Mercy wasn't about to share her relationship status with the prisoner sitting across from her. "Generally that's what a ring on that finger means." Her engagement ring suddenly seemed ten times larger than its actual size.

He deliberately looked at it again, and she swallowed hard at the intensity in his eyes. *This is why they suggest removing jewelry before visiting.* She'd shrugged off the recommendation since she would be interacting with only one prisoner.

"Awfully shiny. Looks brand-new." His dark eyes met hers, and she forced herself to hold his gaze.

"I like shiny things," she answered casually.

Shane Gamble continued to pointedly study her. "For someone who likes shiny things, you aren't wearing any other jewelry. Or much makeup. Seems like those two things go hand in hand with most women." He leaned closer and squinted at her.

Mercy held perfectly still, her hands preparing to aim a powerful thrust at his throat if he tried anything. He was chained to the table, and she knew he couldn't reach her, but her protective instincts couldn't help themselves. The guard standing near the door and out of listening distance cleared his throat. "Gamble," he warned.

Gamble leaned back in his chair. "You wear a little makeup. I was trying to determine if that was a bruise near your eye. You did a good job covering it up."

She did have a bruise. The fault of her inattention and a cupboard door corner. She'd painstakingly been covering it with makeup for days, not wanting strangers to wonder if a man had beat on her.

His words and deep scrutiny made her skin crawl, and she felt as if Gamble were circling her like a predator, probing at her brain for a tender spot. His questions were seeking a weakness.

The guard was right. He likes to toy with people.

"Why are you talking to me without a lawyer?" Mercy asked, knowing Gamble had refused one when Darby set up the interview.

Gamble shrugged. "First of all, I don't want to pay a lawyer to drive all the way out here from Portland and sit for an hour listening to the same old story. Besides, what's going to happen to me? Are you going to discover something new and have me tried for it? I'm already stuck here until I die. You can't add another sentence for me to serve beyond the grave." He chuckled.

"That's right," Mercy said. "You killed another inmate during your first year of prison. How come?" She wanted to find *his* tender spots.

Two can play this game.

"I was defending myself. It can be a zoo in here, and new inmates are the food."

"It says in your file that you attacked the guy. Witnesses claim they didn't know what triggered it."

"Witnesses," he repeated. "Other inmates? You know how reputable we are." He folded his hands, making his chains rattle on the tabletop.

Mercy leaned closer and lowered her voice. "It's just you and me here. You can tell me what really happened," she said in a companionable tone.

Gamble held her gaze and then mimicked her intimate tone. "He tried to bullshit me."

Like I'm doing right now.

She'd have to try harder to get under his skin. A challenge.

"Why are you really here?" he asked. "That murder case is done and settled, even though they never believed he was paid to kill me."

The murdered inmate was hired to kill him? Mercy hadn't read that in his history and wondered if Gamble had made up the reason. Irked he'd diverted her thoughts with the paid-to-kill comment, she searched for one to do the same to him.

"It was a beautiful drive out here today," she said kindly. "You're lucky the prison is so close to the Columbia River. I couldn't believe how blue it was this morning."

Something flashed in his eyes. "I wouldn't know."

She'd figured he never saw the water, and she wondered if the prisoners could smell the river. This corner of northeast Oregon was quite dry, and she'd smelled the crispness and minerals of the water the moment she'd stepped out of her vehicle.

It was logical that the topic of the outdoors would annoy Gamble. He'd been locked up for thirty years.

She'd aptly found a tender spot that made him defensive.

"I'm here because we found a half dozen money bags from the robbery." She dropped the single sentence and watched him.

The slight quiver of an eyelid was all that indicated she'd surprised him. "And?" he asked calmly.

"The bags weren't alone. The money was gone, of course, but a body was left behind."

The eyelid quivered again, and he grew a shade paler. "Whose?"

"Don't know. We're looking into it."

"Where was it found? Was the death recent?"

Wow. Two questions in a row.

She now held the power in the discussion—information he wanted.

"The bags and body were found in a crumbling cabin on private land about an hour outside of Bend. The death scene is old—maybe even a few decades."

Gamble was very still, his breathing slow and calm. He didn't break eye contact. "I don't know anything about a cabin."

"Not a preplanned rendezvous or hideout location?"

"Not that I was aware of. Jerry must have suggested it. Ellis, Nathan, or Trevor never mentioned something like that."

"Maybe you were deliberately left out of the loop."

Anger flashed and then confidence shone from his eyes. "I doubt it."

"Because you knew every aspect, didn't you," Mercy said, tilting her head to the side as if studying him. "That robbery was your baby. You did the planning."

"Everyone knows that." Subtle pride.

"From what I read in your file, you masterminded the whole thing and convinced the other guys to go along. In fact, I think I read that you regarded the robbery as a challenge. Almost a game, to see if you could outsmart the armored car company and the police."

"That's correct. And I succeeded."

"Your plan was solid. Gutsy but solid." She paused. "I wouldn't agree that you succeeded. You're sitting in prison."

"I thought through every detail. We got the money, and the rest of the group got away. I consider that a success." The skin of his throat rippled as he silently swallowed, and curiosity took over his intense gaze. "What else do you know about the body?"

Mercy paused a little too long, letting his question hang in the air, letting him believe she was debating what information to share. "I don't know anything yet. The medical examiner is looking at the remains now."

Impatience flared in his gaze. "Right. But you must know . . . Clothing, shoes . . . Maybe I can help identify the body by those items."

Why is he interested in helping?

"That's very kind, but I doubt you can recall all the clothing your friends owned back then. We'll confirm him with dental records."

Gamble slowly leaned back in his chair and rubbed at a few days' stubble on his chin. "You're probably right."

The tension emanating from him had abruptly vanished.

He's no longer interested.

Or he's a damn good actor.

"I'd hoped the discovery of money bags in a cabin might remind you of some detail you'd forgotten," prodded Mercy. "Or maybe one that you didn't think was important at the time."

"You really think I'd help you find my friends?" He stretched his shoulders, hampered by the chains, and looked away for the first time in the interview.

"Do you believe you're the only one of the five who should be in prison for the robbery and death of the guard?"

"More power to them if they've lived a normal life. I hold no ill will."

Mercy raised her brows. "That's generous."

"They were my friends. Not their fault I ended up here."

"You're saying that after all these years of silence from them as you sat in prison, their friendship still means something to you?"

He was silent.

A minute ago he was gung ho to help us identify the body. What happened?

"You don't want to help us figure out what happened after the robbery?"

"I'd call the case solved. I'm in here paying for the crime, and the cops know the full names of who else was there, except for Jerry. And I doubt there's any money to be recovered after all this time." His tone was pragmatic, and he looked at her as if he were schooling a pupil. "It's over."

He's not going to share anything.

"None of your good friends have contacted you over the years? Maybe to thank you for not helping the police?"

He gave a half smile. "Maybe I did hear from someone. Or maybe I didn't. Sounds like one might have been dead for a long time."

Mercy held his gaze. *He's heard from someone.*

"It's possible the body isn't related to the robbery," she stated, slightly changing the direction of the conversation as she contemplated how one of the thieves might have contacted Gamble. *Letters . . . phone calls . . . what kinds of communication records does the prison keep?*

He nodded solemnly. "I was waiting for you to realize that."

"Of course we'd realized it." She internally flinched at the flicker of enjoyment on his face. *Dammit.* He'd put her on the defensive.

"Then this conversation is truly pointless," he stated. "I'm shocked the FBI is wasting valuable time talking to me when you don't know who the remains are."

"Do you want me to come back when we have an identity?" Mercy shot back, annoyed that she'd reacted to his statements.

He held up his hands in a gesture of *Who knows*, and the clanking of his chains echoed in the room. "It wouldn't hurt to come back when the FBI actually knows something," he said thoughtfully. "Maybe a confirmed identity will trigger a memory. I'll spend some time reflecting on it. I might come up with something." His condescending smile made her toes curl. In a bad way. Not a Truman way.

He wants me to come back.

But is it because he's bored or because he's playing a game with information?

Or both?

She stood, knowing she needed to be the one to end the interview. "I'll be in touch," she said, making one last moment of eye contact with the creep. "Or maybe I won't. I'll spend some time reflecting on it," she mimicked.

Without looking back, she headed toward the exit.

I got nothing.

FIVE

"I told Lucas not to bother you. It's nothing. Probably drunk teens."

Truman took a long look at Bree Ingram, wondering if the woman really believed her statement. When Lucas had asked him to take a look at some vandalism on his mother's property, Truman hadn't hesitated. Now he stood in Bree's small stable, looking at six horse stall doors that had each been spray-painted with a big red X. And that was in addition to the red X on the door of her pickup.

"The symbolism bothers me," Lucas stated, his arm protectively around his mother's shoulders. "To me a red X means something is going to be eliminated."

My thoughts exactly.

"It's on her fucking truck," Lucas went on, anger flushing his usually calm face. "On her driver's door. It feels deliberate. It's not drunk teens," Lucas told his mother. "They'd draw dick pics and write curse words." He tightened his arm on her, and she briefly rested her cheek against his chest. Over her head his glare met Truman's gaze, transmitting his fury about the situation.

Truman sympathized, understanding that the big man felt powerless against a threat he couldn't see.

A horse stretched its neck over the stall door toward Truman in curiosity, and Truman held his palm under its nose. Warm air covered his hand as the animal's nostrils flared, and then its velvety lips nibbled at his hand, the horse oblivious to the threatening X on its door.

I feel as if it's been selected for slaughter.

"There was a horse in each stall that received an X?" Truman asked.

"Yes." Bree pointed at two unmarked stall doors, a tremor shaking her hand. "No horses were in those."

"These horses are like her kids," Lucas said. "Short of marking an X on my forehead, this is like threatening our family."

"The mare in the first stall is Sandy's," Bree added. "But she's like one of mine."

"Sandy boards a horse here?" Truman asked. "Sandy from the bed-and-breakfast in town?"

"Yes," said Bree. "We do competitive trail riding together."

"You mean you sucked her into that craziness," Lucas corrected. "Sandy could barely ride when she moved here, but she hung around with my mom so much, she got horse fever."

Truman faintly recalled Lucas mentioning his mother's horse competitions in the past. "Cameras anywhere?" he asked.

Lucas snorted. "No."

"How much land do you have?" He stroked the horse's cheek, admiring the trust in its black eyes and wondering if the horse had looked at the vandal in the same way.

"Ten acres," answered Bree.

"Have you seen any signs that someone has been on your property recently?"

Lucas and Bree exchanged a look. Both shook their heads.

"Any vehicles you don't recognize hanging around?"

Lucas's expression darkened. "A few times recently I've seen a truck I don't recognize on her road. Old, faded red Ford. Needs some bodywork. Probably from the early nineties. Even though I don't live here anymore, usually I recognize most people out here."

A small chill touched Truman's spine. *Old red Ford?*

"Maybe he's doing work on someone's property," Bree suggested. "We can't recognize everyone."

Truman met Bree's gaze. "I don't know how this would be possible, but have you pissed off anyone lately? Since there is an *X* on your truck, maybe you accidentally upset someone on the road who figured out where you lived?"

She paled. "I—I—don't know. Not that I'm aware of."

"She doesn't make enemies," Lucas snapped. His chest expanded, and he seemed to hulk up a size.

"I know that," Truman said in a calm voice. "But it'd be short-sighted of me not to ask." The horse jerked its head away and paced a circle in its box stall.

Did it pick up on the increase in Lucas's tension?

"The chief is doing his job," Bree stated, covering Lucas's hand on her shoulder with her own. Her voice was still shaky.

Truman rubbed his chin and smelled horse on his hand. Not a bad scent. "There's been some vehicle vandalism downtown. Your place is a good two miles outside of town, so I wouldn't imagine it's related, but I've had multiple vandalism reports in the last two weeks, and before that we'd had none for months."

Lucas looked at his mom. "It was at Sandy's place."

"Sandy told me someone had broken a few guests' car windows," Bree said. "She didn't say anything about spray paint."

"No paint. Just the vehicle damage."

"So someone else did mine," Bree said flatly.

"It's hard to say . . . The close timing of the incidents makes me wonder," Truman said. "Or you are correct, and two different people started vandalizing at the same time. I have to keep both in consideration."

Truman snapped some pictures of the marred doors. "Let's look at the truck again." He followed Lucas and Bree out of the barn and down the short gravel road to the vehicles parked in front of the home.

He inhaled, missing the barn's comforting scent of alfalfa and horse but appreciating the crisp, clean air. The sky was a perfect blue, but Truman was glad for his coat. The weather of the high desert was fickle in the spring. He could wear a short-sleeved T-shirt for a warm walk at lunch and then learn there was snow in the overnight forecast. He loved both elements and enjoyed the unexpected twists in the weather.

"I'm surprised they didn't do more to the truck," said Lucas.

"Maybe they got scared off before they could," Truman suggested. He hated the idea that Bree had been targeted as much as Lucas did.

◆　◆　◆

"I want to read Gamble's old interviews again now that I've met him face-to-face," Mercy told Eddie as they dug through the decades-old Gamble-Helmet files in her office. The files were very neat, and Mercy noticed most of the perfectly printed handwritten entries were initialed "AJ." Art Juergen.

She'd worked with Art in the Portland office. His retirement party over a year ago had been epic, according to the people who'd gone. Mercy hadn't been into huge social events. Still wasn't.

He'd asked her out one time, not long after she'd started at the Portland office, and against her better judgment, she'd agreed. But when it came time for a second date, she'd turned him down, citing the "better as friends" excuse. She had liked Art, just not in that way.

Truthfully, she couldn't get past the age difference. Art was almost twenty-five years older.

She'd kept that reason to herself, but he had to suspect . . .

Yesterday the retired FBI agent had replied with his usual cheeriness to her email asking for help, making her feel as if no time had passed.

41

He planned to arrive in Bend the next day, and she was upbeat at the thought of catching up with him.

Going over Art's reports, Mercy was impressed with his meticulous work. She was still missing a few boxes of files, but they would arrive soon. She couldn't wait to pick Juergen's brain about the case. He'd been obsessed with it for decades.

"What was Shane Gamble like?" Eddie pushed his glasses up on his nose, and then his hair flopped in his face as he bent over a box.

Mercy resisted the urge to tell him he needed a haircut. Eddie always seemed younger than his thirty-some years, and she wasn't his mom, but he was her favorite person to work with, and they formed a good team. His attitude was always positive, and his mind spotted possible investigative paths that hers missed. He also loved talking with people, which complemented Mercy's avoidance of small talk. Eddie could pop into the bank and come out knowing the names of the teller's three kids and that her mother-in-law had been ill for two weeks.

"Gamble was interesting," Mercy said as she flipped through pages. "He loves mind games and must be very bored in prison. He immediately tried to ruffle my feathers, but I was expecting it. He did manage to make me defensive at the end, and I essentially got nothing helpful from him, so he's talented with words. The guard told me his favorite form of entertainment is to mentally mess with his fellow inmates and get them in trouble."

"Well, that corresponds with this high school teacher's note on Gamble," Eddie said. "Sounds like he hasn't changed in thirty years."

The four known robbers had attended a Portland high school together and then moved on to the same local community college. They'd just started their second year at the school when the robbery occurred. Mercy wondered if Gamble had been so bored in college that he decided to dream up the perfect armored car robbery.

"Let me see." Mercy leaned over Eddie's shoulder to study the page.

The high school teacher appeared to have known the four young men quite well. He stated that Shane Gamble was the leader of the group, and that both Ellis Mull and Nathan May were quiet and focused on sports instead of schoolwork. Trevor Whipple was the fast talker, the charmer, and he flirted with the girls. The four were popular, but their grades were never more than average. This teacher said he'd suspected Gamble could easily get better grades but simply didn't care. Gamble seemed more interested in embracing a variety of life experiences than in planning for the future with a solid education. The teacher was convinced Gamble had dragged the other students into the robbery.

What does Gamble think of his life experiences over the last thirty years?

Mercy tried to wrap her brain around the concept of people who didn't prepare for the future. It was like a foreign language to her ears. How could a person not plan ahead? She studied the high school photos in the file, knowing that the men had been barely older than they were in these photos when they'd committed the crime. Not even old enough to drink.

They were children. It was a game to them.

The realizations ricocheted through her skull and combined with Eddie's comment that Gamble hadn't changed over the years. Gamble's emotional growth had essentially stopped when he was incarcerated.

He still played games. Mind games.

She knew an FBI forensic psychologist who would love to pick apart Gamble's words and actions.

Looking at the high school photos, she saw that Gamble, May, and Whipple sported big smiles, but Ellis Mull looked stern. He'd played football all through high school but wasn't good enough to get a scholarship. He had the thick neck of someone who spent excess time in the weight room.

Did he feel lost when football was no longer part of his life?

43

Whipple had the hairstyle of a guy who paid close attention to his looks and grooming. Even from a photo, Mercy felt the flirtation from his eyes. He had that something that made a girl take a second look. And he knew it.

Nathan May ran cross-country and did track. He was lean and looked relaxed and confident in his picture.

The unknown fifth robber left a big void in the file. No one was certain his real name was Jerry. Previous investigators had looked into friends associated with the four, searching for that mystery person—high school friends, coworkers, college associates. No one else had disappeared like Whipple, May, and Mull after the robbery. The FBI had kept a careful watch on friends they believed most likely to have been the fifth man, but the suspicions had faded away as the men went on with normal lives.

"I can't believe they split and never contacted their families again," Eddie commented. "Mull had four sisters. How do you walk away from that?"

Mercy eyed Mull's stern gaze in the photo. "Maybe they weren't close. Two million dollars is a big reason to go silent."

"Forever?" Eddie muttered. "My sister would kill me if I didn't check in every few months."

Or they all died right after the robbery.

Shane Gamble still looked like his high school photo. The hair was different, and he had a few lines on his face, but it was clearly the man she'd met that morning. In a way he'd been caught in some sort of time warp. Nearly thirty years behind bars with limited sun exposure must have preserved him.

"Do you look like your high school photo?" she asked Eddie.

He raised a brow at the random question. "You be the judge." He tapped on his phone a few times and pulled up a photo from a Facebook page.

"We're not supposed to have social media accounts."

"It's my sister's page. She doesn't use my name, and my senior picture is the most recent photo I've allowed her to post."

"Holy crap," Mercy exclaimed as she took the phone. "You haven't changed at all. I look nothing like mine."

"I look totally different now," he protested.

Mercy studied him. "No. Those glasses don't age you like you think they do. You're still eighteen behind them."

"Shit." He snatched his phone back.

"Ask Melissa's opinion. She'll agree with me."

"I'm busy working," he stated, giving Mercy a side-eye. "Not reliving high school. Now . . . here are the interviews with their college professors."

Mercy took the obvious hint to refocus. She scanned the short statements and scowled. "How can these teachers not know their students? Only one instructor says he remembers Mull, because he stood out in his weight lifting class."

"College classes are often larger. You don't spend the one-on-one time like you might with your teachers in high school."

"True," Mercy admitted. "And it's possible that they rarely went to class. These statements are completely different from the high school teacher who gave his opinion. He *knew* them."

"Average grades again in college," Eddie added. "Maybe nothing made them stand out." He opened a thick envelope of black-and-white robbery photos pulled from video. He shuffled through them and stopped on one. "This is Mull. He's the beefiest guy of the four."

"And I can tell from the long legs that the man to his right is Gamble," Mercy said. "He's tall. Even sitting across the table from him, I knew he would tower over me."

"Whipple is definitely the smallest one. Nathan May must be the last."

"What if Gamble hadn't been shot at the last moment by the guard?" Mercy wondered out loud. "Would they all have escaped?"

45

"It wouldn't surprise me. Whatever their plan was for after the robbery sure worked out for the other four."

"Except for the man whose remains Dr. Lockhart is examining."

"If he's even part of this robbery," Eddie reminded her. "I know she was getting results on the dental comparisons today. Hopefully it's one of them."

Mercy couldn't pull her gaze away from Whipple's cheery grin in his senior photo. "What if they're all dead? Maybe that's why they've never been found. Dead men don't talk."

"One would still be alive. The one who killed the others."

Eddie is right.

SIX

Ollie stepped through the door of the Coffee Café, and his heart sped up as he spotted Kaylie bustling behind the counter. Her aunt Pearl was also working in the coffeehouse, but Kaylie moved twice as fast. Kaylie handed a cup to one of the two customers at the cash register, giving him an intimate smile that made Ollie's stomach feel as if it'd tumbled off a cliff.

Ollie recognized one of the tall men from the back. Cade. Kaylie's on-again, off-again boyfriend.

Currently on again.

I have no business wishing they weren't together. She's like a sister to me.

He was pretty sure Kaylie felt the sibling vibe.

Cade was a solid guy, but Kaylie was . . . *more* than him. She had fire and curiosity for life. She constantly analyzed and asked questions, studied the world around her and immersed herself in it. Cade focused only on what was right in front of him.

It wasn't a bad thing. Ollie liked Cade; everyone liked Cade. He just wasn't right for Kaylie.

Cade and the other man turned around to leave, and Cade's face lit up as he spotted Ollie farther back in line. "Hey, Ollie. Fueling up?"

"Yeah."

Cade gestured at the older man next to him. "Dad, this is Ollie. The guy who rescued Truman."

Ollie wanted to shrink into his boots. He wasn't a hero.

Cade's father held out his hand, and Ollie shook it. "Call me Glenn. Let me know if you ever want a construction job somewhere." Ollie had to look up at the tall man, but his eyes were kind, and he dressed like Cade. Carhartts. Work boots. Long-sleeved thermal shirt. Looking between him and his son, Ollie knew Cade would look exactly like Glenn in twenty years.

Glenn seemed just as nice as Cade. No doubt solid and hardworking. "Salt of the earth people," Ollie had heard his grandmother say. He hadn't understood what the term meant until he'd moved to Eagle's Nest. Here he'd encountered many of them.

"Thank you, sir . . . Glenn." Everyone in town had treated Ollie with kindness and respect, but Ollie knew it was because they cared about their police chief. One day he hoped the town would respect him for himself. Out of the corner of his eye, Ollie watched as Kaylie's gaze followed the men to the door while she automatically waited on the next customer.

It'd become a habit to stop into Kaylie's coffee shop several times a week during the afternoon when she was out of school. He'd never cared for coffee, but she'd introduced him to some sweet concoctions that were like drinking a dessert.

Ollie's grandfather would shake his head at what was called coffee these days.

The first time Ollie had stopped in the shop, the scent had brought back memories of his grandfather's old perking coffeepot. Ollie used to stare at the liquid bubbling in the clear knob, wondering what was happening inside that created the bitter drink his grandfather couldn't start his day without.

"Hey, Ollie." Kaylie flashed a smile at him as she grabbed a brownie for the customer in front of him. Her long, wavy ponytail fell over one shoulder, and he realized he missed the pink color. Now it was back to dark brown. His gaze stuck on the green sparkle of her nose stud. She changed the color every day.

His stomach did a bungee-jump thing.

Kaylie had introduced him to the modern teenage world. She'd told him what to do with his hair and what socks to wear with his tennis shoes, along with other instructions on practical things like digital books and streaming videos. No matter how stupid his questions, she never made fun of him. She was smart and kind and patient.

Pearl stepped into his field of vision, blocking his view of Kaylie. "I think my son and his friends are going to a movie this coming weekend. You should go with them." She held his gaze, projecting her auntly concern. For weeks she'd been after him to do things with Kaylie's cousin.

Ollie never knew what to say to Pearl's son. The one time they had gotten together it'd been awkward, and they'd eyed each other as if they were from different planets. Ollie didn't care to repeat the experience. He'd rather talk to Kaylie or Truman. Or Shep.

"I'm probably working. And I have a big test on Monday."

Disappointment flitted across her face, and she nodded, accepting his answer. Ollie knew she meant well, but he didn't need the companionship of guys his own age. They seemed like children to him. Foreign children.

"Did you want the caramel frappé, Ollie?" Kaylie called from behind the counter, the plastic cup already in her hand.

"Please." He gave a silent sigh of relief as Pearl headed for the small back office beyond the counter.

"You just missed Lucas," Kaylie told him as she worked on his drink. "His mom's property was vandalized overnight. He said Truman checked it out."

Concern for Bree overtook him. *She's such a tiny woman.* "Was the damage bad?" Ollie asked as he watched Kaylie dart around. She had a swipe of chocolate on one cheek and he couldn't bring himself to tell her. For some reason he liked seeing it. It made her green eyes pop more than usual. She had the same eyes as her aunt Mercy, but Kaylie's were relaxed. Mercy's constantly studied her surroundings. When Mercy turned them to him, he felt as if she could see his exact thoughts.

When she looked at Truman, they softened.

Truman's eyes did the same thing when he saw his fiancée.

Sometimes they forgot Ollie was in the room, they had their attention so focused on each other.

It wasn't a bad thing. One day he hoped for that type of personal connection.

"Lucas was pretty steamed," Kaylie answered. "None of the animals were hurt, but the damage to her truck could cost quite a bit."

"That sucks. I really like Bree. She's helped me a lot." Ollie appreciated the tutoring time she'd spent with him. Especially with English. He'd had no idea that sentences were made of dozens of parts of speech, and he needed to learn to label each one. To him sentences were just strings of words that created pictures in his mind. She was also good with chemistry, which made his brain hurt. He frowned, thinking of Bree's remote farm. The thought of her out there alone with someone harassing her angered him.

Kaylie handed him his drink, and their gazes met as he realized the gem in her nose matched her eyes.

Bungee jump.

Suddenly she looked past him, and her face lit up. "Truman."

The loss of her eye contact left him hollow, but he turned and raised a hand to Truman.

The lines on Truman's forehead looked deeper than usual, and stress lurked in his eyes. But he looked a million times better than when he'd been holed up in Ollie's cabin, a fever racking his body.

Truman greeted both of them and accepted the cup of brewed coffee that Kaylie had pulled the moment he stepped inside.

"Got a second, Ollie?" Truman took a careful sip and held Ollie's gaze.

Something's wrong. His stomach lurched.

Truman tipped his head toward the side of the room, and Ollie followed him.

"What time did you finish up at Lake Ski and Sports last night?" Truman asked softly, his eyes dark.

Ollie frowned. "Ten, like always."

"Did you go straight home?"

"Yes. I had an early class today." Truman hadn't been at the house last night. He'd been at Mercy's.

Truman glanced around the empty café. "Do you ever drive out on Simpson Road?"

"Of course. When I have sessions at Bree's place." His palm sweated against his cold cup. "What happened?"

His shoulders rose as he took a deep breath and met Ollie's gaze. "A truck like yours has been seen out there recently."

"So? I just said I've been out there."

Truman grimaced. "There's been some vandalism in the area, so I had to ask."

Ollie froze and felt his world crack. "You thought I did it?" His voice was too high. "Are you talking about the vandalism at Bree's?"

He doesn't trust me.

Truman's gaze narrowed. "Yes. How did you know that?"

Ollie pointed at Kaylie, his mouth instantly dry. "She just told me. Lucas was in here." Hot anger flashed, and he stared back at Truman. "I would *never* do anything like that."

"I know that, Ollie, but I had to ask because your truck fit a description. I don't deserve this job if I don't follow up."

"Lots of people have shitty trucks like mine."

51

Truman's expression went blank, and Ollie knew he'd gone too far. Truman had bought him the truck.

Bile rose in his throat. "It's not shitty. Fuck. I'm sorry. I think it's an awesome truck." He really did. The powerful growl of the engine made him smile every time he started it. "I didn't mean it," he muttered, wanting to take back the last ten seconds.

"I know." But the usual warmth in Truman's eyes hadn't returned. "I can't be surprised that you reacted that way to my questions."

"I'm sorry," Ollie repeated and longed to vanish. *Did Kaylie hear me be an ass?*

Truman clapped him on the shoulder. "It's over. Now I can look for other beat-up red trucks."

Ollie tried to smile, but his facial muscles refused to cooperate. "I hope you find who did it."

"Me too. I'll see you at home later tonight." Truman waved at Kaylie and made his exit.

Ollie looked back at Kaylie, who studied him from across the room, her hands on her hips, a small frown on her face. He felt two feet tall.

Did Truman really consider me a suspect?

◆ ◆ ◆

"It's Ellis Mull." Dr. Natasha Lockhart's dark eyes sparkled as she shared the news.

"Are you sure?" Mercy asked as her inner child cheered. She'd held her breath during most of the evening's drive with Eddie to the medical examiner's office, fingers crossed for an identification. The doctor had stated on the phone that she had information but wanted to share it in person.

"Sweet," said Eddie with a grin. "The pieces are falling into place."

The petite doctor nodded enthusiastically, looking as young as a first-year medical student, not like the experienced forensic pathologist

52

she was. Mercy liked the smart and witty woman, who was dedicated to scientifically cutting up bodies for answers.

"I can't believe we're celebrating someone's murder," Mercy murmured, guilt swamping her excitement.

"You're not," said Dr. Lockhart firmly. "You've identified someone who's been missing for a long time. His family can now have some closure."

Mercy eyed the broken eye socket of the skull, where Mull had been shot. *What will his family think of that?*

"You're doubting me," Dr. Lockhart said. "I've heard from too many families that not knowing is the absolute worst." She gently touched the skull. "This is horrible, but it's an answer. It will fill a gaping void for his family. Now they can start to heal."

"Did the dental X-rays provide the confirmation?" Eddie asked.

"Yes. The medical examiner's odontologist found Mull's old films and did the comparison. She's one hundred percent positive. The records match perfectly. She says that Ellis Mull hasn't had any dental work done since the original films. I'd suspected the remains were quite old, so the lack of dental work may reinforce my theory that he died not long after the robbery." She took a breath. "I'd already determined the remains weren't Whipple. He was too short based on the length of the femurs. Age and race hadn't ruled out Mull."

"Is the gunshot the cause of death?" Mercy asked. "Did anything else happen to him?"

"Solely working with skeletal remains limits my conclusions," Dr. Lockhart said, picking up the skull. "There's no soft tissue to determine other injuries. I studied every inch of bone that we have and didn't find any marks to indicate a stabbing or bludgeoning. Of course, not every bone is here. I'm missing several small ones from the hands. Probably carried off by some sort of vermin. The hyoid bone of the neck is missing. If it'd been present and broken, it could indicate a strangling." She set the skull down and picked up a lengthy bone that had to be from a leg. "He has heavy bones. Very thick. I read he'd played football and was into weight lifting. His long bone structure supports that." The doctor ran one finger down the length of the femur, stopping about halfway. "See this groove? It's the linea aspera. He's developed a hypertrophic lesion along it from heavy muscle use. He has similar lesions on his humerus at the deltoid insertion. This boy worked his body hard."

Compared to the medical examiner's tiny hands, the bone looked gigantic.

"His right clavicle and right fibula both had old, healed breaks, but I found nothing out of the ordinary on the rest of the skeleton to indicate how he died."

"Except that." Eddie touched the ravaged eye socket. "This is the entrance wound, correct?"

"Yes," said Dr. Lockhart. She turned the skull to view the back. "See how this hole has circular layers of bone missing around it? It's beveled. That tells me it's an exit. It'd be a clean hole if it was the entrance wound."

"The bullet continued through the wall of the shack," added Eddie. "We haven't found it yet."

Mercy suspected they never would. She looked at Eddie. "So where are the other two friends?"

"And the mysterious Jerry," he added. "The impression I've formed is that the four main guys were the best of friends. My money is on Jerry to be the hothead with a gun who wanted a bigger piece of the money pie."

"I would have picked Gamble as the shooter if he wasn't behind bars," said Mercy. "He's devious, and I can see him getting greedy."

"Think Gamble will be any more forthcoming once he knows Mull is dead?" asked Eddie.

Mercy remembered Shane Gamble's eyes. He craved information. His active brain was locked in a prison, and he was starving for more stimulation. Once Mull's identification was picked up by the media, they could lose some leverage with Gamble. "It's very possible. He enjoys the mind games. Now that I know how he thinks, I might be able to get something useful."

"How can someone who's been locked up for nearly thirty years help your investigation?" asked Dr. Lockhart.

Mercy pointed at the skull. "He was possibly stuck in a shed for thirty years. Has he been of help?"

The woman's dark eyes turned thoughtful. "Touché."

"Getting inside Gamble's skull will be tough," Eddie pointed out.

"I'll let you borrow my Stryker saw," offered Dr. Lockhart.

"I don't think the prison will allow it." Mercy grinned at the doctor, imagining the bone-cutting saw being used on Gamble.

"The media would love to hear you tried," Eddie said dryly. "I can see the headline: 'FBI Agent Threatens Inmate with Saw.'"

"Hopefully we'll have more time to investigate before the story breaks," said Mercy.

"I can't believe it hasn't broken yet," said the doctor. "I've kept things quiet here, and I know the odontologist in Portland won't talk, but the word is going to get out. People have wanted this mystery solved for decades."

"We've been very lucky so far," said Mercy. Her phone chimed. She glanced at the screen, and her heart sank. "I spoke too soon."

"What happened?" asked Eddie as he tried to see her screen.

"It's a text from Jeff. The office got a call from the *Midnight Voice*."

Dr. Lockhart wrinkled her nose. "The tabloid? They got the story first? That doesn't seem right."

"I'm sure the reputable news outlets will be right behind them," said Eddie.

Mercy sighed.

My job just got more difficult.

SEVEN

The next morning before work, Mercy darted across a street in Eagle's Nest to Rose's preschool and realized she should have scheduled a different time to see her sister. Parents were unloading their children from minivans and sedans. It was the morning drop-off rush.

Cindy, Rose's parent assistant, was just inside the door, greeting children as they went in. She spotted Mercy hesitating and frantically gestured for her to enter. Cindy's smile filled her face. "Rose is impatiently waiting for you."

"What's going on with Rose?" Mercy whispered as a tiny girl backed into her leg. She grabbed the child's shoulders before she toppled and steered her in a new direction. "I can't stay long. I need to get to work."

"I'll let her tell you." Cindy looked ready to burst with her secret.

Mercy wandered into the organized chaos of Rose's preschool, stunned as usual that ten small children could make so much noise. Rose sat on a chair in the center of the room. Children rushed her for hugs, tugged on her arm for attention, and talked all at once. Mercy watched as Rose greeted each one, knowing which children needed to stick close for reassurance and which needed to immediately immerse themselves in the toys. Her blind older sister was amazing. Once Rose was down to only two children glued to her side, Mercy approached. "Rose?"

"Mercy!" Rose turned toward her voice and her face lit up.

Mercy took one of her hands. Rose also looked ready to burst, but not in the I've-got-a-secret way that Cindy had. Rose's stomach was huge. She was starting the last month of her pregnancy, and it appeared she'd hidden a giant basketball under her dress. One of her students gently patted the side of Rose's belly, a blissful look on her small face.

Damn, Rose will be a great mother.

Mercy bent over to kiss her sister's soft cheek. "What did you need me to stop by for?"

Rose tugged at her necklace, pulling the chain out, and Mercy saw a diamond ring dangle and sparkle in the light.

Glee surged through Mercy, and she hugged her sister. "Nick proposed? You said yes?" The questions tumbled off Mercy's tongue, their answers apparent from the happiness on Rose's face.

"We had a long talk about getting married a few days ago and made some decisions. I thought that was the end of it until after the baby came. Instead he surprised me last night. I thought we were going out to eat, but he took me to his home. He'd made dinner, and afterward, he took my hand and laid the ring on my palm."

Mercy lifted the silver ring. "It's lovely, Rose." The center diamond was nestled in a delicate filigree setting and was encircled by six smaller stones and elaborate engravings.

"It belonged to his grandmother."

"It's an amazing heirloom—a work of art. The intricate setting is from a different era."

"We aren't getting it sized until my pregnancy fingers shrink back to normal," Rose said with a grin. "Nick also thought ahead to have the chain ready last night."

"He's very thoughtful. Nick's a good man, Rose." *An understatement.* "Do you have a wedding date?"

"My due date is thirty-two days away. Everyone tells me I'll need three months after that to feel halfway human again, so that puts us in fall. We're tentatively planning on mid-October." She leaned closer to Mercy. "He asked Dad for permission to marry me," she whispered.

Mercy bit her lip, holding back a laugh. "How did that go over with Dad?"

"He was thrilled but wasn't about to show it. I could hear the restraint in his voice." She laughed. "He got his wish to marry me off."

"We both know how ridiculous that was." Mercy had been furious at her father's awkward attempts at matchmaking for his pregnant daughter. He'd believed Rose should be married because she was pregnant. Who the man was hadn't seemed to matter.

"It was. But I'm sure he'll take credit for the match after the wedding."

"It was all Nick," said Mercy. "He's been googly-eyed over you for ages."

"I just couldn't see it," she quipped.

Mercy choked on laughter. "Jeez, Rose, I love you so much." She hugged her sister again and squeezed her eyes shut against the tears that threatened. "You deserve this. Nick is freaking lucky." Mercy pulled back and studied her sister's beautiful face, wishing she had half the peace that Rose shared with the people around her. "You're confident in him now?" she asked in a soft voice, hating to bring up Rose's worst fear.

The father of Rose's baby was a murderer and rapist, killed by Mercy and Truman as he held Rose hostage. Rose had worried that no man could ever accept her and her child.

"Yes." Beaming, Rose set her hand on the head of the little girl who was now using both hands to pat Rose's baby basketball. Rose frowned. Her hand slid over the girl's hair to her forehead. "Addie? Are you okay?" She moved the child to stand in front of her knees and ran inquisitive fingers over the child's face as her frown grew deeper. "She's burning up."

Mercy squatted and placed her hand on the girl's forehead. Addie stared silently at her with tired eyes. Rose was right. "She looks exhausted."

"Cindy?" Rose called out.

Cindy appeared, holding a small boy with one hand and a headless doll with the other. "Yes?"

"Call Addie's mom. She's got a fever. Let's keep her away from the other kids."

"I'm on it." Cindy set down the headless doll, and Mercy spotted the head in the boy's grip behind his back, shame on his face.

Someone was about to get a lecture.

"I need to get to work," Mercy told her sister. "Let's meet for dinner this week to celebrate."

"I'll call you," Rose promised, her attention still on the feverish child.

Mercy slipped out of the preschool, cheered by the happiness she'd seen in her sister. No one deserved it more than Rose.

"Agent Kilpatrick?" A young woman with a pleasant smile and dark-purple streaks in her blonde hair leaned against the door of a dusty little sedan. Parked illegally.

"Yes?"

"I understand you're working on the Gamble-Helmet Heist." Her smile didn't change.

An alert went off in Mercy's brain, and she stopped, eyeing the woman. She wore denim capris, a white T-shirt, and flip-flops. She looked young enough to be a friend of Kaylie's.

"Do I know you?" Mercy asked cautiously.

"No. It's true, though, right? Did you identify the body yet?"

Annoyance shot through her. "Excuse me. I was just leaving." She stepped into the street to cross to her car.

The woman shoved a business card in front of Mercy's stomach, making it impossible to move past the woman without either hitting her hand or taking the card. Instead Mercy stopped and gave the woman her best glacial glare.

"My name's Tabitha Huff. I work for the *Midnight Voice*."

"Move your hand, please." Ice water dripped from Mercy's tone. The woman worked for the tabloid that had contacted her office last night.

"What can you tell me about the remains?" Tabitha showed no fear, tilting her head in interest as she held Mercy's gaze.

Why are reporters so pushy?

"Nothing. Go bug a Kardashian." Mercy didn't take the card, yet the woman continued to hold it in front of her.

"You don't deny your case is related to the robbery." Cunning entered Tabitha's eyes.

"I deny and confirm nothing." Mercy pinned the woman with her gaze. "Why are you the only reporter here if you believe this is such a big story? Did someone leak you a false tip?"

The slightest quiver of Tabitha's lashes told Mercy she'd struck a nerve, so she pushed on. "I would think the local news would be hounding us—maybe even CNN or Fox. Sounds like your source isn't very reliable."

Tabitha's face blanked, her pleasant smile gone. "The public deserves to know. The Gamble-Helmet Heist is part of American lore. If you have the first lead in decades, it's going to change history."

Mercy blinked. "Isn't that a little extreme? The Civil War is history. Not one robbery with a dead victim. I think the correct description is *notorious* or *infamous* . . . or how about *senseless murder*?"

"America won't see it that way."

"Then you're doing your job wrong, because that's all it is."

"I'll check in to see if you've changed your mind later. You could be the national face of this investigation," she said earnestly.

That doesn't hold the appeal you think it does. "Call the office. I don't talk to media." With one finger, she gently pushed the woman's hand out of the way and crossed the street.

Who is the leak?

And why would they call a tabloid?

◆　◆　◆

Sandy physically hurt at the sight of the graffiti on the back wall of her B&B.

Her chest was full of pain. *My beautiful building.*

It wasn't just a building; it was her heart. The amazing result of years of hard labor.

Echoing in her head was her comment to Truman two days ago about wanting the vandal to stay away from the old home. It was as if someone had spray-painted the words in reaction to her wish.

Now Truman and his officer Samuel stood with her. Their silence spoke volumes.

Someone had scribbled BITCH! and WHORE! in angry, three-foot-tall letters.

"Thanks for coming," Sandy said, needing to fill the awkward silence. She put her hands on her hips, trying to hide the subtle quiver in her hands. "I didn't spot it until I took the garbage out at nine this morning." She gestured at the small dumpster and recycling bins to the right of the graffiti. "I don't know when it happened. I haven't been out here since early yesterday evening. As you can imagine, I'm rattled." *That's putting it mildly.* She'd seen the dark half-moons below her eyes in the mirror and noticed the cracked and dry lips. She'd had trouble sleeping since the start of the vehicle damage two weeks ago.

Beside her, Samuel abruptly let out a string of curses. Truman flinched and shot him an irritated glare.

61

"It's red paint," Samuel muttered, his tone heavy with menace for the culprit.

Truman nodded. "It's darker than the paint at Bree Ingram's farm, but still . . ."

"Bree?" Sandy's heart stopped. "Someone did this at her farm too?"

"It was different," Truman told her in a calm voice. "No words. Just some markings on the stalls and her truck yesterday."

Sandy fumed. Bree was her closest friend but hadn't said a word. "She'll be getting a phone call from me," she stated. "Any broken car windows?"

"No," answered Truman. "Yesterday was the first incident, and it was just paint."

WHORE. Sandy stared at the huge letters. *Why would Bree be targeted too?*

"Who does shit like this?" Samuel swore again. Fury radiated from him, and Sandy knew he wanted to hit someone. His anger didn't make her nervous. She was pleased he'd responded with Truman.

"Did you find some cameras?" Sandy asked Truman. It hurt to rely on someone's kindness to help protect her property, but she simply didn't have the money. She'd been in the red for months. If she had an accountant, he'd be in deep shock.

Good thing I can't afford one.

"Uhhh . . . I should have some by tomorrow."

Sandy didn't miss the glance Truman exchanged with Samuel. She narrowed her eyes at the two men, who she suspected weren't being completely truthful.

That makes three of us.

"I would have installed one to cover this area." Truman indicated the entire back side of her building. "It ticks me off that I'm too late. But we'll definitely have them up by tomorrow evening."

"Absolutely," Samuel chimed in. "We'll have the asshole the next time he tries anything."

Why am I not reassured? She didn't want to think about what the offender might do next time.

During Truman's last visit she'd been frustrated. Today that frustration had been replaced by . . . fear. A shudder shook her entire body.

It can't be . . .

"Do you have more of the house's original paint?" Samuel asked. His dark gaze bored into her skull, and she knew he'd seen her flinch a moment ago. She wondered if he suspected her . . . her lies . . . her facade . . .

"I do. I painted it by myself two years ago." Her voice fell. "I've worked so hard . . ."

"You have," Samuel agreed. "I'll help you cover it up." He stepped closer, his gaze locked on her face. "You have a feeling you might know who did this," he stated softly.

Sandy looked away, trying to control the tremble in her chin. "No. I told Truman the other day I have no idea what's going on."

"Sandy." Samuel touched her upper arm. "Look at me."

She did and crossed her arms on her chest. The concern in his eyes took her breath away, but she stayed stoic, not wanting him to see the true depth of her fear. The silence awkwardly stretched for a few seconds.

"Tell me what you think is going on," Samuel said patiently. "I can't help you unless you talk to me."

Tell him. Every fiber of her being told her she was wrong and then a split second later screamed that she was right. The conflict was tearing her apart.

She looked at her boots and rapidly spoke before she could change her mind again. "It could be my ex." A weight lifted from her shoulders, and she tentatively met Samuel's gaze again.

Samuel's expression hadn't changed.

"Ex-boyfriend?" Samuel asked.

"Ex-husband," she whispered.

"Why do you suspect him?" Samuel's voice maintained its calm tone.

Sandy finally glanced at Truman. "I'm sorry I didn't mention it sooner."

"You thought he was a possibility when I was here the other day?" he asked.

"I didn't want to consider it. It's been over ten years since . . ." She swallowed and tightened her crossed arms.

"Since what?" Samuel asked sharply, his brows coming together.

"Since I've heard from him."

"Why so long?" the officer pressed.

"Because I changed my name and moved here without telling him." Only two other people in Eagle's Nest knew those facts. Now the number had doubled. It felt as if she'd stepped off a pier into black, fathomless water, her deepest secrets dragging her down.

"What did he do to you?" Samuel asked gently.

"I'm jumping to conclusions," she forced out in an upbeat voice, trying to pull herself up to the surface. "I'm sure it's just teenagers." She smiled, knowing it was fake.

Neither was fooled.

"You don't believe that," said Truman as Samuel nodded. "Why would your ex do this?"

Sandy closed her eyes for a long moment, a rushing sound in her ears. "Almost no one knows about this."

"We'll keep it as quiet as we can," Samuel promised.

Can I do this?

"I left an abusive situation in Portland. I was terrified he would injure me in a permanent way if I didn't get out of there."

"Or kill you." Samuel's tone was flat, but anger projected from his eyes. Sandy looked away from the heat of his fury, but it comforted her instead of scaring her.

She'd been lucky to have a fresh start in Eagle's Nest. Now she had true friends and a spine of steel. But as soon as her ex-husband entered her thoughts, she'd become *that* woman—the woman who watched every word she said and tiptoed around her husband for fear of reprisal.

An abused wife.

Sandy despised the woman she used to be. She had fought and cried and struggled to get rid of that woman. But with a few broken windows and spray paint, she had reappeared.

What doesn't kill us makes us stronger.

I should be fucking Wonder Woman.

"I was stupid to stay as long as I did, but I was barely eighteen when we married, and he was ten years older. He'd convinced me that I was the one with the problem—I was the one who needed to learn to make our marriage work." She shook her head in disgust. "He was the king of gaslighting. It took a lot of therapy before I understood how he'd manipulated my thoughts and actions for twenty years. The physical stuff started toward the end. *Damn*, I was such a stereotype. I believed him when he said a punch was an accident. And then I believed him when he promised it'd never happen again. He begged and pleaded for me to forgive him as he explained how much strain he was under at work. Over and over I gave him more chances. I hid bruises, a broken arm, and black eyes. I honestly believed it was my fault. But when he knocked me unconscious, I knew I was done."

Both men watched her with wide eyes, no blame or pity present.

Thank God.

She couldn't stomach pity. Pity was for victims, and her days of being a victim were far in the past.

"I moved out while he was at work. I hired a divorce lawyer who also helped me start a new life. With a new name." She raised her chin, making herself look both of them in the eye. "During our divorce he threatened multiple times to kill me. My spousal support payments were removed from his paycheck because he refused to pay." She gave a nervous laugh. "That turned out for the best. The state sent the payments to me, so he never knew where to find me."

"What's his name?" Samuel spoke softly, but his command was clear.

Sandy cocked her head as she met the officer's gaze and paused before answering. "Lionel Kerns."

"What's your real name?" he continued in the same gentle tone.

"Jada." She pressed her lips closed. The name hadn't crossed her lips in years; it belonged to another woman. And she'd sworn she'd never say Jada Kerns again. Lionel's last name was like a brand that'd been forcibly burned into her soul. It was best forgotten.

"Jada. That's lovely," Samuel said.

Truman jerked his gaze from her to Samuel, confusion on his face. She took little notice. Samuel's compassion felt like a lifeline, one that was slowly hauling her out of the rough, black water.

Samuel understood and didn't seem to think any less of her.

Male judgment about her previous life was one of her worst fears. It'd kept her single and avoidant, believing no man could understand. Or, worse, that any man would be the same as Lionel.

Samuel looked at Truman, a desire to hunt in his gaze. "Let's find out where Lionel Kerns is these days."

EIGHT

Mercy decided that Art Juergen looked like a man who enjoyed retirement.

He wore a pink golfing shirt and tan pants, appearing as if he'd just stopped in after nine holes. His hair had a little more silver since she'd last seen him, and his skin indicated he'd spent a lot of time on the course.

After shaking his hand, she watched as he met Jeff and Eddie. Within thirty seconds the three men were talking as if they'd known each other for years. Art had a knack for putting people immediately at ease. Eddie hadn't crossed paths with Art in Portland, and Mercy saw he was making up for it. He peppered the former agent with questions.

"You don't know how stoked I was to hear that something turned up after all these years," Art told them as he took a seat in the small conference room. "It's *that* case for me. The one that I've always wondered about."

"I don't know if the new lead will take us anywhere," Mercy said. "Yes, we've got the remains of one of the robbers and some money bags, but will it help us find the other men?"

"Won't know until you try," Art said earnestly. "Every few years the robbery would be featured on a TV news show or turn up in a magazine, and the leads would start pouring in again." He stroked his chin, a faraway look in his eyes. "When the investigation started, there were over a hundred agents working it. Stories were in the news every day, and tips flooded our phones. It took a lot of manpower to follow up on every call, but we did."

"I can't imagine," Jeff stated. "Hopefully it won't hit as hard this time."

"You've heard from the press?" Art asked.

"Just one tabloid so far. We've done our best to keep a lid on it for now."

Surprise lit Art's face. "You're lucky. You'll have time to get organized before the rush."

"I don't think anyone can be prepared enough for that," added Eddie dryly.

Mercy had watched footage of the FBI's old press conferences on the robbery. Art Juergen had spoken at each one. He'd been unflappable and serious, projecting firm control of the investigation. A good television face for the FBI.

"How helpful was Shane Gamble in the beginning?" Mercy asked.

"Shane Gamble." Art leaned forward, resting his hands on the table, and met each investigator's eyes. "Gamble was always cocky, never repentant for the death of that guard or the loss of the money. I swear he looked forward to our conversations . . . I've never met anyone quite like him. He seemed to get off on bantering with me."

"Yes." Mercy blinked as she realized she'd spoken out loud. All eyes turned to her. "He's still the same."

"Part of me admired him," Art admitted. "This young punk had orchestrated one of the boldest robberies in the States and succeeded in stumping the FBI. Not a lot of people have done that."

"He murdered another inmate," Mercy stated. "He deserves no admiration."

"I know." Shame flicked across Art's face. "Does he still claim the inmate was paid to murder him?"

"He does," Mercy said. "For someone who's pretty smart, why does he make such an outrageous claim? It doesn't fit with the rest of his personality."

"I'd wondered the same thing," Art told her. "We investigated and found nothing to support it. No payments to the murdered man or his family. I think he made it up to cover for losing his temper. Maybe he believes it himself by now."

"I can see that. Maybe it *does* fit with his psyche." Mercy thought hard, remembering Shane's confidence during her interview. "He acts like he's completely successful even though he's been in prison for nearly thirty years. Maybe he has a mental block to admitting failure on his part. He has to cast the rationale for the murder on someone else."

"Very possible," Jeff agreed. He looked to Art. "What about the search for the other four men?"

Art blew out a huge breath and slumped back in his chair. "We had so much data rolling in, we must have missed something. We got nowhere on the other four. It was like they vanished into thin air."

"But your gut said . . . ," Eddie prompted.

The older agent grinned. "Canada. I couldn't get it out of my head that they'd vanished into a remote part of Canada."

"That describes most of the country," Eddie said.

"They were all avid campers," said Art. "Snow or sun. Gamble's parents told me their son and his friends loved to disappear into the Oregon wilderness for a few days. Gave his mom sleepless nights, but his father supported it. I kept imagining the other thieves in a remote cabin, toasting their success." He shook his head, a touch of wonder in his eyes. "The image still sticks with me."

"Well, we know that one of the thieves was in a remote cabin," said Eddie. "At least two were there if Mull was murdered by one of the others." Eddie turned to Mercy. "Do you want me to inform Mull's family? Dr. Lockhart emailed me about the notification this morning, and I told her we'd handle it in person. They live in Salem."

"Can you do that today?" Mercy asked.

"Absolutely," said Eddie.

"I wish Gamble's parents were still alive," said Mercy. "I want to talk to them."

"Good people. But they were never the same after their son committed murder." Art's face fell. "His mother developed lung cancer a few years ago. I visited Gamble's parents several times while she was sick to offer my support. We'd gotten to know each other over the years, and I could relate to their struggles. I swear Gamble's father died of a broken heart after his wife died." Art swallowed audibly, dropping his gaze to the table. "My wife died from lung cancer too."

Mercy's heart sank. She'd forgotten that part. Art had rarely mentioned his wife during her time in Portland. His wife had been in her early thirties when she died—Mercy's age now. The bits and pieces Mercy had learned of her death, she'd heard from other agents; Art hadn't wanted to talk about it. The pain of his loss flooded the room.

"I'm so sorry, Art."

Eddie and Jeff echoed her words.

He gave a brave but weak smile. "It's been over twenty years. Time helps but doesn't fully heal, you know?"

The room was silent for a long second, and Mercy couldn't figure out a polite way to continue the robbery conversation.

"Sorry about going off track, folks." Art's voice was stronger. "Back to the Gamble robbers . . . I wouldn't be surprised if they were all dead by now."

Mercy admired how he pushed past a topic that was clearly painful for him.

"The case has been too quiet," said Art. "Dead people don't talk. With four missing people, someone should have talked or bragged by now."

"Three missing people since Mull has turned up," Eddie corrected him. "What was the consensus on the mystery driver? New friend?"

"That was a weird one. Honestly, I don't know what to think. I suspect Gamble wasn't lying about Trevor Whipple bringing in someone at the last moment, but why did this person's family never claim their son or father was missing?"

"Surely there were male missing person reports of the right age," argued Mercy.

"None that panned out," said Art. "I spent more time trying to figure out the mystery driver's identity than on any other aspect of the case."

"The guard who survived didn't have a description of the driver, right?" asked Mercy.

"Nope. He said the driver never stepped foot out of the car. He faintly remembered that there was even a car. The guard was really rattled."

"With good reason," said Eddie. "His partner was murdered. What was the surviving guard's name again?"

"Gary Chandler," supplied Mercy. His interviews in the file were nightmareworthy. His trauma painfully echoed through his words.

"Gary hated dealing with us," said Art. "It brought back the ordeal he'd suffered every time. I know he got psychiatric help after the robbery, but I swear the incident altered something fundamental in him. He reminded me of the guys who came back from war with PTSD."

"Can't blame him," Mercy said quietly. "The other guard died in his arms." A shudder shot through her, and out of the corner of her eye she saw Eddie's and Jeff's concerned gazes. She'd been in Gary Chandler's shoes when her brother Levi died. "I hope he's willing to speak with us."

"Might be better if I call him," Art suggested, scrolling through his phone. "He knows me. I'll tell him to talk to you."

"Perfect. Hopefully I can see him today while Eddie notifies the Mull family."

"I don't think Gary has much on his schedule these days," said Art. "Never had another job as far as I know."

"For thirty years?" Skepticism rang in Jeff's voice. "That seems extreme."

"Can't judge what's going on in another man's brain," the retired FBI agent stated.

"True," said Mercy.

Gary Chandler was forever altered. The children of the murdered armored car guard had lost their father. The families of the thieves had been left in limbo for thirty years.

At least today Ellis Mull's family would get an answer. But not the answer they'd hoped for.

How many lives has this robbery shattered?

Truman had to Google the town of Gervais, Oregon.

Sandy's ex-husband, Lionel Kerns, currently resided in Gervais and worked for an RV manufacturer.

Truman eyed the online map. Gervais was about a three-hour drive from Bend and sat an hour south of Portland. The location didn't eliminate Lionel as a suspect in Sandy's vandalism. Looking through Lionel's priors, Truman found a DUI conviction from four years ago and a recent assault conviction. He dug a little deeper and discovered there were no arrest records from the time when Lionel had lived in Portland with Sandy.

But Sandy said he assaulted her.

72

She never pressed charges?

He sighed and slumped back in his desk chair. He'd seen it before. He couldn't count the number of times he'd pushed for a battered wife or girlfriend to press charges against her partner. A blank look would take over the woman's face, and she'd avoid his eyes. Sandy didn't seem like the type to let assault slide, but she might be a different woman today than she'd been a decade ago.

Did she change out of necessity?

He'd never seen Sandy on a date or heard her name associated with a man's in the rounds of town gossip. This morning was the first time he'd given half a thought to Sandy's personal life, when Samuel surprised him with his obvious feelings toward her.

How long has Samuel been interested?

Since Truman had known Sandy, she'd been one of the unofficial town leaders, joining Ina Smythe, Pearl and Rose Kilpatrick, and Barbara Johnson in their frequent plans to better their community.

From the police department lobby came a familiar voice and the distinctive thumps of a cane on the floor.

Speak of the devil.

Truman stepped away from his desk, headed down the hall, and found Ina Smythe giving her grandson, Lucas, a lecture about the dust that had built up behind his desk's monitor. Truman bit the inside of his cheek as his big office manager promptly ran a damp cloth over the offending area while Ina pointed out other places he'd missed.

"Truman!" Ina turned her cheek for a kiss and he obeyed.

Ina had been a pseudoaunt to him during the high school summers Truman had spent in Eagle's Nest with his uncle, his yearly escape from San Jose city life. Later Ina had recommended Truman for the chief of police job after a serious injury as a cop in the big city had nearly killed him. He'd been left wondering if he'd ever return to police work until Ina's offer came through.

"Let's talk in your office." She painfully headed in that direction, leaning heavily on her cane. Arthritis and bad knees had troubled her for years.

Not "Do you have a minute?" or "Can we talk?"

He smiled. That was Ina. This was her town.

As he followed the determined woman, a small pang vibrated through his heart; her usual limp was more pronounced, and she seemed more frail than usual.

He put the thoughts out of his mind. Ina Smythe wouldn't allow death to tell her what to do.

With a heavy sigh, she sat in a chair across from his desk and waved him to his seat with her cane. He grinned and sat.

"How's the boy?" she asked, fixing her hawklike stare on him.

"Ollie? Good."

Frustration flashed, and she waggled her cane at him. "You know what I mean. He found that body two days ago. He handling it all right?"

"Ollie's an outdoorsman . . . and this wasn't his first encounter with death. He's doing as well as can be expected for an eighteen-year-old."

"I get a good feeling from that boy. He's terrified to make eye contact with me, but he's got better manners than my own kids ever did."

"He likes cookies," Truman suggested. "And you should offer a treat to his dog next time you see him. Those two things will win him over."

"He's got a past."

It wasn't a question, but Truman knew she wanted an explanation. Curiosity shone in her eyes. Few people knew Ollie's history, and he liked it that way. The orphan didn't want anyone feeling sorry for him.

"That's Ollie's story to tell. Like I said, try cookies."

"Hmph." She didn't care for his answer, but she accepted it. "They identify the body yet?"

"They did yesterday evening. He wasn't a local."

"Who was it?"

Truman shifted in his seat, making his chair squeak, knowing the FBI hadn't released the identity. They were waiting to notify Mull's family and trying to keep the media coverage to a minimum.

She held up a hand. "Don't worry about it. I'll find out soon enough."

Relief flooded him. It was still ingrained in him to answer Ina's questions.

I'm not a teenager anymore.

"Why are you waiting so long for a wedding to that woman?"

The question out of left field didn't surprise him. This was typical of conversations with Ina; she collected information.

"I assume you're referring to Mercy. We both know she doesn't rush into anything, and we wanted to wait until—"

"Rose has her baby and marries Nick."

Truman nodded.

"I heard about their engagement. Took him long enough. I had them pegged as a couple almost two years ago."

"What?" Ina had managed to surprise him.

"I saw the way he looked at her at the Fourth of July picnic the year before last and knew it was just a matter of time. Like your Mercy, Nick doesn't rush into anything. He takes his time. Does things right. But I knew he'd made his mind up back then."

"Huh." Truman was speechless. Mercy had believed Nick's interest was relatively new.

"He's got good character, that one. I remember when his wife died, and I wondered if he'd ever recover. I knew he'd wished they'd had children. Now with Rose pregnant, that man will have two people to cherish. That baby couldn't have a better father."

Truman could only nod, his throat thickening. Some men would struggle with the parentage of Rose's baby. Nick wasn't one of them.

Why am I surprised when Ina reveals how well she knows her people?

75

"What do you know about Sandy's time before she moved to Eagle's Nest?" he asked, hoping for Ina's insight into the woman's past.

Her eyes narrowed at him. "Is this about the vandalism at her place?"

"Partially."

"What has she told you?" Ina asked cautiously.

She knows.

But he saw she was holding back, not wanting to betray a confidence. Ina knew when stories were appropriate to spread and when to hold her tongue.

Unlike some of the other gossips in town.

"She told us about Lionel."

Ina relaxed back into her chair, tucking her cane between her knees as she considered Truman's question. "It took me a few years to get the story out of Sandy. Anyone who met that woman could tell she had a past. I swear she looked over her shoulder for years, always expecting something horrible to come for her."

"She's suggested her ex might be responsible for the vandalism."

Ina gazed out the window, her fingertips tapping the arch of her cane. "Maybe. But she hasn't heard from him in ten years." Her sharp eyes abruptly met his. "Right? Don't tell me she knows he's creeping around." Fury burned in her gaze, and Truman worried for Lionel.

"She's not positive about that. We had to pull the story out of her, she seemed—"

"Who's 'we'?"

"Samuel and me."

"Ahhh." A knowing look crossed her face, and she nodded.

"Don't tell me . . ."

"Oh yes. I've noticed how your officer looks at her."

"I feel like I'm constantly in the dark in this town. Not a good place for someone in my position," Truman groused.

She brushed aside his comment with a flick of her wrist. "Don't worry about it. I'd tell you if it was important. This is just people stuff."

"The people of Eagle's Nest are my business."

"Their personal lives aren't."

He bit back his next comment. *But they're yours?*

She narrowed her eyes at him. "Yes, they're mine. You're in charge of the laws and enforcement. The happiness of the people is mine. If I can do something to improve someone's quality of life, I'm going to do it. Sometimes that means asking a lot of questions and maybe sticking my nose into places people don't like. Anyway, Sandy told me about that jerk who beat on her and made me swear to keep it silent. I have until now. Do you think there's any chance it's him?"

"He's got a recent assault conviction and lives about three hours away. It doesn't rule him out." He paused. "He doesn't have a record from the time he was married to Sandy."

Ina pressed her lips together and slowly nodded. "She wasn't up to it. She has a lot of regret about not pressing charges. I hope that hasn't come back to haunt her."

"I'll keep looking into it. We're putting up cameras at her B&B tomorrow."

"You're looking into the problems at my daughter-in-law's place too, right?"

This is the real purpose of her visit. Bree.

"We are . . . It's possibly connected to the issues at the bed-and-breakfast," Truman said. "We haven't had vandalism reports for months, so it's hard to believe that two completely unrelated but similar vandalism cases occurred within a week."

"Doesn't feel right."

"I agree." Truman sighed. "All the graffiti feels personalized to the victim. But it still could be the same person with two axes to grind."

"Bree is upset. She feels her horses are in danger." Exasperation filled Ina's tone. "She's more concerned about them than the *X* on her truck."

77

"She has every right to be upset. I suspect it's easier for her to focus on the horses than consider that the vandal intended a message for her. No one wants to feel targeted."

"Lucas can't be out there all hours of the day, watching out for his mother."

"Neither can we," Truman said gently.

Waves of dissatisfaction rolled off his visitor, and her knuckles whitened as she gripped her cane.

"I know you're concerned," Truman stated. "Bree is a priority to me. Sandy is too, and I'm doing my best to figure out what's happening."

Ina had the grace to look away. "I know you're good at your job . . . but I *had* to say something," she said in a low voice. "It's my family."

"You wouldn't be the Ina I've always known if you hadn't said something," Truman said with sympathy. "I'd be worried if I hadn't received a phone call or visit over this."

"Not asking for special treatment."

"Everyone gets the most special treatment I can give."

The corners of her mouth slowly turned up. "You're a good chief, Truman Daly."

"Why do I feel like you're not complimenting me?" he asked, raising his brows.

"Mighta been a compliment for myself. I knew you were the best for the job." She stood, pushing up with one quivering arm to keep her balance.

"How are you doing, Ina?" Watching her struggle hurt something integral in his soul.

She glared at him, dark eyes flashing. "Why?"

He held up his hands. "Just asking."

"Don't want to be fussed over."

"But you'll keep me in the loop?" He held her gaze, relaying his concern.

She paused. "Of course. Now get back to work and let me say goodbye to my grandson." She turned her back to him and shuffled out to the hall.

Truman stayed put at his desk, following her order and wondering if she'd actually tell him if she had any serious health problems.

She protected her privacy with an iron wall but could easily convince others to share their biggest secrets.

He turned back to his computer screen and studied the image from Lionel Kerns's driver's license, committing it to memory. He sent the photo to the rest of his officers. According to Kerns's stats, he was six foot three and nearly three hundred pounds. He had a silvering beard and a wide nose. Truman studied the eyes, growing angry that the large man had believed he had the right to beat on his wife. Sandy was tall and strong, but not enough to defend herself against a man of that size.

If Lionel Kerns was messing with Sandy or Bree, Truman wanted to be the first person to lay a hand on him.

My town.

NINE

Sandy picked a bench in the sunshine, plopped down, and closed her eyes, lifting her face to the sun as she waited for Bree. After Truman and Samuel had left, her first phone call had been to her best friend, asking why she hadn't mentioned her vandalism. Bree had gone quiet on the phone and asked if they could meet in person.

Toddler shouts made Sandy open her eyes. A young mom play-chased her two tots, who screamed in joy. Twin boys. And the mother's stomach bulged with another new life. Sandy admired her. Kudos to a mom who would get pregnant when she already had toddler twins.

I can't imagine her life.

Not that Sandy's life was easy street. Guests frequently woke her in the middle of the night. Issues with their beds, outdoor noises, spiders, and one time a ghost. Even with the extensive variety she served on her breakfast buffet, someone always requested—demanded—something different. Then there were the guests who expected food to be available all day long. Sandy had tried to accommodate her hungry guests the first year she was in business and then realized they were taking advantage of her. Now she provided fresh cookies, tea, and coffee at all hours. Nothing else. No kombucha, no popcorn, no mangos, no "just a sandwich."

Learning not to be a pushover had taken time.

It wasn't easy when submissiveness had been pounded into your psyche for years.

The boys tore past her bench, and the mother grinned as she made eye contact with Sandy. Sandy smiled back.

No children for me. I'm nearly fifty and married to my work.

She had no complaints about her current life, but she couldn't help the small pangs of envy when she saw babies.

"Sorry I'm late!" Bree slid onto the bench next to her and shoved a paper coffee cup into Sandy's hand, and they hugged. Bree's hair smelled of hay and horses.

Mine must smell of Clorox.

Sandy took a drink of her hazelnut coffee. The fact that Bree had added the perfect amount of cream sparked a small joy in her heart. It reflected their close relationship. They knew each other's likes, dislikes, and most intimate secrets. Bree's friendship was at the top of Sandy's favorite-things list.

"Now." Sandy looked her friend in the eye. "Tell me everything about the vandalism. I'm wondering if the same person did mine."

Bree's happy expression faded into one of caution. "I'm sure it's not related to yours. That wouldn't make sense."

"I'd like to form my own opinion about that. Talk." Her tone left no room for Bree to protest.

Bree turned to lean back on the bench, her gaze focused across the small playground.

Sandy mentally sorted through possibilities as Bree described the scene at her farm.

When she was finished, Bree finally looked at Sandy, an odd expression in her eyes. "What are you thinking?"

"I'm wondering if I was followed when I went to ride at your place last weekend," Sandy said.

"Why would someone follow you?"

"To see what's important to me. I'm pretty sure my love for that horse is obvious when I'm there."

Bree's face was blank. "You think my damage was aimed at you? Why?"

Sandy cocked her head; Bree's flat tone made no sense.

Why isn't she more concerned?

"You know my history," Sandy said slowly. *And you're about to hear a lot more.*

"You're referring to your ex."

"Yes. I can't think of any other reason someone would spray-paint *bitch* and *whore* on my building."

"But he doesn't know where to find you." Bree's eyes crinkled in worry. "Does he?"

"I don't know," Sandy whispered. "I haven't told you everything." Her voice shook.

Bree took her hand and squeezed. "Talk away."

Comfort flowed from her friend's hand. "You know he physically abused me. I told you how I had to sneak away and change my name."

"Yes."

The care in Bree's gaze nearly undid her. "You don't know how bad it was . . . It wasn't just the physical stuff. It was mental and emotional too."

"Of course it was," Bree said gently. "They go hand in hand."

"I had no money. He wouldn't let me work. He gave me some cash at the beginning of every month and that was to buy all our groceries and anything else the house needed." The words spilled out of her. She'd opened a gate that'd been locked for a decade. "I knew how to stretch every dollar. I planted a garden to make the grocery money last longer. I traded with neighbors for fruit from their trees and firewood for heat.

When he realized this, he cut the cash back more because I clearly didn't need it. It wasn't about the lack of money—not completely. It was the mental abuse. Everything was my fault. The reason he couldn't give me more money was my fault. The reason the meals were never tasty enough was my fault. The reason he had to work was my fault. Nothing was ever good enough."

"That's horrible."

"I was stuck. I didn't know how to leave. He wanted children . . . I never understood how he could be so disgusted with me but also want children from me." Her heart pounded. "Of course it was my fault I never got pregnant."

"Asshole."

One corner of Sandy's lips curved up. "It was my fault," she admitted. "I got birth control. I might not have been able to do anything else, but you can be damned certain I would do anything to keep from having his child. I guarded those pills with my life. I had nightmares that he'd find my hiding spot and beat me, throw out the pills, and then rape me." Revulsion racked her.

"Oh, Sandy." Bree looked ready to cry.

"His mission was to keep me down. If I was under his foot, it supported his ego. He felt strong and powerful." She laughed. "I can see it so clearly now. I look back and can't understand why I married him in the first place."

"But you told me that he wined and dined you at first. Bought you flowers and jewelry."

"I was so stupid."

"You were young. He sounded like a dream."

"In a way he was. He was older and mature. His truck was new, and he took me to the nicest restaurants. But it all stopped once we got married. It didn't just stop, it turned 180 degrees."

"Like I said. Asshole." Bree leaned closer. "I think you're letting your memories take control of your thoughts. Yes, something bad has happened recently, but you don't know that it's him. It's understandable that you're thinking that way, but you need to take a step back and look at the situation rationally."

Bree made sense.

Am I expecting the worst?

Bitch. Whore.

Terror swept through her. "No. I know it's him."

"But Sandy . . ." Bree didn't finish. Instead she set down her coffee and added her other hand to the one gripping Sandy's. "My vandalism is directed at me. I know it. It can't be your ex harassing me." Her tone was flat again. "I told you about the big *X* on my truck door . . . That's *personal.*"

"Who would make it personal to both of us?" Sandy asked. *She's holding back.* "I feel like you're not telling me something."

Bree said nothing, her two hands still tight on Sandy's one.

A chill settled on Sandy's skin. Even in the warm sun, goose bumps rose on her arms. "Do you know who did this, Bree?" Her voice cracked.

Her best friend was silent, a mental struggle reflected in her eyes. She finally spoke. "I have some suspicions."

"Did you tell the police? Because Truman was stumped today. I don't think he has any leads."

"It's too far-fetched." Bree gave a weak smile. "My memories are running away with my thoughts too."

"Tell me," Sandy ordered. "I've told you everything. You know how I had to pull myself up. Lionel *destroyed* my self-worth. How can yours be worse than mine? The police deserve to know . . . I deserve to know. Whoever is doing this is trying to tear me down again." Anger was red hot on her tongue. "He's in for a surprise. I'm not the powerless person I used to be. I will fight back with everything I've got because I deserve better. I never believed that when I was married. I thought I deserved what I had—but now I know I'm worth it."

"You have come so far," Bree told her, her dark gaze holding Sandy's. "You are the strongest woman I know. You put yourself back together and became the type of person I wish I was. You have no idea how much I admire and envy your backbone."

She's not going to tell me. I never thought I'd see the day she let me down.

"Give me a few days. I'm going to look into some things." Bree took a deep breath. "I want to make sure I'm not crazy first before I tell the police my suspicions."

"I might be out of business by then." *Truth.*

"You've got to trust me on this, Sandy." Her eyes pleaded for understanding.

I don't understand.

Bree's head jerked as her gaze shot to the far side of the park. "Did you see that truck?"

Sandy looked in time to catch a flash of red. "The red one?"

"Yes."

"Why?"

"I swear I've seen it five times in the last two days."

Sandy frowned. "A lot of people around here drive red trucks." She studied her friend, who appeared sincerely rattled. "Is this part of our minds running away with our thoughts?"

Bree's laugh was feeble. "I think you're right. I've been looking over my shoulder for a while now."

"You're not the only one," admitted Sandy. "My neck is sore from looking behind me." She stood and tossed her empty coffee cup in the garbage can at the end of their bench. "I think we need something stronger than coffee."

"I'm with you."

TEN

Ollie stepped through the door of the Dairy Queen and inhaled.

Grease. Sugar. Meat.

His mouth watered.

Burgers, fries, and ice cream were some of his favorite highlights of joining the outside world, and the run-down Dairy Queen provided them all. At first he'd visited the DQ a few times a week until he realized a large chunk of his hard-earned money from his new jobs was being eaten away. Literally. Now the DQ was a luxury he allowed himself once every other week. He told the woman behind the counter which burger he wanted and then paused as he struggled to decide on the ice cream. He'd tried every dessert available, but there was something about the combination of vanilla soft serve, hot fudge, and peanuts that kept calling his name.

"Tough decision?"

Ollie turned around. Behind him was a young woman with a sweet smile and purple stripes in her pale hair who stared right into his eyes. His stomach fluttered, and he swallowed hard, unable to form words.

"I like the dip cones myself." She continued to smile, encouraging him to answer.

"Peanut Buster Parfait," he blurted, unable to pull his gaze from perfect green eyes. She looked a little older than he, but that could be all the makeup. Since he'd lived with Truman, he'd learned he was a horrible judge of age.

"Is that what you want today, Ollie?" asked Gloria, the DQ employee patiently waiting for him to decide.

He spun back to the counter. "Yes. Parfait." He counted out cash and handed it over.

"I haven't had a Peanut Buster Parfait in years," said the green-eyed goddess behind him.

He glanced back at her out of the corner of his eye as he shoved his wallet back in his pocket. *Talk to her.*

"It's good." *Brilliant.*

"Then it must be time for me to have one again." Still smiling, she ordered and then joined him at the far end of the counter, where he'd moved to wait for his food. "Haven't I seen you at the coffee place in town?" She looked expectantly at him.

"Probably." How had he not noticed her?

"I'm new around here. Really haven't met anyone."

His mind raced for a witty reply. "It's a nice town."

"I really hate eating alone. Would you mind if I sat with you?"

"No . . . I mean, that'd be fine . . . It'd be great."

Her pleased grin made his knees feel like soft serve.

"Here you go, Ollie." Gloria pushed a tray across the counter to him and winked. A flush heated his face, and he wondered if it was noticeable. "Enjoy your lunch." She waggled her eyebrows.

"Where's the ice cream?" he asked.

"Oh, whoops. Hang on." Gloria grabbed two clear cups next to the soft serve machine and skillfully whipped up two parfaits. She set them together on the counter in front of Ollie and his new friend. "Here you go, you two. Have a *great* lunch."

She'd never delivered his food with such enthusiasm. He moved one of the parfaits to his tray and followed the younger woman to a booth with orange seats. He sat, overwhelmed by the fact that this gorgeous, talkative creature wanted to eat with him.

Conversation topics.

"I'm Ollie."

"Tabitha." She took a huge bite of fudge and closed her eyes in ecstasy. "You're a bad influence on me."

Watching Tabitha eat hot fudge made him slightly dizzy. Unable to move, he stared until her eyes opened. She licked a spot of chocolate off her lip. "You eating?"

He'd forgotten his food. "Yeah." He unwrapped his burger, unable to start his Peanut Buster Parfait. *Is that how I look when I eat one?* He took a big bite of greasy burger and chewed. No flavor. His taste buds had gone on strike.

"How long have you lived here, Ollie?" she asked as she focused on her ice cream.

He swallowed. "About two months."

"You're a newbie like me." Her eyes twinkled.

"I've only been in Eagle's Nest two months," he clarified. "I've always lived in Central Oregon . . . in a more remote area." A pickle crunched in his mouth. He couldn't taste it; he didn't care. "Where are you from?" Composing a solid question pleased him.

"I live in Los Angeles. I'm just in town for a little while."

Disappointment made his heart drop. She wasn't staying. His fantasy of a girlfriend with purple hair burst like a balloon.

"I'd like to learn more about Eagle's Nest before I have to leave," she said encouragingly. "I bet you know some. We could hang out for a while."

"Sounds good." He tried to revive his enthusiasm. *How long is a while?*

She leaned across the table, making her breasts press against her shirt, and held his gaze. "I heard they found a murdered body not too far away." Her voice was appropriately quiet, but fascination burned in her eyes.

Alarms rang in Ollie's head.

"Do you know if that's true?" Tabitha asked. "Or are people making stuff up?"

"It's true," he admitted.

Her eyes widened. "Oh! How scary . . . Did they catch who did it?"

"It happened a long time ago," Ollie informed her, feeling a little guilty for talking about the dead. "It wasn't really a body . . . Just a skeleton was left." An image of the skull's bullet hole flashed in his mind.

"Do they know who it was? Or how long ago it happened?" She took another bite, her gaze never leaving his as she hung on every word. Melted soft serve dripped on the table.

"Well . . . don't tell anyone, but they think it's related to a big robbery that happened in Portland a long time ago."

"You're not talking about the Gamble-Helmet Heist, are you?"

Ollie froze. "How'd you know?"

"Everyone knows about it." She shrugged and looked at her parfait as she scooped up fudge and peanuts. "If it's related to that, then whose skeleton is it?"

Ellis Mull. He'd heard Truman and Mercy discussing it yesterday, but something stopped him from saying it out loud. "Dunno."

"Surely you've heard something."

Is that what it looks like when someone bats their eyelashes? Ollie abruptly felt as if he'd been trapped. "Nothing." He took another bite of his burger and studied the girl through fresh eyes. "What are you doing in Eagle's Nest?"

She looked at her ice cream. "Work stuff."

"What kind of work do you do?" Now that his brain was functioning, the world appeared crystal clear, and a murky cloud of suspicion clung to Tabitha.

"I just need to write up something. Say . . . is there a movie theater around here?" she asked with hope in her eyes.

"No. The closest theater is in Bend. What do you write?"

Her winning smile had lost some of its warmth. "Just little articles. Like what it's like to live in a small town such as this one."

"Usually it's pretty great to live here. Do you have a business card?"

Now her smile vanished. "Why?"

"Because I've hinted several times that I want to know what you do."

"Well, I haven't pressured you to tell me what *you* do." She thrust her chin forward and stubbornly tilted her head.

"I work in the warehouse for Lake Ski and Sports, and I also detail cars at a dealership in Bend. I'm not in school, but I take online courses and plan to start at the community college for summer session. See? It's not hard to be forthright." He held her gaze as he took another bite of burger, thoroughly chewed, and then swallowed. "Why do I feel like you're playing me? I've got nothing anyone could want." *Except access to the police chief and an FBI agent.*

Tabitha slipped a card out of her purse and pushed it across the table.

TABITHA HUFF
STAFF WRITER
THE MIDNIGHT VOICE

"You write for a tabloid." He'd scanned the headlines in stores as a kid, hungry for information. Any information.

"I don't write anything that's not true."

"I recently saw a headline about the president having seven toes on one foot."

"I didn't write it."

"You have higher standards?"

90

"It's a job. My pieces are factual and well written."

"Why did you target me?" *Does she know I found the body?*

She stirred her fudge into the melting ice cream, watching it blend together. "I saw you leave the house where Agent Kilpatrick spent the night. She doesn't live there, right?"

Ollie ignored her question. "You followed me? After you'd already followed Mercy to the house?" Dread crawled up his spine. Mercy and Truman were not going to like these facts.

"I didn't get any information when I talked to the FBI agent, and I figured the police chief wouldn't talk to me either, so I decided on a different approach when I spotted you." She was all business now. The earlier flirtation was completely gone.

"How'd you find out about the remains?"

"I got a tip. Someone created a Twitter account just to tweet at me that they had a big story. I privately messaged them, and after hearing what they had to say, I decided it was worth a look."

"What was in the tip?"

"That the notorious robbery case was about to blow open and reveal all the characters involved. He told me about the money bags and remains that had been found."

"How could he have known that?"

"He wouldn't tell me, but I had nothing to lose by poking around. I saw a chance at breaking a huge story. He said he wasn't sharing it with any other media."

Ollie frowned. "Why not? I'd go to the big-gun reporters, not a tabloid."

She lifted one shoulder. "Anyway, I've been following you since early this morning." She leaned forward, a sneaky gleam in her eye. "Are you following the woman in the silver truck?"

Dry bun stuck in Ollie's throat, and he coughed. *Crap.* "I don't know what you're talking about." He struggled to clear his throat, wishing he'd ordered a soda.

91

Tabitha rolled her eyes. "Do you have some sort of weird obsession with her? She's old enough to be your mom."

He snorted. "That's sick. She's a nice lady . . ."

Tabitha raised a perfectly shaped eyebrow at him as she waited for the rest of his explanation.

How did she turn the tables back on me?

"There's been some weird vandalism at her place. I'm keeping an eye out for anything odd around her."

Tabitha stared. "You're pretending to be a secret protector? That's still twisted."

"It's not like that." Ollie fumbled for the right words to explain. "I'm good at watching people and blending into the background . . . I used to do it when I lived—well, where I lived before."

"You don't blend. I noticed right away."

"Well, it was easier in the woods." Truth. It was difficult to be discreet in his red truck. "I know the police can't always watch out for her, so I help out when I have some time."

"The police asked you to help?" Skepticism filled her tone.

"No . . . I'm just doing it."

"Still creepy." Tabitha pushed away her half-eaten parfait, leaned back in the booth, and crossed her arms.

"How old are you?" Ollie asked, curiosity taking over his tongue.

"Twenty-two. Why?"

"I'm only eighteen. Did you really think I'd fall for your lonely-single-woman routine?"

"You're eating with me, aren't you?" She raised one brow.

"What are you going to do next?" he asked, ignoring that she was correct. "I don't think anyone in Eagle's Nest will give you information for your story."

A slow, wide smile answered him. "People always talk. I'll figure out the right way to approach them."

"You've struck out twice now."

"Then I'll have to keep swinging, won't I? Don't worry about me." She batted the eyelashes again. "I always come out on top. By tomorrow, that FBI agent will wish she'd answered my questions."

Ollie set down his last bite of burger, bile burning in his stomach. "Are you threatening Mercy?"

Her laugh was forced. "Of course not. I meant she'll wish she'd been my source."

Ollie took a long look at Tabitha. Under his stare, she blinked several times and tried unsuccessfully to smile. "That's my family you're talking about," he stated quietly.

"I happen to know you're not related," she snapped.

"Family is more than bloodlines. It's also the people you *choose* to be in your life. I chose them."

"You're not making any sense."

"All you need to understand is that if you do something to embarrass Mercy or Truman, you'll be answering to me."

Boredom crossed her face as she turned away. "Okay, little boy."

But a moment of uncertainty had flickered in her eyes.

Ollie stood and moved his uneaten fries and parfait back to his serving tray, his hunger long gone. "Nice meeting you." He dumped the contents of the tray in the garbage bin behind their booth and headed for the door. He briefly regretted the loss of the parfait but realized he'd never taste one again without remembering this meal. Nausea swirled at the thought of fudge and peanuts.

No more parfaits for me.

He glanced back and saw her tapping on her cell phone.

What's she planning to do?

93

ELEVEN

The guard from the armored car company had agreed to talk to the FBI but insisted that Art accompany Mercy. Mercy didn't mind, and Art seemed pleased he was wanted. During the two-and-a-half-hour sunny drive from Bend to The Dalles, they caught up on each other's lives.

"You look good, Mercy," he said during a break in the conversation. "This rural part of the state must agree with you."

"You know I grew up here, right?"

"I don't think I did. Getting you to talk about yourself was nearly impossible." He shot her a serious look.

"Yeah. I still don't. Well . . . I'm a little better than I used to be. I tried to keep a thick wall between work and my personal life."

"You didn't have a personal life," he stated. "Shocked the hell out of me that you agreed to have dinner that one time."

Mercy chuckled. "Shocked me too. But it was impossible to say no to you." She took a deep breath. "You were very kind to me back then, Art, and I appreciate it. I know I avoided interactions with most people."

"You were a challenge," he admitted. "Rumors flew around about you, you know."

"What?" Mercy clenched the steering wheel in surprise. "What rumors? Who spread rumors about me?" Her heart sped up.

"Calm down. Nothing earth-shattering. Private people always drive other people crazy with curiosity. They don't understand why private people don't share every crumb of their lives."

"You still haven't told me what they said."

He turned his attention out the windshield of her Tahoe. "That you had a secret boyfriend . . . that you left town on the weekends . . . Some people were convinced you had a whole other life."

"Trust me, I had no life. I spent my weekends . . . working on my home. I just didn't like socializing."

"I enjoyed our dinner," he added, a question in his tone.

Here it is. "I did too."

"Remind me why there wasn't a second?"

"I told you . . . friendship fitted us better." She gave him a quick glance. "I wasn't in a mental or emotional place to start something," she said. "I can't explain it better than that."

"It appears you're in a better place now. Congratulations."

His sincerity was unmistakable. "Thank you. I'm very happy. I've changed a lot since I moved here—and all of it is for the better." She pulled the Tahoe to the curb in front of a house. "Would you believe that my teenage niece lives with me?"

"A teenager?" His response was appropriately aghast, and his eyes crinkled with humor.

"I'll fill you in after we talk to Gary Chandler."

Gary Chandler lived in a tiny house. Mercy and Art carefully followed the broken concrete walkway to the front door. *Tiny* was a generous description of Gary's home; it was a dollhouse. The lush green grass was in dire need of a mow, and the warped siding needed paint. More than likely the siding needed full replacement. The glorious day showed every sagging detail of the neglected home. An old minivan was parked under the carport, a faded JOHN KERRY FOR PRESIDENT 2004 bumper sticker peeling from its rear window.

"That might be a collector's item," stated Art, pointing at the bumper sticker.

Mercy doubted it. "Gary's wife will be here, right?" she asked.

"He said she would be. Naomi." Art knocked firmly on the door. Paint flaked off and fluttered down to the welcome mat that read GO AWAY.

"Not very welcoming," Mercy commented.

"Gary's not a fan of guests, but I think it's supposed to be funny."

The joke fell flat for Mercy.

The door opened inward, and a large woman blocked the entrance as she sized them up. She wore a shapeless housedress, and her graying hair was pulled into a tight bun at the back of her head. Her penetrating stare rivaled that of a starchy schoolteacher, and Mercy couldn't pull her gaze away from the small turtle tucked under one arm.

"Evening, Naomi," said Art. "This is Special Agent Kilpatrick. She's in charge of the Gamble-Helmet Heist case these days." He didn't mention the turtle.

Mercy held out a hand, and the woman paused a rude two seconds before shaking it. "Keep it short. Gary's not feeling great today, and talking about this only makes it worse." Her expression indicated she'd hold Mercy personally responsible for giving her husband any grief.

"Not a problem," answered Mercy.

Naomi stepped back and let them in. Embroidered cat faces decorated her slippers.

Pet lover?

It was dark inside. All the small windows were covered with heavy curtains, and the light from the lamp was too dim. Mercy wanted to fling open the curtains. Gary Chandler sat in a battered easy chair in one corner, a calico cat on his lap. The cat's glare rivaled Naomi's.

"Hey, Gary." Art immediately stepped forward to shake his hand.

Gary was thin—skeletally thin—and he had a faded comb-over. The pictures in Mercy's file showed a slender man with a full head of hair and a kind smile. He didn't get out of his chair as he greeted the retired FBI agent. Art introduced Mercy, and the odor of marijuana reached her as she shook his bony hand. His pupils were larger than they needed to be, even for the darkened room.

It's legal. It probably helps his anxiety.

Hopefully it wouldn't influence their conversation.

Gary's knees nearly poked through the fraying fabric of his jeans, and he had several days' worth of stubble. Sunken cheeks and eyes made her wonder if he struggled with a physical illness. One of his hands never left the cat's back. Naomi stood with her arms crossed, a sentry between the tiny living room and the rest of the home. Mercy glanced around to see where she'd set the turtle down. No turtle.

Art gestured for Mercy to take the chair closest to Gary as he pulled up a wooden chair from a corner.

Mercy sat after checking the chair for the reptile. "Thank you for meeting with us, Mr. Chandler."

"Gary, please."

The powerful, low voice from the thin body startled her. He smiled, but it never reached his eyes.

"I don't want to take up too much of your time, Gary, so excuse me if I get right to my questions." She felt as if Naomi's eyes were stabbing daggers in the back of her skull.

"Appreciate it."

"Would you mind giving me a rundown of what you remember the moment you first saw the robbers that day?"

Annoyance filled his face. "I've already told that dozens of times. There must be a half dozen recordings of my story." Panic rose in his voice as he shifted in his seat and his gaze shot to Art. "You said you had something new to talk about. New information."

Art leaned forward, resting his forearms on his thighs, and said reassuringly, "We do. The body of one of the robbers has turned up."

Gary's hand tightened on the cat's back, and he looked suspiciously at Mercy. "That true?"

"Yes."

"Body . . . So he's dead." Gary eyed Art this time.

"Yes," Art said calmly.

"Good." Gary exhaled and relaxed his shoulders. "Three more to go. Which one was it?"

"Mull."

Gary nodded, his gaze distant as he scratched the cat's chin. "The big one."

"Best fucking news we've heard in years," added Naomi.

"I still dream of killing all of them," Gary said in a slow voice. "Sometimes I meet them face-to-face. I've surprised them in a grocery store and in a church—places they never expected to run into me. Other times I dream I shoot them in defense as they break in my house, looking to murder me because I survived."

Thirty years of dreams?

"Understandable," stated Art.

"I fucked up back then. Phil would be alive if I hadn't choked." Echoes of guilt filled the words. "Seeing them die by my hand is the only thing that keeps me sane—even if it only happens in my dreams."

Mercy had a lot of issues with that statement, but this wasn't the time to address Gary's mental health.

"They pepper-sprayed you. I've been hit in the face with that shit," Art told him. "I couldn't see. I physically couldn't open my eyes, and my skin burned like fire. Then the puking and slobbering . . . No one can function during that. They deliberately did it to incapacitate you, and it worked."

Mercy nodded. At the FBI academy everyone had dreaded OC day, named for the irritating agent in pepper spray. It wasn't an experience she cared to repeat.

"Since you couldn't see what was happening, Gary, what did you hear?" Mercy asked.

Gary shut his eyes, and his hand stilled on the cat. "Gunshots. Two of them. Yelling. Cursing. Screams." His voice was monotonic, and Mercy wondered if he'd smoked the pot to get through the interview.

"One gunshot from Phil Palmer and one from Shane Gamble," Art stated.

"That's what I was told," Gary agreed, opening his eyes. "I only saw the results, not the actual shots." He turned stoned eyes to Mercy. "I blindly crawled out of the vehicle, scraped off half my chin when I fell down the stairs, and felt my way to Phil. Half of his face was gone, but I tried to lift him up anyway . . . I guess to comfort him, let him know he wasn't alone. Even with my eyes straining to stay shut, I could see inside his skull. I touched his brain." He shuddered.

She nodded, the photos and the autopsy report fresh in her memory.

"Gamble was bleeding from the thigh. Couldn't walk. Asshole." Gary muttered the last word. "He screamed while Phil was dying. It was all about him. He didn't care that I was ten feet away holding my part-ner as his blood drained onto my uniform. I wish I hadn't been blinded. I would have finished off Gamble. I still had my weapon." Bitter regret filled his face. "I frequently have that dream too."

"Then you would have been in prison," Mercy said gently. "Instead of home with your wife." She glanced back at Naomi, hoping for some support from the woman. She simply stared past Mercy at her husband, her face like stone.

She's probably heard this a million times.

"You didn't see the getaway driver?" Mercy continued with Gary. "Did you see the vehicle before you were sprayed?"

"I didn't see shit," stated Gary. "My fucking eyes were barely work-ing, and before that I was focused on the job."

"You said Gamble was making it all about him," Mercy continued. "Why did you describe it that way?"

Gary rubbed the back of his hand across his lips. "I'll kill them all," he said in a monotone. "Gamble was screaming that he'd kill them all. I thought he meant kill all the guards. But then he started screaming about being left behind and calling the others cowards."

"Oh." Mercy sat a little straighter, her mind racing. Gamble had defended his accomplices when she interviewed him. He'd given the impression that his loyalty to his friends had never wavered. *Maybe he felt differently with a fresh bullet hole in his leg.*

Art scowled. "Outside of their names, he never gave us shit on his friends. He's protected them until this day, right?" he asked Mercy.

She agreed. *Gamble had nothing to lose by cooperating with the prosecutor. In fact, he could have received a lighter sentence.*

Before he killed another inmate.

"Does the media know about Mull's body?" Gary asked.

"It hasn't reached the mainstream media yet," Mercy told him. "But it probably will."

"Vultures. All of them. Every few years they come poking around my house, camping out front, wanting to relive the story." He held Mercy's gaze, implying that she was a vulture too.

"Dammit," swore Naomi. "We can't deal with that again."

A click from Naomi's direction made Mercy turn. Naomi had lit a cigarette and then exhaled a cloud into the small dark room.

Not a cigarette.

"I'd get out of town for a while," suggested Art.

Naomi gave a choking laugh. "Easy for you to say. We don't have money to waste on a hotel. Not even for one night. Vacations are for rich people."

"What about some relatives or friends?" asked Mercy. "Could you stay with someone for a while?"

"No," she snapped. Another cloud billowed from her mouth.

"Here." Art removed a key from his key ring. "This is a key to my place in Lincoln City. It's pretty small for a condo, but it's right on the beach. No one will think to bother you there." He wrote an address on the back of a receipt and handed it and the key to Gary, who accepted them with a stunned look.

"We c-can't do that," Gary stuttered as his eyes stated how badly he wanted to escape.

"Of course you can," said Art. "You got somewhere you need to be this week?"

"No," cut in Naomi. "Take it, Gary," she ordered.

"Just clean up after yourselves . . . and please smoke outside," Art requested. "I don't have plans to use it for a while, so it's yours as long as you need it."

Mercy wondered if they'd bring the turtle.

She asked a few more questions, but with each one Gary's answers grew shorter. His lids were half-closed, and Mercy decided to end the interview.

Outside a few moments later, Mercy inhaled the clean air and then sniffed at her sleeve, wondering if the marijuana smell would stick to her for the rest of the day.

"That was very generous of you to loan your place," she told Art. The kind move had touched her.

A thoughtful look filled his face. "I bought it after my wife died. Should have done it long before that. We'd talked about finding a place at the coast for years but never did anything about it." He met her gaze, his eyes distant. "Don't wait to do what you want to do. You never know how long you'll have."

He sounded haunted.

"I understand." She did. After she'd almost lost Truman two months ago she'd tried to live in the present a little more, instead of focusing on how to live in the future. A future that might never happen.

What else have I put off?

TWELVE

"You smell like pot."

Mercy snorted at Truman's observation as he took the take-and-bake pizza out of his oven. "I haven't had time to shower and change since the Chandler interview." Out of the corner of her eye she watched Ollie take a step closer to her and discreetly sniff. He grimaced.

"If you can tolerate how I smell, I'd like to eat first. I'm starved."

Truman leaned over the steaming pizza and drew in a deep breath through his nose. "Oregano and garlic will block it." He ran a pizza cutter over the pie and slid a melting, cheesy slice to a plate. He handed it to her and dished up more for himself and Ollie.

"Bless you," she mumbled, aching to devour the piece in three bites, but knowing she'd burn every surface in her mouth. The three of them took seats on stools at the high counter in Truman's kitchen, all tentatively checking the temperature of the slices. Ollie gave in first and took a huge bite.

Before Ollie joined their lives, a medium pizza would have fed both her and Truman. It was even enough for the nights Kaylie ate with them. Now they ordered the giant size, and Mercy worried it wouldn't be enough. Pizza mysteriously evaporated around Ollie.

Shep gave a low whine at Ollie's feet, his eyes pleading. "Later," Ollie told his dog, intent on his food.

"How late is Kaylie studying at her friend's?" Truman asked.

"She promised me she'd be home by nine." Mercy checked the time. "I promised the same." She had a half hour to eat before she needed to leave.

"What's your opinion on Art Juergen after spending the day with him?" Truman asked between bites. "Is he going to be any help?"

"Definitely," stated Mercy. "He knows the case inside and out."

Truman eyed her. "What happened? I hear a *but* in there."

Mercy looked straight at him. "I guess I should mention that I had a date with him one time." Her lips twisted with amusement.

He flinched. "Wait. He's retired. Isn't he . . . old?"

"Yes, he's *older* than me by about twenty-five years."

"Why only one date?"

She saw only curiosity in his eyes, no jealousy. "I was rather antisocial."

"Uh-huh."

"I only liked him as a friend—and the age difference was a big thing to me. Does that make me a horrible person?" The guilt felt as fresh as it had when she'd turned down a second date.

"No. You can't make yourself feel something for another person." He paused. "Am I giving my fiancée dating advice?"

She snorted. "I learned today that the armored car driver's life hasn't been the same since the robbery. It really screwed him up, and he still can't cope with it."

"That sucks," Truman told her. "Does his lack of coping skills explain why you smell like pot?"

"Maybe. Could be for medical reasons too."

"Did the driver offer any new information?"

Mercy was silent for a moment, remembering Chandler's words. "The Shane Gamble he described didn't sound like the same man I met or the one who is portrayed in all the other interviews."

"How accurate could Gary Chandler be? He only saw the guy during the most stressful minutes in his life."

"Most stressful in Gamble's life too," Mercy added. "Anyway, it struck me as weird. It was the first time I'd heard that Gamble had lashed out at his friends."

Ollie set his pizza slice down and broke off a corner of crust for Shep. Mercy watched, waiting for the rest of the slice to vanish into Ollie's perpetually hollow stomach and for the boy to take another. Instead he picked morosely at his slice. He gave another chunk to his dog and then popped a tiny piece of pepperoni in his mouth. She glanced at Truman. He was focused on his own food and didn't seem to notice Ollie.

"On the way home from the Chandler interview, Art suggested I contact the police in Prince George," she said.

Truman stopped chewing and wrinkled his forehead. "Canada?"

"Yes. There were several leads of sightings from there during the first year after the robbery. More in that single city than from anywhere else outside Oregon. They all fizzled out to nothing, but Art told me he's always had a feeling about the location. He's hoping a new look might get us somewhere."

"Sounds like a good place to start," agreed Truman.

"Sounds like a faraway place to start," groused Mercy. "I know this is essentially a cold case, but I'd rather focus my time around here. There're plenty of people nearby to interview again—like the Mull family. Eddie drove to Salem today to inform Ellis Mull's parents." She checked Ollie, who didn't flinch at the name of the skeleton he'd discovered. But he still was picking at his first piece of pizza. "Eddie said the parents were relieved to finally know what'd happened to their son. One of Mull's sisters was there and claimed she'd always known he was dead since he never contacted any of them. According to her, they were a close family, and the lack of contact was completely out of character."

"Are you going to interview each one of them?"

"Eventually. I'll give them a little more time to absorb the news."

"What else is on your list?" Truman asked.

Mercy wasn't listening. "Ollie, is the pizza okay?" Ollie was usually quiet, but tonight he was utterly silent.

He jerked on his stool, his concentration clearly elsewhere. "It's good."

"Typically you've finished three pieces by now." A picked-over half slice still sat on his plate.

Truman leaned forward to look past Mercy at Ollie. "You sick?"

"Nah. Just a weird day. I'm fine." He crammed the rest of his slice in his mouth with a nervous glance at Mercy.

If her brothers didn't eat at Ollie's age, it meant they were sick or . . . nothing else; only illness kept them from food. But Ollie wasn't like her brothers. "What's bugging you? Was it because I mentioned Ellis Mull?"

"You talked about him?"

Not Mull.

Truman elbowed her and gave her a leave-him-alone look. Mercy acquiesced. She was used to Kaylie needing a little prodding to spill her troubles. Ollie would talk when he was ready. A soft chime made her reach for her purse and check her phone. "A text from Kaylie," she told the others. "She says she found something I need to read." Mercy waited for the next text, and her heart fell as she read it. "Ugh. Kaylie sent me a link to the *Midnight Voice.*"

Ollie leaned toward her, trying to see her screen. "What is it?"

"I don't know yet." Mercy's lungs tightened as she waited for the page to load. "It can't be anything good. I refused to talk to one of their reporters this morning." Mercy scanned the story. "Shit."

"What?" Ollie practically stuck his head between her and the phone. She turned away.

"What's going on in the sleepy tiny town of Eagle's Nest, Oregon?" Mercy read out loud. "Ancient secrets are crawling out of the woods in the forms of skeletons and money bags." She choked on a cough. "Give me a break. The reporter is the one I met this morning."

Truman chuckled. "Think anyone will believe when a tabloid is actually printing the truth?"

"She states that the skeleton found was related to the robbery and could possibly be the first step in solving a thirty-year-old mystery."

"True," stated Truman.

"She also writes that the money bags were confirmed as being from the robbery."

"Also true. You sure that's a tabloid?"

Positive. Mercy took a deep breath. "She points out that the FBI brought an agent out of retirement to help the current lead agent. That this 'backwoods FBI agent'—me—'could be bumbling the biggest mystery in thirty years. *Is she capable of handling it?*'" Fury rocked through her. The reporter hadn't been able to find more on the investigation, so she'd dug into Mercy instead. "She's striking back at me for refusing to talk to her today."

"She's a bitch," Ollie stated clearly.

Both Mercy and Truman turned in surprise toward the teen. *I've never heard him talk like that.* Ollie's eyes were heated, and understanding swamped Mercy. "You met her."

He lifted his chin and nodded. "She followed me. Tried to talk to me at lunch. I didn't tell her anything." His eyes narrowed as he met Mercy's gaze. "She knew you spend the night here sometimes, and she hinted that you'd regret not speaking with her."

Mercy glanced at the article on her phone. "I don't regret it, but I am rather pissed at her."

"I should have told you . . . Maybe you could have stopped the article. It's been on my mind all afternoon." He sagged on his stool.

"I sincerely doubt anything I could have said would have stopped her. It's not your fault." Mercy patted him on the shoulder, hating to see him so down on himself. "Did she think this article would win her an interview with me? I'd also like to know why she's the first one on the story."

"She said she got an anonymous message through Twitter," Ollie stated.

"What else did you learn at lunch?" Mercy asked in surprise.

Ollie shrugged. "She's determined."

"But why did someone contact her at the *Midnight Voice* when they could have tried CNN or Fox?"

"Maybe they did and were ignored," suggested Truman. "How did Kaylie find that article? Don't tell me she reads that rag."

"She has online alerts set up for my name. Yours too." Mercy slid off the stool and paced in the small kitchen. "Who tipped off the reporter? One of the county deputies? Someone at the medical examiner's? Who else knew about the money bags?"

"My guys have mentioned the remains a time or two, but they don't know about the robbery connection."

"Shane Gamble knows what we found." Mercy halted her pacing, a feeling of dread in the pit of her stomach. "I told him."

"He wouldn't have access to Twitter," Truman pointed out.

"He can make phone calls. He could have someone else do it for him."

"But what's his motivation?" Truman asked. "He's sitting in prison. Finding the other thieves won't affect him. He's not going anywhere."

"He's complicated," Mercy told Truman. "He loves a game and he loves attention. *Dammit!* I gave him confidential information on a silver platter, and I bet he's using it to stir things up. He's bored and needs entertainment."

"That fits with what you said about his character," agreed Truman.

"I probably made Gamble's day with my visit yesterday—I probably made his decade. How could I be so stupid?" She ran her hands through her hair and tugged until her scalp protested. "I thought I was

107

so smart during our interview, but instead I gave him something big to play with, and he put himself in the spotlight."

"You're jumping to conclusions," Truman pointed out. "Anyone could have leaked the story."

"The fact that it was leaked to a tabloid means something—and I suspect it's Shane Gamble who deliberately chose it." *Why?* Her mind raced. "I could interview him again . . . and not let him know that I suspect he leaked the story. Maybe I can find out what he's up to. We'll see how he likes it when—"

"I think you need to focus on finding the other thieves and money," Truman said gently. "Not picking the brain of a convict to satisfy your personal curiosity."

Mercy took deep breaths instead of giving in to her impulse to reject Truman's point. *He's right.*

"Don't let him get to you. And do the same with this reporter. Ignore them. Focus on the information that's in front of you."

"I don't like being used," she grumbled. "And yes, I know you're correct." She shot him a rueful side-eyed glance. "How can you be so levelheaded and not upset?"

"I don't see much to be upset about. But I'm annoyed that she called you a bumbling backwoods FBI agent." His brown eyes warmed her. "That's not true at all."

"And she claims she only prints facts," complained Ollie. "I should talk—"

"No one is talking to her," Truman stated firmly. He pointed at Ollie. "Eat your pizza."

Mercy bit into her own piece, glaring at her plate.

Tabitha Huff is in for a surprise if she talks to me again.

THIRTEEN

The next morning Truman was almost to the Coffee Café when Kaylie stepped out the front door with two men. The three of them stopped to talk outside, and Kaylie put her hands on her hips and pushed her chin forward, presenting a profile that Truman had seen a dozen times on Mercy. In other words, something had pissed Kaylie off.

As he drew closer, he recognized Cade Pruitt and his father, Glenn. *Uh-oh. What did Cade do now?*

Kaylie spotted him and relief crossed her face. Glenn turned and held a hand out to Truman. "Hey, Chief."

"Glenn. Cade," Truman replied, quickly checking Cade's expression. The young man didn't appear upset. In fact he'd just set a comforting hand on Kaylie's shoulder. "What's up?" Truman directed the question to Kaylie.

"Reporters," she said grimly. "They all seem to think the local coffee shop is the place to slyly probe the employees with questions." She rolled her eyes. "They're so obvious."

Truman understood. "Seen a few today?"

"Three so far. The story has spread far beyond that tabloid," Kaylie said. "They act as though I'm their best friend and then ask if I know the way to where that body was found." Her nose wrinkled. "Please. How stupid do they think I am?"

"I heard the same thing happen to a waitress in the diner," Glenn told Truman. "They're descending on the town like vultures."

"Tell everyone to ignore them," he advised. "They'll eventually leave when they realize no one is talking."

"I wouldn't be surprised to hear someone had taken a reporter up there for money," Glenn said. "I can think of a few people who can be bought."

Truman could too. "I'll get word to Christian Lake to put some security in the area." *He can afford it.*

Cade leaned toward Kaylie, heavy concern on his face. Truman lifted a brow. "Is there more to it than that, Cade?"

Frustration crossed the young man's face. "I don't like people harassing her."

"I can take care of myself," Kaylie said pointedly. No eye roll was visible, but Truman heard it in her voice. Mercy had told him one of the things that bothered Kaylie about Cade was his overprotectiveness.

"I know you can." Cade didn't sound convinced.

"I need to get back to my customers," Kaylie stated, breaking the quiet. She gave Cade a kiss on the cheek and went back inside the coffee shop.

"She'll be fine, Cade," Truman told him. "Reporters aren't threatening. Just nosy. They have bosses to answer to if they step out of line."

"You're not even together now," Glenn told his son. "Or are you?" He looked at Truman. "I can't keep track."

Truman couldn't either.

"We are," answered Cade. "I need to get to work." He lifted a hand at Truman and headed toward his vehicle. As he left, Truman noticed

Cade walked with the same left shoulder tilt that he'd seen on Glenn. He'd call Cade Glenn's Mini-Me, but both men were well over six feet tall.

"Do you have a minute?" Glenn asked Truman, a worried look in his eyes.

"You concerned about those two kids?"

"Nah. They're good friends whether they're dating or not. Kaylie knows how to keep Cade in line."

"They're like a teeter-totter," Truman said. *I swear they broke up recently.* There'd been some sort of romance drama that made Mercy bang her head against the wall.

"They'll grow up." His expression grew serious. "I heard threats were made against Bree Ingram."

"What? When?" Truman's stomach dropped.

Glenn frowned. "I thought you saw them. The *X*s on her property."

"Oh. That." Truman exhaled. "When you said threats, I assumed something verbal."

"I'd call red *X*s on my stock and vehicle threats."

"I agree, and I'm looking into it."

"Do you have any leads? She lives alone. I don't like it."

"There've been some possibilities," Truman hedged. He wouldn't discuss Lionel Kerns.

Glenn waited a long second. Disappointment shone in the man's eyes when he realized Truman wasn't going to expand on his comment.

"Do you have an idea who did it?" Truman asked, studying the man carefully. He didn't know Glenn all that well. The Pruitts had lived outside of town for a long time and were well regarded. Most of his encounters with Glenn had also involved Cade and Kaylie. He'd never heard a bad word said against the man. And in a town that gossiped as much as Eagle's Nest, that was something.

"I don't," admitted Glenn. "If I find out it's a bunch of stupid teen-agers, their parents are going to hear from me."

"They'll hear from more than just you."

After a brief discussion on the weird behaviors of today's teens, the men shook hands, and Glenn left.

We sounded like a couple of old men.

As Glenn walked away, Truman's attention was caught by a young woman in a car across the street and a few buildings down. She sat in the driver's seat of a small Ford and abruptly turned her face away as she realized he was staring at her. Purple flashed in her blonde hair.

"Well, I'll be damned," he muttered as he strode toward the car.

Both Mercy and Ollie had mentioned the *Voice* reporter's purple hair, and the white car looked like a typical rental to Truman.

Which one of us was she watching?

Assuming she had been watching any of them at all, but Truman's gut told him the young woman had been keeping an eye on someone. If it was Kaylie, the reporter was in for a session with an angry stepfather . . . stepuncle . . . whatever Truman was to Kaylie.

The reporter started the car, and Truman held up a commanding hand as he moved closer. *If she takes off . . .*

Luckily she rolled down the window and smiled as he approached. "Can I help you, Officer?" Her sugary tone didn't fool him.

Truman rested his hands on the top of her door and leaned down toward her window. "Why are you parked here?" was his greeting.

Concern filled her face. "Uh . . . I didn't realize I couldn't park here. I didn't see the signs."

"Let me rephrase that," Truman stated, putting on his best stone-cold-cop face. "Who are you following? If you say Kaylie Kilpatrick, we're going to have a serious discussion."

Her hands tightened on the steering wheel. The engine was still on, but he could see the car was in park. "I'm not doing anything. I just got a cup of coffee back there." Unease settled in her features.

As she spoke, a spicy scent that he recognized as Ben Cooley's favorite coffee drink reached him. Sure enough, a cup from the Coffee Café was next to her seat. But she didn't deny following anyone or ask who Kaylie Kilpatrick was. No doubt she was one of the reporters who'd spoken with Kaylie that morning.

"I know who you are, and I know what you wrote yesterday." Truman struggled to keep his temper in check. "And by the way, Special Agent Kilpatrick is one of the sharpest agents I've ever worked with."

"Worked with or slept with?" Snark replaced her discomfort.

"Both. If you need information for your story, why don't you ask for a media release instead of writing crap about the agent who ignored you? That's what a professional would do."

"I know what I'm doing," she snapped.

"No, I don't think you do. Act like a professional and stay away from my family. All of them." He glanced up as engines rumbled. Two white vans had pulled up and parked down the street, a local news station logo on their sides. *Damn. The gate has been opened.*

He knew it was just the beginning.

"Looks like my story got some attention," the reporter stated. "That's what happens when you print the truth."

Truman pinned her with a glare. "Write the truth. But pay attention to how you frame it. If you'll excuse me, I have some real reporters to talk to." *Like hell I will.* "And don't forget what I said about my family. Kaylie and Ollie are kids. Don't mess with them."

"Ollie is eighteen."

"Don't mess with them."

Truman pushed away from her door and headed back to the Coffee Café, where a small crowd had gathered outside to eye the news vans in curiosity.

Dammit.

◆　◆　◆

113

Mercy was cautiously optimistic. A man had walked right into the Bend FBI office and asked to talk to the investigators of the Gamble-Helmet Heist.

"He says he heard people talking about an old body that was found with a bunch of money bags," Eddie told Mercy. "And that made him remember a guy who bragged about money. He claims he saw the stacks of cash a long time ago."

Mercy looked across the conference table at Art Juergen. "What do you think?"

"He's a local?" Art asked.

Eddie nodded, scanning the information he'd found on Larry Tyler. "He's sixty-two. Has a current driver's license, but I don't see any work history. No tax issues. No arrests. No property in his name." He looked at the other two agents. "Sounds like someone who likes to stay off the grid."

"We have a few of those around here," Mercy said, trying to make a joke. "Let's hear what he has to say." She didn't recognize Larry Tyler's name, but she understood the people who tried to live under the government's radar. Eddie left the room to get Larry Tyler.

"Have you dealt with this sort of person before?" she asked Art.

"What type of person?" Art asked. "According to what Eddie found, all we know about him is his age."

Mercy controlled her smile. "A lot of people out here avoid anything that has to do with the government. Most of them are good, solid families who just want to be on their own, but some are fervently antigovernment. The fact that Larry has an up-to-date driver's license makes me hope he's one of the calmer ones."

Art looked baffled.

He'll just have to watch and learn.

Art Juergen had been in robbery at the Portland FBI office during his time there. A department that didn't see the number of sovereign citizens or militia members that the domestic terrorism department did.

Mercy's experience with both groups had increased since she'd joined the Bend office, but she was hoping that Larry Tyler was neither.

Eddie appeared with Larry. The small man shook hands with Mercy and Art and then took a seat. He was a rancher. Mercy saw it instantly in his sun-aged skin, his durable clothing, and his well-used boots. His gray hair was a touch too long, but his eyes were blue and clear.

"What can we do for you, Mr. Tyler?" Mercy asked. Her pencil hovered over a yellow pad, showing the man she would listen carefully to anything he offered.

"I heard about the remains found in that old cabin that were linked to the robbery." Larry was missing several lower front teeth. Black tobacco stains covered the rest.

"Yes, it's been on the news," Mercy pointed out. The local stations had covered the story on the day's noon broadcasts. She was relieved they'd been more balanced than Tabitha Huff's piece.

"People were talking about it before that."

Mercy wasn't surprised. Central Oregon was fertile for gossip.

"I understand it reminded you of something," she prompted.

Larry looked at his hands clasped in his lap. "It did. I used to live . . . with some other families. We had a group ranch about an hour outside of town. We believed in relying on ourselves . . . didn't need the government looking over our shoulder."

Mercy said nothing. He'd described a communal setting of like-minded people—possibly survivalists, possibly a militia. *I'm not here to judge.*

He rapidly glanced at the other agents, clearly concerned that they would ask for more details. The other two men sat as silent as Mercy.

"There was one guy who was kinda new. I wasn't in charge, so I didn't make any decisions about who lived where, but . . . I don't think I would have let him join."

"Why not?" asked Eddie.

"He wasn't much use. Didn't know shit about animals or crops."

115

"Sounds like more of a burden than an asset," agreed Mercy. Living off the grid with other people wasn't easy. Everyone had to contribute. There was no room for dead weight or laziness.

"Anyway, one night over beers he was bragging that he'd bought his way in and that he was actually rich. A couple of us called bullshit—excuse me, ma'am."

Mercy ignored the apology. "How long ago was this?"

Larry rubbed his wrinkled cheek. "Must be close to thirty years now."

I wonder if he remembered that fact before he heard about the connection to the Gamble-Helmet Heist.

Larry kept talking. "Why would anyone who was rich live in the middle of nowhere in the way that we were? He took two of us back to his place. He made us wait outside, swearing he had proof. We waited for at least twenty minutes before he came out with a couple of bundles of cash."

"How much cash?" asked Eddie.

"Twenty thousand dollars," Larry said in a hushed but awed voice, his eyes wide as he looked from agent to agent.

Few of us have ever seen that much cash at once.

"That's a lot of money," agreed Art. "And he said it came from . . . ?"

"He wouldn't say," Larry said. He glanced behind him and then leaned forward. "But he pulled it out of a thick cloth bag. I saw a part of a bank name on it."

"Which bank?" Mercy matched his quiet, weighty tone.

"Couldn't tell. Just saw the word *bank*."

"Not a leather-looking zip bag?" asked Eddie.

"No," Larry said firmly. "Cloth. Like pale, thick muslin."

"Wasn't he worried about being robbed?" Art asked. "Seems pretty stupid to show off that much money."

"Well, I'm not that type of person. And neither was Bert. He probably showed it to the only two real honest people at the ranch. We didn't tell no one."

"Where is Bert these days?" asked Mercy.

"Dead. Heart attack."

"And what was the name of Mr. Moneybag?" asked Eddie.

"Victor Diehl. When I moved off the ranch a few months later, he was still there."

"Be right back." Eddie left the room. Mercy knew he would track down Victor Diehl.

"Where did you go?" Mercy asked.

"My own place. I was done with putting up with other people's problems. Wanted to make our own decisions. I had my wife and two teenage sons. We did good on our own."

"Good for you." Mercy genuinely commended him. "It's not an easy life."

"Nope."

"What's the address of the ranch where you met Mr. Diehl?" Art asked.

A muscle in Larry's cheek twitched, and he looked out the window, his mouth firmly closed.

"I don't think we need to know that, Art." Mercy kept a curious eye on Larry. "It was a long time ago." Clearly the small man wasn't going to share his old address.

"It might help us find Victor Diehl."

"Let's wait and see what Eddie comes up with," Mercy suggested. She didn't want to pressure the rancher. It wasn't easy for a man like him to talk to federal investigators. She was very familiar with people like Larry Tyler. In him she saw echoes of her father and uncles. If he didn't want to share information with the FBI, nothing they could do would get it out of him. "We appreciate what you've told us today, Mr. Tyler."

His blue eyes studied her. "You're the agent who helped take down the McDonald militia."

"I am."

"They say you were related to him."

117

Mercy flinched. "Who says?" *Who else knows that?* She'd believed that her uncle, the leader of that militia, had taken that secret to his grave.

"Just people." He continued to stare at her curiously.

"Don't believe everything you hear." She evenly met his gaze. "How could I be related to the dead leader of a militia? Sounds like a conspiracy theory to me."

Eddie yanked the door open, a big grin on his face. "Got him."

Art bounced out of his seat, his enthusiasm matching Eddie's. "What are we waiting for? Let's go ask Mr. Diehl a few questions about some bank money."

FOURTEEN

"What else do we know about Victor Diehl?" Mercy asked as she drove Eddie and Art to Diehl's home.

"It appears he lives alone. No other name is associated with the address," started Eddie.

"How long has he been there?"

"About twenty-two years."

"Employment?"

"Self-employed. Has made less than twenty thousand a year for the last five years. But he pays his taxes, including his property taxes. He has a few driving infractions, otherwise his record is clean."

"Has Deschutes County had any interactions with him?" Art asked.

"A neighbor complained that Diehl shot his dog."

"What?" Her SUV swerved the tiniest bit as Mercy turned to look at Eddie. "He shot a dog?"

"Watch the road," ordered Eddie. "Allegedly shot the dog. When confronted by the neighbor, Diehl threatened to shoot their cats too. But when county responded, he denied shooting the dog and making the comment about the cats. Although he did confirm he's not fond of dogs."

"Should we have requested backup?" Mercy asked.

"Nothing indicates that he's violent. I think we'll be fine politely knocking on the door." Eddie looked at Art. "I assume you're not armed?"

"I'm a private citizen now."

"That didn't answer my question." Amusement danced in Eddie's eyes.

"I have a concealed carry permit. I felt naked after being armed for all those years."

"Understandable."

"Please remember that you are a . . . consultant," Mercy told Art.

"I won't forget," he promised. "What actually happened to the dog? I'd strangle someone who did that to my pet."

"According to the deputy, it was clear the dog had been shot. The neighbor claimed that Diehl had complained several times about the dog getting into his food supplies."

"Ahhh." Mercy sympathized. If Diehl was a prepper, supplies were gold.

"And the neighbor didn't see or hear the dog get shot, so it was his word against Diehl's."

"That doesn't make for a hospitable neighborhood," added Art.

"As you'll see, it's not a neighborhood. These two properties are in the middle of nowhere. They're the only people around for several miles."

"Then it makes more sense that the neighbor would suspect Diehl," said Art. "I'm surprised Diehl doesn't have his own dog. If it's as remote as you say, I wouldn't like living alone."

"The same neighbor has complained that Diehl trespasses on his twenty-acre property."

"How many acres does Diehl have?"

"Two."

"Small," Mercy commented.

"It backs up to state forest land."

"This isn't how you're supposed to live out here," Mercy muttered, focusing on the winding road.

"What does that mean?" Art asked.

"A person needs good neighbors. You might have to rely on each other one day."

"For what?"

Mercy glanced at Art in her rearview mirror. His expression was curious. He sincerely didn't know what she meant. She eyed the teal golf shirt and Bandon Dunes golf cap. *No, he wouldn't get it.* "If there is an emergency, it'd be nice to know that your neighbor has your back . . . not wants your supplies."

Understanding swept over his face. "You're talking about an apocalypse."

She hated that word. It was associated with preposterous box office blockbusters and survivalist nutjobs. "No, I'm talking about survival if the usual way of life is interrupted."

"Interrupted," echoed Eddie. "That's a polite way of putting it." He turned around to Art. "She's talking about the electrical grid going off-line or food supply lines being disrupted. Maybe water contamination or martial law. Shit happens." He moved to face the road again. "There's a lot of people out here who spend all their time getting ready in case that happens."

"I've seen them on TV shows," said Art.

"Real survivalists wouldn't go on TV," said Mercy. "They don't want the public to know they have food and fuel supplies, because guess who people will run to when things get tough? It's hard enough to prepare for your own family. They don't want to share their hard-earned work with the world. It's a very me-first type of life, but they often include a like-minded community. Depends on the individual situation. The people willing to talk on TV are simply looking for their fifteen minutes."

Art was quiet for a few moments. "Sounds like you've met a few."

Mercy forced a grin. "Just ask Eddie. You can't work out here without being aware of them." Her GPS announced they'd reached their destination. She pulled onto the dirt shoulder of the narrow road and leaned forward to look out Eddie's window.

"This can't be right," said Art.

On their right was a wide, empty field, but on the west side of the field was a large group of trees. Mercy squinted.

"There. Deep in the grove of trees."

"Wow." Eddie was surprised. "I would have never seen that." He opened his door and stepped out, scanning the road's edge. "There's a small track going toward the trees about twenty yards back. I assume that's a driveway." He hopped in the SUV, and Mercy turned the vehicle around.

The narrow dirt road was easy to miss, and the SUV bounced through the ruts. Eddie grabbed the handle above his door as the truck rocked.

"It looks abandoned," Art said as they drove closer. "Your information must have been old."

Mercy was silent, her gaze cataloging the property. It did look abandoned. Hence, perfect for someone trying to live unnoticed. Two small outbuildings flanked the single-wide mobile home. Tall grasses and weeds surrounded the house, but Mercy noticed the ground was clear closer to one of the outbuildings.

I bet there's a vehicle in there.

The wooden stairs and tiny porch at the front door sagged, indicating a visitor risked a broken leg if they tried to climb them.

"Is there another entrance?" Eddie asked quietly, studying the home.

"Legally there should be, for safety reasons," Mercy answered. "But this might be older than those laws."

"How old would that be?" asked Art.

"A good decade older than me," replied Mercy.

"Want me to cover the back in case?" said Eddie.

Mercy thought it over. "We're just here to talk. We don't know that he's done anything criminal, and I don't want to spook him." If he was the survivalist type, as she suspected, Diehl might have some sort of bolt-hole to avoid visitors. Most likely under the home, which was slightly raised instead of sitting on a concrete slab. If he hid, he wouldn't be far.

"No one is here," asserted Art. "We need to research more."

"Let's take a look first," stated Eddie.

Mercy parked a good distance from the house, and Eddie was the first one out of the vehicle. He cupped his hands around his mouth. "Hello! Anyone home?"

Art stepped out on the same side as Mercy, a resigned look on his face. She didn't care if he thought they were wasting time.

She sniffed the air, searching for any hint of civilization: smoke, motor oil, gasoline. All she smelled was grass, pine, and soil, and she noticed it was a few degrees cooler in the shade of the trees. Eddie repeated his shout, and Mercy watched the home for movement in the windows, looking for a place where someone could spy on visitors. Everything was still except for a soft rush from a small breeze in the pines overhead.

"I'll knock," she said as she moved toward the home. "Stay back a bit and keep watch." Art and Eddie moved in opposite directions, each keeping a side of the home in view.

Mercy held tight to the rail and tentatively stepped on the first riser. It was solid. A closer look showed the collapsing stairs had been discreetly reinforced. *Someone is definitely here.* She knocked. "Hello?" she said loudly.

Silence.

She knocked again. "I'm a federal agent from Bend and would like to ask you some questions about—"

The loud crack of a rifle made her drop to her stomach, knocking her breath out of her lungs. *That came from behind the house.*

Adrenaline pumping, she whipped out her weapon, and male shouts reached her. She twisted to look in Eddie's direction. He writhed on the ground, his hand clasping his shoulder. Her heart stopped, and panic briefly flared in her chest.

He's shot. Get him out of here.

Straining to stay focused, she turned to find Art. He was crouched low and already moving toward Eddie.

"Eddie?" she shouted as she darted down the stairs. "Where is he?"

"West outbuilding!" His voice cracked with pain, and she cringed.

Art stopped at the corner of the house and rapidly glanced around the corner. As Mercy joined him, he gave her a quick look over his shoulder. "I don't see anyone. You cover. I'll go."

She nodded and swapped places with him. She stole a peek around the corner. No one. Stepping out, she could see the outbuilding, and she aimed her weapon in that direction. "Go!"

Ducking low, Art ran twenty feet, grabbed Eddie under the armpits, and dragged him past Mercy to the cover of the building, close to the stairs.

Tuning out his shrieks of pain, she covered the two men, her gaze darting about their surroundings as Art ripped open Eddie's shirt and checked his injury. "Gunshot below his collarbone. Not spurting. But bleeding heavily."

Thank God.

Ignoring Eddie's howling protests, Art rolled him to one side, checking his back. "Clean exit. Got a first aid kit?"

"Back of my truck. I'll get it."

Thankful she'd parked out of the line of sight from the west outbuilding, Mercy raced to the SUV. Flinging open the rear, she stretched to grab the huge kit next to her Get Out of Dodge duffel. Her duffel contained a smaller kit, but the big one had supplies for almost any injury. It wasn't a first aid kit; it was practically a portable emergency room. One she'd carefully stocked with whatever gadgets she wanted.

Move faster.

She ran back and landed on her knees next to Eddie. "How you doin'?" she asked with a smile, taking in his pale skin and sweaty forehead. His wound continued to gush. She dug in her bag, ripped open a silver pack, and pulled out what looked like a giant plastic syringe full of tablets. "Call 911," she ordered Art, who had shifted to cover their surroundings as she focused on Eddie. She plunged the wide tip into Eddie's wound and pushed the plunger, injecting the centimeter-wide tablets deep into his wound.

Eddie screamed. Mercy shuddered but continued to fill the bullet hole.

"What the hell is that?" Art asked, sneaking rapid glances at her work as he covered them.

"Sterile bits of sponge made from crustacean shells."

"The fuck?"

"They'll pack and clot. Even if he was bleeding from an artery, this would stop it."

"I've never heard of that."

"It's rather new," she muttered. She tossed the half-empty syringe to the side and started packing stacks of gauze over the wound. No new blood seeped into her gauze.

Yes!

Strong persuasion had been used to convince her doctor to write a prescription for the lifesaving device.

She applied pressure to the gauze and taped it in place. *I need to do the same to his back.* She dug in her duffel, pulled out a small box, and ripped it open, dumping out a green tube and a small bottle. Her hands shook as she poured the contents of the bottle into the tube and gently rotated it to distribute the contents. It seemed to take forever as Eddie writhed on the ground. She placed the narrow end in Eddie's mouth and brought his hand up to hold it. "Inhale," she ordered. "And keep inhaling."

His terrified gaze held hers, tears still leaking from his eyes. *Hang on, Eddie.* Panting, she counted the seconds in her head until she spotted a measure of relief in his eyes. Again, time took forever. Agitation rushed through her veins. *Hurry up. Hurry up.*

"I'm going to roll you onto your side again."

He nodded, still inhaling from the green tube.

The analgesic inhalant in his hand wasn't approved for use in the US, but she'd wanted it in her medical kit, so she'd gotten it illegally from Australia.

She doubted Eddie cared she'd used an illegal drug on him. In fact he was beginning to look comfortably stoned. *That won't last.*

She rolled him and picked up her original syringe. Swallowing hard, she pushed it into the exit wound as he shrieked, and she pressed the plunger.

More gauze. More tape.

Eddie wouldn't bleed out on her watch.

A shuddering breath filled her lungs as she waited to see if blood would seep out. *I pray I never have to do this on a friend again.*

She looked up at Art, who had his back to her and Eddie. He had his feet firmly planted and his weapon ready in case the shooter came around the corner of the house. Mercy glanced behind her, hoping the shooter wouldn't come from the other direction. She drew her weapon again, keeping one eye on Eddie and the other on the far side of the house.

"*Get off my property!*" came the male shout from the side that Art covered.

Mercy flinched. The voice sounded much closer than the outbuilding.

"We are federal agents," Art called out. "Do not come closer."

"I know who you are! Fucking FBI! Now get out!"

He spotted our jackets.

All three of them wore the thin windbreakers with FBI emblazoned across the back.

"We'll leave as soon as we can move our injured man," Art stated.

"You've got thirty seconds!"

Anger burned through Mercy. "He's bleeding from your shot," she yelled. "Have a little decency and let us keep him from dying!"

"You're just stalling to bring in more agents!"

"Why did you shoot?" she shouted back as she checked Eddie's gauze. Still no fresh blood.

"You're not taking my land or my guns!"

She and Art exchanged another glance. "We're not here to take either," Art answered the man. "We had some questions for you."

"Bullshit!"

"Are you Victor Diehl?" Art asked.

"You know I am!"

"No, actually we didn't. We haven't seen your face," Art said in a calm tone. "For all we know you're squatting on Victor's land . . . maybe already killed him."

"I am Victor Diehl!"

His hysteria disconcerted Mercy. He didn't sound balanced. *He shot at us. Of course he's not balanced.*

What will he do next?

"He's fucking crazy," whispered Eddie, screwing his eyes shut. Tear tracks raced down both sides of his head.

"Do you always shoot first and ask questions later, Mr. Diehl?" Mercy hoped her question wouldn't push his buttons.

"I do when I know the feds are coming for me!"

Eddie's eyes opened and met Mercy's gaze in confusion. "Who told you we were coming?" she yelled. "We didn't know we were coming until an hour ago."

"That's a load of crap! I was warned yesterday!"

"By who?"

"None of your Goddamned business! You'll just take away his rights and liberty too!"

"Mr. Diehl, I think there's been a mistake—"

"Shut up before I put a hole in another one of you!"

"We need to get out of here," Art whispered. "His voice is getting closer."

"Can you walk?" she softly asked Eddie.

He pulled the green tube from his mouth. "Yeah."

I don't believe him. She looked up at Art and shook her head. They'd have to carry him to her vehicle. The back hatch was still open. They could load him into the back and get out. But first they had to get Eddie over the thirty yards between him and her truck. And hope Victor Diehl didn't choose that moment to come around the corner of the house.

"I can get him," said Art.

At first Mercy thought he meant he could carry Eddie by himself to her Tahoe. But the intent expression in his eyes told her he meant he could shoot Diehl.

The shooter is a threat.

Their backup and ambulance were probably another twenty minutes out unless a county deputy happened to be in this rural area.

She was torn.

Victor Diehl made the decision for her.

She heard Diehl before she saw him. Boot steps. Grunts. Heavy breathing. As if in slow motion, the barrel of his rifle appeared at the corner of the house, and Mercy rose to a stance but froze; Art stood between her and the corner. *I can't fire.* Then Diehl's hands and wrists showed. Arms of a grimy chambray shirt. Dusty brown boots. Tan canvas pants.

Then she saw Diehl's eyes. Blue, squinting, and crazed. His mouth was open.

He will shoot.

The barrel swung their way and Art fired.

Diehl jerked and spun to one side, losing his weapon. He fell to the ground with a howl that made the hair rise on Mercy's neck.

Art stepped closer, his weapon still trained on the shooter. Diehl was silent and motionless.

Mercy dashed past Art and knelt next to Diehl. His eyes were shut, and he still breathed, but the wound in the center of his chest rapidly bubbled with blood. "Hand me my bag," she ordered Art as she unbuttoned Diehl's shirt. *Center mass. From six feet away.* Art's shot had been dead-on. This wound wasn't like Eddie's. Diehl's wound was gaping and angry and spewed blood in a way that terrified her. She glanced over her shoulder. Art hadn't moved to get her kit; his arms were at his sides, his weapon in his right hand and his gaze fixed on the dying man.

"Art!"

He didn't look at her.

Mercy surged to her feet and pushed past him to grab her kit, taking a split second to assess Eddie. His eyes tracked her, the green tube clenched in a fist on his chest. "I'm okay," he said as she paused.

Like hell you are. But he was in better shape than Diehl. She snatched her bag, spun in the direction of her newest GSW, and deliberately ran one shoulder into Art as she passed. "Get moving! Call 911 again. Tell them we've got two injured now." She collapsed next to Diehl and dug for another clotting syringe. Ripping the box open, she noticed the bubbles in his chest wound had stopped.

His open mouth was full of blood. He wasn't breathing.

Airway first.

How . . .

Dumping equipment out of her duffel, she grabbed a CPR mask. She placed it over his mouth and nose and blew through the one-way valve. Blood splattered the underside of the mask, and she jerked away. *The blood can't get through the mask.* She sucked in a deep breath and blew again. New bubbles formed at the wound in his chest.

Oh no.

She sat back on her heels and picked up the clotting syringe again. Her heartbeat pounded in her ears, and her stress level surged, urging her to do *something.*

There's no point.

A voice came through the adrenaline-hazed cloud around her head. Art was talking to 911 again. She needed to tell him Diehl was dead, but she couldn't move. Couldn't speak. All her energy had vanished as quickly as it'd come. All she could do was stare at the man who'd died beneath her hands.

The gray hair on Diehl's chest was covered in blood. His face sagged, wrinkles forming near his ears and around his neck. The angry blue eyes that had locked on her as he came around the corner were shut but crystal clear in her memory.

Mercy briefly closed her eyes as memories of her brother Levi's death swamped her. He also had died under her hands. Shot. Bleeding.

Nothing I could do.

Mercy forced herself to her feet. Turning, she met Art's gaze. She held it for a long second, words escaping her. They'd both have their own demons to deal with tomorrow.

Eddie moaned, breaking the moment.

She went to him, taking his hand, and was pleased to see he still had good color in his fingertips and lips.

"Thank you, Mercy." He inhaled from his tube again. "This green thing is awesome." His eyes struggled to focus.

The effects would be gone by the time he got to the hospital. Hopefully the EMTs could do something else for him. "That's what I've heard," she answered, as an emotional wave nearly knocked her over. *Eddie could have been the dead one.*

She tightened her grip on his hand, dizzy from the crush of relief and fear.

But he's not.

FIFTEEN

The EMTs were pleased with Eddie's condition and approved of Mercy's field dressing. "Usually when it takes us over a half hour to get to a gunshot wound, it's too late," one of them had told her. He'd glanced at the body of Victor Diehl. "Like that one," he said quietly.

"If you'd been here immediately, there'd still be nothing you could have done," Mercy told him.

"I see that."

Both of the EMTs had heard of the clotting agent she'd pumped into Eddie's chest and the illegal analgesic inhalant but had never seen them used. Mercy had given them the packaging for the surgeon who'd eventually have Eddie on the table. They'd want to know what was inside the patient.

It happened so fast.

Anxiety and relief had made her vomit once the ambulance left with Eddie.

After Eddie had been driven away, Mercy and Art had sat silently on the tailgate of her Tahoe, waiting for Jeff and more county deputies to arrive.

"I choked when you asked for help," Art had said quietly, staring at his feet. "Your reactions were amazing."

Mercy leaned against him and gave a one-armed hug. "You got Victor before he got either one of us. I couldn't get off a shot without it going through you."

"I've never shot anyone," Art admitted. He hadn't responded to her hug. It was as if he hadn't even noticed her touch. "All those years on the job, and the only time I ever drew my weapon was for practice."

"That's why we practice."

"Can't say I've practiced since I retired."

"You did good, Art." She tightened her arm around his shoulders again. He looked as if he desperately needed reassurance.

"I know I did the right thing. But you know what? It doesn't feel very right."

"It's the adrenaline. You saw how it made me sick," Mercy sympathized.

"No. It's deeper than that. It feels soul deep." He shook his head, still avoiding eye contact.

Mercy understood. "You'll learn how to cope with it." His guilt and sorrow were palpable. "I'm glad you took the shot. It would have been you or me on the ground over there." The EMTs had left Victor Diehl for the investigators. She, Art, and a state trooper who'd been the closest law enforcement officer in the area had quietly waited with the body. Mercy had asked the trooper to keep Art in his sights at all times, knowing he'd be questioned about his actions before, during, and after the shooting. Two law enforcement witnesses would be welcome support for his story.

Once her boss, Jeff, arrived, he moved Art away from the property and into the care of a deputy. Jeff was unhappy that his agent had been shot and that a retired agent had killed a citizen. Mercy didn't blame him. The entire situation was a highly charged emotional mess that would have to be unraveled by an impassive bureaucratic investigation.

He quizzed her on the events, and she recited every moment in a calm voice as he made notes. Then he asked her to tour Diehl's home with him.

Inside the house, Mercy covered her nose and mouth.

How did Diehl live like this?

The odor of Victor Diehl's home was similar to that of a garbage dump.

"He's not a prepper or survivalist," said Jeff with his hand over his nose. "He's a hoarder."

Mercy agreed. The home was a narrow rectangle, one room wide. One half contained a living area and kitchen. The other half had a tiny bedroom, a bathroom, and a larger bedroom. Both bedrooms were crammed from floor to ceiling with boxes and bins, while Diehl apparently had slept in a recliner in the living room, which held its own fair share of junk. The kitchen counters overflowed with empty cereal boxes, frozen dinner containers, and empty food cans. She didn't know how he'd used the sink. It was packed with filthy dishes. She jumped back as a roach darted out from under a dish.

"No, no, no." Mercy brushed her hands on her thighs, trying to wipe off nonexistent slime and debris. Simply being close to the mess made her feel as if she were coated in it.

"Here's one piece of technology," Jeff announced, spotting a flip phone on top of a toaster. "Looks like one of the phones you can pick up at Walmart for ten bucks." He flipped the phone open with gloved hands and pressed a few buttons. Mercy watched over his shoulder. "The phone log is only three days old," Jeff commented. "I wonder if he erases his calls or doesn't get that many." He opened the contacts and Mercy's heart stopped. The sole contact was "Karl."

She stared at the unfamiliar phone number, fully aware she didn't know her father's. She had her mother's and siblings', but she still didn't feel welcome to call her father. *It could be any Karl. Maybe his brother's name is Karl.*

133

"There are two calls to Karl," Jeff stated, oblivious to Mercy's inner turmoil. "The other two are unidentified."

"So far," she said weakly. "We can have them identified by tomorrow. And get a list of his previous calls from his wireless provider."

"Does anything in this home make you think he's connected to the Gamble-Helmet Heist?"

"I would say no, except I told you he said he'd been warned the FBI was coming for him," Mercy said slowly, staring at the phone log. "The only reason we're here is because of Larry Tyler's tip. Would Larry have told him we were coming? But he didn't know yesterday we were coming . . . We didn't talk to him until earlier today." She sighed. "This is making my brain hurt."

"I'd like to know who warned him yesterday when we didn't even know ourselves."

"I don't think he was quite right in the head. He could be one of those people who always expects that we're coming for their land and guns."

"I plan to talk to people who knew him and get their opinion on that," Jeff told her. He pulled a copy of two old photos from his pocket. "Shane Gamble's missing associates Trevor Whipple and Nathan May. Take a good look. Could Victor Diehl have been one of them?"

Mercy studied the familiar images. "His eyes were very blue. Nathan's could be the same blue . . . but it's hard to tell in a photo. Whipple's are definitely the wrong color. The shape of his head seems wrong . . ." *Or does it?*

"We still have one unknown guy. The driver. Diehl could have been the driver."

"Could be," Mercy repeated, frustrated they didn't have a name or face for the driver. It could be anyone. Her brain lit up as inspiration struck. "What about showing a picture of him to Shane Gamble? Maybe he will recognize Diehl."

"Good idea. Think he'd tell us the truth?"

Skepticism replaced the excitement of her idea. "I don't know," she said. "I'm sure he'd love to be asked—you know, feel as if he is involved in our investigation. But he might see it as an opportunity to mess with us again."

"I think it's worth a try," said Jeff. "Let's get you in there tomorrow." He gave her a side-eye. "Be ready for him this time."

"I thought I was last time," she griped. *At least I got an education on how he thinks.*

A Deschutes County deputy entered the kitchen wearing a face mask. He had two rifles in his hands, both wrapped in ancient towels. He stopped to show the weapons. "There're quite a few guns in the closet in the smaller bedroom," he told them.

"You got the closet doors open?" Mercy was stunned. He would have had to move several stacks of junk.

"Barely." He paused, looking from Mercy to Jeff. "I'm sorry about the other agent."

"He should be fine," Jeff answered as acid in Mercy's stomach churned anew. She was glad it was empty.

"I still can't believe I've got a fatal shooting with a retired agent," Jeff muttered as they escaped from the cramped home. "Pretty certain there's no precedent for handling this."

"Imagine he's a civilian—which he is. I had no shot, and the actions of the civilian saved his own life and mine. Nothing wrong happened."

"I know . . . It just doesn't sound good."

"It sounds better than 'officer-involved shooting,'" Mercy pointed out.

"True." Jeff brightened the slightest bit. But maybe the fresh air helped too.

The outbuilding west of where Victor had fired at Eddie contained a small pickup. And piles of rusting car parts.

The other outbuilding was packed to the rafters with cracked bins, old fuel cans, and sagging cardboard boxes.

135

Mercy rolled her eyes at the sight of the mess. One box to her left was labeled *Beans. 2001.*

Ugh.

"I don't know how we're going to sort through all this." Jeff rubbed the back of his neck.

"Do we need to?" Mercy asked faintly, overwhelmed at the thought. "So far we have the word of one person that Victor Diehl flashed a lot of cash many years ago. Victor didn't tell Larry that he'd robbed a bank. For all we know, he hoarded cash for many years."

"And kept it in a bank bag?"

"Seems as good a place as any."

Jeff turned in a slow circle, surveying the property. "Let's start by talking to people who knew him. Maybe he bragged to one of them."

Karl.

"I'll get moving on the numbers in his phone."

Unease crawled up her spine. *Please don't be my father.*

SIXTEEN

Sandy tipped her head back and looked up into the pines as the strides of her horse gently rocked her in the saddle.

The sight of the green branches against the blue sky and the small chill of the early-morning air instilled a peace she couldn't find anywhere else.

There was something about nature and being on horseback. No vehicle noise, no electronics, no entertaining her guests.

Once a week she rode in the early morning with Bree. Not for training, just for pleasure. It was a break Sandy desperately needed to disconnect from her business. Running a bed-and-breakfast was 24-7 work, so she'd trained a reliable neighbor to supervise the buffet after Sandy prepared all the food.

Now she smelled pine, scrub brush, horse, and leather instead of scones. She inhaled deeper, letting the natural scents ease the residual stress that hid in her spine.

A mental health break.

Even the worry from vandalism and thoughts of her ex felt far away. Right now it was just her, Bree, and their horses. No one else existed.

A relaxed smile on her face, she twisted in the saddle to see Bree.

Bree wasn't experiencing the same level of relaxation. Her forehead was wrinkled in thought, and her jaw was clenched in a way that meant she was thinking hard. Very unlike Bree on their rides. She'd been quiet that morning as they groomed and saddled the horses, but Sandy hadn't worried about it. Her friend wasn't a morning person. It always took a couple of cups of coffee from their thermoses before Bree was ready to socialize.

There was something very extravagant about pouring a cup of coffee on horseback as the animals ambled down the trail. It was slightly awkward, but the leather cup holders Sandy had attached to the saddle horns helped.

Sandy pulled gently on her reins until her mare, Abby, stopped and waited for Bree to come up beside her. Abby turned her head to sniff and blow at Bree's gelding, Cyrus.

"What's going on?" Sandy asked. "You look like you have a big math test in an hour. Did something else happen at your place?" She gave Bree her sternest look. They'd agreed to share updates on the vandalism at both of their homes.

Bree snorted. "I'm so glad I'll never have a math test again. It's one subject I'll never be able to teach, and I couldn't even help Lucas when he was in high school. And no, nothing new has cropped up."

It'd been quiet at Sandy's since Truman and Samuel had installed cameras. She'd wondered if the vandals had watched the cameras go up or spotted them the next time they came to cause trouble. She didn't care as long as it'd stopped.

"Then why are you so preoccupied?"

Her friend looked away. "I had an odd encounter yesterday."

"What kind of encounter?" Abby sidestepped as Sandy's calves tightened on her sides.

"It was a woman. She was a reporter, and I didn't think it had anything to do with the damage."

"Where did you run into a reporter?"

"At the hardware store. She approached me and asked if I was Bree Ingram."

"You admitted it?" Sandy fought back a shiver as she put herself in Bree's shoes. She'd had frequent nightmares about being approached and asked if her name was Jada Kerns. Granted, Bree wasn't living under a new identity, but it still made Sandy nervous.

Bree shrugged. "I didn't see why not. She was young and appeared friendly."

Sandy briefly closed her eyes. "And? Who did she work for?"

"That's the weird part. She worked for a tabloid called the *Midnight Voice*."

"She had purple in her hair," Sandy stated.

Bree turned to her, eyes wide. "You know her?"

"She came to the bed-and-breakfast late last night. She had questions about the spray paint and broken car windows."

"So she hunted down both of us," Bree stated. "She asked about my vandalism too. I didn't tell her about yours," she added quickly. "Something about her felt off."

"How did she know to come ask me?" wondered Sandy. "She must have heard from someone else that I'd been targeted."

"I asked her how she heard about my vandalism. She just smiled and said she'd heard about my troubles around town."

"Jesus Christ."

"Yes. It gave me the creeps. I know stories travel like the wind through town, but usually outsiders like a reporter don't hear them."

"Why would a national tabloid be interested in vandalism?"

Bree was silent for a long moment. "I don't know. When I asked the same question, she said she was just investigating and asked if I *still* read the *Voice*."

Sandy struggled to find words. "Damn, Bree . . . *Still* read that paper? Like she *knows* you? What the hell does that mean?"

"I don't know," she whispered.

"You must have misheard her. She probably only asked if you read the paper, not *still* read the paper."

"When I was a teenager, I read the *Voice* every week," Bree admitted. "Cover to cover. I loved the sensational stories. It threw me off that she was from that paper. It was like an echo from my past . . ."

No wonder Bree's been distracted.

"Why would she ask if I still read it?" Bree mused out loud, her voice shaking. "Is that something they ask everybody? Or was it meant just for me? *But how would she know?*"

Sandy studied Bree's face. She looked . . . guilty. *What isn't she telling me?*

"We've been best friends for years," Sandy said slowly, not wanting to make her friend clam up. "Does this have anything to do with your suspicions about the vandalism? You mentioned you had a suspicion the other day."

Bree wiped her eyes. "I still don't know." Tears ran down her cheeks, alarming Sandy. She'd never seen her best friend cry.

"You need to talk to the police," Sandy stated.

"No. It's stupid . . . Just old fears cropping up. I can't talk about it."

"It's not stupid if it's making you cry. Jeez, Bree. Why don't you talk to Truman? You'll feel better telling someone." It broke her heart that her friend didn't trust her enough to share. *You never know what's going on inside another person.*

"I can't. Not yet."

Anger touched Sandy's nerves. "This is ridiculous."

Bree squeezed her calves and moved Cyrus ahead of Sandy. "I'm fine. I don't want to talk about this right now."

"I'm fine." The biggest lie ever uttered by every woman.

Sandy knew. She had used it plenty of times in the past.

"Let's get moving," Bree said in a lighter voice. "I want to get to Horse's Head Rock before it gets warmer. That's all I need . . . I need to see that vista. It fixes everything. You need to promise to bury me up there. I like knowing that I'll always have that view." She glanced back at Sandy. "Promise me."

Every time we go to the rock she makes that ridiculous request.

Sandy gave a short nod, refusing to be distracted by Bree's sudden change of topic. She clucked her tongue, urging Abby after Bree and Cyrus.

She needs to tell me what's going on.

Confusion raced in Sandy's brain. A tabloid reporter had tracked Bree through town to ask about her vandalism. Why? And why had the reporter asked the same questions of Sandy?

"Bree." She raised her voice. "I understand you can't tell me what you're afraid of, but can you tell me what you fear will happen if you tell?" She moved Abby to walk beside Cyrus.

Bree turned her head, and Sandy saw her deep need to say something, anything. She'd felt it herself when she hid her secret about her ex. Embarrassment and humiliation were why she'd hidden her story. What was Bree's fear?

"I'm afraid of ruining my life. My life and my son's."

Sandy caught her breath. *She's completely serious.* "That sounds like a good reason," she said faintly, processing Bree's words. Sandy understood. She'd kept her own secrets out of fear for her life. "Two good reasons."

"It is." Bree faced forward, her jaw stubbornly tight. "You see my problem now."

"Can I help?"

Bree was silent for a long moment. "No."

That morning Truman was face-to-face with the purple-haired reporter again.

141

But this time blood had mixed with the purple and dried on her face.

"My dear Jesus in heaven," Ben Cooley muttered beside him. "Who would murder such a young girl?"

Tabitha Huff had been shot in the head. Her Ford rental car had been found on a quiet road with her body in the passenger seat.

"She wasn't shot in the car," Ben continued in a respectful tone. "They put her in it after. There's no spray or spatter. Just some blood smears on her seat and door from loading her in."

Truman had arrived at the same conclusion. He shone his flashlight on the steering wheel and gearshift lever. No bloody prints. Someone had cleaned up.

I just spoke with her.

His threat to Tabitha echoed in his head. *Stay away from my family.*

Clearly she'd gotten too close to someone. Someone who hadn't controlled their temper with Tabitha as well as Truman had.

He allowed the guilt and sorrow to swamp him for a moment. Guilt for getting angry with her and sorrow for the end of her young life. Both logical emotions.

Taking deep breaths, he firmly put away his sentiments to focus on the nuts and bolts of her murder. He'd used Ben's car to block the road in one direction and asked Royce to block traffic in the other until more help could arrive. Lucas had already requested a crime scene team from Deschutes County and let the FBI know that a reporter digging into the Gamble-Helmet Heist had been murdered.

Is the case hotter than the FBI realizes?

What did she find out?

The FBI wouldn't be pleased if a tabloid reporter had discovered something the federal agency had missed.

Truman stepped away from the car, the scent of blood and worse still in his nose. The crime scene team arrived in a white van at the same time Mercy pulled up. His heartbeat stuttered happily at the sight of her even though she was responding to a murder. He'd been asleep in her bed when she finally arrived home near midnight after Eddie's shooting. She'd collapsed in his arms and shed a few tears as he held her and stroked her hair until she fell asleep. This morning she'd barely stirred as he kissed her goodbye three hours ago.

It's odd seeing her work without Eddie. He silently sent good wishes to the recovering agent.

"Go brief the team from Deschutes County," he ordered Ben. Even though the car had been found within the Eagle's Nest city limits, Truman wasn't going to attempt to process the scene. A murder investigation like this couldn't afford any errors on his part.

I'll stick with my simple vandalism cases.

Mercy approached him, concern in her eyes as she looked him up and down. She gave him a brief hug. "You look like crap," she told Truman.

"Dead twenty-two-year-olds do that to me. Excuse me a minute." He walked to his vehicle and popped open the back, then dug around until he found wet wipes. He cleaned out his nostrils. The baby-fresh scent wasn't his favorite, but it beat the odors of death clinging to the inside of his nose.

Mercy moved closer to Tabitha's car. Her face was grim, and Truman wondered if she was reliving her conversation with the reporter, as he had. At least Mercy hadn't threatened her . . . he assumed.

Ollie.

Truman wondered what else the teen had discussed with Tabitha. Could it have been related to what got her killed?

Is there danger to Ollie? Or Mercy?

Both were approached by the reporter.

Dread settled in his lungs, and he counted to ten. He watched as Mercy bent over to look through the car window, the bulge of a weapon at her side. Her lips moved as she pointed and spoke with a deputy. She was a good investigator and capable of taking care of herself.

Doesn't mean I'm not allowed to care.

He joined her at the car. "I poked around a bit for her phone and didn't find it."

Mercy grimaced. "Not surprising. We'll get her cellular records from her provider and see who she talked to recently. I've already put a call in to her boss at the *Voice*. I'd like to hear his version of what she was doing up here." Her gaze went past Truman. "Uh-oh."

He turned. Fifty yards away, two local news vans had stopped, blocked by Royce's patrol unit. The young cop was already approaching the drivers. "Ben!" Truman waved over the older cop. "Go make sure they don't con their way past Royce." Ben immediately jogged toward the vans. Royce was the most gullible man Truman had met. He put in a good day's work and had a huge heart, but an experienced reporter would dip him in batter, deep-fry him, and then eat him for dinner.

Truman had turned away reporters yesterday. Sure enough, they'd been following up on the *Voice* story. Truman had directed them to the FBI, stating the Eagle's Nest PD was not involved in the investigation of the remains found on Christian Lake's property.

Now they were back. Two men shouldered cameras and pointed them in the direction of the car. One of the crime scene techs spotted the cameras and pulled a collapsible screen out of her unit and set it up between the car and cameras. *Good.*

Ignoring the press, Mercy spoke into her phone, circling the car and studying the inside. She gestured at a tech and pointed into the back seat as she continued her phone call. The tech understood and took several photos. Curiosity got the better of Truman.

"Find anything?" he asked Mercy as she hung up her phone.

"Did you notice the notebook on the floor of the back seat?"

144

"No." Truman took a look. The notebook was mostly hidden under the front seat.

She picked up the book with gloved hands and flipped through it. "It's packed full of scribblings. Looks like notes for her articles."

"Sounds helpful. Maybe it will show what she's been up to for the last two days."

I hope.

"I called in the request for her cell records. We should have them by tonight."

Truman looked at the little car. "This is a rental, so I bet she used the GPS system to get around. That will give you some of her destinations, and then ask the rental company if the car has a tracking device. Hopefully her phone will turn up. Possibly she uses apps that track where she's been."

"Crossing my fingers you're smarter than whoever dumped her here. I doubt they considered the GPS might tell us where she met him," said Mercy, handing the notebook to the tech for evidence collection. "You mentioned you talked to her?"

"Caught her watching Kaylie and me yesterday morning . . . Well, I assume that's what she was doing. She claimed to be getting coffee."

Mercy wrote something in her notebook. "What time?"

"About ten a.m."

"Did Kaylie notice?" Her voice hitched on her niece's name.

"No. She'd already headed back to work when I spotted Tabitha parked on the street."

"You had words?" She lifted a brow.

"A few."

Mercy waited, her pencil poised over her notebook.

"I told her I knew what she had written the night before about you. Told her to stay away from my family and the kids. She had some snarky comeback about Ollie being eighteen. Then I might have told her not to mess with Ollie and Kaylie."

"Did you say it as politely as that?" Mercy asked, a knowing tone in her question.

"No."

"Are you saying you threatened her, Truman?"

"Hell no. I was . . . firm."

Mercy nodded.

I didn't say anything wrong to her.

But seeing the dead young woman made him feel as if he had.

SEVENTEEN

"I need more people on the Gamble-Helmet Heist," Mercy stated for the third time as she stood before Jeff's desk.

"I know. Believe me, I know," Jeff answered. "But with Eddie's injury and Art's shooting investigation, the whole office is straining to keep up."

"Art didn't even count. He was a lucky bonus for the robbery case," Mercy complained. "I can't do this by myself, and I'm being pulled in a half dozen directions. This is a high-profile investigation, and I know the media interest is getting deeper."

"I'm setting some things aside so I can help you," Jeff said, eyeing his cluttered desk.

Mercy folded her arms and cocked her head to the side.

"I'm the best you've got right now."

"Find me some more help."

He looked sharply at her. "You mean ask Portland for more agents? You do know we have a budget, right?"

"You do know this is one of the biggest cases we've ever had, right?" she threw back at him. She understood part of his job description was to control costs, but she also knew he could get more money for a case like this one.

Mercy was encouraged by the speculation in Jeff's eyes. "Let me know what the Portland office says." She gave him a sugary smile and tapped a finger on his desk phone. *Call now.*

"Go talk to Tabitha Huff's boss," Jeff ordered. He picked up his receiver but didn't push any buttons.

Good enough. "On my way."

Mercy strode back to her office. *The editor of the* Midnight Voice. *Victor Diehl's phone calls. Autopsy report for Tabitha Huff. New interview with Shane Gamble.* Deciding which took priority was driving her crazy. Every task needed to be done *now.*

She dropped into her desk chair and wiggled her mouse to activate her computer. A photo of her and Truman hiking filled her screen and transported her back to that mountain and the wonderful feeling of lack of responsibility. No murders. No phone calls. No government bosses. The two of them had stood on a peak in the Cascade mountain range, and Truman had extended a long arm to snap a selfie of them with Mount Bachelor in the background. A clump of her long hair had blown into Truman's mouth, and happiness radiated from them. Truman had taken another without her hair in his mouth, but this was her favorite.

Her heart ached for the lightness of that moment.

The past week had been all work. Every time she and Truman spoke it was about work. At this very second, that carefree mountain moment felt light-years away. And the expectation of another day like it was drastically low.

We should be planning a wedding.

Each time she sat down to browse venues or dresses she was interrupted. At this rate they'd marry at city hall, and she'd be in her usual black garb.

Rose has a wedding to plan too.

Mercy realized she could kill two birds with one stone and pulled out her phone to dial her sister.

"Hi, Mercy."

The sound of Rose's voice instantly relaxed Mercy. Her sister spread peace through her presence even over the phone.

"I only have a minute, Rose," Mercy said. "I'm swamped here—"

"I heard about Eddie," Rose cut in. "I'm so sorry, Mercy. And I heard about the reporter who died too. Is that case yours also?"

"We think it might be related to something I'm working on."

"That poor girl. So young." Rose coughed.

Mercy frowned. Rose sounded horrible. "Are you sick?"

"A little. Lots of bugs going around the preschool."

Mild alarm slid into Mercy's thoughts. "Maybe you shouldn't be working there . . . with the pregnancy."

Rose laughed. "I stayed home today, but it's a little late to avoid germs while I'm pregnant."

"It can't be good for the baby to have you sick. You can't take any medication, can you?"

"My doctor says I can take some things, but I'd rather not. I can stick it out."

Mercy's inner mama bear stepped forward. "What are your symptoms?"

"I'm fine, Mercy, really—"

"Symptoms, Rose."

Her sister sighed. "Okay. You heard the cough. I've got a sore throat and fever. Nothing big."

Mercy knew it was big if Rose had stayed home from work. "Body aches?"

"I'm pregnant, Mercy." Amusement rang in her voice. "Everything always aches. Especially my feet. Don't get me started on trying to find a comfortable position to sleep."

"Does Mom know you're sick?"

"I can't get her off my back."

Good.

"Say . . . can you give me Dad's cell number?"

Rose was silent for a long moment. "Are you reaching out? That's good, but maybe talking to him in person—"

"No, I have a question for him," Mercy hedged. "It's about a case."

Rose rattled off a number, and Mercy's fingers grew icy as she scribbled it down.

It's the same number as in Victor Diehl's phone.

"I don't know if calling him is the best idea, Mercy. He's not one to say much on the phone."

Mercy wasn't surprised. A phone conversation with him would be awkward. "I'd rather talk to him in person."

"Well, I know he has a doctor's appointment today at one. You could probably catch him after that."

"Same doctor?"

"Do you really think he'd see anyone else?"

Mercy smiled in spite of herself. Her father was still a creature of habit.

She ended her call and sat staring at the number from Rose, her brain spinning in a million directions. *Is my father involved in this?* Her heart pounded in her ears, and everything in the room faded away except for the phone number.

She glanced at the time. It was too early to catch her father at the doctor's office, and she knew Jeff expected a statement from Tabitha Huff's boss. She did a quick online search and found a name and phone number for the managing editor of the *Midnight Voice*. Within a minute she had Gordon Kelly on the phone and had identified herself.

"You said Bend, Oregon?" Kelly had a distinctive smoker's voice. "Where is that?"

Mercy paused. *Wouldn't he know where he sent a reporter?* "Sort of in the middle. Did you send Tabitha Huff here to investigate a story?"

"Tabby? No. I looked over her latest story, but she'd written it during some personal time off. Why? Is she in trouble with the FBI?" Curiosity filled his tone. "Does she need some help?"

Mercy steeled herself. "No. Tabitha was murdered yesterday."

"*The fuck?* Are you bullshitting me? Tabby? She's dead? How?"

"She was shot. We don't know much else. I wanted to see if you knew what she was investigating in our area."

She was here because of her own curiosity?

"I know shit." His voice grew rougher. "She asked for some personal time, and I gave it. I didn't ask what she would be doing during the time."

A dead end? Who else would know why Tabitha Huff came here to ask questions?

"Why is the FBI involved? That seems odd . . ."

Mercy flinched as Gordon's voice took on a what-are-you-hiding-from-me inflection.

"We work closely with all the law enforcement agencies in the area." Mercy scrambled for noncommittal phrasing. "If they ask for a hand, we give it."

"Uh-huh." Gordon wasn't convinced.

"If you have next-of-kin information, that would be appreciated."

"I'll transfer you to my secretary. She'll help you with that . . . although I can't recall Tabby ever mentioning family."

"Sometimes people just don't talk about it." Mercy knew all too well.

She thanked the editor and waited on hold as he transferred her call. *I've stirred up his curiosity. He'll start digging.*

Why did Tabitha come here on her own dime?

Resting her head on one hand, she listened to the scratchy hold music, growing impatient. She had work to do.

Next up was a visit with her father.

EIGHTEEN

Mercy leaned against the door of her Tahoe, keeping one eye on the doctor's office door and feeling guilty for lying in wait for her father.

Please talk to me.

Victor Diehl had died, and his last two calls had been to her father. She crossed her fingers that Victor's death would convince him to open up. More guilt piled on her shoulders for using a man's shooting to get information for her investigation. But with her father, all normal requests for help would be useless. Especially coming from his youngest child.

Karl Kilpatrick didn't have any use for the federal government. Or for the daughter who—in his eyes—had abandoned her family when she was eighteen.

The fact that his daughter was employed by federal law enforcement meant she received double the disdain.

The Eagle's Nest medical building was a relic from the 1970s. One level. Flat roof. Mustard paint. Ugly stone accents. According to its sign, the building housed two family practitioners and a pediatrician. No pediatrician had worked in town when Mercy was growing up—not that her family had visited the doctor much anyway. Doctors were expensive, and her mother's amateur medical knowledge went a long way. Even her father's veterinary know-how came in handy when his kids were ill.

The doctor her father was seeing today had to be near retirement, and she wondered how her father would handle the young doctor who would likely replace him one day. New ideas. New routines.

New and Karl Kilpatrick didn't mix.

The door opened, and her father stepped out. He placed his cowboy hat on his head and started down the cement steps. Every time Mercy saw him, he seemed to have aged a bit more. More lines on his face, thinner through the chest, looser pants.

Is he ill?

She froze as a million deadly maladies fought for attention in her mind. *Surely Mom would tell me . . . Rose definitely would . . . unless she doesn't know either.*

Squaring her shoulders, she pushed off her SUV and crossed the parking lot. "Dad?"

He'd reached his truck and was digging in his pocket for his keys. He turned toward her, and his surprise rapidly vanished, replaced by an emotionless facade. Annoyance had flashed too. Mercy set her chin and forced a smile. "How are you?"

"Were you waiting for me?" His brows shot together as he glowered at her from under his hat. The expression reminded her of her oldest brother, Owen. No one could intimidate with a single glance the way Owen could. Her father was a close runner-up.

"I admit I was. I have a work question for you." *Please talk to me.*

"I can't help you." He shoved his key in the door to his old truck.

"Victor Diehl died yesterday."

His hand stilled on the door handle. He didn't look at her. "How?" he asked, still facing the door.

Mercy knew he'd cut her off and leave if she said the wrong thing. "He was shot."

Now he looked at her, his eyes hard under the tan brim. "By who?" His words were mangled.

"Why did he call you twice in the last few days?"

Understanding flickered on his face and quickly turned to anger. "That's why you're here. Don't people have privacy anymore? You guys pry into everything. Feel you have the right to spy on what the little man is doing."

Mercy bit the inside of her cheek and struggled to keep a pleasant expression on her face. "His cell phone was found at the scene. It's normal procedure to see who a victim spoke with before he was killed. Could your conversation shed any light on why he died?"

"Who killed him?" Her father's voice was low and direct. The voice he'd used when she was in trouble as a child. It still triggered obedience.

"He was shot in defense by a law enforcement officer. Victor had already shot one agent and was about to fire at two more."

Her father studied her face, his gaze moving from one of her eyes to the other. "So they say. Damned police twist everything to put themselves in the right light."

"I was there." *The fact that I'm calm is amazing.*

"Why were you there?" he snapped. "You saw what happened?"

Her calm shattered. "I did. Even though I was fighting to keep my bleeding partner from dying from a gunshot wound, I saw Victor come around a corner, his gun pointed at me, verbally threatening to shoot me and another agent." She sucked in a breath, holding his gaze. "I saw his eyes as he aimed at the man standing in front of me. Victor wasn't right in the head. His eyes were crazy, and he was ready to kill. If Art hadn't taken the shot, we'd both have been injured. Or worse."

Her father said nothing but continued to listen, still expressionless.

"Victor had been told the government was coming to take his guns and land. He was so convinced of this lie that he shot Eddie without warning." She tilted her head. "Who told him that, Dad? Who would put that idea in his head? Or was he always a supremely paranoid person?"

"You were there," he stated slowly.

Mercy saw his pressure building. He was motionless but seemed to expand and grow taller with the anger.

"Death likes to follow you."

A low roar started in her brain. *Don't go there . . .*

"You blame Victor's paranoia for the bullet your agency put in him? Just like how it wasn't your fault that Levi was murdered? Victor Diehl never had a chance, did he?"

"Leave Levi out of this," she uttered through clenched teeth. "My brother died in front of me due to his poor decisions. Not because of me."

"Everything was fine until *you showed up!*"

She flinched as if he'd slapped her. A slap that bared all the guilt she felt for Levi's death. The roar in her head grew louder, and she fought to hold his gaze.

"You'll never forgive me for Levi, will you? It gives you something to gnaw on when you're angry, someone to heap blame upon since the man who was at fault is dead. That's fine, Dad. If it makes you feel better to hate me, go ahead. But put it aside for five minutes. You've got a bigger problem. Victor is at the center of a major bank robbery investigation, and you are too—unless you have a clear explanation of why he called you."

"Are you threatening me?" He moved closer, using his height to intimidate her as he had when she was a child.

But now she was an adult. An adult who'd done nothing wrong and had no reason to back down. She didn't budge and leaned toward him, unafraid. "No. I'm telling you how it is. Why don't you make this easier and tell me about your conversations? If you're protecting a conversation about . . . the weather . . . or a sick animal . . . you're simply being stubborn." She lifted her chin. "You've always been the king of stubborn. A trait I inherited."

He was in her personal space, and his presence pricked every nerve in her skin.

After a long moment, he looked away. "Victor was a bit simple, but we always look out for *our own*." He threw the two words at her, emphasizing that she no longer belonged in that group. "He's always functioned at a lower level. That's why his house is the way it is. He called me ranting and raving that he'd been told the government was coming for him. He called me twice, saying the same thing. He was more worked up than I'd ever heard him. He knew my daughter was an FBI agent and wanted me to stop you."

Mercy silently exhaled, knowing her father had long been embarrassed by her government job. When she'd returned to Eagle's Nest after fifteen years away, no one had known her profession. Many had been surprised to hear that Karl Kilpatrick had a third daughter.

"I assured him that the government wouldn't do that . . . but look what happened . . . My daughter was involved in his death." He met her gaze as he whispered the last words. "I don't know if that is irony or simply tragic."

Mercy didn't contradict him. He was talking, and she wanted to keep it going. "How long have you known him?" she asked in a quiet voice.

Karl shrugged one shoulder. "He approached me years ago— decades ago—for help in getting off the grid. I can't remember who sent him my way. He didn't have any skills I could use, so I gave him some basic information and let him go. I still get a couple of people every year who come to me to get started. I can tell who will succeed and who won't."

"Which category was Victor?"

Her father gave a short laugh. "I expected him to turn tail and go back to wherever he came from within a year. He surprised me. He worked hard, I sold him a few necessities, and he made it out of sheer luck."

"You don't know where he was from?"

"Nope. Never asked."

"You sold him some equipment? How did he pay you?"

He frowned. "Cash. No barter."

Mercy knew that was unusual. Barter was the most common currency in her father's world. She paused and asked delicately, "Did he seem to have a lot of money?"

He stared, comprehension growing in his gaze. "You mentioned a bank robbery."

"Yes. An old one. But recently—"

"I heard about the skeleton and bank bags. You think Victor knew something about that?"

"That's what we were trying to find out when he fired at us."

"I'm sorry about your friend Eddie."

Mercy grew still as his words spawned a hole of anger in her chest. *He knew about Eddie before I mentioned him. He waits until now?* She wondered how much he'd already known before she approached him. *Am I just a game to him? Someone to pluck for information?*

"Thank you. He's going to be fine."

"I heard."

"It could have been me." She held his gaze, wondering what he'd say.

"Coulda." He didn't look away.

He's done talking about Victor Diehl. "Why are you at the doctor's? Are you ill? You seem thin."

An invisible wall shot up between them. "I'm sixty-five. I go to the doctor when your mother makes me."

"Why'd she send you? What's wrong?"

"Nothing." He dropped her gaze.

Liar.

He has pride. Heaven forbid I rattle his ego.

He hung on to his pride as tightly as he hung on to his anger toward her.

He turned his back and opened his truck door, signaling their conversation was over, and she stepped back.

Dad, one day you'll learn that protecting your pride isn't worth the price.

Truman had been about to sit in a chair across from Mercy's desk, but when he spotted her bleak gaze, he walked around and pulled her into a hug.

What on earth happened?

"You look like your best friend died," Truman said.

She nestled into him, burying her face in his shoulder. They were alone in her office, and the door was open, but no one was in sight. She sighed, and he felt her muscles relax.

"How do you do this to me?"

"Do what?" he asked.

"Before you got here, I was ready to go home and crawl in bed . . . maybe binge watch something and eat ice cream." She raised her head and looked him in the eye. "But it's as if I get energy from simply touching you. I feel like a vampire, sucking away your personal stamina."

"I'll let you know if I get completely drained."

Her lips curved. "My point is that you make me feel better by simply appearing. Maybe I should hire you to pop into my office once a day."

"Why are you so exhausted today?"

"It's been one of those days. I can't get Eddie out of my mind, *and* I talked with my father . . . and I have so much work to do and not enough help."

Aha. She spoke with her father.

"A typical day. What happened with Karl?"

She pulled out of his arms and gave him a peck on the lips. "Have a seat."

"You need me to sit down. That's not good." But he sat, and she did the same.

She leaned her chin on her hands as she stared across the desk at him. "Victor Diehl called him twice in the days before he died."

"Why?"

"Someone told Diehl the FBI was coming for his guns and land, and he wanted my dad to stop it through me."

"No wonder Diehl came out with guns blazing when you three showed up."

"I've been sitting here thinking about my father's explanation, and now I'm wondering if we were set up," she said quietly. "It can't be a coincidence that Victor was warned of the FBI before we showed up."

Truman's back stiffened as surprise shot through him. "What? Someone wanted one or all of you shot?"

If I find out that is true . . .

"My father told me Diehl isn't quite right in the head. He wasn't surprised at all that Diehl flew off the handle when he saw us. It's possible someone else expected the same thing."

"What led you to Diehl in the first place?"

"A local came to the FBI with information."

"He walked in on his own?" *Was that more than luck?*

"Yep. Said the news about the money bags reminded him of an incident he had with Diehl a long time ago."

Truman let the information percolate in his brain for a long moment. "Any way to back up your informant's story?"

"I've been trying. It happened too long ago, and the other witness is conveniently dead."

The two of them sat in silence.

"You think someone is trying to lead the FBI in the wrong direction? And get you killed at the same time?" The thought made bile stir in Truman's stomach. "The FBI must be getting too close. Someone wants the investigation stopped."

"Why?"

She knew why as well as he did, but he suspected she wanted him to say it out loud. "The same reason most crimes are committed. Money."

"The robbery money has to be all spent by now . . . or nearly spent," Mercy pointed out.

"Then the reason is the protection of someone's ass. He doesn't want to end up in prison."

"You're right." Mercy leaned back in her chair and rubbed at her bloodshot eyes.

"You need to go back to the person that led you to Victor Diehl."

"That would be Larry Tyler. Who lives off the grid about an hour away from here."

"Mercy?" Jeff knocked on the frame of her open door. "Hey, Truman."

Truman lifted a hand in greeting.

"We got the cell phone records from Tabitha Huff's wireless provider," Jeff stated.

The murdered young reporter's face popped into Truman's mind. Something he wouldn't forget for a long while. If ever.

Jeff glanced at Truman, clearly hesitant to speak in front of an outsider. "I'll step out for a few moments," Truman offered.

"Stay, Truman," Mercy ordered. "You were the first officer at the scene."

As if he didn't know. She'd said it to remind Jeff that Truman was involved.

Jeff's face cleared. "You'll never guess who she had multiple phone calls with."

"Just tell me."

"Two Rivers Correctional Institution."

Mercy nearly rose out of her chair. "Shane Gamble."

"The first call is from her to the prison in the evening of the day you visited him."

"Something I said stirred him up." Mercy spoke rapidly, lost in thought but with excitement growing on her face. "She said her source reached her through Twitter, right? Whatever he told her pushed her immediately into action."

"What did you tell Gamble?" Truman asked. "What would make him reach out to a tabloid?"

Mercy stared back at him. "I'm not sure. It must have been something about the skeletal remains that meant more to him than he let on."

"But what was Tabitha's purpose?" asked Jeff. "You said she didn't have an official assignment here, so Gamble must have sent her on a mission."

"I need to speak to him." The determination on Mercy's face told Truman she *wanted* to go head-to-head with the convicted felon again.

Jeff checked the time. "It's too late today. Tomorrow you can drive out there. I'll set it up."

"I won't let him in my head this time," she promised.

Truman wished he could be a fly on the wall when Mercy told Shane Gamble the reporter had been murdered.

Did he purposefully send Tabitha to her death?

Picturing the close-range shot to the reporter's face made anger burn through Truman. No one deserved that kind of death. Especially a young girl.

Shane Gamble has some explaining to do.

NINETEEN

It was the same interview room as last time.

Shane Gamble wore the same prison garb and rested his hands in the same way on the same table.

Mercy had fancied up a bit. A little extra mascara, a neutral lip pencil that she'd never used, long beachy-looking waves in her hair that took twenty minutes with a curling iron she'd had to borrow from Kaylie. White blouse, jeans, boots, and a sporty violet suede jacket she kept for special occasions.

The unusual sensation of the thin layer of color on her lips was distracting.

Am I trying to flirt? Hope I distract him and get him to spill his story?

She sucked at flirting.

But she'd use whatever weapons she had, whether they worked or not.

"Nice to see you again, Special Agent Kilpatrick." The cadence of Gamble's speech was still slow and relaxed, but she knew he considered every word before it came out of his mouth.

"Thank you," she answered with a polite smile. "You'd suggested I return when we had an ID on the body."

"You're too late. I already heard from the news. Ellis Mull." His look of contrite sorrow made her skin crawl. It felt rehearsed.

"Yes."

"How long ago was he shot?"

"There was evidence that some time was spent at the cabin—sleeping bags, food cans—but the medical examiner backs up our theory that he was killed close to the time of the robbery."

"That's very sad. I wonder what went wrong." The affected remorse stayed in place on his face.

"Did he have issues with the other men?"

Condescension replaced the remorse. "Now, Agent Kilpatrick . . . how do you expect me to answer a broad question like that? Unless we were miraculously in agreement on every little problem in our lives, of course we had issues. Who doesn't?" The disappointment in his eyes at her question made her feel like a child.

"Issues that would cause one man to kill another," she clarified, keeping her serene demeanor, while she mentally rolled her eyes hard enough to cause permanent damage.

"Ahhh." Dramatic comprehension.

More invisible eye rolling.

Broadway has nothing on us.

His chains clanked and then stopped him as he tried to raise one hand to his chin. Fury flashed. Then the thoughtful, helpful convict reappeared.

He's still dangerous.

For a brief second, she'd seen the man who'd killed another inmate. He was good at keeping his temper in check—in fact, he presented himself as a man without a temper. But she'd seen his truth.

Shane Gamble was a very angry man.

"I can't see any personality traits that would have driven one of them to kill another," he answered seriously. "Maybe he was killed by someone outside of our group."

"Maybe." Mercy removed some photos she'd tucked in her jacket pocket. One was Victor Diehl's current driver's license photo—the only photo they'd been able to find of him. Another was a recent photo of Gary Chandler—the guard who'd survived. She'd also brought photos of her father and Ben Cooley to create a lineup.

She spread out the photos. "Do you recognize any of these men?"

Gamble leaned forward, studying the photos in all seriousness. *Perfect.*

She wanted him to feel he was of assistance, as if he had a little power over the interview.

He picked up the photos one by one, eyeing them as if they were precious jewels. "Obviously you're asking if I knew these men when they were younger. Decades ago."

"Yes."

"That's not easy. People change."

"I know. Do your best."

He laid the photos in a perfect line, paused, and then tapped a finger on Gary Chandler. "This is the guard who survived. Clearly he's older now, but I'll never forget those eyes from my trial. How's he doing?"

She'd expected the answer.

"Do you recognize anyone else?" she asked.

He didn't look down at the photos. "No."

"The guard is doing just fine," she lied.

His mouth twitched on one side. "That's good. Having your partner die in front of you could scar some people for life. Really screw them up mentally and emotionally."

She scooped up the photos. *He said nothing about Diehl. Is he holding back or telling the truth?*

Her gut told her it was the truth. Diehl's eyes were the same color as Trevor Whipple's, but the shape of the face was wrong.

"You're thinking hard," Gamble said. "Did I disappoint you?"

"No. Just thinking about other new leads in this case."

He tilted his head in polite interest. "What kind of leads?"

"The usual. Claims of money being flashed around. Sightings of Trevor Whipple or Nathan May. Nothing has panned out yet."

"That's too bad."

"I'd hoped showing you the photos would give us some help."

Gamble went very still, his gaze locked on hers, and Mercy knew he wanted to see the photos again, wondering what he'd missed.

His reaction confirmed that she'd been right that Diehl wasn't Whipple; otherwise his need to see the pictures again wouldn't be flooding the air around them. Instead he would have apologized for being unable to help, keeping Diehl's identity close to his chest.

"Not sure how you expect me to be of any help," he said modestly. "I've been locked up for decades. Other than you, I haven't talked to anyone about the case in years."

Bingo.

"Then what did you speak to Tabitha Huff about?"

Until now, she'd never experienced the air being sucked out of a room. Every ounce of oxygen was drawn into the man across the table from her, fueling his anger.

"Tabitha Huff reached out to me."

Liar.

"There are several calls between the two of you." She dug a sheet of paper out of her other pocket and pretended to study it. "The calls on her cell phone coordinate with the times you made or received calls here."

"What else do you have in your pockets?"

She grinned, appreciating his wry comment. "Nothing."

"She's a reporter. She was digging into the story just like someone does every few years. I usually speak with them—I've got nothing better to do. I never have anything new to share with them, but usually they're thrilled and get off on the fact that they spoke with me. It makes them feel accomplished." An empty smile. "It's the least I can do."

Feeding his ego.

Then it hit her: *He wants this case to never be solved.* As long as America still wondered what had happened to the money from the notorious robbery, he would be relevant. Once the robbery was solved, he would fade into obscurity. No more visits from the FBI, no more attention from reporters.

I wonder if he gets fan mail.

"You're saying Tabitha learned nothing useful from you."

"Everything I know has already been in print. Several times."

"Is she going to contact you again?"

"Who knows?" He shrugged, looking away.

His answer was too breezy. He cared. He cared very much about continuing his conversation with Tabitha Huff.

"She was murdered yesterday. Shot in the head and left in her car."

Is it wrong that I love his look of surprise?

She'd finally coaxed a genuine reaction out of the felon. The score on her side of the board increased tenfold.

"Who killed her?" he whispered. His gaze darted about her face as he desperately sought for something to regain control of the conversation.

"We don't know."

They sat silently for a long moment, each regarding the other. A subtle dawning in his eyes told Mercy that he'd finally realized she was a worthy opponent in his constant game.

"Maybe you should try to remember the conversations between the two of you," she suggested. "Perhaps you'll recall something that can help us find this young girl's killer."

The prison randomly listened to and recorded phone calls. Two of Gamble's four conversations with Tabitha Huff had fallen through the cracks. The recorded two had been listened to and deleted due to nothing of note. Standard procedure.

166

Mercy had cursed up a storm when she found out.

"I don't understand how something I told her could have gotten her killed . . ." His voice trailed off.

"Think of something?"

"No."

Behind his gaze, Mercy sensed his wheels were spinning at top speed. He'd stumbled onto something and was weighing whether or not to share.

Damn, I wish we had the recordings.

She'd have to speak carefully if she wanted to hear what had just occurred to him.

"Who did you suggest she talk with to find more information on her story?"

"No one." He moistened his lips; the brain cells were still in full frenzy.

"Why would someone kill a reporter?" she asked.

Now his gaze truly focused on her. "Because they've discovered something that someone wants to remain hidden."

Mercy waited.

"She must have gotten close to the money," he said quietly. "But not because of what we talked about . . . She must have done it on her own." Wonder filled his tone.

He's surprised a reporter found something?

"I agree."

His eyes narrowed on her. "You might be getting close too, Agent Kilpatrick. Maybe you should be looking over your shoulder. I'd hate for something to happen to you."

Ice encased her. "Is that a threat?"

He shook his head, his gaze never leaving hers. "No. I have no power over what happens outside of these walls." His voice quieted. "It's a sincere concern for your safety."

Ugh.

The creep factor in his gaze scattered over her skin, and she ached for a shower to clean it away.

"Seriously, Agent Kilpatrick, be careful. It sounds like someone will do anything to protect their secrets."

"What did you tell her to do?" She tried to speak normally, but it came out as a whisper.

He sat quietly, a silent struggle on his face. "I offered her an inside scoop on the robbery. Our agreement was that she couldn't tell anyone—even her boss—until she did something for me. I asked her to deliver a message to an old friend. I warned them to be careful because of the finding of Ellis Mull. That discovery could stir up trouble."

That's the most honest statement he's said to me.

"Clearly it did. Who is this friend?"

"I'm sorry. I can't share that. I won't put more lives at risk."

Like he gives a shit about anyone but himself.

"By being silent, you risk more."

He didn't reply, and Mercy was startled by a moment of vulnerability in his eyes that vanished as quickly as it had appeared. His casual mask of indifference returned.

He's done.

Mercy stood. "Thank you for your time. Let me know if you wish to speak with me again."

He leaned back in his seat, his shoulders down, his gaze distant.

Fuming, Mercy left.

Damn you, Gamble. Who or what are you protecting?

TWENTY

Ollie's phone vibrated with a text from Truman.

Where are you?

Dairy Queen, Ollie sent back.

Ollie set the phone on the truck seat beside him and stretched to grab his backpack. He was parked down a dirt track in the woods a little way from Bree's house, nowhere near the Dairy Queen. He'd parked there a few times since her place was vandalized, just to keep an eye on things, hoping he could catch who had targeted her.

A sharp rap on his window made him jump in his seat and turn toward his door.

Truman glared at him.

Oh shit.

Ten minutes later Ollie sat in Bree's living room as the two adults silently stared at him.

Ollie couldn't look Truman in the eye.

The police chief stood with his feet planted far apart and his arms crossed on his chest, his focus drilling a hole in Ollie's skull.

Ollie shrank into Bree Ingram's comfortable sofa as if it could protect him.

"Go easy on him, Truman," Bree stated. "You're scaring him."

Ollie straightened. *I don't need her to protect me.* He looked to Truman. "I didn't do anything."

"Then explain why your truck is tucked into that grove of woods on the edge of Bree's property. And not at the Dairy Queen like you just told me?"

"Not illegal," he muttered, dropping eye contact again. "Just keeping an eye on things."

"Ollie." Bree's voice was kind. "Were you at the park the other day, watching Sandy and me?"

Disbelief hovered around Truman. "Did you do that, Ollie?"

If a giant wormhole abruptly opened next to him on the couch, Ollie would be fine with that. He looked at Bree. It was easier than looking at Truman. "Yeah, that was me. I'm just worried about you. You go everywhere alone."

"You're following me?" she whispered. She fought to keep a look of horror off her face, but Ollie spotted it.

This isn't how this was supposed to go.

"Jesus Christ, Ollie. Is that true?" Truman turned to Bree. "I'm really sorry, Bree. You understand that he hasn't been around people—"

"Stop it!" Ollie ordered, defensiveness tightening his chest. "I'm not some stupid backwoods hick!"

"Then what the hell are you doing?" He suspected Truman would strangle him if Bree weren't present. "Normal people don't follow and spy on others."

Ollie hung his head. *I had good intentions.*

"Answer me."

He'd never heard that tone from Truman. Deep disappointment wrapped up in anger. Ollie cleared his throat and looked to Bree again. "After the vandalism on your property, I felt the need to watch out for you. You've been a huge help to me with my studies . . . I thought maybe I could spot who did it."

Bree didn't speak. Her usual peppy and chatty self had yet to make an appearance. Instead she looked bewildered at his actions. Not like the confident woman who'd taught him for the past six weeks.

Ollie cringed. *I did that to her.*

Truman scratched his cheek, perplexed. "Are you saying you've appointed yourself some sort of secret bodyguard?"

Hot embarrassment rose in Ollie's face. "Not quite . . . Just hoping to prevent anything worse from happening."

"That's very kind of you, Ollie," Bree told him, "but I wish you'd told me what was going on. I was seriously spooked."

Misery flooded him. "I'm sorry. That's the opposite of what I wanted to happen."

"You suck at surveillance, Ollie." Truman sighed and faced Bree, clearly done with listening to him. "What do you think?"

Bree tucked her hair behind one ear, still looking troubled. "I think his intentions were in the right place. But he needs to learn that's not acceptable behavior."

"Agreed. We've been working on social nuances—"

"I'm right here," Ollie muttered. It was embarrassing enough to make stupid mistakes, but he didn't need his lack of socialization discussed in front of him.

"I think the two of you can work this out," Bree said, looking from Truman to Ollie. "Let me pack up some stew to send home with you." Bree's change of subject triggered a wave of relief for Ollie. But she left the room, and the relief evaporated because he was alone with Truman. He didn't know which was worse, angry Truman or disappointed Truman.

"I'm really sorry," he told Truman.

"Do you have some sort of crush on her?" Truman asked in a low voice, his forehead wrinkling.

"No! It's not like that . . . She's just nice and helpful. Besides teaching me, she's always giving us food, and Lucas is really lucky . . ."

"Ahhh." Truman nodded in comprehension. "She's a mother figure."

I'm not four years old.

But Ollie was done with defending himself. "Maybe that's it," he answered, wanting the topic to go away.

"Mercy's not motherly."

Defense shot through him, and he sat up straight. "Mercy's *amazing*." He scowled at Truman and balled his hands into fists. *How could he put her down?*

Truman laughed. "You should see your expression. Ready to beat in my face over a casual comment. Mercy would agree with me if she was standing here. She wouldn't take it as an insult. And you don't need to tell me how amazing she is. I'm well aware."

Ollie relaxed a fraction.

"Bree's not like Mercy," Ollie said slowly. "I know Mercy can take care of herself. Bree's—"

"She's tougher than you realize, Ollie. Bree has run the farm since her husband died years ago. She's not helpless, and Lucas isn't as much help as you'd think. But I get what you're saying." Truman glanced in the direction of the kitchen and lowered his voice. "There's something about her that makes you want to stand guard with a big sword."

"She listens to me and really helps with school. It never feels as if she's doing it because she's paid," Ollie whispered.

"Her heart is bigger than she is," Truman agreed. "Let's establish a rule." Truman put on what Ollie called his lecture face.

More rules. Every day the list grew longer.

"Number one. You don't spy on other people."

Ollie nodded.

"Number two. Don't pretend to be a cop. If you want to do that, you can go to the police academy after you get your degree."

Police academy? "I want to teach."

"Number three . . ." Truman paused, thinking hard. "I can't think of how to phrase number three . . . except 'Don't do stupid things.'"

"You've already put that on my list of rules," Ollie said sourly. "Several times."

"Clearly it needs to be added again."

Bree reappeared, a plastic storage dish in her hands and an innocent look on her face as if she hadn't heard Truman's scolding. She handed the dish to Ollie as he stood. "Now, get on with you, my hidden protector."

Ollie wanted to melt into the floor. Truman's laugh didn't help.

He gave her a weak smile and followed Truman out the door. Ollie's gaze immediately went to the red *X* that was still on Bree's truck.

"Need to get that taken care of," Truman muttered.

Ollie agreed. It made the hair on the back of his neck rise every time he saw it. Like now.

He shifted the dish to his other hand before opening his own truck door. He paused, glancing around the property, feeling watched.

This is why I followed her.

Every time he came close to the property, he felt it.

He opened his door and tossed the stew on the bench seat.

Not my problem anymore.

Mercy leaned against the rail of the wide footbridge that crossed the Deschutes River and soaked in the late-afternoon sun. Her office sat on a bluff that overlooked the river as it flowed through Bend, miles of walking and hiking trails along its banks. The footbridge led to a touristy district of restaurants and shops, and she waited in the exact middle of the span, watching bikers and families pass by.

I feel like a spy in a bad movie.

Art had suggested a meet at the location. He was staying in one of the hotels next to the shopping district.

His removal from the investigation had hampered its progress. His guidance and memories had helped tremendously, but until the internal review of the shooting was finished, he was to stay away.

That doesn't mean we can't have a personal chat.

Actually, it did, but Mercy didn't care about procedure right now. She needed help, and no one knew more about the robbery than Art.

She spotted him a few seconds before he reached her. Today he wore shorts and a T-shirt, making her jealous. Her jeans were soaking in too much heat from the sun. A Portland Timbers cap and aviator sunglasses completed his carefree look.

"I feel like an informant who's meeting to slip you the secret codes," he said as he leaned beside her.

"You look like a retiree whose big decision of the day is whether to play golf or sit on a bar's sunny patio with a beer in your hand."

He flashed a grin. "Both of those have crossed my mind for today. I'll probably do the latter."

"You don't seem like a man under review by the FBI."

The grin vanished. "Trust me. I can't think about anything else. But there's nothing I can do about it. I simply have to wait."

"They'll decide in your favor. It was a solid shooting."

"Still hate the process."

"You seeing someone?"

He grimaced. "Yeah, the department has me hooked up with a local psychiatrist. Nice lady. She's handled problems like mine before. The county uses her."

"That's good. You need to feel you can talk freely to someone."

He was silent for a long moment, and Mercy wished he'd remove the sunglasses that hid his eyes.

"I'm sorry you're going through this, Art."

He leaned more weight on the railing and sighed. "Tell me about your interview with Shane Gamble. Give my brain something else to concentrate on."

Mercy ran through the highlights of that morning's discussion.

Art listened closely, stopping her occasionally with questions or asking for clarifications. When she was done, he was silent, stroking the stubble on his jawline as he thought.

"You think he's protecting someone?" he finally asked.

"Yes. Or something."

"You don't have any ideas of who or what?"

"Well, his parents are dead. He doesn't have any friends. By process of elimination, I'd say he's protecting one or more of his accomplices."

Art continued to stroke his jaw. "Never pegged Gamble to have a sense of honor."

"Definitely not. I'd say his motivation is financial."

Art's brows rose from behind his sunglasses. "You think there is money left after all these years?"

"If he's hiding an identity, I don't see him motivated by revenge. His motivation can't be sexual. That leaves financial."

"But he's in prison for life."

"Maybe it's for someone else?" Mercy had also considered that fact. "Maybe he believes he'll get out one day?"

"Could be." Art sighed. "You said he had the reporter deliver a message."

"A warning. I think the discovery of Ellis Mull's remains meant something to Shane Gamble. Something important enough for him to lure a reporter with the promise of a scoop when his real plan was to use her as his delivery person."

"I wonder if his message was delivered before the reporter's murder," Art speculated.

"Or did the receiver of the message kill Tabitha Huff?" Mercy stopped talking as a boy of about five flung himself at the railing beside

175

her and climbed up partway to look down at the flowing water. Even as she tensed to grab his shirt if he climbed higher, Mercy lost a breath at the absolute joy and wonder on the child's face. *When did I last look at something like that?* The boy's dad called him as he passed by with two other small children, lifting a hand in greeting to Art and Mercy. The child leaped off his perch and dashed after the group, energy emanating from his every movement.

Not a care in the world. A family enjoying a walk in the sunshine. And we stand here discussing murder.

Art resumed their conversation in a quieter voice. "I hadn't thought of that . . . I wonder if Gamble thought the receiver shot the messenger? What would it mean to him if his message had been thrown back in his face like that?"

Mercy thought back to the moment she'd told Gamble of the reporter's murder. "He was shocked when I told him Tabitha was killed. It was the first time I'd seen a true reaction from him. And he seemed to change after that. Would you understand what I meant if I said he seemed human after that point?"

"I do. He dropped the bullshit game he always plays. I don't think I've ever seen it myself."

"Exactly," said Mercy. "And he warned me to be careful too."

"Shane Gamble might know who killed Tabitha Huff. Why protect that person?"

"That's what I want to find out."

"And you have no leads on her murder."

"We should have her GPS information from the car rental company by tonight. We had to jump through their legal hoops."

"You'll be able to see where she went. You should get some good leads out of that."

"I'm crossing my fingers that she visited whoever Gamble is trying to protect. I'm hoping it's one of his accomplices."

"I feel like your case is about to break wide open," Art said slowly. He finally lowered his sunglasses, and Mercy was pleased to see his eyes were calm. "Congratulations."

"Nothing has happened yet."

He looked straight down at the river, watching three kayakers emerge from under the footbridge. "I'm out of the game again, but my gut says you're closer than I ever was."

Is that a bit of envy I hear?

She wasn't surprised. The robbery had been his baby for many years. He deserved to be there at the end.

Whether he was still under review or not, she'd do her best to give Art a taste of victory.

TWENTY-ONE

"It looks like Tabitha Huff stopped at every place of business in Eagle's Nest," Mercy groused to Jeff.

She sat at her desk, staring at the GPS notes from the victim's rental car, as Jeff stood behind her chair and read over her shoulder. She threw her hands up in exasperation. "Am I supposed to go talk to every shop owner? What if she was following someone and she didn't even go into these places?"

"She was in town the day after you first talked to Shane Gamble. She didn't waste any time at all."

"Here's where I met her." Mercy pointed at an entry that coincided with the location of Rose's preschool. "It looks like she stopped by the bed-and-breakfast in Eagle's Nest a few times," Mercy said, studying the map. "But she stayed in a hotel."

"The bank is right there too," Jeff pointed out. "Makes more sense that she went in a bank. Or used the ATM. She drove to Bend too. Looks like she was in our parking lot. She didn't come to the door as far as I know."

"I checked with Melissa. She didn't talk to anyone with purple streaks in her hair."

"She also drove to a lot of places in the countryside," said Jeff. "What's out in these areas?"

"Mostly a lot of nothing." Mercy tried to visualize what was on the route Tabitha had driven. "I'd have to recreate it."

"The second-to-last coordinate is where the car was found."

"Yes. Before we had it towed."

"This last route is crucial. Somewhere along the line she encountered her killer."

Frustration filled Mercy. *This is impossible.*

It'd sounded so helpful—a map of where their victim had gone since she'd arrived in Oregon. It'd started as a long log of coordinates, which they'd translated into a map. The routes looked as if someone had covered the map with scribbles. Almost if the woman had deliberately obscured her route.

Would she do that?

Tabitha was part of the generation who'd never known a world without the internet. Instant information. Digital footprints. "Dammit!" Mercy sat back in her chair. "Tabitha might have been smarter than I gave her credit for."

"She had purple dye in her hair. It was hard to take her seriously."

Mercy silently humphed. She'd liked Tabitha's hair and briefly wondered how her own hair would look with a bit of artfully applied purple.

"You already went through the notebook found in her car, right?" asked Mercy. "Can I take a look at it now?"

"I skimmed it. It feels incomplete to me, and I suspect she used a note-taking app on her phone for her research."

"Like something she spoke into?"

"Could be. Or something that holds photos, links, typed notes, and voice notes," Jeff told her.

"I could use something like that for work," Mercy admitted.

"I have hope her cell phone turns up."

"It wasn't in her hotel room. Deschutes County said there was just clothes and toiletries. They also checked the hotel security cameras. On the day she died, no one else visited her room. Whoever killed her apparently didn't need anything else of hers."

"I'll grab her notebook from my office." He stepped out.

Jeff was helping the best he could, but he was also being pulled in a million directions. She'd asked for the notebook three times.

He never gave me an answer about bringing in help from Portland.

She suspected that was her answer.

He reappeared, a small spiral notebook in his hand. "You talk to Eddie today?" he asked as he handed it over.

"I did. He's hoping to be discharged tomorrow. If he had his way, he'd be sitting in my office right this minute."

The notebook's cover had a big circle around the words BANG HEAD HERE.

"I just might," she muttered.

"The recent stuff is toward the back," said Jeff. "The pages are dated. Most are notes on older stories that are already present on the *Midnight Voice* website."

Mercy flipped pages and then paused as she scanned one. "Looks like notes from her calls with Shane Gamble. She's written a brief history of the robbery and underlined the fact that the money has never turned up."

"Something made him move fast to contact her."

Mercy slowly nodded as she mentally reviewed the first conversation she'd had with Gamble again. *What spooked him?*

Jeff checked his phone at the sound of a soft ping. "Tabitha's autopsy report. You should have it too."

A couple of clicks opened the report on her screen. Mercy scrolled, pausing on the generic drawing of a woman's body. The sketch was clean except for arrows and notes near the skull. *No other injuries.*

"Perforating gunshot wound to the head," she read aloud. "Entrance was left temporal region with evidence of close-range firing. Dr. Lockhart cites stippling." Mercy remembered the tiny powder bits embedded in the flesh around Tabitha's wound. "Someone was very close when they killed her. Exit was above right ear. Direction was left to right and downward." She glanced at the drawing again. "Someone was taller than her or else she was in a lower position . . . sitting, maybe. No projectile recovered, of course.

"Toxicology report is normal. Overall she was a healthy woman." *Except for the holes in her skull.* "Lividity indicated that she was seated. It lines up with her being in the passenger seat for a period of time after death."

"But she wasn't shot there."

"No. The killer must have moved her there immediately."

Mercy took a deep breath as she imagined Tabitha Huff on Natasha Lockhart's stainless steel table. The very alive young woman she'd met had now been sliced open and had her organs weighed and examined, the top of her skull sawed open, her brain removed, and then everything replaced and stitched neatly back together. Slices of her organs preserved in case of future need.

Purple streaks in her hair. Dr. Lockhart had noted the hair color on the report.

She'll never experiment with another color.

This moment felt more final than when Mercy had stood at Tabitha Huff's murder scene.

"Did evidence turn up anything from her vehicle?"

"Nothing of note."

Who did you make nervous?

Mercy turned back to the notebook, flipping to the last page and working her way back. "She has some notes on Ellis Mull. They were written after his identification made the news . . . Looks like she dug into what the thieves were doing in the years before the robbery just like we did. Same with Trevor Whipple and Nathan May. She has the suspects numbered, with Shane Gamble being number one, of course."

A word underlined three times caught her eye. And sent her brain spinning in a dozen directions. "Jeff, what do you think of this?"

She tapped the word. His eyes widened as the possibility sank in.

"Where would she get that idea?" he said under his breath. "From Gamble?"

For the fifth suspect, Tabitha had firmly crossed out the driver's name, Jerry, and written *female*.

TWENTY-TWO

Ollie's demons were in full force tonight.

He'd nearly driven through a red light on his way home from the sports equipment warehouse.

Just keep driving.

He thought of Shep waiting for him at home, probably curled up on Ollie's bed with Simon right beside him. After initial hatred, the dog and cat had formed a bond. One was never far from the other. It made Ollie feel better about working so many hours away from Shep.

But the thought of getting home to his dog wasn't enough to change his mind tonight. He pulled a quick U-turn and pressed the accelerator, his hands confidently on the wheel.

I'll just drive by. No stopping.

Truman's lecture from earlier in the day filled his head. *"Don't do stupid things."*

Ollie wasn't being stupid. He was protecting his sleep. He knew he'd lie awake forever in bed if he changed his routine tonight. It'd become a habit to slowly drive by Bree Ingram's place after work since the day Truman asked if he'd done the vandalism at her property. He cringed as he remembered how Truman had embarrassed him in the Coffee Café with the question. His face heated at the memory.

It's dark. No one will see my truck.

Twenty minutes later, he slowed as he approached the turnoff for the long driveway that wound back to Bree's home. The house was well lit, with strong outdoor lights that showed all aspects of the front of the house. It looked quiet. He spotted Bree's truck in front of the house and relaxed.

Why does driving by make me feel better? I can't see her.

But he swore he'd instinctively know if something bad were going on in her house.

Now I can go home.

Hopefully Truman wouldn't question why he was late. Truman could always tell when Ollie was lying.

Ollie squinted, studying the road's shoulder to spot the dirt road where he'd been parked when Truman surprised him. He would turn around there and head back to Eagle's Nest. It appeared in his headlights, and he pulled off the narrow country road. He stopped a few feet in and threw his truck in reverse, placing a hand on the back of the seat as he twisted and looked behind him before backing up.

He froze and then turned forward again, leaning over his steering wheel to see what had caught his eye.

The headlights reflected off a small chunk of metal down the dirt road.

His heart pounded as he put the truck back in drive and slowly rolled forward. The shiny object grew larger as Ollie rounded a slight curve, and his lights illuminated the rear end of a pickup truck. The original metal he'd seen had been the edge of the bumper.

The truck sat exactly where Ollie had parked.

Big dents damaged the tailgate. The truck was even older than his. And it was red.

I told him it wasn't me!

Fear for Bree sucked away his breath. He grabbed his cell phone, snapped a picture of the license plate of the truck, and then threw his truck into reverse and floored the accelerator, shooting backward. He steered while looking over his shoulder. No fancy backup camera for him. He took a hard turn when he met the narrow blacktop and sped back to Bree's driveway. His brakes screeched as he slowed to take the turn. Gravel flew as he raced to her house.

Call Truman.

Call 911.

Christ. I don't even know if something has happened yet.

He pictured a dozen policemen staring at him for calling 911 on a parked truck. Truman right in front. His arms crossed and his eyes stern.

Am I doing something stupid?

No. He could feel it.

He slammed to a stop behind Bree's truck and raced to the door. Lights were on in the house. *Good.* He rang the bell several times, unable to stand still on her porch. After waiting five seconds he banged on the door with a fist and it swung open.

Oh shit.

"Mrs. Ingram?" he shouted. "Are you here? It's Ollie."

He took one step into the house and listened hard. Silence. *Is she asleep?*

Truman's going to have my head.

"Mrs. Ingram?" he yelled again. "Anyone home?"

A small noise reached him. It sounded like a puppy. "Hello?" He took three more steps into the home, moving past the living room on his right and speeding toward the kitchen at the back of the house. "Mrs. Ingram?" he called in a normal voice.

The puppy whined again.

Ollie took a few fast steps and found himself in the kitchen. And nearly puked. *Dear God in heaven.* Oxygen vanished from the room and he sucked for air.

Bree was tied to a wooden chair, her head slumped forward on her chest. Blood soaked her clothing and had puddled under the chair on the linoleum. One arm was clamped to the table. Her hand flat on its surface. A bloody mallet and a knife lay beside her hand. Along with two severed fingers.

Ollie flung himself at the kitchen sink and heaved, barely making his target.

Her fingers. He vomited again.

Bree whined. A high-pitched, wet, choking sound.

She's alive.

He spun toward her, wiped his mouth with a towel, and knelt next to her chair. He pushed her bloody hair out of her face and clenched his teeth at the sight of the abuse. Both her eyes had swollen shut. Her nose was bloody and split. Bleeding abrasions everywhere. *What do I do?* He made himself look at her hand. The bleeding seemed to have stopped. He quickly scanned the rest of her. She'd been beaten, but he didn't see any active bleeding.

Get help.

With shaking hands, he called 911.

Moments later he set the phone down, switching to speaker. The operator had notified emergency services and wouldn't allow Ollie to hang up. Unable to call Truman, he asked the operator to reach the Eagle's Nest police chief.

"I need to untie her," he told the operator. "I should lay her down."

"Is she breathing?"

"Yes."

"Then don't move her."

"But she's *barely* breathing!"

"If she's been beaten as badly as you say, don't move her. It might make it impossible for her to breathe."

"But . . . but . . . she's tied up!" He wrestled with the rope's knots. They'd moistened and swollen with her blood. The rough texture scraped the skin from his fingertips as he dug at them. He grabbed the knife from the table.

"Ollie," the operator commanded. "Don't move her. The ropes might look horrible, but she needs to stay still."

Ollie froze with the knife in his hand, every cell of his body screaming for him to cut her loose.

"Ollie, is anyone else in the house?"

He jumped to his feet. *I forgot about her attacker.* He checked the adjoining bathroom, the knife clenched in his hand. Anxiety had him ready to stab. *I can kill anyone right now.* But he couldn't bring himself to leave Bree to check the rest of the house. He pushed open an adjacent door and found the laundry room. At the other end was a door wide open to the outdoors. Breathing heavily, he stared out into the darkness. He saw and heard nothing.

He's escaped.

But I have a photo of his license plate.

Back in the kitchen, he told the operator, "The back door is open. I think he left."

"The police should be there momentarily. The ambulance is a little further behind."

"Did you reach the police chief?" An overwhelming need for Truman swamped him, and he felt tears burn.

"One of the other operators did. He's also on his way."

Relief made his knees weak. "Thank you."

"Hang in there, Ollie. How's she doing?"

He knelt beside Bree again, his hands gentle and no longer shaking. She still breathed. He was relieved she was unconscious. The pain would be unbearable.

"Still breathing. Can you hear me, Bree?" he asked softly, hoping on some level she knew he was there. "He's gone. You're safe."

Her breathing stopped. Hitched. And started again.

Ollie collapsed onto his heels in relief, rattled by the long pauses between her breaths. *Did she hear me?*

Sirens sounded in the distance and tears burned again.

She's going to make it.

He jumped to his feet and grabbed the first bowl he found in a cupboard. He scooped ice from the freezer into the bowl and then gingerly buried her fingers in the ice. *I should have done that earlier.*

With luck, she might be whole again.

Who am I kidding? No one would be whole after a beating like this.

TWENTY-THREE

Truman drove back to Bree's home as soon as the sun rose the next morning.

Last night had been a nightmare. After the call from the 911 dispatch center, he'd floored his Tahoe all the way to Bree's, alternating between cursing Ollie and praying for him under his breath. When he'd arrived, county had already secured the scene and Bree had just been loaded into an ambulance. Truman caught a brief glimpse of her, and it'd haunted him all night.

She'd been covered in abrasions and blood. An oxygen mask over her face and an IV in her arm. By the grim faces of the EMTs, Truman knew she was in bad shape.

Her eyes had never opened.

Ollie had been in the process of being questioned by Detective Evan Bolton. The boy's hands were covered in blood, and a tech swabbed and photographed them. His eyes had been wide, confusion and fear in his gaze as he stared from the tech to his hands and then to Detective Bolton. Truman had stridden straight to him and enveloped him in a big hug, ignoring the annoyance on the tech's face.

The teen had trembled in his hug. "She might die." Truman barely heard Ollie's whisper.

Truman had stayed silent, knowing there were no words that would help.

After Ollie was more composed, he'd walked the investigators through his steps from the previous hour. Embarrassment flushed his face as he admitted he'd vomited in the sink. "Most people would have done the same upon finding this scene," Bolton had told him.

Truman agreed. Even with Bree on the way to the hospital, the cut ropes and drying blood on the floor, chair, and table were enough to give his stomach a solid churn. He tried not to imagine how it'd been with her sitting there, dripping and unconscious, with her loose fingers on the table.

"What was the clamp for?" Truman had asked, pointing at the C-shaped piece of metal on the floor.

Ollie's shoulders quaked once as he answered. "It fastened her hand to the table."

Truman wished he hadn't asked.

The teen had showed them the open back door, and then Bolton drove the three of them to where Ollie had seen a truck. It was gone. "Those are my truck's tracks." Ollie pointed at the soft dirt. "You can see how I went in and then backed out to turn around. It looks like the other truck backed out over my tracks."

"It was quick thinking to snap a picture of the truck," said Bolton.

"I'm sorry it didn't help." Ollie's shoulders sagged.

The license plate had been stolen a month before.

"That's where you're wrong, Ollie," Truman told him. "We've got the make, model, and color. We'll find him."

Truman had sent Ollie home with a county deputy and was glad Mercy was spending the night at his house. The teen shouldn't be alone. Truman hadn't wanted him to drive, and he knew Bolton would want to look over Ollie's vehicle.

As Truman steered up the driveway that early morning, Ollie's old red truck sat in front of Bree's house, silently waiting for its owner.

Truman was pleased to see a county vehicle had parked all night at the home. The county deputy's head jerked forward from his cruiser's headrest at the sound of Truman's vehicle. The now-awake man raised a tired hand in greeting, and Truman wished he'd thought to bring the deputy some coffee and breakfast. The county evidence team, their detective, and Truman had worked the Ingram home until three in the morning. Truman now had two hours of sleep under his belt and a drip coffee with three shots of espresso in his hand. Truman parked his Tahoe next to the county deputy and downed the last of his espresso-choked coffee, grimacing at the bitter flavor.

After a few words with the deputy, Truman went to the stables. Horses nickered as he entered, sticking their heads out over their stall doors, dark eyes eager for attention. Or food. Truman nosed around until he found an open bale and then tossed a flake of the alfalfa hay in each stall. A bin of good-smelling grain was next to the hay, so he gave each horse a big scoop, having no idea if he was over- or underfeeding. By the pleased snorting of the horses as he dumped the grain in each feed bucket, he suspected it was more than they were accustomed to.

Lucas can handle the feeding after today.

Right now, Lucas was with his mother in the hospital. She'd had a midnight surgery to reattach her fingers, and the surgeon had been optimistic, stating the cuts had been clean and the fact that the fingers had immediately been placed on ice had made the difference.

Ollie did good.

Truman trudged along the gravel road from the barn to the house, weighing his Ollie issue. *How do I tell him he did good when he purposefully disobeyed?* "We just had that discussion yesterday," he complained to the morning air. "Was I wrong to tell him to stay away from Bree?"

It'd been the right thing to say.

191

"But if he'd obeyed, Bree would be dead." His words dissolved in the quiet morning, and he shuddered. If Ollie had done as Truman commanded, they'd be getting ready for a funeral.

Raising a teenager—a unique teenager—brought up issues Truman had never dreamed of. He'd known it'd be a challenge to acclimate Ollie back into society, but he hadn't expected the boy's protective instincts to override acceptable behavior.

What's acceptable and normal? Maybe Ollie's way is the way it should be.

"Fuck me," Truman muttered. His brain was starting to hurt. There was no getting around the fact that he had to praise and reprimand Ollie at the same time.

Poor kid will be even more confused.

"I can't let him run wild." Truman went up Bree's steps, put on booties and gloves, and studied the front door.

Technically the investigation belonged to Deschutes County. But he and Bolton had come to an understanding after working several shared jurisdiction cases together: two heads were better than one.

No sign of forced entry.

Did Bree know her attacker? How many hours was she tied up?

Truman entered the home. It looked different in the daylight, but the metallic odor of blood still hovered in the air.

The house was meticulously clean and showed Bree's love for horses. Horse decor was everywhere. Prints on the walls, bookends, and even a lamp with a rearing horse for the base. He moved into the kitchen and stopped. Morning sun streamed through the windows, providing perfect light for breakfast at the table in Bree's kitchen's nook.

A brutal attack had clearly taken place. Dried blood covered the table and had pooled on the floor.

I'll never stand in this room again without remembering it this way.

He was determined to have it cleaned up before Bree returned. He'd do it himself if necessary.

The knife was noticeably absent. It'd been sent for processing. Print results could be available in a matter of hours. Ollie had picked up the knife, so his prints had been taken. Truman crossed his fingers that the attacker's prints showed up in the first database search. Assuming he'd left prints . . .

Loud voices came from out front.

Truman left the kitchen and discovered Sandy arguing with the county deputy.

"Truman! He won't let me come in. I need to get some stuff for Bree." Sandy was indignant, her hands on her hips as she stared down the deputy.

"It's a crime scene, Sandy."

Dark circles under her eyes marred her fair skin. He knew she'd been at the hospital all night with Bree.

"Detective Bolton told me most of the evidence had been collected overnight."

"That's true, but—"

"Then I'm good to go in."

Her eyes pleaded with him, desperation in her expression. She was a woman on a mission for her nearly murdered best friend.

"I'll stick with her," Truman told the deputy. "Make a note that she went in with me."

Hopefully Bolton won't have my head.

Enthusiasm made Sandy leap up the stairs, and Truman stopped her on the porch, handing over booties and gloves. As she put them on, he noticed her enthusiasm rapidly waned; she'd realized what she was walking into.

"How bad is it?" Her eyes were nervous, and he wondered if she would change her mind.

"Bad. We'll avoid the kitchen. How is Bree this morning?"

"Still unconscious. Her face and entire head are so swollen." Sandy took a deep breath. "He really beat on her. I hope she doesn't have a serious brain injury. They say her brain has swelled too," she said softly. Moisture glittered in her eyes. "Lucas is with her, so I came to get some clothing and other stuff. She'll appreciate it when she wakes." Her voice broke on the last word.

If she wakes.

Truman hugged the tall woman. "She's going to be fine, Sandy. We know what a fighter she is. She's tougher than this."

"Why does she have to be so damned tiny?" Sandy muttered into his shoulder with a mix of tears, anger, and exasperation in her voice.

"I hear you."

Sandy pulled back, wiping her nose with her sleeve. "She told me she was nervous."

"Yes, I know the vandalism rattled her. She took it very personally."

The woman pressed her lips together, eyeing him curiously. "Did she tell you who she suspected?"

Surprise rocked Truman. "No. She told me she had no idea."

"Damn her. She's so stubborn."

"She told you who she thought did the vandalism?" *And perhaps nearly killed her?*

"She wouldn't tell me." Sandy's brows came together as she concentrated. "She said . . . her memories were running away with her thoughts and that it was too far-fetched. You knew the murdered reporter talked to her the day before she was killed, right?"

"No." Frustration ignited. "What did Tabitha Huff tell her?" He fought to stay calm. Usually people around here couldn't keep their mouths shut about anything. Bree was an exception.

"Bree was confused by the interaction. The woman approached her in the hardware store and asked if she was Bree Ingram."

Truman ran a hand through his hair. *How is Tabitha tied to this?* "And?"

Sandy wrinkled her nose. "Bree swears Tabitha asked if she *still* reads the *Midnight Voice* . . . but that can't be right. She must have asked if she'd ever read it."

Truman blinked. "How . . ."

"Right?"

"Did Bree know Tabitha from somewhere?"

"She swore she'd never met her before . . . but Bree said she used to read the paper religiously when she was younger. It was always there at the checkout stand, you know? Before it went digital. I guess it was a guilty pleasure for Bree."

"What does a tabloid have to do with this attack?" Truman muttered.

"Tabitha Huff talked to me about my vandalism on the same day." Sandy looked away, biting her lip.

"And you're just telling me *now*?" It was getting harder to keep his temper in check. Usually stories ran rampant around town. *Why are people choosing now to keep quiet?* "The woman was murdered, and you didn't think to tell anyone? Jesus, Sandy. Bree was nearly killed . . . You could be attacked next. We need to get you somewhere safe."

Could Sandy be the next victim?

"I can't leave right now. But don't worry, I'm very careful."

Unable to stand still any longer, Truman paced in a small circle on Bree's porch and shot glares at Sandy. "Careful. Define *careful* for me. Are you armed?"

"I left it in my car."

"Lot of good it does there," he muttered. "Do you know what you're doing?"

Her chin went up. "I have a concealed carry permit. I practice. I've been careful for ten years."

Since she escaped from her husband.

"And if he wrestles the weapon away from you?"

"Then I'll have to shoot first, won't I?" Her gaze told him she'd do exactly that.

He studied her face. This wasn't the time for a lecture. Sandy's stiff back and planted feet told him she wouldn't listen anyway.

"We aren't done with this topic," he warned her. "But right now, tell me what else Bree said. You mentioned memories."

Sandy nodded. "I could tell she was thinking about a past incident. But she wouldn't give me any details."

"I wonder if Lucas would know anything."

"I had the impression this was something she kept close to her chest. She wouldn't tell me . . . I don't know if she'd tell Lucas. She's rather protective of him."

"Like mother, like son," said Truman. "I wonder if she's had a similar attack in the past." He took a deep breath. "I wish she'd told me if someone had broken in or physically attacked her before." He gave Sandy a side-eye. "How come it's so hard to drag information out of both of you?"

A nervous smile touched her lips. "Must be why she's my best friend. We're alike. Can we go in now? I'll be fast."

Truman opened the door and watched as Sandy squared her shoulders. She stepped carefully over the threshold and headed toward the hallway that led to the bedrooms. She put her hand over her nose and turned to Truman, her brown eyes stunned. "Is that smell . . ."

He nodded.

Her jaw tightened, and she continued down the hall. In Bree's bedroom she stopped. "Can I touch things?"

"What do you need to do?"

"Just get a change of clothes out of her drawers and closet."

"Touch only what you need to."

Sandy opened a drawer with one finger and removed underclothes and a pair of black yoga pants as Truman watched. At the open closet she took a shirt and sweatshirt. Truman was about to mention how warm the weather was but kept his mouth shut. Sandy had picked comfort clothing, the type of clothes to wear while watching TV from the couch all day. It'd be quite a while before Bree could wear the clothing. The task was more for Sandy; she needed to do *something*.

"I'll grab her Kindle," Sandy murmured. "She'll like that. I'll run this stuff back to the hospital after I stop by my place. I had someone new set up the breakfast buffet, and I want to look it over." Sandy nervously chatted away, and Truman knew she wasn't looking for conversation. She was simply filling the silence of the house. She found the Kindle in a nightstand drawer and rooted deeper for the charger, still talking about the buffet food.

Truman watched. The room had been lightly searched overnight. Everyone had agreed it appeared the attacker hadn't entered any of the bedrooms.

Abruptly Sandy's monologue stopped. "Truman . . ." She had removed a few folded pieces of paper from inside the cover of the Kindle and was scowling at one. It was wrinkled, as if it'd been balled up at one time. Her hand shook as she gave it to Truman.

You'll do it if you want your son to live.

His blood turned to ice; his hands were numb on the paper. "What do the others say?"

"More of the same," Sandy whispered. "Oh my God. What did he want her to do?"

Truman took the three sheets of paper with gloved hands. They were slightly smudged as if they'd been rubbed in dirt. *Found outdoors?*

Each one threatened Bree or her son. None specified what she was to do.

Did she already know what to do?

"Do you think the same person attacked her?" Sandy whispered and then turned accusing eyes on him. "Why didn't you find these earlier?"

Guilt swamped him. "We were looking for evidence left by the attacker."

"I'd say he left these at some point in time."

"Why didn't she come to us with these?" Truman silently cursed at Bree. "Why didn't she tell Lucas?"

"Because he's threatened in the notes too."

"All the more reason to tell someone." He eyed Sandy. "Don't hide this kind of shit."

"Never." Her hand trembled as she took a page from him and read it again. "Why wouldn't she say anything? What would she lose by taking these to the police?"

"Maybe she didn't take them seriously."

"Then she would have thrown them away."

Truman stared at the words *if you want your son to live.*

He whipped out his cell phone and called Lucas's number.

TWENTY-FOUR

Standing in the warm late-morning sun, Mercy looked at the notes.

Inside plastic sleeves was paper that had been ripped out of a spiral notebook, the left-side edges still tattered. She met Truman's calm gaze. He'd called her to Bree Ingram's home to discuss Tabitha Huff's possible link to Bree's attack. Detective Evan Bolton had arrived a few minutes after. Both he and Truman looked as if they'd been up most of the night. Their faces were long and their eyes were tired.

Is Bree's attack part of the Gamble-Helmet Heist case?

Truman thought so.

"Has Lucas been warned?" she asked.

"Yes. He's at the hospital. County has a deputy at the door of Bree's room. I told the deputy to stay close."

"Did Lucas ask why?"

Truman looked grim. "He did. I told him we found some threats at his mother's house that included him. He was shocked. I had to repeat several times that he's to stick by the deputy. He wanted to drive right out here and take a look."

"I understand why he believes that he doesn't need protection." The office manager was the size of a professional linebacker.

The sound of tires on gravel caught her attention. Her boss had arrived. Jeff joined their group, looking as exhausted as the first two men.

"We're a sad-looking bunch," Mercy commented. "Looks like none of us got much sleep last night." She handed the threatening notes to Jeff.

"I'm not sure I follow what these have to do with the robbery," Jeff said, blinking wearily at the handwriting.

"Shane Gamble brought in Tabitha Huff after Ellis Mull was found. Tabitha met with both Bree and Sandy to ask about their vandalism," Truman stated. "Tabitha was murdered, and now Bree has been attacked—nearly killed."

"Where's Sandy?" Mercy asked.

"She's checking the buffet at her place, and then she'll go to the hospital to stay with Bree. She found the notes."

"Sandy discovered these? Did she lead you right to them?" Mercy asked, the hair on the back of her neck standing up.

"Why was she allowed at the scene?" Detective Bolton asked with a hard look at Truman.

Truman raised his chin the tiniest bit. "I was with her at all times. She was getting clothing for Bree and found the notes in her room. I saw it happen."

"I thought Ms. Ingram was still unconscious," Jeff added. "Why did Sandy take it upon herself to get clothes for a woman who couldn't ask for them and won't need them for a while?"

"I get it," Mercy replied, feeling a guilty need to back Truman. "Sandy's a doer. She's the type of person who can't sit still. I can see her pacing in Bree's hospital room, needing to do *something*."

"That's pretty much the impression I got too," answered Truman.

Mercy didn't miss the glance he flicked her way. He didn't need her to speak for him.

"Shane Gamble said he gave Tabitha a message to deliver," Mercy reminded Jeff. "Could it have been for Bree or Sandy?"

"Tabitha Huff talked to nearly every person in a ten-mile radius of town," Jeff muttered.

"But Bree was clearly in some sort of danger." Mercy pointed at the notes in Jeff's hand.

"How would Gamble know Bree was in danger and want to warn her?" Truman asked. "Why would he know anything? He's sitting in prison."

"He contacted Tabitha after my first interview. Something I said must have been relevant—that we missed or didn't understand—that made him want to warn someone."

"It could have been anyone Tabitha talked to," Detective Bolton stated as he looked at Mercy. "Heck, she talked to you."

Jeff gave a tired sigh. "What do we know about these two women? Could they have known Gamble or some of his gang in the past?" He swayed slightly.

Suspicious, Mercy reached over and placed her hand on Jeff's forehead. "Dammit, Jeff, it's got you too! Your forehead is hot enough to fry an egg." *Why is he working while sick?* "Go home. Rose has it and so does one of her preschoolers. I don't want it."

Truman and Evan both took a step out of their circle.

"You need help—" Jeff started.

"What I need is to not get the flu," Mercy interrupted him. "Then no one will be able to work this case."

"I can't just—"

"Yes, you can. Now leave." She shot a get-out-of-here glare at him. "You're welcome to call and email me all you want. Just don't breathe the same air as me. Or touch the same stuff." She took the notes out of his hands, glad she still wore gloves. Truman had removed his gloves, and out of the corner of her eye she saw him surreptitiously rub his hands on his pants.

Jeff looked at her a moment longer, defeat in his eyes. "I'll go. But tell them."

Truman and Evan's interest was piqued.

"I will," she promised. *I'd already planned to share our new information with them this morning.*

Jeff quietly left the group, making Mercy realize he was sicker than he'd let on.

"Should he be driven home?" she asked the other men.

Both shook their heads.

Men.

"I'm holding the two of you responsible if he gets in an accident." Neither looked concerned.

"Okay." Mercy looked at the notes in her hands. "There're enough correlations here for the FBI to consider that Bree's attack might be related to the robbery. Let's get these notes to the lab. Have we heard anything on fingerprints from the knife he used? Who is working on whittling down red trucks in the area?"

"I have a guy on the trucks," said Evan. "And I expect to hear from the lab about fingerprints any minute. But first I want to know what Jeff wanted you to tell us." Truman nodded in agreement.

Mercy cleared her throat. "One of Tabitha Huff's notes suggests that the driver at the Gamble-Helmet Heist was a woman."

And now that I know Bree's attack could be related to the robbery, it makes her a possible suspect.

Their surprise was palpable.

The two men exchanged a glance. "But even Gamble refers to the driver as 'him' or Jerry," said Truman, his eyes skeptical.

"Maybe he had a good reason to do so."

"He's been protecting someone for thirty years?" Evan asked. "I can't see it. Maybe he'd do it for a year or two, but why for so long?"

"Who knows?" said Mercy. "If he has protected her, that means she's someone very special. All the investigating done in the past didn't turn up a girlfriend for Shane Gamble. Trevor Whipple had a few, but all their alibis checked out."

202

"You think Bree could be that woman?" Truman said faintly.

Mercy saw it was hard for him to wrap his brain around the idea that the petite mother of Lucas could have been involved in one of the biggest heists of the twentieth century.

"Now that I've seen this attack, I think she's a possibility."

"This is ridiculous. I've known Bree—"

"For barely two years," Mercy said firmly.

"But Lucas—"

"Might know absolutely nothing of his mother's past." She sighed. "I know this is difficult, Truman. I want to get Art's opinion on the female theory."

Both Evan and Truman frowned. "Wasn't he removed from the investigation after the shooting?" Evan asked.

"Yes, he's in bureaucratic limbo. But I can't let that stop me. No one knows this case better than him."

"What about female relatives of the thieves?" Truman asked. "Mull had four sisters, right? I assume the other men had some too. Were they even looked at back then?"

"There was extensive investigation into the families and friends of the thieves. I spent hours looking into their last ten years overnight. Twelve women. I checked sisters, cousins, and mothers," said Mercy. "That's why my eyes are completely bloodshot. But I can't find anything that suggests any relatives came into money after the robbery."

"Maybe she didn't get paid," Evan suggested. "Once the plan fell apart, maybe she decided to cut her losses and play it quiet."

"Help me out here," Mercy asked. "Assume for a moment that Bree was the driver. Which person wrote these threatening notes and what do they want her to do?"

"As I see it," said Truman, "they're threatening her life and Lucas's, so it's got to be about big money or else the note writer's own life feels threatened."

"But if the note writer feels threatened," continued Mercy, "don't you think he'd tell her to *not* do something . . . instead of telling her *to* do something?"

"You're leaning toward this being about money, not his life," added Evan. "Most likely money from the robbery."

"The writer wants money," Mercy asserted. "It fits."

"Why did he wait thirty years?" asked Evan. "Why now?"

Mercy shrugged. "Maybe he recently ran out of money? He's ordering her to give him money or he'll kill Lucas . . . or her. And it's a good possibility he tried last night."

"If he wanted to kill Bree last night, he had plenty of time to do so," said Truman. "Her attacker *tortured* her—he cut off two fingers. I think he wanted information and she wasn't sharing—or she didn't know the answer."

"I bet that information is the location of money. If she was the driver in the robbery, would she still have money after all these years?" asked Evan.

"Maybe she doesn't have any," said Mercy, "but he doesn't believe her. I'm going to request her financial records as far back as I can. See if there are any red flags."

"Was he involved in the robbery or not? It could have been someone else who heard a rumor that Bree had money." Truman passed a hand over his forehead, and Mercy sympathized. Her brain hurt from the possibilities too. "We don't even know who this 'he' is that we keep talking about."

"I'll request to have the high school photos of Whipple and May aged. I keep thinking of them as young men when they're closer to fifty."

"That would help," Truman agreed.

"We really need to hear what Bree has to say," she said. "What's the latest on her condition?"

"Earlier Sandy told me she was still unconscious."

Mercy pressed her lips together. *Sandy again.* "Maybe Sandy needs to be kept out of Bree's room."

Truman swung his head her way, anger in his eyes. "That's ridiculous. She's her closest friend."

"Close friends share secrets. Maybe secrets about money."

"Sandy would have said something," Truman argued.

"I don't know either of these women," said Evan. "But what Mercy has suggested is logical. If Sandy knows Bree has a large sum of money, she has motive for Bree's attack. I'll call the deputy at the hospital."

"What about the notes? Sandy's the one who found them," Truman pointed out. "Someone threatened Bree and Lucas."

"Maybe Sandy planted the notes," suggested Evan. "It takes the focus off of her."

Truman crossed his arms, clearly wanting to argue. "I know both these women." He looked at Mercy, disbelief in his eyes. "You do too. This is insane."

"We're just speculating, Truman. We have to consider all the possibilities, and I'll look at Sandy's background too. That might clear some things up."

"Her previous name was Jada Kerns," he offered. "I don't know what it was before she married."

"I'll figure it out."

"She's a good person, Mercy."

"I agree. But good people commit crimes too," Mercy stated.

He said nothing, but his disappointment settled over her like a heavy blanket.

TWENTY-FIVE

Glass from a second-story window at Sandy's bed-and-breakfast shattered as a woman screamed. Truman ducked behind his truck, shoving his hat tighter on his head. He had just returned to Eagle's Nest from the investigation at Bree's home and immediately he, Samuel, and Ben Cooley had been called to an incident at the B&B.

A guest had reported that a man with a rifle had burst into the old home and waved his weapon around, threatening to shoot unless Sandy came out of the kitchen. When she did, he forced her up the stairs and locked himself and her in a guest room while the rest of the guests evacuated the property.

The officers had barely stepped out of their vehicles when the glass shattered.

"I knew this was going to happen!" Samuel shouted at him, frustration burning in his eyes.

Truman glared at the officer crouching beside him, their backs against his vehicle. Samuel's face had gone white with anger, and his hand hovered over the gun at his side. He shook with outrage. Exactly what Truman—and Sandy—didn't need right now.

"No one could have predicted this," Truman snapped. "Now shut the fuck up and pay attention." Truman stole a glance at the broken second-story window in Sandy's bed-and-breakfast, glad he'd parked across the street. Ben was twenty feet to Truman's left, taking cover behind his own vehicle.

"Has Lucas called county?" Samuel asked in a calmer voice.

"Yes. They're sending their SWAT team and hostage negotiator. Did you see what he broke the window with?" Truman asked.

"The butt of his rifle. Not the smartest move. Maybe the gun is damaged now."

"I think we figured out he wasn't the brightest character a few days ago with all the vandalism."

Is this the same guy who nearly killed Bree?

Angry shouts came from the window, male and female. Truman recognized Sandy's voice but couldn't make out the words. All he knew was that she was pissed and letting her attacker know it.

I'd rather hear that than terrified screams.

Is it her ex-husband?

"Are we just going to sit here?" Samuel couldn't hold still. He continuously ran his hands over his utility belt, taking a subconscious inventory, his energy distracting Truman.

"Tell county to set a perimeter around this block. We don't need pedestrians strolling into the area."

Samuel grabbed the radio mic at his shoulder and relayed Truman's message.

Truman's mind was spinning. If this attack was from Sandy's exhusband, did that mean he'd tortured Bree too?

Is Sandy's ex involved with the Gamble-Helmet Heist?

Ben calmly watched Truman, waiting for orders.

"Is it okay if I go in and get my phone? I'll just be a minute," came a female voice.

207

Truman and Samuel both spun to their right to see who had spoken. A woman stood near the rear of Truman's SUV—her back to the B&B—looking curiously at them.

"Ma'am! Get out of the street!" Truman sputtered as Samuel darted to the back of the SUV, grabbed her arm, and pulled her to crouch next to Truman.

She was about fifty and wore faded denim along with white laceless Keds tennis shoes like the ones Truman's sister had worn in elementary school. She yanked her arm out of Samuel's grip and shot him a death glare. "You don't have to be rude!" She tried to stand, and Samuel pulled her back down.

"Please stay behind cover, ma'am."

"This is ridiculous. The couple is locked in a room upstairs. My phone is on the first floor. No one will notice if I sneak back in. He hasn't even fired his gun." She met Truman's gaze, waiting expectantly.

Truman couldn't speak.

Samuel could. "Hey, Ben!" He waved the older officer over. "Please take Ms. . . ."

"Leggett."

"Please take Ms. Leggett to a safe area and help her understand she's not to enter the bed-and-breakfast."

"Now, wait a minute—"

The roar of a shotgun filled the air, and they all dropped closer to the ground.

"Get her out of here, Ben. Now!" Truman snapped. Ms. Leggett glared at him again but kept her mouth shut.

"Jesus Christ," Samuel said under his breath as Ben guided her past his vehicle, both of them keeping their heads low. "What is wrong with people?"

". . . Demand a refund . . ." Truman heard her say as the two of them moved farther away.

Sandy let loose with more furious shouts, and Truman and Samuel exhaled. She didn't sound injured; she sounded angry about her broken window. The male attacker yelled back at her. Sirens sounded close by, and Truman watched county vehicles block the street on both ends.

Truman refused to picture Sandy with injuries similar to Bree's.

"Is this a domestic or an active shooter?" Samuel muttered.

"Both. He's shooting, so we're going in." Truman held Samuel's gaze, asking a silent question.

"About damned time."

Truman had known that'd be his answer.

Ben darted back, crouching as low as his seventysomething back would let him.

"Samuel and I are going in. All activity has been at that window."

"Got ya, boss. Go get our girl." Ben propped his arms on the hood, his weapon trained on the broken window from where shouts still persisted.

Truman opened his SUV's door, grabbed the rifle on his dash, and slung it over his shoulder. "Let's go."

Their pistols in hand, he and Samuel dashed across the street and up the wooden stairs of the porch. Voices in altercation still sounded from above.

Is he acting alone?

No assumptions. No one had reported a second attacker, but one could be waiting inside. They paused, Truman on one side of the closed front door and Samuel on the other. Truman nodded. Samuel whipped open the door and Truman entered, weapon leading, covering the blind spot to the right as Samuel moved smoothly after him to catch the left. The large lobby area was empty. Truman checked behind the huge wooden desk as Samuel moved to one side of the swinging door that led to the kitchen. His heart pounding but his focus razor sharp, Truman paused at the other side of the door, and they repeated their front-door maneuver. A rapid pass through the kitchen showed they were alone.

Stomping and shouts had continued above during the twenty seconds it took to methodically clear the first level. They carefully moved up the stairs, weapons leading, covering all blind spots. On the second level was a hallway with five doors. A small crash and the sound of breaking glass came from behind the door labeled CASCADE SUITE. More angry shouts from Sandy.

Truman and Samuel moved cautiously down the hall, checking each doorknob as they passed. All the suites were locked. They stopped on each side of the Cascade door, breathing heavily. Sweat ran down one side of Samuel's face as he gently tried the knob.

Locked.

Samuel's gaze met his, concern in his eyes.

This is where everything could go wrong.

Truman took a deep breath. "Eagle's Nest police!"

◆ ◆ ◆

Sandy had felt someone watching her. Even before the graffiti had started, she had felt someone's gaze on the center of her back.

After leaving Bree's home with a change of clothes that morning, she'd stopped in at her B&B to see how the morning buffet had gone. In the kitchen she'd been putting away food when a rash of angry shouts came from her lobby. She grabbed a rolling pin and marched out, determined to put a stop to the ruckus. As she went through the door into her lobby, she froze.

Lionel stood there.

He was older and grayer and fatter. But it was him.. And he pointed a rifle at her head.

Two of her guests hovered in the far corner of the room, the man standing protectively in front of his wife, unable to get a clear path to the front door without passing Lionel.

"There's the bitch." He grinned through his beard, his teeth more yellow than she remembered.

Every ounce of her old fear of him clogged her nerves. She couldn't speak. She couldn't walk.

All she could do was stare.

He's going to kill me this time.

Dear Lord. Did he torture Bree?

Her legs quivered. She might have led her ex to Bree's doorstep.

He took four quick steps and grabbed her hair with one meaty hand, nearly pulling her to the ground. She dropped her rolling pin and wrapped her hands around his wrist. The male guest in the corner moved forward, a need to help her on his terrified face.

Lionel will shoot him.

She'd seen him fire his rifle one-handed while drinking a beer with the other. A talent he was proud of.

"What do you want, Lionel?" She forced the words between clenched teeth, feeling her scalp rip. He'd always grabbed her hair as he abused her.

He yanked backward, forcing her face upward to look at him. He leaned close, the rifle still held in his one-handed grip, ready to fire. But now it pointed at the couple in the corner. The male guest had stopped, his hands raised.

"Maybe I just wanted to see *my wife.*"

Vomit rushed up her throat, and sweat broke out under her arms.

His words were worse than the pain on her scalp.

He moved his mouth to her neck, his breath smelling strongly of alcohol. His lips were wet, and she nearly spewed the vomit pooling in the back of her mouth. "Where's your bedroom, sweetheart?"

Her nerves and muscles shrieked at his words, and her thighs instinctively clamped together. The male guest took another step in her direction, not caring that Lionel had a rifle aimed at him.

Get Lionel out of the lobby.

"Upstairs."

Delight crossed his face. "Let's go, darlin'. Just like old times."

Old times . . .

Memories of his brutal sexual attacks flooded her. Tears. Bruises. Blood. She'd learned the hard way to never say no. And to never fight back.

That was the old me.

Ripping her scalp, he dragged her toward the stairs.

I'm not the victim I once was.

She tripped on the first step and fell hard on a shin, drawing a cry from her lungs. His answer was another yank on her hair and to slap the butt of his rifle across her face. Tasting blood, she stumbled up the steps after him, and out of the corner of her eye she saw the couple dash out the front door.

Stall him until the police get here.

She focused on Lionel, searching for a weakness. He huffed as he moved up the stairs, his thighs and stomach jiggling with excess fat. He wasn't as fit as he used to be, and she was lean and powerful. Anxiety had driven her to develop and maintain physical strength in case she ever had to fight back again.

Today was that day.

I've spent ten years preparing for this moment.

She breathed hard, her heart slamming against her chest. *I can do this.* She would put an end to his control over her. She was done looking over her shoulder.

No matter the cost.

They reached the top of the stairs. "Which room?"

She pointed at the Cascade Suite, which she knew was empty. He tried the handle and then shoved her face into the wall next to the door. Blood streamed from her nose. "It's locked!"

"Pocket." She spit blood and cringed as his huge hands dug into her pocket, coming up with her ring of master keys. He pressed them into her hands.

She fumbled with the jingling ring, her brain screaming for her to place the keys between her fingers and drive them into his eyes. Instead she plunged one key into the lock and pushed the door open. *Not yet.*

He dragged her inside, pushed her toward the bed, and slammed the door, locking it behind him. He pointed the rifle at her. And smiled.

Did he torture Bree because of me?

◆ ◆ ◆

Truman listened. The room behind the locked door had gone silent at his shout of "Eagle's Nest police."

A split second later loud thumps sounded, and the wooden floors vibrated through Truman's boots. *Did someone fall?* The thumps were followed by deep gasps for breath. "Fucking bitch!" A gunshot roared from inside the suite.

Truman flinched at the shot but never dropped Samuel's gaze. He nodded at his officer and gestured at the knob. Samuel immediately positioned himself and thrust a power-packed kick near the doorjamb above the knob. He stepped left into the room and Truman followed to the right. Both men froze, their weapons trained on Sandy.

The rifle was in her hands, aimed at the head of the man on the floor. His shaking hands shielded his face as he peered at her through his fingers. Lionel Kerns.

Dust filtered down from a large hole in the ceiling above Sandy, and the odor of a freshly fired rifle hung in the air. She didn't look at the officers. All her intensity was focused through the weapon's sights and on her target. "It's not so fun when you're on the wrong end of a gun, is it?" she said in a low voice. Her chest heaved, and her arms quivered. Chunks of red hair had loosened from her ponytail and dangled in her face. Blood ran from a cut on her cheek and a split lip.

But she was no victim; she was empowered. And dangerous.

213

"I'll end this nightmare," she muttered, never looking away from her target on the floor.

"Sandy," Truman said gently. "Put down the rifle." His own gun was still fixed on the woman.

"Not yet, Truman," she breathed. "You don't know what this asshole has done to me."

Her finger is on the trigger.

Truman tightened his grip.

Don't make me do this, Sandy.

"This is Lionel, your ex, right?" Truman asked.

"Yes."

Lionel was a big guy, as Truman had seen on his license, but he was flabby around the middle and upper arms. Fresh blood streaked his full silver beard.

"He's not worth it, Sandy," said Samuel. "Don't go to prison for the rest of your life because your anger got the best of you."

"Shoot the bitch!" begged Lionel as blood flowed from his nose. "She's gonna kill me."

"Fuckhead," Sandy said in a low voice. "You have it coming. You deserve it for breaking my arm. You deserve it for all the bloody lips and bruised cheeks. You deserve it for purposely screwing with a young woman's mind and emotions for your own pleasure." Her breathing hitched, and the rifle shook in her hands. "*You broke me.* You played an egotistical stupid game, and you *broke me.*"

The pain in her voice rattled Truman.

"Sandy . . . ," Samuel said gently. "Look at me."

She ignored him and moved the gun an inch closer to her objective. "I worked my ass off to build a damn good life after you ruined me. And you think you can waltz in and fuck it up *again?*"

"I'm sorry, I'm sorry . . ." The words slurred out of Lionel's mouth as he spit blood.

A sharp odor reached Truman. Her ex had pissed himself.

Sandy froze as she saw the spreading wet stain on his jeans. Then she smiled. A wide, pleased smile that made the hair rise on Truman's arms. "Well, God damn." She took a half step back, moving the barrel of the gun away from her ex. "Look at you now, big tough man."

She looked over at Truman and Samuel. "I'm done." Her grin was radiant, but her eyes were slightly crazed.

Truman exhaled, lowered his weapon, and held out a hand for her rifle. With a contented look, she handed it over and touched her lip, frowning when she saw the blood on her hand.

"Roll onto your stomach," Samuel ordered Lionel. The man obeyed. Samuel easily cuffed him and then searched him for more weapons. Finding a pocketknife, he tossed it aside. He spoke into his radio mic, informing Ben the suspect had been apprehended, and then studied Sandy with concern. "You okay, Sandy?"

"I am now." She blotted her bloody lips with the hem of her shirt and then pulled the fastener out of her ponytail and redid it, getting the hair out of her face.

"What happened?" asked Truman. Sandy seemed ready to get back to her kitchen.

"When you announced yourself at the door, he got distracted. I yanked the rifle out of his hands and rammed the butt into his nose. He went down like a dead elephant."

"I meant, what happened when he first arrived here?" Truman said faintly. *She's got some balls to grab a loaded gun by the barrel.*

"Oh." She frowned at the figure on the floor. "I heard someone shouting in the lobby, but I was in the kitchen. When I came out, Lionel was waving the rifle and threatening my guests. He grabbed me by the hair and forced me upstairs. Once he got in here, he decided to see how much of this room he could destroy while mouthing off about this and that." She kicked Lionel in the ankle. "I've always *hated* it when you grabbed my hair. And you'll pay for that broken window and vase."

"Jesus." Samuel ran a hand over his buzz cut. "Remind me never to get on your bad side."

"Sorry about that bit at the end there, Truman," Sandy said in a quieter voice, a contrite look on her face. "I'd never had power over Lionel before. You don't know how many times I've dreamed of that moment."

"Next time an officer tells you to put a gun down, *put it down.*" A full-body shudder rocked through Truman as he relived how close he'd come to shooting her.

"She never fucking listened," muttered Lionel. He twisted his head, trying to look at her over his shoulder while lying on his stomach. Samuel crouched down next to her ex's head and bent close, whispering something.

Truman didn't want to know what he was telling the big man.

Lionel's face paled under its smears of blood as Samuel's lips continued to move.

With a tip of his head, Truman directed Sandy closer to the suite door, away from the men. "Did he do the damage to your guests' vehicles?"

"Yes. He told me he did."

She looked calm and collected for a woman with blood caking on her lip and cheek.

Maybe being on the right side of a gun was good therapy for her.

"He'll probably end up in prison for what he did here today," Truman told her.

"That'd be great."

Truman didn't miss the subtle quiver in her answer. The reality of her last few minutes was sinking in. Samuel noticed too.

"I'll walk you downstairs. Let's get someone to look at your cuts," Samuel told her as he placed a gentle hand on the back of her arm. "You got Lionel?" he asked Truman.

"Yeah. Send Ben up when you get a chance." He watched the two of them leave the room, pleased with what he'd seen in Samuel today. His officer had willingly gone into an active shooter situation and now was handling the victim with a gentle touch and patience.

Truman knew emotions would sneak up and swamp Sandy once she realized what could have happened today. Her body was running on adrenaline, and she would crash. He made a mental note to ask Ina Smythe to stay with her for a few days.

"He gone?" muttered Lionel into the carpet. "Can you sit me up?"

"I think you should stay in this position a little longer." Sandy's analogy of a dead elephant was on point.

"He threatened to smash my fingers. And my dick."

"I didn't hear anything."

"Bullshit. I'm gonna file a complaint against the asshole. Guys like that shouldn't be cops."

Truman grinned. "Funny. I was just thinking what a great officer he is."

"I'll get him fired."

"Good luck with that." He took a deep breath and confronted Lionel dead-on. "Did you attack Bree Ingram last night?"

"Breed what?"

A chill shot through Truman's nerves. "Last night. You assaulted another woman."

"Bullshit. Sandy's the only one who had it coming."

Truth rang in the big man's words. *It wasn't Lionel?* "We've got your fingerprints on the knife," he lied.

Lionel twisted his head to look at the pocketknife Samuel had tossed aside. "Well, you should. It's mine." His tone indicated Truman was an idiot.

Truman's chest tightened, and he tried a different approach. "You spray-painted Sandy's B&B, right? Then you did Bree's stable."

"I didn't do no stable. Why are you asking me this shit?"

Truman stepped closer to Lionel's head and squatted as Samuel had minutes earlier.

"*You* gonna threaten to break my bones now?" Lionel asked.

"You didn't spray-paint red Xs in a horse barn or on a truck?"

"Horses? Fuck no. Who said I did? They're lying."

Truman stared at the prostrate man for a few long seconds, his mind racing.

I believe him. Sandy's vandalism isn't related to Bree's.

Was Bree attacked because of something that happened thirty years ago?

TWENTY-SIX

"What the hell is going on?" Mercy muttered as she strode into the Eagle's Nest Police Department. "First Bree's attack last night and now Sandy's today? Is the moon full?"

"Not full," replied Ben Cooley from where he sat at Lucas's desk. "I already checked. Trust me—our calls double when it is full. Hospital ERs swear they experience the same thing." He was completely serious.

Mercy smiled at the older officer, pleased he appeared fine after dealing with the attack on Sandy. "What's the word from Lucas?" she asked.

His face fell. "No change in Bree's condition," he said in a glum tone. "I've had twenty phone calls asking about Bree—and now more calls are coming in about Sandy. Those two women are important to this town."

"They are," Mercy agreed. "I know a lot of residents have been students of Bree's over the years and remain friends with her. Ollie says she's a great teacher."

"She is. Got awarded teacher of the year for Oregon last year." His chest puffed as if he'd won the award himself. "She has a gift for working with teenagers. And everyone knows Sandy sits on that *secret town council*," he finished with a whisper and a wink, pulling another smile from Mercy. She'd attended a few monthly meetings with the group of women who met to discuss the needs of the people of the town. They were amazingly effective given that they operated without a tax base. They relied on the kindness and generosity of the residents to make a difference.

"Where is Sandy now?" she asked.

"Truman sent her to Ina's. He told her Ina shouldn't be alone while her daughter-in-law is in the hospital. Getting to the hospital is too hard of a trip for Ina," he added in a confidential tone. "But he mainly wanted someone to be with Sandy after her attack."

And to keep Sandy away from Bree's hospital room.

Her suggestion to Truman that Sandy could have been involved with Bree's attack now felt a bit foolish in light of Sandy's own attack.

"Truman in back?"

"Yep. Go ahead."

She heard Ben answer a call as she headed toward Truman's office. "Eagle's Nest PD." Pause. "No, I don't know how Bree Ingram is doing, and no, Lucas isn't here to answer questions."

She knocked lightly on Truman's door and pushed it open at his call. He was eating a big takeout salad that she recognized as being from the pizza parlor. She sniffed the air, smelling oregano. He was eating lunch late.

"Sorry, I already ate the pizza," he admitted. "Do you want me to order some more?"

"No, I grabbed a sandwich." She plopped into a chair. "Are you as drained as I am?"

"Hell yes." He put down his fork and came around his desk, pulling her up out of the chair and into his arms. "I just need to feel you for a bit."

She closed her eyes. He smelled of pizza and Central Oregon sunshine. Some of her stress from the last twenty-four hours melted away.

Without changing position he reached past her and shoved his office door shut. His lips covered hers and she let all thoughts of robbery, murder, and money escape for a few minutes.

"We've had no time alone," he said against her mouth.

"Trust me, I've noticed."

"We're supposed to be planning a wedding."

"Other things have taken priority lately. We still have over six months."

"According to my sister, we're already six months behind," he answered, running his hands over her as if he hadn't touched her in days.

"The bridal magazines Pearl keeps giving me say the same." Mercy sighed. "I think things operate a little differently here in Eagle's Nest. I'm not worried about booking a venue or caterer a year in advance."

"Nope."

They spent a few more seconds in each other's arms, and when he took a deep breath, she knew those stolen moments were over. "Evan Bolton says the county lab didn't get a hit on the fingerprints from the knife used on Bree yet. According to him, there were a few good ones set in the blood."

Blood. Their romantic respite was definitely finished.

"Good prints, but not in any major databases." Every officer's frustration.

Truman let her go with one final kiss and returned to his seat, focusing on his computer screen. "They're expanding the search, checking other localized databases."

One day there will be one central database for all prints.

"What about the search for the truck?"

Truman brightened slightly. "He's got a solid list of about six trucks from the immediate area. They're visiting each address in person."

"Hopefully it's from around here," Mercy said. "If it's from out of town or state, that list is going to grow. Say, I've got something for you."

She removed a file from her bag. "Here are the photos we had made up. The aged ones of Whipple and May. I wanted to see if anyone looked familiar to you or your men."

Truman took the folder. "Shouldn't you get these to the media?"

"We're planning for tonight's newscast."

He scanned through the pictures. Mercy had found the images fascinating. The computer program had created several different options for Trevor Whipple and Nathan May. Some had glasses, or facial hair, or excess weight, or were bald.

"It's clear that these aged photos are still these two guys, isn't it?" Truman said in awe as he flipped between the pages. He stopped on the one of Nathan May with excess weight and facial hair. "This one's bugging me. I feel like I should recognize him, but I can't come up with a face or name."

Mercy took the sheet. The eyes in the photo were the only things familiar to her. She compared it to the original teenage picture. *His eyes feel familiar because I've stared at his high school photo a million times.* "Let's see what your officers have to say."

"I'd also like to show them to a few people in town. Nick Walker comes in contact with a lot of local men. Same with Pearl in the coffee shop."

"Those copies are for you."

Truman leaned on his forearms, and his desk creaked with the weight. "Talked to Ollie today?"

His voice and tone were deceptively normal. She knew he was ripped up inside about how he'd handled Ollie's surveillance of Bree.

"I haven't. You did the right thing, Truman," she said firmly. "Ollie was out of line."

He leaned back in his chair, rubbing the stubble he hadn't removed that morning. "I fucked up, Mercy. I should have listened to Ollie's instincts. And I should have had better protection on Sandy with her vandalism. Her ex could have killed her."

"You can't be everyone's personal bodyguard 24-7. You're taking blame for things out of your control." Her voice was harsh. He needed to snap out of this guilt-ridden mind-set.

"Tabitha Huff was murdered, Bree *nearly* murdered, and Sandy could have been shot. I feel like I have no control."

"Get over it. You *don't* have control of what assholes do."

Subtle amusement crossed his face, and a familiar heat appeared in his eyes. "That's why I love you."

"Someone needs to stop you from thinking you're Superman."

"I prefer Iron Man."

"Me too, but you know what I'm saying." She pointed at the computer-created images on his desk. "Now. Let's figure out who attacked Bree."

Truman picked up an image. "Lionel Kerns has an airtight alibi for last night. He was drinking at the bar right here in town. The bartender remembered him and said he had to kick him out when he closed at eleven."

"It's coincidence that both women had graffiti?"

"As much as I hate to say it, it sure looks that way." Frustration radiated from him. "They were different shades of red, and Sandy's graffiti felt sloppy and angry, while Bree's felt deliberate."

Mercy agreed. "But I haven't ruled out Sandy as our missing getaway driver."

"Assuming the driver was female." He was skeptical. "Your theory is based on a single notation in a tabloid reporter's notebook."

"I need to set up a time to talk to Sandy."

Truman looked at the clock on the wall. "I expect her any minute."

"Thanks for the heads-up," she said dryly. "Are you going to ask her flat out if she drove for a robbery thirty years ago?"

"No, that's your case. I want to talk to her about Lionel."

"Ben said Sandy is at Ina's."

"She is, but she sounded ready for a break already when I called her a half hour ago." A knock on the door immediately followed his statement. "Come in!"

Samuel opened the door. "Sandy's here to talk to you." Mercy spotted the tall woman behind Samuel's bulk, and Truman waved them in.

"Hey, Mercy. I didn't know you'd be here too," Sandy said as she took a seat beside Mercy in the tiny office. Samuel leaned against the open door, his arms across his chest in his usual stance.

Truman glanced at the officer but didn't ask him to leave, and Mercy wondered if Sandy would speak openly with Samuel hovering close by. She was about to suggest he leave when he exchanged an encouraging look with Sandy. *Hmmmm. I'll keep my mouth shut for now.*

"Sandy," Truman began, "you want to press charges against Lionel, correct?"

"Absolutely. Who knows how many other women he's terrorized over the years." Her voice was firm, and she had a determined set to her chin. She showed no emotional signs of being a woman who'd been attacked a few hours ago.

But there was no avoiding the physical signs. Several bruises had started to color her face and darken around one eye. She'd have a black eye for certain. A bandage covered her cheek, her lip had black stitches that made Mercy shudder, and her nose was swollen. Her sleeveless top exposed scratched arms, and more bruises were blooming on her legs. She hid nothing.

Admiration swelled in Mercy. This was one tough woman. *Tough enough to drive the getaway car for a robbery?*

"How are things at your B&B?" Mercy asked.

Sandy rolled her eyes. "Three people checked out, but one couple stayed, claiming it was the most exciting thing that'd happened to them in years."

"I wanted to ask you about Bree again," Truman said. "The lab is analyzing the threatening notes you found, and Deschutes County

224

is going to send a team through the home to look for other similar evidence."

"You mean evidence that she was being threatened?" Sandy asked.

"Or blackmailed," Mercy added, watching the woman carefully.

Sandy's eyes widened the smallest bit.

"Has Bree done or said anything that made you wonder what was happening in her life?" Mercy asked. "I know you're the closest of friends. Did she seem off lately? Maybe upset before the vandalism?"

Sandy fingered the bandage on her cheek. "A few weeks ago I found her in tears. She claimed she was simply having a tough day with one of the horses and feeling emotional." She raised her shoulders. "I've cried over less, so I didn't think much of it. Maybe it was related to those notes. Who knows when she got them?"

"She having any financial issues?" Mercy asked.

"We didn't talk about things like that. I'd complain when things were tight at the B&B, but she didn't ever mention money. I assumed her teaching job was sufficient for her and the horses." She looked at Mercy. "You think she was being blackmailed for money?"

"I looked into her financial records earlier today," Mercy said. "I didn't see anything that indicated that. Everything looked pretty normal for a single person. I've also requested her credit information."

Sandy was puzzled. "Why?"

"Standard." *Not really.*

The woman's eyes grew more thoughtful. "Why are you here, Mercy? Aren't Truman and Deschutes County handling Bree's attack? Why would you be looking at her bank accounts?"

Mercy exchanged a glance with Truman. His gaze seemed to say, "You opened this can of worms; you handle it."

"It's a bit complicated, Sandy . . ." She made a quick decision to not ask Sandy about her background. Yet.

The woman looked at her expectantly.

"Do you know much about Bree's past? Before she got married and had Lucas?"

"Can't say I do . . . I know her husband passed away when Lucas was pretty young."

"She ever talk about who she dated before her husband? Or what she did for work?"

"I think she's always been a teacher. You could ask Ina. She might know what Bree did before she became her daughter-in-law."

Why didn't I think of that?

"Have you heard of the Gamble-Helmet Heist?" Mercy decided to jump in with both feet.

"Who hasn't? It's been in the news a lot since they found that body." She looked from Mercy to Truman. "What's that have to do with Bree?"

"We're following a possible lead," Mercy stated. "Bree might have known one or more of the men." *Keep it vague.*

Sandy's red brows shot up. She winced and touched a bruise near her hairline. "Wow. She's never mentioned anything like that to me. Did she live near one of them? Or work with one?"

"We don't know," Mercy answered. "We don't have much information."

"What is the point of Bree knowing—" Sandy stopped talking and confusion covered her face. "I don't get it. I assume you're investigating her attack, but what would that have to do with an ancient robbery?"

"That's what we're trying to figure out . . . We haven't found a connection."

"Then why are you looking?" Her annoyed gaze focused on Mercy.

"I can't disclose much," said Mercy, putting on her business face. "But I can tell you that the murder of Tabitha Huff led us to this point. She talked to Bree . . . She talked to you too."

"She did," agreed Sandy.

"The reporter was doing a follow-up on the old robbery. We're looking into Bree's background because the reporter met with her. It's been hard to find any records for Bree thirty years ago." Mercy paused, holding Sandy's gaze. "It's been hard to find any for you either."

Sandy didn't move. No facial change. No shift in her gaze.

"You're looking at my past because a reporter talked to me," she said slowly.

"A murdered reporter."

"You think I murdered her?" Shock weighted her tone.

Samuel unfolded his arms. "Wait a minute—"

"Not now, Samuel," Truman ordered. The officer snapped his jaw shut, but his eyes burned daggers at Truman.

"That's not what I said," Mercy answered Sandy, keeping her tone calm. "I'm asking why you're so hard to find on paper thirty years ago. I know you were Jada Kerns when you were married and Jada Glover before that."

Sandy paled, and her mouth opened the slightest bit.

"I can't find much on Jada Glover at all," Mercy added.

Anger flashed in Sandy's eyes.

"I was eighteen when I got married. I didn't have the name for long." She gave a short, bitter laugh. "I grew up poor. We had absolutely nothing. When it was time for me to get my driver's license, no one could find my birth certificate. I remember being terrified that the government wouldn't believe I existed. I even wondered if I was who my parents said I was. It took months to straighten out." She turned haunted eyes on Mercy. "Does that answer your *paper* problem?"

Samuel stepped forward and set a gentle hand on Sandy's shoulder. Her hand slipped up to grip it, her gaze never leaving Mercy's.

"That explains things quite a bit. Thank you," Mercy answered calmly. "But it doesn't explain why I'm having the same problem with Bree."

"I can't help you with that," Sandy snapped. "I've only known her for about ten years."

Mercy said nothing.

Sandy did the same, their gazes locked.

Truman cleared his throat. "Thank you, Sandy. You've helped a lot."

Sandy turned to Truman and stood, her legs slightly shaky. "I'll fill out the paperwork to press charges against Lionel, and then I'm going back to the hospital. I don't need Ina to babysit me."

She turned and left without a word to Mercy. Samuel raised a single brow as he looked at both her and Truman, then followed her down the hall.

Mercy blew out a breath. "I don't know if she'll speak to me again." The thought of losing Sandy's friendship hurt, twisting a knife in a fresh place in her heart.

"She'll come around," Truman said evenly.

"No, maybe men can do that, but not women. I broke a level of trust between us that will be near impossible to rebuild. I dug into her history, and she thinks I accused her of murder." She frowned. "Which isn't what I meant to do at all."

"What do you think of her as the possible driver?"

Mercy shifted gears in her brain, shoving the hurt away. "Her reaction felt genuine when I mentioned Bree might know one of the robbers. She didn't grab that bait at all. If she's a liar, she's awfully good."

"Could Bree's attacker be the same person as Tabitha's killer?" Truman asked.

"That's a question I've wondered about since Bree's attack," said Mercy. "It's a possibility, but outside of the two women meeting, I've found no other connection. Do you think anyone else is in danger?"

"If we follow Tabitha's path, that would be everyone in town." His face darkened. "Including Ollie and Kaylie. And you."

"Don't forget yourself."

Truman shrugged one shoulder. "Where does that leave us with Bree?"

Mercy thought. "Waiting for Bree to wake up and tell us who attacked her. Or waiting for results from the list of red trucks."

Both were silent for a long moment.

"I'd put my money on the truck," said Truman, his eyes sad.

"Me too," Mercy agreed. Bree's medical condition was up in the air. She could have memory loss from the attack.

Or she might lie and state she didn't know the person.

"I'll show these images around town," Truman said, shuffling the papers back into the folder.

"I'm headed back to the office. I'll call Evan and see if he needs more manpower to follow up on the list of trucks."

"Be careful," he ordered, coming around to kiss her goodbye.

"Right back at you."

TWENTY-SEVEN

Mercy couldn't get Sandy's shocked face out of her mind.

She sped back toward her office, mentally going through Sandy's interview and still feeling sad that her questioning might have ruined their friendship.

Tabitha is dead. Bree nearly was.

Mercy had been doing her job.

But damn, her female friends were few and far between.

She gave a short laugh that echoed in her Tahoe. *Since when have I worried about maintaining friendships?*

Sometime over the past few months, they'd become important. She'd planted roots. Roots that had replaced the ones she'd ripped out years ago.

My father ripped out those roots, not me.

That wasn't completely true. She'd nursed her role as victim after her father had ousted her from the family. A little effort on her part might have repaired most of that break years ago.

Might have.

She pushed the what-if scenario out of her head. For years that type of thinking had dominated her spare time, and she wasn't about to get caught up in it now.

Focus on the case.

She asked her vehicle to call Art Juergen. Listening to the phone ring, she refused to worry that she was stepping over a department line again.

If I have a question, I should be able to ask.

"Hello?"

"Art. It's Mercy. You have a minute?"

"Always for you."

"We found an odd notation in Tabitha Huff's notes that I wanted to run by you."

"Go for it."

"Did you ever consider that the getaway driver was female?"

Silence filled her vehicle.

"Well . . . that's an odd one, Mercy," he said in a voice full of contemplation. "I can't say we investigated that angle specifically, but we looked into every female associated with all the men. Relatives, girlfriends, coworkers. We always operated under the assumption that the driver was male because Shane Gamble told us it was a man. Didn't have any reason to doubt him. I think he would have noticed if it was a woman."

"What if he didn't want you to know it was a woman?"

Art was silent again. "I guess it's possible. But what would be the point? I don't see what we would have done differently if we thought it was a woman. We questioned all the female connections while trying to locate the thieves."

She thought about the pages and pages of information and interviews of the women who'd been investigated as the FBI searched for a lead on where the men had vanished with the money.

"That's true," she admitted. "But you'd have to see the page in her notebook. It's hard to explain, but by the way she wrote it, I believe she was convinced the driver was female . . . and she had been in touch with Shane Gamble. I suspect he said something that made her go that route." As she said the words out loud, she realized the basis for her theory was very weak.

One notation.

"Well, she might have found something to make her believe that . . . and maybe it's true. Now what?"

"I've got two women I'm looking at," Mercy told him. "You heard about the attack on Bree Ingram, correct?"

"Yes. She's lucky that kid showed up when he did."

"Tabitha talked to Bree the day before she was murdered, and she also spoke to the female owner of a B&B in town. Gamble told me he asked Tabitha to deliver a message to someone to be careful because the body of Ellis Mull had been found."

"Are those the only people Tabitha spoke to?"

"Well, no, but since a safety warning had been sent and then Bree was attacked, it was worth following up."

"What did you find out?"

"That Bree Ingram is nearly impossible to track before she got married nearly thirty years ago. The same is true for Sandy, the B&B owner. It's almost as if both women didn't exist."

"You think they have new identities. And they got new identities because they were avoiding investigation for the robbery."

"Sandy does have a new identity, but it's only ten years old, and we know she did it to escape an abusive husband. It's odd because these two are the closest of friends. I honestly don't think they knew each other before Sandy moved here. Bree's lived here at least thirty years, and Sandy lived in Portland with her husband."

"Doesn't rule it out." A pencil scratched in the background as he took notes. He was taking her theory seriously.

"It doesn't," agreed Mercy. "Sandy was assaulted earlier today by her ex-husband. He had her at gunpoint, but she managed to turn the tables on him."

"She hurt?"

"A few cuts and bruises. Sandy's ex has a firm alibi for Bree's attack. He didn't attack Bree."

"Still odd that two best friends suffered attacks so close together. They were tight?"

"Very," said Mercy.

"Any new leads on who attacked Bree Ingram?"

"No hits on the fingerprints—"

Art laughed. "He left fingerprints?"

"Yeah, not the smartest guy. They're expanding the search on the prints. The other lead is a red truck that was seen near Bree's home at the time of the attack. The plate was stolen, so we're narrowing it down by the make and model of the vehicle."

"That sounds promising." Enthusiasm rang in his voice. "Stolen plates. Someone was up to no good."

"Exactly."

"I'll go through my notes with your theory in mind about a female driver," Art told her. "Can I check in with you later?"

"Yes, I'm headed back to the office right now. Leave me a message if I don't answer."

"Will do."

The call ended.

Pleased Art hadn't punched too many holes in her female-driver theory, Mercy placed a call to Evan Bolton. *Think of all the time wasted in vehicles before hands-free conversations.*

"Bolton."

"Evan, it's Mercy."

"Hey. I was about to call you. So far we've only eliminated two of the six trucks in the area."

"I'd hoped to hear a better number than that."

"That makes two of us. I've sent deputies to four of the homes, but no one was home at two of them and no signs of the truck. I'm following up on employment locations, but we've got a marijuana bust situation south of here that's gotten out of hand. That takes priority and a good number of the deputies."

"Marijuana is legal now. Why are people still growing it on illegal farms?"

"Most of it is shipped out of state."

"I see. How about you give me a couple of those addresses for the trucks and I'll check them out?"

"You sure?"

"I am. It feels like our strongest lead to discover who attacked Bree Ingram—and hopefully will give us some insight on the Gamble-Helmet Heist."

"That's a long stretch."

"I know. But it's one I'm willing to check out. Email me the addresses. I have some work at the office, but I should get to them within an hour or two."

"Will do."

Mercy ended the call as she pulled into her office parking lot.

I've got a good feeling about that truck.

TWENTY-EIGHT

"You're sure you don't need a change of clothes?" Ollie asked Kaylie again.

She laughed, making his stomach twist in a pleasant way. "I never get wet."

"But you believe I will?"

"Absolutely."

Kaylie had talked him into paddleboarding this afternoon. He'd watched people float down the Deschutes River on the long boards, standing with tall paddles in their hands.

It looked easy.

He'd handled the equipment at Lake Ski and Sports, wondering what it would be like to stand on one. One of his personal goals was to try out a half dozen new activities that he'd learned about since working at the warehouse. The job had exposed him to a whole new world he hadn't known existed. He'd also learned that sports and communing with nature were expensive. Some of the price tags had blown him away, making him wonder who could afford to spend that sort of money on "fun." Today he and Kaylie were going to rent boards near the Old Mill District.

Like hell he could afford his own board.

"Maybe we should have waited for a super-hot day. That water is going to be icy," Ollie muttered as he pulled into the parking lot of the Bend FBI office.

"It will definitely be cooler out on the river," Kaylie said. "I'm glad I wore yoga pants, but I should have brought a sweatshirt." She eyed his cargo shorts and short-sleeved shirt. "You might need something more."

"I don't get cold."

She gave him an odd look but didn't say anything.

He parked at the Bend FBI office. Kaylie had one errand to run.

"You coming in?" Kaylie asked as she gathered up her day-old baked goods. She dropped off muffins and pastries at the Eagle's Nest Police Department and Mercy's FBI office on alternate days. Mercy grumbled when Kaylie brought in the sweets, but her coworkers were delighted.

"Nope. I'll wait right here." He had an odd fear of Melissa, the office manager. No one could be that perky and happy all the time.

"I'll just be a minute. I'll see if Mercy has a light jacket I can borrow."

He rolled down the windows, turned up the music, and tapped his fingers as he waited. Kaylie had picked a good day for him to try paddle-boarding. The sky was a brilliant blue, but he knew the river would be frigid from the Cascade snowmelt. He hadn't lied when he said he didn't get cold. Long before, out of necessity, he'd taught his mind to ignore it. But he had to admit it'd been nice to sleep in a real bed and under a solid roof for the last two months.

He was getting soft.

Kaylie had been gone for a full ten minutes, and he imagined her talking with Melissa. That was another thing he feared about Melissa. She could carry on a one-sided conversation for a half hour. It'd happened to him twice, and he still hadn't come up with an escape technique for the next incident. He was better off staying out of the FBI office.

Kaylie finally reappeared, pushing open the heavy glass door of the office. She wore a lightweight white jacket that he frequently saw on

Mercy. She tucked some of her long hair behind her ear as she walked toward him.

She stepped off the curb and stumbled. A loud crack filled the air, and her body folded in half as she collapsed.

Ollie stared, his mind scrambling to put the sound together with her abrupt drop.

She's been shot.

He was out of his truck before his brain completed the thought. A faint voice in his head warned that he could be shot too, but he pushed it away, his gaze locked on Kaylie lying on the blacktop as he sprinted toward her.

Dropping to his knees, he turned her over, and his heart stopped at the sight of the blood on her stomach. Her green eyes were wide, and her hands pressed into her belly. "Ollie," she whispered, terror in her gaze.

"You're gonna be fine." He ripped off his shirt, balled it up, and pressed it into her stomach, adjusting her hands to hold the bundle.

"Kaylie!" He'd know Mercy's voice anywhere. She and an FBI employee with her hair in a long braid dropped next to him. Mercy elbowed him out of the way as she assessed her niece, keeping pressure with Ollie's shirt. The other woman was on her phone. "What happened?" Mercy shouted at Ollie as her hands flew over her niece.

"I don't know. I heard a gunshot and she went down."

Mercy froze and scanned their surroundings, her gaze hard, ready to kill for her niece.

"Ambulance is on its way," said the other woman.

"Darby, keep pushing on this," Mercy ordered. She leaned closer to Kaylie, taking her face in both hands and staring into the girl's wide eyes. "Stay with me, Kaylie. You're going to be fine."

"Hurts," Kaylie whispered. "Am I going to die?" Her gaze flew from Mercy to Darby and then to Ollie.

I don't know what to say. His tongue was as frozen as the rest of his body.

237

"Fuck no!" Mercy informed the trembling girl. "We'll get you to the hospital." She turned to Ollie, dug a remote out of her pocket, and pressed it into his shaking hand. "In the back of my Tahoe, there's a medical kit . . . *Dammit! I already used it!*" Her face went white, and she struggled to speak. "I haven't restocked. Get the bag anyway," she finally said. "I'll improvise."

Ollie sprinted in the direction she pointed, recognizing her SUV. He clicked UNLOCK on the remote and flung open the rear hatch. He grabbed the medical bag and slammed the hatch closed, ignoring the bloody handprint he left on her vehicle. The sound of squealing tires made him halt and spin toward the noise. Trees blocked his view of the road, but he followed the sound of an engine as it sped away. A flash of silver was all he saw.

Someone's in a hurry.

Sirens sounded in the distance. *They need to know about that vehicle.* He ran back to Mercy and dropped the bag next to her, and she immediately unzipped it. "The cops need to know a silver vehicle just sped away," he told Darby. "I couldn't see what it was, but it was definitely silver."

"Hold this," Darby ordered, and Ollie applied pressure on his balled-up shirt again. But now it was soaked, and more blood covered his hands.

Kaylie's eyes closed, but she moaned, her lips pale.

Is she going to die?

He looked from Mercy to Darby, his heart in his throat, unable to ask the question out loud. Mercy had her head close to Kaylie's, speaking rapidly, but Ollie couldn't hear the words. Darby was on her phone again, her lips pressed together, her eyes grim.

They look terrified.

Not good.

238

I have to go with her.

"No, ma'am! I'm sorry, ma'am!" The EMT unclasped Mercy's fingers from the handle of the ambulance door. "Meet us at the hospital. You can't ride inside."

Mercy barely heard him, her gaze locked on Kaylie through the small windows in the rear doors. Another EMT rapidly worked on her niece, ripping open sterile packets and injecting something into her IV.

She's not going to make it.

Why didn't I immediately restock my kit?

The EMT who had dislodged Mercy's hands dashed for the driver's door of the ambulance, and the vehicle sped away, lights flashing. As he pulled out of the parking lot, the sirens began to wail. Bend Police Department cars started to flood the parking lot, their lights flashing and their sirens drowning out the ambulance.

Don't just stand here. She touched the pocket where she kept the remote to her Tahoe. Empty. "Ollie! Give me the key!" The teenager stared at her. His eyes were huge and his hands bloody. Smudges of blood marked his bare stomach, and his shirt was in a bloody heap on the ground where the EMTs had dumped it. He didn't appear to have heard her.

"Ollie!" Mercy took three long steps and grabbed his arm. "Where's my key?"

He jerked and ripped his arm away as if she'd cut him. His mouth opened, but no words came out.

"Hang on." Darby put a hand on Mercy's shoulder. "You're not driving anywhere right now."

Fury raged through her, and she spun toward Darby, knocking her hand away. "I need to get to the hospital!" Her vision blurred, and she angrily wiped away the tears that streamed down her cheeks. Her lungs hurt, her brain throbbed, and her heart was shredded. "I need to go!"

"I'll drive you," said Darby. "Now calm the fuck down."

Red clouded her gaze. "Do *not* tell me to calm down," she said with deadly intent, feeling fire burn in her eyes.

Amazingly, Darby didn't turn to ash. Instead she took a deep breath and held up her hands. "I know. I know." She pointed across the lot. "Go wait at my car. I'll be right there." She ran back to the office.

Her heart pounding, Mercy watched her leave. She took several deep breaths and looked at the ground. "Oh my God," she whispered.

Kaylie's blood was everywhere. Pieces of packaging and red-stained gauze dotted the ground.

Something bad happened here.

I need to protect the scene.

I need to get to Kaylie.

Thinking clearly felt far beyond her grasp. She needed to do everything at once. More police cars arrived. Officers in dark uniforms streamed her way.

"Mercy."

She barely heard Ollie's whisper, but she saw him shiver in the warm air, bumps covering his bare skin. "Sit down," she ordered, her brain snapping back online. She helped lower him to the ground and pushed his head between his knees.

"Is she going to die?" It was the voice of a seven-year-old.

"Of course not," she told him. She wrapped her arms around the lost boy, rubbing her hands up and down his back to warm him. "She's tough."

"I know . . ." A huge shudder racked him.

Poor kid watched it happen.

"Ollie. You're going to talk to the police. They need to know what you saw." She lifted his head, making him look her in the eye. "Tell them about the car you saw too."

Glancing behind her, she saw Darby dash back out of the office. "I need to go. I'll call Truman on my way and have him meet you here, okay?"

He nodded, his eyes unseeing.

Ollie had filled out a lot in the two months he'd lived with Truman. He no longer looked three years younger than his eighteen years. But right now Mercy saw a terrified teenager who'd been alone for too long. The thought of leaving him to sit in a parking lot crime scene killed her.

"You did good, Ollie. That was quick thinking to get pressure on her stomach."

"There was so much blood," he whispered.

"The best thing you can do now is tell them what happened. We need to catch who did this."

His chin lifted as cognizance entered his eyes. "I'll kill him."

The bleak tone stabbed deep in her chest. "Get in line," she whispered.

She looked up as a patrol officer approached. Standing, she showed him her badge, handed him a business card, and pointed at Ollie. "There's your witness. He saw the shooting and a car that sped away. The victim is on the way to the hospital, and I'm following. Tell your detective to call me when he gets here." The officer had a few years on him and appeared competent. He nodded and immediately started to direct the other officers to protect the scene.

She squatted by Ollie. "Stay tough." His eyes widened as he looked past her. Mercy looked over her shoulder and saw Melissa approaching, a spare jacket in her hands for Ollie.

Good.

"I'll call you," she told him. He nodded, his nervous gaze still on Melissa.

Darby was at her car, the door open as she watched and waited for Mercy.

Mercy sucked in a deep breath, forcing herself to walk away from Ollie.

It was tougher than she'd expected.

I'm coming, Kaylie.

TWENTY-NINE

Truman's initial phone call from Mercy had been abrupt and short. Kaylie shot. Ollie waiting at the scene. Mercy following ambulance. He could tell from her tone that she was in survival mode. No time for lengthy explanations or emotional breakdowns.

That would come later.

He understood where she was; he'd been there.

But a halting break in the cadence of her words told him she was near the edge of reason, and the slightest misstep would push her over. The only way he could help was by acting.

After asking Samuel to find more details of the shooting and fill him in on the way, he'd sped toward the Bend FBI office. Samuel's news hadn't been good. Kaylie was seriously injured, and the police were looking for a small silver sedan. Ollie had watched it happen, and both he and Mercy had tried to stop the bleeding. The prognosis for Kaylie was unknown.

The unknown was ripping Truman apart.

Will she live?

When Truman arrived, part of the parking lot was taped off, and a few officers kept people and press away. Truman parked, signed his name in the scene log, and headed toward a small group of people. A crime scene tech took photos as two plainclothes detectives talked to an officer. Bloody clothing and ripped medical supply packaging were strewn not far from their feet. Truman lost his breath and looked away.

He shuddered, struggling to keep his professional composure.

This isn't the crime scene of a stranger; it's Kaylie's.

Our Kaylie.

Ollie sat in the back of a nearby squad car with the door open and his feet on the pavement. He wore a navy windbreaker with FBI stamped above his heart.

Truman embraced the boy and looked firmly in his eyes. "You okay?"

"Yes."

What a fucking week for this kid.

For all of us.

Ollie was slightly shaky on his feet, and his eyes were swollen and red. His hands had been washed, but something dark was still under most of his fingernails. Something that hadn't been there when Truman saw him at breakfast.

"I heard you did good," Truman told him, wanting to erase the despondent look in the teen's eyes.

Instead Ollie's face crumpled.

"Ah, jeez." Truman pulled him close again. His heart cracked as the boy shuddered in his embrace.

"They don't know if she's going to live." Ollie's words were wet and low.

What would we do without her? Mercy . . . me . . . Ollie too.

"She's a tough girl." Truman fought to keep his voice even.

I have to be strong for Ollie.

"Chief Daly?" came a voice behind Truman.

He gave Ollie a final squeeze and turned to face one of the detectives.

"I'm Detective Ortiz. We're done with this young man. He can leave." The detective's face was grim but flashed with sympathy as he looked at Ollie.

"What's the word on the shooter?" asked Truman.

"No word."

Truman stared at Ortiz for a long second as his heart dropped.

That's it?

The man held his gaze. He had no news for Truman.

Truman was nauseated. "Got it." He gave Ortiz his card. "Keep me updated."

"I understand the girl is your niece," Ortiz said as he glanced at the card.

"Yes." *Not quite true. But feels like it.* "Practically my daughter. I'm going to take Ollie home to get cleaned up and then head to the hospital."

"Good luck, Chief."

Truman didn't like the guarded hope in the detective's gaze, but he understood it.

At the house Truman tried to get the teen to eat something. Ollie picked at the food, took two bites, and then pushed it away. Shep sat at his feet, his back pressed against Ollie's shin. Lots of head rubs and scratches for his dog had perked Ollie up more than his shower. Even Simon walked a dozen figure eights around Ollie's legs, her tail hugging his jeans.

Now in the vehicle with Ollie, Truman was nearly back to Bend and the hospital.

"What's happening, Truman?" Ollie asked, his voice so low Truman almost missed it.

He glanced at the boy in the light of the setting sun, not understanding his question.

"Why is everyone around me getting hurt? Or dying?" Ollie's voice cracked.

The words were like a mallet slamming into Truman's chest. He'd watched Ollie open up and accept people into his life over the last several weeks. It'd been a big step for someone who'd been alone and suspicious of others all his life.

"I know how painful it is to see someone you care about get hurt."

Ollie was silent but wiped his eyes.

"Don't let this make you keep people at an arm's distance. Shit happens, and we deal with it when it comes. The benefits to having people you care about far outweigh the pain."

"Doesn't feel like it right now."

"No. It doesn't."

The Tahoe rocked as he turned into the hospital parking lot. He stopped the car. He and Ollie sat staring at the hospital for a long moment, neither making a move to get out.

"I don't want to know what's happened," Ollie whispered.

"Mercy would have called me . . ." *If Kaylie had died.* He swallowed hard. *Assuming Mercy could function after that news.*

He clapped a hand on the boy's shoulder. "Let's go give Mercy some support."

Ollie nodded, a look of determination on his face, and he opened his door.

Mercy couldn't sit in the damned chair any longer. She got up and paced the room again. Someone with good intentions had decorated the surgical waiting room in muted greens and blues. Even the artwork was mellow, landscapes and seashores. The room was long and narrow, with several groups of furniture, giving a sense of privacy for each arrangement. The tissue boxes on every flat surface negated the notion that this room was for relaxing.

It'd been almost two hours.

She wanted to scream.

Pearl, Owen, and her mother shared the airless room with her. It was a good-size room, but Mercy had felt the need to step out into the hallway multiple times. She swore the air pressure was different. Eddie was still in the hospital somewhere with his gunshot wound. She had considered popping in to see him, but she knew that if she left the waiting room, that would guarantee the doctor would show up.

I could call Eddie. She immediately rejected the idea. The thought of telling him about Kaylie made her want to curl up in a ball and hide under one of the room's sofas.

"Let me get you another cup of coffee, Mercy." Pearl stood and stretched her back. Her oldest sister looked exhausted, and she'd been up since 4:00 a.m. to get the Coffee Café open. It was on the tip of Mercy's tongue to refuse, but the hope in Pearl's eyes told her she needed something to do.

"Another cup of coffee might launch me into space. Maybe something else."

"Decaf, then. Or I'll see if that machine has something else that won't wire you. Maybe chicken broth?"

Chicken broth out of a coffee vending machine? Her stomach stirred in a disquieting way.

"Not broth."

"Anyone else?" Pearl asked, looking from Owen to her mother. Both shook their heads. She vanished out the door, her tennis shoes making no sound in the hall.

Owen shifted in his seat. He looked as uncomfortable as Mercy felt. He played with his cowboy hat, spinning it in his hands, fingering the brim, probably wishing his wife had come with him, but she had the flu. Mercy's mother, Deborah, glanced at Owen's hat several times, but he didn't pick up her silent plea to stop the constant fiddling. Her mother looked as composed as always. The rock in every storm of their lives.

Her father was absent. "On a call," her mother had said. "Twin calves and no vet. I talked to him on the phone, and he said he'd be here as soon as he could . . . but you know how it can go." Mercy did. Her father had helped ranchers with calving for as long as she could remember. He was who they called when they couldn't get a vet. Some called him first.

The door clicked, and Mercy spun. Surprise made her mouth open. A very pregnant Rose and a very concerned Nick entered. Sweat dotted Rose's temples and neck. She was breathing hard . . . and looked like crap. Mercy had told her not to come. She was still sick. Mercy touched her sister's hand and was immediately enveloped in a hug. Heat radiated from Rose.

Mercy glowered at Nick, thankful Rose couldn't see her.

"Don't get mad at Nick for bringing me," Rose ordered. "I gave him no choice."

"Oh, Rose." Deborah stood and approached her second daughter. "You shouldn't be here! In fact, you shouldn't be out of bed."

"I'm fine, Mom. How's Kaylie?"

For the seconds Rose had been present, Mercy had been distracted from worry. With one question, Mercy's stress and anguish came rushing back. "We haven't heard anything since she went into surgery."

Rose's face fell. "Well, no news is good news, right?"

A phrase Mercy had silently repeated a hundred times in the last hour. Her heart had jumped every time the door opened.

Deborah guided Rose to a chair, sat beside her, placed a hand on Rose's forehead, and began questioning her in depth about her symptoms and the pregnancy. Owen rose and shook Nick's hand, clearly grateful for a male presence in the room.

The urge to scream overwhelmed Mercy again. Instead she walked the long room, from one end to another, trying not to remember Kaylie's laughing face as she'd told Mercy goodbye that morning. Or to think of Dulce the cat sitting at home, wondering where her bedmate was. Or of Kaylie bleeding out in a parking lot.

Nausea swamped her, and she grabbed the back of a chair.

The door swung open, and Truman entered with a crestfallen Ollie tagging behind. His gaze instantly found her, and she locked on to it like a life preserver. He strode to her, ignoring the rest of her family, and took both her hands. "Is she okay?"

"We don't know." Her voice was a shadow of itself.

Strong arms surrounded her, and the nausea abated. She relaxed into him, digging her face into his shoulder, feeling the anxiety start to dissolve. But with it went her strength. Her extremities went cold. She wavered, and he sat in the chair and pulled her onto his lap. No speaking. No questions. Just his rock-solid dependability. It was practically a physical entity, and she clung to it, desperate for someone to help shoulder the load.

"She's mine," Mercy whispered, her icy cheek pressed against his warm one. His internal furnace felt different from the sickly heat from Rose. "She's mine to take care of."

"She is."

"I let him down." *Levi.*

"He knows what happened. He knows it had nothing to do with you."

She shuddered. "I love her so much. I had no idea . . ."

His smile moved against her skin. "We all do."

They sat silently for a long moment. Simply being.

Then she remembered that most of her family was in the same room. Looking over her shoulder, she saw they were politely ignoring her and Truman. Pearl had returned and taken charge of Ollie, seating him beside her.

"How is Ollie?" she whispered to Truman. The lost look on his face in the parking lot flashed in her memory.

"He's a wreck. It's been a lot for him lately." He paused. "He wanted to bring Shep. I didn't think I was going to get him out of the house without the dog."

"I can see that." She took a settling breath and leaned back so she could see Truman's face. *A good man.*

"Tell me what the doctor said," he said gently.

Mercy looked away and focused on a painting of the ocean. "I can't remember everything they told me. It all happened so fast, and the ER team sent her to surgery immediately. I know they said the bullet went through her liver before exiting out her back."

"No wonder there was so much blood."

"The team should be able to find the bullet and hopefully the cartridge at the scene." *And then the shooter.*

A realization slammed into her, and she gasped for breath.

Why didn't I think of this before?

Because I was fixated on Kaylie's survival.

She spun to him. "Truman. *What if that shot was meant for me?*"

"Why—"

"Kaylie was wearing my coat. Who shoots a random teenager?" Her fingers dug into his shirt, her theory feeling stronger by the second. "They were ballsy enough to shoot in the FBI parking lot. Their motivation had to be huge . . . two million dollars huge?" she whispered.

"You think it's the robbery case?"

"It could be . . . I don't know. My brain won't stop spinning." Guilt racked her. "And I hadn't restocked my medical kit after Eddie's shooting. I didn't have the right things to save her." Regret flared in her chest. "If she dies because they thought she was me, and I wasn't prepared—"

"*Stop.* Stop right there." He held her gaze. "The only person responsible for Kaylie's injury is the shooter. You can't take any of the blame."

"I don't." She straightened on his lap, trying to make him understand. "The supplies I keep—"

"Dammit, Mercy. Stop it," he repeated. "I don't want to hear another word about what *might* have happened. It's done. It's over."

She pressed her lips together. *He doesn't understand. If I'd restocked, Kaylie would have a better chance.*

Was I the target?

The door opened, and she saw a long white coat. She was off Truman's lap and halfway to the door when the doctor spoke.

"Kaylie Kilpatrick," the doctor said, looking from face to face.

"That's me. I mean I'm hers—actually, all of us are hers." The words tumbled off her tongue.

"She came through the surgery just fine."

A sound like the roar of the ocean started in Mercy's ears. "She's fine?" Behind her, Truman rested his chest against her back, and his arms sneaked around her. She tentatively touched his hands, feeling his warm skin.

The doctor's brows came together. "The surgery went well. Watching for infection is our next priority. She'll be in the ICU."

The roar in her head grew louder. *The surgery went well.* Mercy covered her face with her hands, his words echoing in her head. The doctor continued to speak, but she caught only bits and pieces . . . *massive blood transfusion . . . packing quadrants . . . gall bladder shredded . . . repaired the vein . . .*

If she made it this far, she'll make it all the way.

Mercy's sheer willpower would force Kaylie to heal the rest of the way.

"She's going to make it," Truman whispered into her ear.

Mercy could only nod, her face still buried in her hands. Her emotions were simmering just under her skin. The wrong word or movement could turn her into a blubbering mess. She refused to do that in front of Truman and her family.

The sound of the door closing made her lift her head. The doctor had left.

Everyone in the room was looking at her. Even Rose.

"Kaylie's going to be fine, dear," her mother said, looking at Mercy tenderly. "She's got strong blood in her veins. Just like you."

Mercy dissolved into a blubbering mess.

THIRTY

Her phone was ringing.

Groggily, Mercy dug in all her pockets trying to locate the offender. The sound had pulled her out of a dead sleep.

Kaylie.

Phone forgotten, Mercy bolted upright in the chair she'd slept in and took a step to the girl's hospital bed. *Still breathing.* Blinking sleep out of her eyes, Mercy scanned the flashing and beeping equipment hooked up to Kaylie. She didn't know what she was looking for, but no alarm was wailing, and the cadence of the beeps felt pleasant to her brain. The steady rhythm slowed her racing heartbeat. *Everything is okay.*

Her phone rang again, and she located it in her purse under her chair.

Evan Bolton.

"Evan?" she answered. Checking the time, she saw it was nearly 8:00 a.m. She'd slept off and on for six hours.

"Mercy. We've got a good lead on one of the trucks."

She slapped her hand to her forehead. The robbery investigation had completely slipped her mind. "I'm so sorry I didn't get to the address you gave—"

"Forget it. I know what happened to your niece. Ortiz told me last night it looked like she would pull through. How's she doing?"

Touched that he'd kept apprised of Kaylie's condition, Mercy studied the face of the sleeping girl. Her lips were dry and flaking, but she looked peaceful. She breathed normally, and her color looked good.

"I think she's fine. I'm with her now. They repaired the damage to the vein in her kidney and she lost her gall bladder. We're just waiting and watching her heal at the moment. The doctor says infection is their next concern."

"Good. She won't miss her gall bladder. My mother and sister both had theirs removed decades ago and don't think twice about it."

Mercy blew out a breath. "That lines up with what I Googled last night."

"*Don't* Google medical issues."

She smiled in spite of herself. "I know."

"This morning I sent two more men to a home on the list. One of my deputies went last night, but the truck owner cut off their conversation and slammed the door in his face."

In spite of her worry over Kaylie and her exhaustion, Mercy slid back into work mode. "Did the deputy see the truck? Did it have the stolen plate that Ollie photographed?"

"He didn't see the truck, but the man verified that he owned a truck like the deputy described before cursing him out and slamming the door. He locked the door and refused to answer again. My deputy peeked in the garage behind the home, but it was empty."

"I wonder where it is." Her mind sped through possibilities.

"The guy's name is Silas Dillon. He's fifty-one and currently unemployed. His record includes two DUIs and an assault conviction. He's renting the house. I'm trying to contact the owner."

If he was involved in the Gamble-Helmet Heist, the age is about right.

Pearl stepped into Kaylie's small room and gave Mercy a silent wave when she saw her on the phone. Her focus immediately went to Kaylie, and she laid a hand on the girl's forehead, leaning close, whispering something Mercy couldn't hear.

"Mercy? Hang on a second."

She listened as Evan spoke to someone in the background. Her gaze wandered over Kaylie and Pearl, appreciating the mothering look on Pearl's face as she straightened Kaylie's sheets and light blanket.

The voices in the background rose, and she heard Evan curse. Her focus whipped back to the phone call.

"Evan? What happened?"

"He took a shot at one of my men—"

"Is he okay?" Her heart rate started to rise again.

"He missed. We're pulling SWAT together. Looks like we've got a hot one."

Mercy's mind split, torn between Kaylie and the investigation. "I'll be there. Text me the address."

"No! I know you've got more important things to do." Evan exchanged more words with someone else, their tones heating up.

"Pearl is here, and Kaylie is stable. It doesn't help if I just sit and stare at her."

Kaylie's shooter.

I'm losing my mind. I forgot the hunt for her shooter.

"Evan, have you talked to Ortiz about Kaylie's case?"

"Yep. Ortiz works a desk across the room from me. I think he's been there most of the night."

"Let me talk to him."

"Hang on." Murmuring voices in the background.

"Agent Kilpatrick." A new voice came on the line. "Ortiz here. Evan says your niece is stable this morning. I'm glad to hear it."

"Yes . . . thank you. What have you found on her shooter?"

He cleared his throat. "We found the bullet and a nine-millimeter casing. The casing was in the dirt adjacent to a narrow side street on the west side of the parking lot."

Mercy knew the location. From her building, trees and shrubs blocked a view of the street. It was perfect cover for a shooter, and it was dense enough to hide a waiting vehicle.

"And the car?"

"We've got security video from a business down the street. It shows a silver Camry speeding by at the time of the shooting."

"Plates?"

He paused. "Not on the video. We're searching for a way to identify the car."

Mercy waited a long moment and then realized he was done. "That's all you have?" Her voice cracked.

"Agent Kilpatrick—"

"Mercy, please." *This is personal.* "Detective Ortiz . . . I might have been the target of Kaylie's shooting."

"I was about to ask you about that possibility. According to the receptionist I interviewed from your office—"

"Melissa."

"Yes, Melissa." He paused. "She stated Kaylie was wearing a white jacket of yours when she left."

"Exactly. I wear that coat all the time." Mercy closed her eyes. A vision of Kaylie's blood seeping onto the jacket had slammed into her brain. The red stark against the white.

"Your niece bears a very strong resemblance to you," Ortiz stated carefully.

"I know. Someone could have mistaken her for me," she whispered. *Her new hair color.* Kaylie had been wearing black yoga pants that were similar enough to the black slacks Mercy still wore from yesterday.

"The big question is who and why," Mercy went on. "It could be related to the robbery case I'm working." Indecision swamped her. "Or it might be something else . . . But I can see someone trying to stop my robbery investigation." She rubbed her hand across her forehead. "I don't know what to think."

"Thinking about this is my job, Agent Kilpatrick. We'll get to the bottom of this. I'll keep in touch."

"Mercy?" Evan was back on the line. "I'm heading out to that house. The situation is heating up."

"Evan . . . what's your opinion on Ortiz?"

His answer was immediate. "He's the best. After me, of course."

Determination shot through her, and she set Kaylie's shooter aside for the moment.

Kaylie is safe. I need to let Ortiz do his thing while I do mine.

"I'll meet you there."

"Now, Mercy—"

"Don't argue with me, Evan. Get me that address. All I need to do is change my clothes."

She was done sitting in chairs.

THIRTY-ONE

Mercy beat SWAT to Silas Dillon's home.

The home was set back from a winding road off one of the main highways. His neighbors were few and far between. Their properties were acres of flat land peppered with lava rocks of all sizes intertwined with the scrub brush. Mercy knew the rocks had come from ancient volcano flows. The rocks were a common sight south of Bend.

The home was a one level with a small garage behind it. It appeared someone had plopped the little house down in the middle of nowhere. It had boring views of rocks and low, brown hills.

Four county vehicles waited on the winding road, set far back to create difficult targets for Silas Dillon. A deputy stood at each vehicle, shotgun casually in hand. Mercy pulled in behind an unmarked Explorer that she recognized as Evan Bolton's. He approached as she stepped out of her vehicle.

"You didn't need to come."

"Good to see you too," Mercy replied. "I'm tired of sitting still. I need to feel like I'm doing something."

She opened the back of her truck, grabbed her bulletproof vest, and strapped it on as tension went up her spine. An hour ago she'd been sitting by Kaylie's bed. Now she was at a SWAT situation.

Before she left the hospital she'd stopped by Bree Ingram's room. A bored-looking deputy still guarded Bree's door, and Lucas Ingram had been sitting in a chair like the one Mercy had spent the night in, a Lee Child novel in his hand. He'd stood as Mercy entered and hugged her. "I'm so sorry about Kaylie."

"She's stable. How's your mom?"

"The swelling on her brain has gone down. They're hoping she'll start coming around." His tone was somber, his usual happy demeanor nowhere to be found.

"We'll find who did this to Bree," Mercy promised. "I'm following a lead as soon as I leave."

Lucas was startled. "What about Kaylie?"

"Pearl is with her. She won't be alone."

He'd studied her eyes and then nodded. "Good luck. And thank you, Mercy."

"You should go home occasionally."

"Sandy and I trade off."

"Good."

She'd clutched her duffel, hugged him goodbye, and dashed to change in a restroom.

Now, as she studied the skepticism on Evan's face, she wondered if she should have left the hospital at all.

What if Kaylie takes a turn for the worse?

She pushed the thought out of her head. "Where are we at with Silas Dillon?"

"He fired once when the deputies pulled into his driveway. Hit the grille of that one over there." He pointed at one of the vehicles. "They immediately backed out to this road and called it in. One of them tried to reason with him through the bullhorn, but he told them to fuck off."

"Lovely. Did you reach the actual owner of the house?"

"No."

"What else do we know about Dillon?"

Evan handed her a sheet of paper. "This mug shot is from last year."

Mercy stared into Silas's eyes, searching for a resemblance to Trevor Whipple or Nathan May. She couldn't see one. *Could this be the driver? Was Tabitha wrong about it being female?* "You have deputies checking out the other addresses for the red trucks?"

"Yes." He frowned as he took the sheet. "I can tell that you don't think this is the guy who hurt Bree Ingram." It wasn't a question. "Why?"

"I didn't say that."

He raised a skeptical brow at her.

"We have a theory that Bree might have been assaulted by someone involved in the Gamble-Helmet Heist."

Evan's brows shot up. "Why?"

"It's complicated . . . and it's only a theory. I'd hoped to see a resemblance between Silas and one of the men from the robbery in this mug shot, but I don't. That doesn't mean Silas didn't assault her."

"He's got the right type of vehicle, and he's clearly violent," Evan pointed out. "And stupid enough to fire at a law enforcement officer."

"But no one can find his vehicle. The deputy said the garage was empty?"

"Yes."

"How's he getting around, then?" Mercy frowned. "And where is the truck?"

"Maybe he ditched it, suspecting that it'd been seen the night he attacked Bree."

Mercy turned to study the quiet house again. The flutter of a window curtain indicated they were being watched. "How far out is SWAT?"

"Another twenty minutes. They're bringing a negotiator."

"Twenty minutes? Dammit." She needed results now. "Where's that bullhorn?"

"Now, Mercy—"

"I'm going to ask some questions. Don't worry. I have negotiation experience. The most important part is to not say the wrong thing."

Like it's that simple . . .

Evan turned around and swore under his breath. He strode to a county vehicle and got a bullhorn from the deputy.

"Tell them to put their shotguns back in their vehicles," she said as he handed her the bullhorn. "I don't want him to believe we're ready to attack."

"No one will attack." His glare stated she was ridiculous.

"I know that, but to him four deputies with shotguns look threatening."

Evan considered, nodded in agreement, and gave the order.

Mercy considered what to say and then brought the horn to her mouth. "Silas Dillon. I am Special Agent Mercy Kilpatrick from the Bend FBI office." She paused. "We're looking for a truck that fits the description of yours."

Put the focus on an object. Not him.

"I understand the truck is not here. Can you tell us where to find it?"

"Why is the FBI here?" The shout came from the open window where Mercy had seen the curtain flutter.

"The truck may be linked to a federal investigation. We'd like to confirm it's the correct truck."

"It's not here!" Another shout.

Mercy sighed. "If it's not the right truck, we'll be done here, Silas. Can you tell us where to find it?"

Don't remind him that he shot at an officer. Shift his focus.

"I don't know." Uncertainty was in his shout.

Mercy and Evan looked at each other. "He's lying, of course," stated Evan.

"Silas, do you have a cell phone?" Mercy asked through the bullhorn. "I'd much rather talk instead of yelling. I'd like to understand why you don't know where your truck is."

"I have a phone."

Mercy rattled off her cell phone number through the bullhorn.

"Why the hell would you do that?" muttered Evan. "Now he has your number."

"I'll get a new one. Not important at the moment."

Her phone rang. "Silas?" she answered.

"Yeah. I don't know where my truck is."

"I appreciate your call so we don't have to yell."

Let him believe he's helping the situation.

"When did you last drive your truck?" She switched her phone to speaker so Evan could hear.

"What's this about?" he asked nervously. "Is someone hurt?"

He sounds confused.

"Not exactly," she lied. "We saw a truck like it parked next to a . . . house we're investigating."

"You're just looking for my truck," he said slowly. "No one was hit."

Hit?

"Hit by your truck?" Mercy frowned. She exchanged a confused look with Evan.

"Yeah."

"No. We aren't looking for a vehicle that was in an accident."

Silas exhaled loudly over the phone. "Thank God. I thought I fucked up."

261

"Silas . . . I feel like we're talking about two different things." The suspicion that she was talking to the wrong man grew stronger and stronger. "Was your truck in your possession the day before yesterday?"

"Yeah."

She didn't want one-word answers. "Did you drive it somewhere that day? Where did you go?" she added quickly before he answered with another *yeah*.

"Timbers."

Evan grimaced. Mercy was familiar with the dive bar on the outskirts of Bend. The run-down building with the dozen garbage cans out front had never encouraged her to venture inside, and the absence of windows gave her the creeps.

"And then where did you go?"

"I don't know. I woke up when I hit the rock."

Mercy and Evan stared at each other. "Where's this rock, Silas?"

"Well, that's the problem. I remember getting out and looking at how I'd smashed into the rock, but the next thing I know I woke up in my bed. No truck."

"Did you walk home?"

"I guess so. Don't know who'd drive me. I live alone."

Mercy muted the phone while she spoke to Evan. "Get three of your deputies to drive the roads between here and Timbers—closer to here, I assume, if he walked home drunk."

"Silas," she said back into the phone. "We're gonna help you out and send some guys to locate your truck, okay?"

"Sure would appreciate that. You sure I didn't hit no one?" His voice wavered.

"We haven't had a report of that recently." She looked at Evan for verification. He shook his head.

"Sorry about firing at that county vehicle," Silas said. "Thought I'd hurt someone, and they were here to take me to prison."

"Silas, now that we've got this cleared up, I'd like you to come out. Leave any weapons in the house, okay?"

"What's going to happen to me?"

"Well, you did admit to driving drunk, right?" *And firing at officers.*

"Yeah."

"But no one was hurt. So you've got that going for you. You understand you'll be arrested when you come out, right?"

He didn't answer.

"I promise they'll keep it simple." *Don't give up on me now.*

"I want you to do it."

Surprised, Mercy looked at Evan, who shrugged with one shoulder. "You established a rapport," he whispered. "He thinks he knows you."

"You got a deal, Silas," she said. "Here's how we'll handle it. I want you to come out with your hands up, so I can see they're empty, okay? And when you get past that first rock in front of your house, I want you to lie on your stomach with your hands on the back of your head. Got that?"

"Hands. Rock. Yeah."

"I'll have to cuff you, but you already knew that, right?"

"Yeah."

"I'll do a quick search of your pockets after that, and we'll be done. Smooth and simple."

"Okay."

"You can hang up now. Leave your phone in the house."

"I don't like to go anywhere without my cell phone."

Mercy briefly closed her eyes in exasperation. "Me too. But I'd have to take it away from you anyway, so let's leave it in the house."

"Okay. Hanging up now."

"See you outside, Silas."

Mercy ended the call and exhaled. "Think he's being honest?" she asked.

"We'll find out soon enough."

"His truck still could have been the one at the Ingram house," Mercy speculated. "Someone else could have driven it. Even if he'd been drinking at Timbers, someone could have borrowed his truck and brought it back. Sounds like Silas was smashed enough to not notice."

The front door of the house opened, and Mercy held her breath.

Evan positioned himself, his arms on the hood of his vehicle, his handgun pointed at the door. The deputy who stayed behind was in the same position. "We'll have you covered," Evan told her. Mercy nodded, her gaze locked on the figure who'd stepped out with his hands up. Silas Dillon was short and round, with his gray hair in a ponytail and a beard halfway down his chest. He followed Mercy's instructions perfectly. When he was in position on the ground, she walked down his driveway. She felt confident with Evan as her backup, but her nerves were on high alert. Too much confidence caused people to miss signs.

She glanced at the windows of the house. *We didn't ask if anyone else was in the home.*

Her protective vest suddenly felt small and feeble.

He said he lived alone.

Not good enough.

Her gaze locked back on Silas, she moved closer, her heart pounding as she thought about the open windows of the home.

Silas watched her walk the entire way down his drive. As she drew closer, she smiled. "You did perfect, Silas."

"Holy shit." His eyes widened. "You're fucking hot. Are you really an FBI agent?"

She bit her lip. "Yes. Now move one of your hands to the small of your back. I'm going to slip on the handcuffs."

"You can cuff me anytime." If his voice hadn't been so pathetically whiny, she would have taken offense. Instead the situation was too ludicrous to be real.

She locked on a cuff. "Other hand now." He obeyed, and she did the other.

"You into dom and sub roles?" he asked hopefully.

"No. I'm going to search your pockets now. You got needles or anything in them that can hurt me?"

He leered. "Only one big thing, and I promise not to hurt you too bad with it."

She stopped, fighting an urge to whack him on the back of the head. "You always talk to women like this, Silas?"

"Depends."

"Let me give you a tip. It's not a turn-on. Ever. It's creepy. Maybe talking like this is the reason you live alone." She started to check his back pockets.

"I'll finish that." Evan squatted next to Silas. "You get to enjoy my hands instead."

Silas glared. "I said I wanted her to arrest me."

"She did. The cuffs are on. Now you belong to me." Evan did a quick, thorough search and stood, leaving Silas facedown in the grass. "I canceled the SWAT callout. Nice job."

"I didn't have the patience to wait. My niece is in the fucking hospital, and we've got more trucks to check on."

"I've got something to show you," Evan said. He held out his phone, showing a picture of a red truck. Its front end was smashed against a large lava rock in the center of a field. "A deputy spotted it within minutes."

The red color was too dark. *Silas wasn't at Bree's.* Disappointment radiated through her.

"Guess this is the wrong one," Evan said regretfully. "We'll keep working down the list of trucks. At least we got a drunk off the road."

"Dammit." Time was slipping away. "I thought we were so close."

"Maybe the next one will be our lucky strike." Evan nodded at the house. "Now go delete your number from this jerk's phone before you start getting nightly calls."

"Getting a new number will be worth it." Mercy strode toward the house. "Have a deputy take him in," she said over her shoulder. "We'll go find the next truck." She pulled out her phone.

As soon as I check on Kaylie.

THIRTY-TWO

Sandy took her turn at Bree's bedside.

Oh, Bree. She looks worse.

"Any changes?" Sandy asked Lucas as they both stared at his mother. The bruising was now a rainbow of colors, and her scabs were turning black.

"The surgeon is pleased with her fingers," Lucas said. "Circulation is established, but the nerves could take a full year to regrow . . . if they do."

"I'm happy for that," Sandy whispered, brushing the hair from Bree's forehead. "But she'll remember what happened every time she sees the scars."

Lucas studied her for a moment. "Where are your scars, Sandy?" he asked gently.

Sandy couldn't look him in the eye. "Mine are hidden."

Not hidden from me. She saw them every time she changed her clothes. They were her private little secrets.

Not secret anymore.

Lionel was behind bars, and everyone knew she had been a battered wife. *My scars are hard-earned medals for survival—not something to hide.* She slid up her sleeve, exposing her upper arm and the twisted tissue.

She met Lucas's gaze. "It was a compound fracture."

The big man shuddered. She understood. Bones weren't meant to be seen; even broken bones were supposed to stay below the muscles, not ram their jagged edges through the skin. She lowered the sleeve.

"I'm sorry, Sandy."

"It's history. I learned to deal with it long ago, and your mother helped me ease into a new life in Eagle's Nest. I'll always be grateful for that."

Silence filled the small room.

"I'll be back at one for my lunch," Lucas finally said. His struggle to leave was apparent on his face. "I feel like I'm about to miss something."

"I'll call you immediately with any change."

He gave her a careful hug. "I'm not breakable, Lucas," she said with a wry smile.

"If you say so."

The air squeezed out of her lungs as she got what Bree called a Lucas rib crusher.

He left, and Sandy pulled up a chair close to the bed and took Bree's hand. The undamaged one. "Hey, lady. How's it going? I fed and watered the horses, and then let them out. You should have seen Cyrus run. He's getting antsy. He needs you to take him for a long ride."

Bree didn't respond.

"Abby is going to get fat. She won't tear around the pasture like Cyrus does. She just eats. I'll have to take her out on my own pretty soon."

Come on, Bree. A squeeze. A blink. Something. "I'd much rather we went riding together."

Sandy sighed in the silence and considered her friend's injuries. Bree's damaged hand was heavily wrapped, making it look like the bulbous end of a chicken leg. *Will she be able to ride with damaged fingers?*

She snorted, knowing that would never stop someone as horse crazy as Bree.

"We'll head up the same trail we took last time. Remember? It was a gorgeous day. You showed me the rock that looks like a horse's head gazing out over the valley." She squeezed Bree's hand. "We'll go back real soon, you hear me?"

Bree's eyes opened, and Sandy froze. Bree stared directly at Sandy with terror in her gaze, and her cracked lips moved. As Sandy's heart attempted to hammer its way out of her chest, she leaned closer to the patient. "What did you say, Bree? I couldn't hear you."

Bree's words sounded like rustling leaves, but Sandy finally made them out. "Killed . . . him . . . buried . . . buried. Bury me," she whispered.

Sandy's stomach dropped. "You're not dying, Bree. And no one is dead." She pressed Bree's hand to her own chest. "You're going to be just fine," she ordered. "The doctor fixed your fingers, and your bruises will go away."

Bree continued to stare at Sandy in dread as she mouthed the same words over and over.

It feels as if she's staring through me. Who does she see?

"Sorry . . . ," Bree whispered. "Sorry . . . dead. Buried."

"Bree. *You're not going to die!* You're safe. No one is going to hurt you again." Sandy searched for the CALL button and hit it. "Everyone will be so happy you're awake. Lucas just left, but I'm going to call him right now." She kept talking, afraid Bree would drift away if she stopped. The woman gripped her hand like a lifeline. "Bree, honey, you can relax. Are you in pain? Do you need more medication?"

"Lucas?" she croaked with a new fear in her eyes.

"Lucas is safe."

Bree's lips stopped moving, and her eyelids fell closed. The grip on Sandy's hand eased.

"Bree?" Sandy touched an unharmed spot on Bree's cheek. "Bree. Open your eyes again for me."

"What's going on?" Sandy's favorite efficient nurse bustled in, wearing purple scrubs and running shoes. The deputy on guard stood in the doorway, his face hopeful.

"She opened her eyes and talked to me!"

"That's great!" The nurse leaned close to Bree. "Hey, Bree. Sandy claims you talked to her, is that true?" she cajoled as she checked Bree's pulse and started the automatic blood pressure cuff. "Wake up for me again, would you?"

The two of them watched Bree's closed eyes and waited. Sandy swore her heartbeat was louder than the machinery in the room.

Nothing.

It was as if it had never happened.

"She was terrified she was dying." Sandy wanted to weep. "She kept saying 'buried.' Do you think she's in pain?"

"Hmmmm," the nurse said noncommittally. "I'll mention it to her doctor." Satisfied with Bree's vitals, she straightened the sheets and laid a caring hand on her patient's shoulder. "Keep talking to her," the nurse said kindly, smiling at Sandy. "Keep reassuring her she is safe. No doubt she's very traumatized." She frowned. "I've seen patients open their eyes and even speak, but then fall right back into their unconscious state. Sometimes that is the best medicine as the brain tries to process the trauma."

"Lucas missed it." *But would Lucas have wanted to see his mother like that?*

Sandy decided it was best he hadn't. She still struggled to catch her breath after the sight of Bree's fear.

Lowering herself into her chair, Sandy kept a grip on Bree's hand and stared at the battered face as the nurse left.

Buried.

Had Bree been more concerned than she let on about the threatening notes? Had she wanted someone to know her final wishes?

A shudder shot up Sandy's spine.

Had Bree expected to be murdered?

Why?

Sandy had spent a decade looking over her shoulder, always waiting for Lionel to jump out of the dark. But she'd never felt the need to express her last wishes to someone.

I really should make a will.

The gentle hum and beeps of the equipment were reassuring, and Sandy relaxed into the chair. As long as the machines were calm, everything was all right with Bree.

But something in her head is tormenting her.

Understandable after the torture she'd endured.

But the distress was there before the torture.

Sandy leaned forward, rested her arms on the metal rails of Bree's hospital bed, and started to think.

I can figure this out.

◆ ◆ ◆

Truman pulled open the door to Leaky's Tavern, stepped inside, and paused as his eyes adjusted to the dim light. He'd shown the digitally aged images of Trevor Whipple and Nathan May in every shop in town and come up empty.

Over and over people studied the pictures, frowned, shook their heads, and then handed them back with a "Sorry, Chief."

Currently Truman was on the hunt for Nick Walker, Rose's fiancé. At one time or another, every man within several miles had passed through Nick's business, and Truman knew he could find Nick at Leaky's for lunch.

He spotted Nick in a booth near the back, a club sandwich in hand and a gigantic soda on the table in front of him. A bar like Leaky's was an unlikely lunch spot for a man on the job, unless that man knew about the awesomeness that was the Leaky turkey club.

Truman knew.

His stomach growled.

A few other people sat at the bar, their eyes glued to a basketball game. Nick was the only customer at a table. Truman slid into the booth across from him, and Nick wiped his mouth. "Hey, Truman."

"Rose holding up after last night?"

"Yeah, but she calls the hospital nurses' station every hour to check on Kaylie. What's the latest?"

"Stable. Doctors are optimistic." *That's such a relief to say.* Truman had repeated the same phrase multiple times that day. Everyone cared deeply about the young, peppy owner of the Coffee Café. It made him proud to be a part of this town.

"Catch the asshole that shot her?"

"They will. Deschutes County, Bend PD, and the FBI are all over it." Truman itched to be on the hunt, but it wasn't his jurisdiction. He couldn't sit still, so with renewed vigor he'd thrown himself into finding who'd attacked Bree Ingram.

"Good." Nick took a drink of his soda.

"Rose definitely has the flu?"

"Yep. Doc started her on some medication as soon as she went in." Nick looked glum. "She didn't want to take anything, but he said there's more risk to the baby from the fever than the drugs, and Rose is also at risk for getting something worse. He said something about changes in a pregnant woman's immune system that makes them more prone to bad shit."

"That sounds awful." Pregnant women were a mystery to him. Perplexing changes happened in their bodies.

"They say it's a good thing she's in her last trimester. Just need to keep her hydrated, eating consistently, and her fever down." He scowled. "And no more late-night stressful visits to hospitals. She was exhausted when we got home."

"I know how persuasive Mercy can be when she wants to do something. I assume Rose is the same way. There's no changing their minds."

"Exactly." Nick took a fierce bite of his sandwich. "You here for lunch?" he asked after he chewed and swallowed.

"No. I wanted to show you these." Truman laid out the images one by one. "Recognize anyone?"

Nick picked one up and wrinkled his forehead. "Why are they so weird looking?"

"They're computer generated."

"Oh." He carefully studied each one, continuing to make quick work of his sandwich. "Help yourself to some fries." He pushed his plate closer to Truman.

Leaky's fries were a close second to the club. Crisp outsides, tender insides, and tossed with a secret spice recipe. Mercy claimed the secret was cumin and chili powder, but hers tasted nothing like Leaky's. Truman took a few from Nick's plate and flavor exploded in his mouth.

He must have made a noise, because Nick looked up from a page and grinned. "Good, huh?"

Truman could only nod.

Nick sat back in the booth. "I don't recognize these guys, but I keep coming back to this one." He tapped the overweight Nathan May. The same photo that felt familiar to Truman. "Don't know where or how, but I've met him. I think." Nick looked less than positive.

"I had the same type of reaction."

"Hmph," Nick said with his mouth full. "Did you try Ina?"

"I'm headed there next."

"She knows everyone."

"She can't get around like she used to."

"Doesn't stop her," Nick said. "One of my guys sprained an ankle at home. Ina called to tell me he'd been hurt before my guy did. And he lives a half mile away from her. Don't know how she knew."

"I think she has a network of spies."

Nick solemnly agreed, his eyes serious.

"I'll let you finish your lunch. Thanks for the fries." Truman shoved himself out of the booth.

Nick lifted a hand and focused on his food.

Truman walked the four blocks to Ina Smythe's little house, taking the time to check in with his office. Eagle's Nest was eerily quiet, and not a single car passed him. Odd for a lunch hour. It felt as if the entire town were waiting for news on Kaylie Kilpatrick before it could return to normal.

My visit with Ina should get that gossip train moving.

He opened the little white gate and ducked under the low arch. At her front door, he knocked, knowing she wasn't fond of doorbells.

A moment later the door was open, and she happily ushered him in, her cane thumping. She guided him to the kitchen table, where she had a pot of coffee and a plate of cookies ready. Truman sat and recognized Kaylie's triple chocolate cookies.

His gut churned, and he lost his appetite.

Ina tipped her head to one side, her sharp gaze on Truman. "Yes, those are from her place. I buy them by the dozen, and Pearl usually delivers them every Monday."

Truman struggled to speak; his mind was blank.

"She's a good kid. Mercy has done a wonderful job, considering what Kaylie went through."

"The doctors are optimistic. She's stable." His fallback statement.

Ina's face lit up. "Good! I'm so glad to hear it. They won't tell me anything when I call the hospital. They just quote privacy laws. Sheesh. How's a person supposed to check up on a neighbor?" She poured coffee in his mug. "Good thing they answer my questions about Bree since she's family, or they'd have the wrath of Ina coming down on them. Now. You said you had some pictures to show me. Where are they?"

Always gets right to the point.

Truman handed her the small stack and reluctantly took a cookie. He stared at it for a moment and then dunked it in his coffee the way Kaylie had urged him to do the first time he'd tried one. He took a bite. Still delicious. A subtle wave of peace came over him as he chewed and watched Ina. He didn't know if it was the cookie or being in Ina's home. He and his uncle Jefferson had sat at this table for dozens of meals during his high school summers. Only later did he figure out that Ina and Jefferson had a *thing*.

Good memories.

Ina set the images aside, except for one.

Truman stretched his neck to look. In his head he'd started to call the image Fat Nathan.

"This one," Ina said slowly. "I can't say who it is, but it's familiar." She scowled. "It's old. My memory of this man must be from a long time ago. I see him in my head as young."

"Any idea how long? Were you married at the time?" he prompted, trying to help her associate the memory with something else.

"Which marriage?" she snorted gleefully.

Only Ina could have four marriages and never suffer from malicious town gossip. Gossip stopped and started with her.

"Good point."

She carefully laid the image on the table, her face thoughtful. "Let me stew over it a bit. My memory needs a kickstart every now and then."

Truman cleared his throat. "I understand the latest news on Bree is positive."

"Did you hear she woke up and spoke today?"

"No!" Truman's mind raced, and he forced himself to stay in his seat instead of rushing to interview her at the hospital. "Did she say who beat her?"

Ina's face fell. "No. She mentioned Lucas, but the rest made no sense. Sandy told me she asked to be buried." Ina shook her head. "That poor girl. She must have thought she was dead. After saying that, she fell unconscious again. Sandy said it didn't last more than fifteen seconds."

"It's a good sign."

"Agreed. I ordered Sandy to ask the name of the son of a bitch who hurt her so we can catch him." Her eyes were ferocious. "I want two minutes with a sharp knife and his fingers . . . Make that a dull knife."

Truman had to smile. This was the Ina he'd always known. "I'll see what I can do. What can you tell me about Bree when your son, Hollis, met her?"

"Hmmm." Her gaze went distant. "She was always a pretty little thing. Hollis was instantly crazy for her."

"Do you know how they met?"

"No . . . Maybe they met at the college in Bend. She was attending full-time, and he'd take a class here and there. He didn't live with me then." She chortled. "I always told Hollis she was too good for him. She got her teaching certificate in record time. That girl was driven. She knew exactly what she wanted to do with her life."

"She was damned good at it," agreed Truman. "Ollie loved their tutoring sessions."

"I was so pleased when the state recognized her last year for her teaching talent." Ina took a long sip of coffee. "When Hollis died, I thought she'd get married again one day. She was such a gem that I figured another man would snap her up right away. But she told me she only had room in her heart for Hollis . . . and Lucas, of course. He's the spitting image of his daddy."

"Was she originally from around here?" Truman asked.

Ina's gaze sharpened. "Is that the point of this trip down memory lane? Bree's history?"

"We're trying to catch who attacked her. It helps to know her past. It's been difficult to find any data before she married Hollis."

"She wasn't from around here . . . Northern California." Her face brightened. "She'd lived in a town called Paradise. Can you believe that? She always joked that she moved from one paradise to another. Have to respect a girl who embraced the beauty of our area."

"She ever go back to visit?"

"No. She said her parents had passed a few years before she moved, and she didn't have any other relatives she cared to keep in touch with. I always felt bad for her . . . When she talked about her parents you could tell it hurt. Hollis told me not to pester her with too many questions." Ina twisted her lips. "I did my best."

Truman tried to imagine Ina holding her tongue.

"Well now . . ." Ina twisted her hands on the arch of her cane and frowned as she turned to look out the window. "I had it a second ago . . . Dammit."

"What was that?"

"Shush. Let me think."

Truman took another cookie and let her think.

Ina picked up the Fat Nathan picture and glared laser beams through it. "This was Hollis's friend . . . Well, more like an acquaintance . . . High school?" She muttered under her breath for a moment. "Maybe. Or from the real estate office? Nah, that's not old enough." More scowls.

A friend of Hollis's? Hollis had been dead for at least fifteen years.

"Your memory sounds darn good to me, Ina."

"Stop with the sweet talk." She waved a hand at him. "I keep associating the picture with high school . . . but my gut tells me that's not right, and I can't come up with anything else." Exasperation crossed her face.

"Any chance you still have Hollis's high school yearbooks?" Truman asked, crossing his fingers.

"Of course." She braced her hands on the table to stand, and Truman immediately jumped out of his chair to help. "Sit down. I'm not dead yet." She slowly left the kitchen.

Nathan May can't be a high school friend of Hollis. Mercy told me Nathan went to school somewhere in Portland.

Truman wouldn't pass on the yearbooks. Someone who looked similar must have attended Eagle's Nest High School. That would explain why a few people had zeroed in on the same picture.

But I didn't live here back then. Why is it familiar to me?

Ina reappeared with two books. They were startlingly thin compared to Truman's high school yearbooks. His books were heavy beasts, but he'd attended a school with nearly two thousand kids. Eagle's Nest High School wasn't a tenth that size.

"Here you go. I grabbed his junior and senior year." She placed the books in front of him. "I'll let you do the exciting job of going through them."

"Thank you, Ina."

"You need anything else?"

"I don't think so." Truman stood and took a last sip of his coffee. "I appreciate the information on Bree."

"Anytime." She tapped her cheek, and he grinned as he bent to kiss it.

Just as he'd done a hundred times.

He said his goodbye and strode back toward the main part of town, the yearbooks tucked under his arm.

I'll tackle these first thing when I reach the office.

THIRTY-THREE

Every red truck on the list had been eliminated.

Mercy wanted to hit something. Expanding the search to nearby counties had more than tripled the list and meant a lot of driving.

Now she sat in the parking lot of the hospital, trying to calm her frustration before she went in to check on Kaylie. And Bree Ingram. At least Eddie had been discharged that morning, but he hadn't left the hospital. Instead he'd gone to sit with Kaylie. He'd called Mercy to explain that he and Kaylie had a shared experience, and she would need someone to exchange gunshot jokes with.

Mercy hadn't known whether to laugh or cry at his remark.

Her mother and Pearl had updated her hourly on Kaylie's progress. Thankfully each of their reports said the same: no infection yet. Kaylie was awake and had some issues with getting her pain under control, but Mercy's mother had handled it. Mercy easily imagined her mother riding the nurses until her grandchild was out of pain. Pearl's report a half hour ago had said Kaylie was sleeping. She'd added that Eddie was sleeping in a chair in Kaylie's room due to his own pain management.

At least Kaylie wasn't alone. Her support group was strong.

Mercy started to get out of her Tahoe and stopped, watching a red-haired woman leave the hospital.

Sandy.

Her gait was rapid and determined. Her head down, her arms swinging with purpose as she walked straight to her SUV.

Something is up.

Mercy jogged to intercept the woman. "Sandy!"

Sandy stopped. Fear flashed on her face and then vanished as she recognized Mercy.

Guilt poked Mercy. *The woman was just assaulted. I shouldn't have startled her.*

"I heard Bree woke up," Mercy said as she reached Sandy at her vehicle.

"She did. But it was brief, and it hasn't happened again yet." Something odd flickered in her eyes, and she scanned the parking lot, clearly wanting to be on her way.

"What's going on, Sandy?" Mercy crossed her arms. "You look like you've got somewhere to be."

The tall woman's gaze grew confrontational. "Of course I do. I have a business to run."

Mercy waited. Sandy's gaze bounced everywhere, and an air of urgency swirled around her.

I don't think it has anything to do with her B&B.

"Sandy," she said in a low tone. "What happened? I can tell you've got something on your mind."

"Last time we talked you practically accused me of murder. I can't say I want to repeat the conversation."

"I was doing my job . . . and I didn't accuse you of murder. I asked you about your past. It was a simple connection. Tabitha was murdered while digging into a nearly thirty-year-old crime. She talked to you. Therefore, I looked into what you were doing thirty years ago. And I did the same with Bree."

The woman exhaled and looked at Mercy head-on. "That's what's bugging me. Bree's past. Today I had a thought."

"And?"

"Do you know what Bree said when she woke up?"

"I heard she thought she was dying and wanted to be buried."

Pain flashed in Sandy's gaze, and her mouth tightened. "That's correct. She also said 'sorry' a few times, 'killed him,' and then asked for Lucas."

"'Killed him'?" The hair on Mercy's arms rose. "What the hell?"

"I know. It's been bouncing through my brain all afternoon."

"And it's made you think of something to check out." She looked hard into Sandy's brown eyes. "Do you have an idea of who attacked her?"

Her head jerked. "Oh no! It's nothing like that . . . I have no idea who did that."

Disappointment rolled over Mercy. "Then what is it?"

"I'm not sure . . . but I need to take a look."

Mercy couldn't interpret the expression on Sandy's face.

"Can you spare three or four hours?" Sandy asked, sounding hopeful.

"It depends. Where are we going?"

"Can you ride a horse?"

Mercy snorted. "I was born on a ranch. Hell yes I can ride."

◆ ◆ ◆

But Mercy hadn't ridden a horse since she'd left Eagle's Nest at the age of eighteen.

As she followed Sandy's Explorer to Bree's ranch, she wondered if it would be as easy as riding a bike again. The body never forgets how to move with the motions of the horse. *Right?* She crossed her fingers it was so.

Mercy didn't know when she'd learned to ride; it'd always been a part of her life. All her siblings had ridden. As kids they'd hold competitions to see who could ride backward and bareback the longest, who could best guide a horse through a complicated course without a bridle, and who could run and vault up over the horse's hind end to land in a sitting position on its back.

That only worked on one of the small, older geldings. He didn't care what the kids did. They could hang upside down under his belly and it didn't faze him.

Any other horse would have freaked.

Memories flooded her. Her siblings, the ranch animals, the diverse nature around her home where she and her siblings found their daily entertainment. No handheld screens to constantly stare at.

I had a good childhood.

She'd thought it was horrible and suffocating—and parts of it had been, but she'd had a breadth of experience that the kids of her coworkers in Portland would never have.

I can see that now.

She parked beside Sandy at Bree's barn, the home in her rearview mirror. It looked like a happy place to live. Well maintained, with a few feminine touches of country decor.

It felt like a facade.

Mercy had been inside the house and seen the bloody kitchen. She was aware of the crime scene investigation's findings, which hadn't amounted to much. They desperately needed more evidence from Bree's attack. The battered red truck had been their best lead.

I'll look at every red truck in the state if I have to.

Sandy waited for her at the barn door. "Feels too quiet, doesn't it?" she said with a glance at the home.

"It does. Are you sure this is the only way to get where we're going?"

"I'm positive. Unless you can scale tall, perfectly vertical cliffs. There are no roads to where we're going, just horse paths."

A chain and combination lock held Bree's two barn doors together. Sandy spun the combination. "Bree added it after her stalls were marked up."

Mercy didn't say anything. A good pair of bolt cutters would make fast work of the chain.

Throwing her weight against one of the doors, Sandy slid it to the side.

Mercy inhaled. Hay. Horse. Manure. Her mouth stretched into a wide smile.

"What?" asked Sandy.

"The scents of my childhood."

"Are they good memories?"

"Yeah, they are. At one time I would have said no, but looking back now, I know they are."

The barn lit up inside as Sandy hit a light switch. When Sandy opened the main door, shadowed heads had appeared over the stall doors, but now Mercy saw the alert ears and dark eyes fixed on her.

God, I've missed this.

Sandy immediately opened one of the stalls and led out a bay mare. She crosstied her in the center aisle. The horse rotated its ears toward Mercy, and its nostrils widened as it inhaled, searching for her scent. "This is my Abby," Sandy said with a fond rub on the mare's head. "I think Justin would be a good mount for you." She pointed at a chestnut with a wide white stripe down his face. "He's unflappable and solid. I know you said you can ride, but I assume it's been a while?" Sandy raised a brow at her.

"It has," Mercy admitted. "Show me his tack, and I'll get him started."

It was like riding a bike.

Her muscles remembered the movements to lift the heavy western saddle and settle it on the gelding's back. How to tighten the cinch and knot it. How to slip the bit between the teeth and manipulate the soft ears to slide the headpiece behind them.

She'd traded her shoes and slacks for the hiking boots and heavy-duty black pants from her SUV's clothing stash. After adding a light jacket she was ready to go. Sandy surprised her by tying a shovel to each of their saddles. "We'll be digging?" Mercy asked. The long shovel handle was parallel to Mercy's back. She had an urge to fasten a flag to the top as if she were in a parade.

"Maybe."

I will expect a clear answer before I go much farther.

The pensive look in Sandy's eyes, and the constant stress in her jaw, kept Mercy from pressing the issue as they saddled the horses.

Minutes later, she was on horseback and following Sandy across a field. Her thighs immediately complained about the unusual position, and Mercy knew she'd be sore tomorrow. Sandy was right about Justin. He didn't care a whit about the shovel or when Mercy adjusted the length of her stirrups three times. He simply plodded forward.

She gave him a squeeze with her calves and clucked her tongue, moving him even with Sandy and Abby. "Start talking," she ordered the other woman.

Sandy took a large breath. "Seven years ago, my business was about to go under. Hospitality is not an easy game. I had no funds for a website for guests to find me, my roof needed to be replaced, and two of my refrigerators were close to death. The stress had me nearly pulling out my hair.

"Bree knew I was sinking. She saw the anxiety was affecting my health. I couldn't sleep, I could barely get out of bed, and I suddenly had no joy in my work." She shrugged. "Who would? No one likes to see their dreams circling the drain."

"I'm sorry, Sandy."

The redhead gave her a weak smile. "It's water under the bridge now."

"What happened?" Mercy had a feeling she knew what Sandy was about to say.

"Bree gave me a stack of cash."

Bingo.

"I refused to take it, convinced she was giving away her life savings. She was a widowed mother with a growing son. She had to need the money."

"But she didn't."

"No. She told me Hollis's death had left her money from a huge life insurance policy, and her investments had nearly doubled the amount in the eight years he'd been gone. I still didn't want to take it, but I felt like my life was about to implode. I finally swore I'd pay her back, and she agreed. When you and Truman interviewed me after Lionel's attack, it struck me as odd when you said her bank records looked normal for a single working person. You didn't mention a huge investment account."

"I didn't find one."

"And you said that Bree might know one of the thieves from the Gamble-Helmet Heist." Sandy turned clear eyes on Mercy. "That stuck in my head. Bree doesn't seem the type to hide cash in her mattress, but a thick wad of cash was exactly what she gave me."

"You think she has money from the robbery."

"Maybe . . . and maybe someone else who knows about the money wants it. Enough to cut her fingers off to get her to talk." Her voice went ragged as she spoke.

"Are we going to dig up that money?"

"There's a place I want to look." Sandy took a deep breath. "I could be totally off base, but Bree and I have ridden to one particular ridge at least a dozen times. She calls it her happy spot, but it's called Horse's Head Rock. As you can guess, it's a huge rock that looks like a horse's head. A few weeks ago we were up there, and she dug a gorgeous crystal out of the dirt."

"The dirt? Like, found it randomly?"

"No. She knew exactly where it was. It was in a little tin box not far from the horse."

"That's really weird. Why hide a crystal?"

"That's what I asked her, and she laughed and said she hid it next to the horse for good luck—like an offering of some sort, I guess, but she tucked it in her pocket. I don't think it was worth any money, but I could tell it was special to her. She said she'd originally found it on one of her rides."

"And you think she might have buried something else—like money," stated Mercy. "I can see that. It's worth taking a look, but it's a long shot."

"I know. That's why we could be wasting our time. But repeating 'buried' and 'bury me' has to mean something."

"Bree also said 'killed him' when she woke," Mercy pointed out.

"I don't know what to think about that." Sandy met Mercy's gaze. "Do you think she killed someone because of this money?"

Mercy thought of Ellis Mull's skull with its bullet holes. "Hard to say. We don't know for certain that the money exists."

Sandy blanched. "Maybe she killed and buried someone up there?"

"I hope not," Mercy said firmly.

What are we going to find?

They rode in silence for a few minutes, following a faint trail through rocks and sage that steadily led upward toward a pine forest. Sandy's mount pulled ahead as the trail narrowed.

"How far is it?"

"At least another hour or so."

Mercy pulled out her phone, grateful to see she had service. "I need to make some calls."

"Do it now," Sandy said over her shoulder. "There's no reception near the ridge."

Dialing Truman while sitting on a horse in the middle of nowhere made her smile. A collision of two eras.

His voice mail answered.

"Hey, Truman. I'm calling you from horseback." She grinned. "I'm with Sandy. We're riding from Bree's ranch, and we're headed to a place called Horse's Head Rock. Sandy has a theory about Bree that we're going to check out."

I can't explain Sandy's idea in a voice mail.

"I'll tell you about it when we're done. I'll be out of range for a few hours."

Her phone beeped in her ear and she checked the screen. Art was calling.

"I love you," she said rapidly to wind up her message to Truman. "I'll call you as soon as I can." She switched over to Art's call.

"What's up, Art?"

"After you told me your theory on a female driver, I started reviewing interviews of some of the women from back then and taking a more recent look into their lives."

Mercy glanced ahead at Sandy's back, straight and tall as she sat on her horse.

"What did you find?"

"You knew Ellis Mull had four sisters, right?"

"Yes."

"The youngest, Shawna Mull, started some heavy spending about seven years ago. She was seventeen when the robbery happened. I can remember her terrified face during our interviews. I chalked it up to her being a high school student with the FBI in her face, but now I wonder if I didn't look hard enough at her because of her age." He sighed. "Sometimes our personal mind-sets work against us."

"What kind of spending?" asked Mercy. Shawna's face was blurry in her mind. The pictures of the four sisters had blended together.

"Trips to Europe. Cruises."

"What's she do?"

"She's a checker at a grocery store. Her bank accounts look normal—there's nothing to reflect she earns enough to do this. I'm getting this information from her social media accounts. People document every step they take these days."

"Sounds like we need to talk to her."

"You busy this evening?"

Mercy looked behind her. She and Sandy were already in the middle of nowhere. "I'm tied up for several hours. You should take . . . Dammit. You can't take anyone to the interview because you're officially off the case."

Eddie's out of the loop. Jeff is sick.

"It'll have to wait until I get back."

"What are you doing?"

"Would you believe I'm on the back of a horse? It's for work, I swear."

"Where are you going?"

"I'm on a wild-goose chase."

Sandy turned around and grinned.

"But no geese are involved," Mercy continued. "A friend has a hunch about where Bree Ingram might have buried some money—if she was actually involved in the robbery."

"Mercy," he said slowly. "Do you know how many times I followed up on a lead about buried money? They all led to squat."

"This might too. There's a lot of dirt out here."

"Where is it?"

"Bree called it Horse's Head Rock."

"Don't get your hopes up, but let me know how it goes."

"I will. But I really like your lead on Shawna. It's very promising. We can set something up with her tomorrow." Mercy ended the call.

I like the information on Shawna. Part of her wanted to turn around and go interview the woman, but Sandy's story about a stack of money from Bree had to be checked out.

She called Pearl next and learned Kaylie was sleeping, no infection had appeared, and Eddie was still crashed out, to the amusement of Pearl.

Relief tinged with worry wove through her chest. She'd hoped to hear the doctors had declared Kaylie completely in the clear.

No change is good. Better than sliding backward.

The horses entered the pine forest, and the temperature dropped in the shade. The trees were denser up ahead, and the trail was noticeably steeper. Justin increased the power in his legs as he moved up the slope, and Mercy leaned forward, shifting her weight to help.

"It opens up on the other side of this stretch of forest," Sandy said. "More open, flat areas and then the ridge. You'll love the view."

Mercy wiggled her hips, searching for a comfortable place in the saddle, wishing the ride were shorter.

Sunlight struggled to penetrate the forest. Mercy could see clearly, but the dimmer light and the loss of the ability to see for miles were unsettling and threatened to trigger some claustrophobia. She took deep breaths, searching for a distraction. She settled on Sandy's red hair, admiring the woman's long ponytail.

I'm embarrassed I thought she might be involved in the robbery.

She patted her horse's neck, and his ears swiveled in her direction.

Actually Sandy's done nothing to wipe out that theory. Instead, my focus has been moved to Bree as being involved in the robbery.

Her hand paused on Justin's warm neck.

Sandy moved that focus. To a woman who is currently unable to speak.

Apprehension shot through her, and she stared at Sandy's straight back.

No cell service. Remote.

I've been talked into a buried treasure hunt.

Mercy touched the weapon at her waist. Echoing through her head was Detective Ortiz's assertion that Kaylie's bullet might have been meant for Mercy.

Someone might want her off the investigation.

Am I riding into a trap?

THIRTY-FOUR

A beat-up red truck passed by as Ollie waited to pull out of the Eagle's Nest Dairy Queen.

Instantly his gaze went to the license plate. It wasn't the same one he'd seen that night at Bree's, but he didn't care. The previous plate had been stolen; this one could be too.

He'd followed two other red trucks since the attack. The first had had a SAVE A HORSE, RIDE A COWBOY sticker in the rear window and been driven by a teenage girl. The other had been driven by a senior citizen who walked with a cane. Ollie had wasted two hours following these trucks until the drivers exited. Possibly either vehicle could have been driven by someone else the night of Bree's attack, but Ollie's gut told him neither red truck was right. He knew Deschutes County was doing its own search, but he couldn't sit still when he spotted one.

With his hot dog in hand, he cranked his wheel and pulled out after the red truck, cutting in front of a blue sedan whose driver expressed his displeasure with a long honk.

Ollie ignored him, his gaze glued to the back of the truck.

He finished his hot dog in two bites and wiped his mouth with the back of his hand.

He'd studied the photo he snapped of the license plate at Bree's a hundred times. The photo had shown only a small section of the tailgate, but the hint of a dent had shown in one corner of the picture. The tailgate was open on this truck, an ATV extending onto the tailgate and held in place with several straps.

Could be another false alarm.

He swallowed his pessimism and settled in to follow the vehicle, his plans to go back to the hospital postponed. He couldn't see who was driving the truck. The ATV blocked his view. After a few turns he was positive it was a man but couldn't guess at the age. The truck turned onto a two-lane highway heading out of town, and Ollie frowned. *Please don't drive to Eastern Oregon.* He had less than a quarter tank of gas. Truman's rule to always fill the tank before only a quarter was left rang in his head.

Dammit.

He knew he should follow Truman's advice. But there was *so* much of it.

He hung back, not wanting to raise suspicion in the light traffic. After twenty minutes the red truck slowed and turned on its blinker.

Ollie's hot dog threatened to come back up. The truck was turning onto the road that passed by Bree's home.

It's a coincidence.

Sweat ran down his ribs under his shirt.

If this is the guy, he'd be stupid to drive by Bree's house.

Ollie barely breathed for the next two miles. When the truck turned down Bree's driveway, his vision tunneled, and dizziness attacked him. He drove past the driveway, too terrified to look down it.

I've got to call Mercy.

A quarter mile ahead, he parked at the same small turnout where he'd seen the truck the night of Bree's attack. With shaking hands, he dialed Mercy. It went immediately to voice mail, and he left a jumbled, nervous message, his heart pounding in his chest.

He dialed Truman next. Voice mail. He left another scramble of a message.

What the hell?

Do I call 911? He shook his head as he imagined explaining to an operator that he'd seen a red truck.

He sat still, a million options running through his head. His hand seemed to creep to the door handle of its own accord, and he knew what he was going to do. He got out of his pickup and darted through the underbrush toward Bree's. *I won't get too close. I'll just get a photo and hope it's the real license plate. Bree's not there. No one can get hurt this time.*

Pleased with his plan, he increased his speed.

It felt as if he ran forever. His lungs hurt, and he tripped twice, nearly landing on his face. The house finally came into sight, and he spotted the truck down near the barn. It was parked next to a Ford Explorer and a black Tahoe.

Ollie squinted at the Tahoe's license plate. *That's Mercy's vehicle.*

Confusion swamped him. *Was she meeting the driver of the red truck? Why here?*

Nothing made sense.

Two men had already unloaded the ATV from the long bed of the truck, a pair of narrow ramps tossed aside. Mercy was nowhere to be seen.

I've got to get closer. He stuck to the shadows of the home and then followed a hedge toward the barn, his back hunched as he tried to stay hidden.

"We should have brought two," one of the men complained.

Ollie stopped and lowered himself to the ground behind the hedge. The men were out of sight about twenty feet away.

"You can stay here."

"Like hell. I'm going."

"Then you'll have to deal with riding behind me. Get over it."

"Fuck you."

Silence stretched for a long moment. "Is that really how you want to talk to me?"

"I've taken all the risk. I've about had it."

"What exactly are you trying to say? You done? Because you can just say the word, and you're out."

Bitter laughter. "I'll never be out, and you know it."

"It was your choice."

"Don't I fucking know it. But it wasn't my choice to shoot that girl."

Ollie stopped breathing. *Kaylie?*

"She was about to blow everything open and put it online. She got too close. We didn't have a choice."

Tabitha Huff. Ollie closed his eyes.

"If *we* didn't have a choice, then how come I do all the shit work?"

"You didn't help me with Leah."

Who?

"That was your fucking ugly business."

The engine of the ATV came to life, and Ollie scooted closer, trying to listen over its noise. He could still hear the men's voices, but not the words. He peered through a thin spot in the hedge. Mercy's Tahoe was between him and the men. Moving to his hands and knees, he crawled through, the wiry branches scratching his face and arms. He dashed to the Tahoe and crouched low, moving around to the front of the vehicle.

"You sure you want to do this? She's a federal agent."

"I've got no choice."

The ATV's tires crunched over some gravel, and after a moment Ollie saw the men head south on the ATV through one of Bree's fields. Each had a rifle slung over a shoulder.

Mercy.

He dialed her number. Voice mail. "Dammit!"

He hit Truman's number again.

295

Truman waited at the bar for his sandwich. He hadn't been able to get Nick Walker's turkey club out of his head after his talk with Ina. On the walk back to town, he'd stopped back into Leaky's and ordered a club to go for dinner, knowing he'd be working late. He pulled out his phone as he waited and noted he'd missed a call from Mercy and one from Ollie. He listened to Mercy's recording. *Horseback? With Sandy?* He grinned at the thought of her on a horse, and his curiosity was piqued by her vague reference to a theory.

Must not be worth mentioning yet.

Fine with him. He started to open Ollie's voice mail.

"Evening, Truman."

Karl Kilpatrick pulled out and sat on the stool next to him. He held up a finger at the bartender, who nodded.

Truman put his phone back in his pocket. "Evening, Karl. On your own for dinner tonight?"

"Yep. Deborah didn't want to leave the hospital, but I've got animals to feed."

"Gotta feed yourself first," Truman said with a grin.

"Damn right. Deborah is an incredible cook, but sometimes I just want a beer and burger by myself."

Truman nodded. "Any news on Kaylie?"

"No change. The doctors say that's good news. She was awake while I was there. Poor kid." His face was glum.

"She's tough, but it will take a long time to move past this."

"She's had enough trauma in her life." Anger flashed in Karl's eyes.

Does he still hold Mercy responsible for his son's murder?

Truman kept his mouth shut. Karl and Mercy's issues were their own. He noticed Karl seemed thinner than usual. He'd always been a tall, lanky man, but his face was narrower and the skin under his chin looser. Mercy had mentioned her father hadn't looked well the last time she saw him. Truman had to agree.

He knew better than to ask. You didn't ask men like Karl about their health. That was private. He would stay mum about an illness until he fell over dead.

That's his right.

Besides, Deborah would inform the family if there were a real problem.

"That agent get fired for shooting Victor Diehl yet?" Karl asked, his eyes sharp under bushy eyebrows. "Man was just living his life."

Truman counted to ten. "Diehl shot Eddie Peterson. And then pointed a gun at two agents at close range." He purposefully didn't mention that one of those agents was Karl's daughter. Karl knew that fact; Mercy had told him herself.

"They had no business being on his property."

"I'm not the person to talk to about this. If you have a problem, take it up with the FBI."

"Hmph." The bartender set a beer before Karl, and he took a long draw. The tavern briefly lit up as the front door opened. Truman did a double take as he recognized Samuel's profile in the light. He held up a hand in greeting to his officer. Samuel's jaw was tight and his eyes hard.

Uh-oh. What happened?

"Truman. Karl." Samuel nodded at Mercy's father and then focused on Truman, his expression completely businesslike. "I've been looking into the finances of Sandy's B&B like you asked me to." His tone was grim. "That place almost went tits up several years ago."

"That doesn't surprise me. Sandy said it's been a hard road," said Truman, unease growing in his belly. Samuel clearly had something on his mind.

"She had a lot of repairs and remodeling done one year. I hunted down her contractor because I found it odd since she was virtually broke. He said she paid every single bill immediately—and some of them were pretty big invoices—in cash."

Truman's skin crawled. "That's what cash is for."

Exasperation crossed Samuel's face. "One time she invited him into her office to pay him. Shocked the hell out of him when she opened a small safe right in front of him and counted out three thousand dollars."

Truman stared at Samuel.

"And he could see more cash in the safe."

"That's a lot of money," said Karl, who'd been blatantly eavesdropping.

Truman's phone rang. *Ollie.*

"Hey—"

"Truman! I found the truck and I found the guy and he and another guy are headed out on an ATV and Mercy's truck is here too and they've got rifles—"

"Ollie. Slow the fuck down. What are you talking about?" *Did he say "rifles"?* Anxiety bloomed in the base of his spine.

The boy sucked in a breath. "I followed a red truck. They went to Bree's," he said in a staccato. "I think Mercy is here somewhere and they said they're looking for her."

The anxiety shot up his spinal cord, giving him an instant headache. "Did you see Mercy?"

Karl turned and looked at him sharply.

"No. Her Tahoe is here. They got on an ATV and headed across a field . . . One of them said he shot Tabitha Huff. And one asked the other if he wanted to *do this* to a federal agent."

Holy shit. Truman steadied his breathing. "Did you say 'rifles' before?"

"Yes. Each had a rifle."

Mercy said she was going somewhere on horseback with Sandy.

"Ollie, is Sandy's Ford Explorer there?"

"There's one here. I dunno whose it is."

"Shit." Truman's mouth went dry.

"What do I do, Truman? I can't follow them." Ollie's voice shook.

"I know. It's okay, Ollie. Mercy told me where they were going." His mind raced with panic as he tried to calm the teen. *I have no idea how to find the place she mentioned.*

"Where?"

"Horse's Head Rock."

Karl's eyebrows shot up.

"You know where that is?" Truman asked Karl, who nodded. "Ollie, stay there. I'm going to send Ben to get you."

"I can drive."

"Stay put anyway."

THIRTY-FIVE

"How do I get there?"

Adrenaline pumped through Truman. He and Samuel focused on Karl Kilpatrick. The closest person at his disposal who knew how to get to Horse's Head Rock.

"Helicopter would be the best way," Karl said, rubbing the back of his neck, his eyes pensive.

"*Helicopter?* Karl . . . do you really think I can afford a helicopter? I'm lucky to have all our department vehicles running smoothly at once."

"How about asking the FBI to pay for it? I'm sure they have the big bucks."

"Is this horse head location that remote?" Samuel asked.

"Yup." Karl looked from one man to the other.

"Mercy said she was riding in," Truman told him. "If you can get there by horseback, you should be able to get there by four-wheel drive."

"Nope. Not happening. There's a dense forest and rocks to wind through. Got a dirt bike?"

"Jesus Christ." Truman felt time ticking away. "Mercy is being followed by two guys with rifles. One of them killed that reporter, and I'm wondering if one of them shot your granddaughter." He glared at Karl. "One theory is that they thought they were firing at Mercy. Ollie just told me they mentioned Mercy specifically."

Karl held his gaze. "Your best bet is getting in on horseback."

"How do I do that?"

"I can loan you a couple of mounts. You ride?" He included Samuel in the question, who nodded immediately.

"I rode when I was a teen," Truman said. Summers with his uncle had included many hours on horseback. Usually drunken escapades with friends.

"Then you'll do fine. The best way in to Horse's Head Rock is off Old Sherman Road."

"Mercy and Sandy left from Bree Ingram's house."

Karl nodded. "I can see how they'd get there from that location. Old Sherman is a lot faster. Still remote and dense but faster."

"Perfect. You can get horses there?"

"Yep. Let me call one of my guys. He can load them up and meet us there."

"Thank you, Karl." Truman's heart slowed the slightest bit. *We have a plan.* Karl pulled out his cell phone, and Truman glanced at Samuel, who didn't look pleased. "What?"

"Those guys are on ATVs. They'll be way ahead of us."

"Got any other ideas?"

"No." He looked away, a muscle in his jaw twitching. "Was I wrong about Sandy?" he asked in a low voice.

Truman understood. Nothing like finding out you might be infatuated with a criminal. "We don't know the full story. Her money might have been legitimate."

"Don't know how," Samuel muttered. "Everything I saw and heard from her says she's always struggled."

"Maybe she got a loan back then."

"But paid people in cash?" Samuel was skeptical.

"How about we wait and ask her instead of jumping to conclusions?" Even as he said the words, Truman worried he'd missed something. An answer to the Gamble-Helmet Heist might have been living in his town for the last ten years. An answer that wanted to stay a secret.

Enough to murder?

Tabitha Huff was the answer to that question.

"Call Ben and tell him what's going on. We'll need county backup . . . if they can find the place."

Karl turned back to the two men. "Let's go." As he stood from his bar stool, his phone rang again. "Deborah," he mumbled, but he motioned for Truman and Samuel to start walking. He followed the two men out of Leaky's and then stopped. *"What?"* Karl shouted into the phone. "Why did she do that?"

Truman and Samuel both turned to listen. *Who?*

Karl's eyes widened. "Are you sure? That bad? Shit!"

Kaylie?

"I'll be right there." He hung up the phone, concern filling his face. "I gotta go."

"What?" Truman grabbed his arm as the man started to leave. "You need to show us how to get to Horse's Head. What the hell just happened?"

"Rose is in labor. She's been in labor all fucking day and didn't tell anyone, but she finally called Nick, who took her to the hospital. The baby is breech, and Rose is severely dehydrated from the flu. She wasn't taking care of herself, and they think that's why she went into early labor." He pulled his arm out of Truman's grasp and turned his back. "I gotta go."

Truman took a hard step and spun the older man around. "We've got to get to Mercy."

Fury shot from his green eyes. *Mercy's eyes.* "She's gonna have to wait."

"She can't wait!" Samuel moved into the man's face. "She doesn't know she's being followed by two killers. You have to see that takes precedence over Rose's labor."

A struggle raged in Karl's eyes.

He's always had a problem with Mercy. "Are you going to let your pride endanger Mercy, Karl?" Truman asked softly. "This isn't the time to hold old grudges."

"Rose—"

"Is in the hospital with doctors. What are you going to do there? Deliver her baby? She has professionals to help her." Truman paused, his gaze hard. "Mercy only has you. No one else."

The war in Karl's eyes continued. He didn't move.

"Jesus fucking Christ. She's your daughter," said Samuel. He unsnapped his weapon, and Truman shot an arm out to block him.

"Don't," he ordered his officer. "Does your guy bringing the horses know how to get there?" he asked Karl.

"I doubt it."

"Then we need you a hell of a lot more than Rose does right now."

Karl looked from Truman to Samuel, and resignation filled his gaze.

"Let's go."

Truman exhaled, shaking his head, and followed Mercy's father. Samuel caught up to him. "Was he really headed to sit uselessly in a hospital waiting room?" Samuel whispered.

"Yes."

"I had no idea his anger went so deep." Samuel's gaze shot daggers at Karl's back.

"I think it's more habit now than anything." Truman hoped that was true.

"He will regret that habit if something happens to Mercy."

Truman had his doubts.

◆ ◆ ◆

Thirty minutes later, Truman watched Karl and his hand back two horses out of a trailer.

"Wait a minute," Truman said. "Only two horses? Aren't you going with us?" he asked Karl.

"I don't ride anymore. My back can't take more than five minutes in the saddle."

"Don't you think you should have told us that to start with?" Samuel snapped.

Karl snorted. "I'm sure two intelligent *officers* like yourselves can follow a map."

"What map?" Truman ignored the sarcasm. Time was ticking loudly in his head.

Karl squatted and smoothed a stretch of dirt. He picked up a thin stick and started to draw.

You've got to be kidding me. Truman adjusted the rifle on his shoulder and moved closer to watch.

"We're right here." Karl made an *X* in the dirt. "Head south from here until you clear this part of the forest. Then go southeast for about . . . oh, say about twenty minutes at a trot, shorter at a canter. You'll see rock formations start. You'll need to loop this way for a bit and then look for a narrow pass between two of the tallest rocks." He continued to make scratches in the dirt. "When you come out of the pass, go east for another ten minutes—"

"At a trot?" Samuel asked, sarcasm heavy in his voice.

Karl just looked at him. "After ten minutes or so, you'll be at the ridge and can easily spot the one that looks like a horse's head. Lots of rocks, but only one looks like a horse."

"How much time total?" Truman asked.

"Depends how fast you go. Somewhere around forty minutes, I'd guess." Karl scowled. "Don't overwork my horses."

Truman stared at the dirt, trying to memorize Karl's marks. Samuel snapped a picture with his phone, making Truman feel like an idiot.

He looked at Mercy's father. "Thank you, Karl. For the horses and everything."

The man looked away. "Hope it works out for the best."

Not what I expect to hear from a father about his daughter.

"I'll be thinking of Rose," Truman told him. "A birth a month early isn't too bad. Lots of babies come that early."

Karl just nodded, his expression flat.

"Ready?" Truman asked Samuel, who nodded. He had a rifle on his shoulder and his game face on. The face that stated he was ready to kick butt.

Truman took the reins from Karl's helper, gripped them in place on the saddle's pommel, and slid his left foot into the stirrup. With a grunt he lifted himself up and threw his right leg over the horse's back. The horse didn't move a muscle as Truman's rear awkwardly slammed into the saddle.

Karl picked a good one for me.

He glanced at the sky, figuring they had a few hours of daylight left. Samuel and his mount moved beside him, and Samuel sat as if he'd lived in the saddle all his life.

"About time you showed us you really deserve that cowboy hat," Samuel joked, touching the brim of his own hat.

Truman snorted. "At least we've got the white hats."

Samuel's face went solemn. "Hope that's enough."

Truman lifted his reins and clucked to his horse, who moved straight into a jarring trot.

"I'm not relying on my hat."

Hang on, Mercy.

THIRTY-SIX

The view took Mercy's breath away.

She moved as close as she dared to the edge of the cliff. Dizziness swamped her as she looked straight down, and she jumped back two steps.

The face of the cliff was rock, but she couldn't see the bottom because trees growing on a gentle slope covered it. Beyond the trees, the land leveled out and extended east forever.

Sage and rocks and dirt. A few clumps of trees. A stretch of river far in the distance. It seemed to wind off the edge of the earth.

She looked over her shoulder, expecting to see the Cascade mountain peaks she loved so much, but trees on the top of the ridge blocked them.

"Stunning, isn't it?" Sandy asked, appearing beside her.

Mercy studied the tall redhead, her earlier doubts still percolating in her mind. Mercy had become on edge, watching Sandy for any sign of deception. But Sandy had seemed to grow more relaxed the longer the trip went on. Mercy relaxed too.

But not too much.

"This was Bree's happy spot, but it's become mine too," Sandy told her with a genuine smile.

"It's amazing." Mercy turned to admire the horse head formation. "I can see where it got its name," she said. "But it needs more of a neck."

That drew a snort from Sandy. "Right? It's rather stumpy looking. Still obviously a horse, though."

The formation towered a good thirty feet over Mercy to her right. The outline of its face was a gentle downward slope east toward the cliff. At the top, two triangular extensions formed ears, and then the rock sloped down again for the neck. It even had hollows for nostrils and a round bulge where its left eye should be.

"There's no eye on the right side," said Sandy. "But the shape of the cheek is much more pronounced."

"It's amazing," said Mercy. "I can't believe I've never heard of it before."

"Bree said even Indians referred to it as the horse's head."

"I can imagine the reverence they felt for this figure. It's majestic. No wonder Bree buried stuff next to it for good luck. It makes me feel like I need to leave an offering."

"Right here is where Bree dug up the crystal." Sandy strode over and pushed her shovel into the dirt not far from the horse. "Oh God. This is going to suck. It's nearly as hard as the rock."

Mercy copied her movement and found her statement to be true.

They dug in silence for a few minutes, occasionally hitting rocks and not making nearly the progress that Mercy had hoped. Mercy took off her jacket and tossed it aside. At least it wasn't boiling hot. It was a warm day, but plenty of fluffy clouds kept the sun from being unbearable.

"I'm sorry I upset you the other day in Truman's office," Mercy told Sandy as she tossed aside a tiny shovelful of dirt and watched Sandy's reaction out of the corner of her eye.

"You were doing your job." Sandy huffed as she spoke. "I can't be offended by questions when that young woman was murdered, Bree was beat up, and your niece was shot. I overreacted."

Kaylie flashed in Mercy's mind. Hopeful, she pulled out her phone. No service.

"Told ya," Sandy said.

"Just checking." Mercy looked up as she heard the engine of a far-off plane. The blue of the sky and the white clouds looked fake—as if from a painting.

Sandy stopped and used the hem of her shirt to wipe sweat from her brow. "This is a pain in the butt."

"Just think of all the money you might find."

Sandy laughed. "I don't think I'll get to keep it." She gave Mercy a hopeful look. "Or would I?"

"I don't think so."

"What I would do with two million dollars," Sandy said softly as she plunged her shovel into the ground. "No more problems."

"I suspect that was what the robbers thought too. I'd say the money brought them some problems." She pictured Ellis Mull's skull. "And worse."

Mercy's shovel clinked. Her heart racing, she bent down and brushed away the dirt. Rock.

Disappointment radiated through her. They'd hit rock at least a dozen times. She leaned on her shovel and looked around. "There's got to be an easier place to bury things."

"We can scout out the right side, but there's more rock than this one." Sandy put her shovel on her shoulder and looked to the horses they'd tied up in the little grove of pines. "I don't think they're going anywhere." Neither horse had moved, and they both looked bored.

"This way," said Sandy. She led Mercy along the rock horse's neck and into another small grove of pathetically ratty-looking pines. They looked exactly as one would expect with little access to water and rich soil. Mercy followed, threading between the trees. They rounded the rock that formed the neck and came out on the south side of the horse. Sandy was right. No eyeball.

The ground was all rock. Mercy's heart sank.

"You're right to call this a wild-goose chase," Sandy said softly. "I'm sorry I took you away from your niece in the hospital. I jumped to stupid conclusions based on Bree saying 'buried.'" Sandy slammed her shovel tip into the dirt. "*Really* stupid conclusions. When you told me Bree might know one of the thieves, I couldn't get it out of my head that she'd loaned me money from the robbery."

Mercy plopped down on a rock bulge. "Where else would Bree have hidden money?"

"We're assuming she had the money," Sandy pointed out as she sat next to Mercy. "I hope we can ask her at some point." Her voice cracked, and sympathy filled Mercy.

"She's a tough woman. Bree will pull through this." She patted Sandy awkwardly on the shoulder, unsure of how to comfort the woman. Mercy wasn't a hugger. Although Kaylie and Rose had pulled more hugs out of Mercy in the last eight months than she'd given in the previous fifteen years.

"They say the longer she's unconscious, the worse her chances of full memory recovery," Sandy whispered, wiping her eyes.

"Don't give her problems that don't exist yet," ordered Mercy.

"She's so strong," said Sandy, staring at the amazing vista. "There have been several times when I've fallen apart over money . . . stress . . . customers, and she was always there to pick me up." She turned to Mercy. "You know how many times I've picked her up? None. The closest I've seen her come to cracking was the other day, when she told me about the reporter confronting her."

"Everyone adores her."

"I'm sorry I brought you up here on a stupid whim." Sandy sighed and wiped her eyes. "I was so sure . . ."

309

"It was worth checking out. Why don't we look around a little more?" she suggested, looking at the spread of rock under their feet. *Art was right. This lead was a disappointment.*

"How about over there?" Sandy pointed at a patch of dirt with a few scraggly weeds. It was a good twenty feet from the horse.

Why not?

◆ ◆ ◆

Sandy was embarrassed.

At least Mercy has been a good sport about it.

She and Mercy had dug for a good hour and turned up squat.

How did I come up with such a wild idea?

Mercy paused, leaned on her shovel handle, and wiped the back of her neck. But Sandy could tell she wasn't giving up.

"I'll dig some more near our first spot," Sandy told her. "You keep on this one." Guilt was making it hard for her to work next to the agent.

Mercy nodded and continued to dig.

Sandy worked her way around the horse's neck, fighting back tears. *How could I be so stupid?* And she'd convinced an FBI agent to join her on the quest. Mercy would never take anything she said seriously again. Sandy eyed the large patch of ground they'd disturbed. They hadn't gone very deep—they couldn't. The type of soil and the rocks made it impossible. Sandy inhaled and looked around. *Where would I bury treasure?*

She thought back to the times she'd been here with Bree. *Was there something Bree had always checked out?* As lovely as the spot was, Bree insisted they visit a little too often. Sandy had always assumed it was because of the beauty—because it was drop-dead amazing—but now she wondered if Bree had been checking on her prize.

She leaned her shovel against the horse's neck and ran her hands over the cracks and grooves, working her way to its head. Bree had often petted the horse's head. Sandy looked up at the ears nearly thirty feet in the air. *There's no way I can get up there. And I've never seen Bree go up there.*

The money would have to be reachable but hidden well enough from casual visitors.

She climbed up a few feet, still checking the grooves.

"You find my money?" A male voice spoke behind her.

Instant sweat bloomed under Sandy's armpits. Hanging on by her fingertips, she looked over her shoulder.

I don't know him.

He wasn't a big man. In fact, he was compact and wiry. But the rifle in his hands seemed huge. His clothes were well worn, his denim a grungy white in places. His salt-and-pepper hair was a good month past needing a cut, and he'd last shaved at least a week ago. His eyes . . .

Sandy swallowed.

Wrinkles and heavy lids spoke to his age, but his eyes were the most intense she'd ever seen. Icy blue and staring lasers through her skull.

"Answer me," he said calmly.

"No money." Her voice was hoarse.

He took in the large dirt area she and Mercy had overturned.

"Not for the lack of trying, I see. Where did Bree say the money was?"

A dozen scenarios ran through her head. The first showed him shooting her as soon as the money was found.

I'm dead if it's found.

She put her finger to her lips and jerked her head, indicating the other side of the horse. The man's eyes narrowed on her. "What? It's on the other side?"

Sandy shook her head, shushing him as she held her finger to her lips.

Understanding flashed. "I know you're not alone." He grinned. "Don't want the feds to find it, eh?"

He believes me.

She nodded and slowly stepped down from her perch, attempting to hide how badly her knees shook.

"Well, we'll take care of her and then you can show us."

Us?

Mercy peered from the scrubby pines and caught her breath. A man stood near the rock formation, his rifle aimed at Sandy, who had climbed partway up the horse's head.

Sandy's eyes were wide, her mouth slightly open as she stared down at him.

Mercy drew her weapon. *I have cause.* She lined up her shot, her heart strangely calm, his torso in her sights.

Metal dug into her temple.

Her heart stuttered as she froze.

Who?

"Can't let you do that, Mercy."

That voice. Mercy briefly closed her eyes and lowered her weapon. *It can't be.* A stabbing sensation rose in her chest.

It's him.

Art snatched the gun out of her hands and flung it into the trees.

She turned her head the slightest bit, pressing her temple harder into the gun, and met his gaze. "Fuck you. You fucking rat." Anger shook her voice.

He smiled, but the emotion didn't reach his eyes. "You know nothing about me." Art roughly searched her with one hand, taking too much time at her breasts.

"You've been wanting to do that for years, right?" she snapped.

"In my dreams every night, babe."

Realizations swamped her brain.

"You screwed up this investigation at every turn. You tried to get me to go to *Canada*, for God's sake." Anger flooded her. "Have you done that since the very beginning? *For thirty years?*" Her fingers flexed, aching to squeeze and destroy something. Preferably his black heart.

"Walk," Art ordered, moving the gun to press her spine. "Over by her."

Refusing to raise her hands, she marched over to where Sandy now stood, below the horse's cheek. Sandy blinked rapidly but seemed in control of herself.

Mercy crossed her arms and took in the second man, who still held a rifle on Sandy, recognizing the eyes and shape of his face immediately. She'd stared at his photos a thousand times. "Trevor Whipple," she stated. "I've been looking for you." She tilted her head and frowned. "You look *a lot* older than the photos we had digitally aged."

Art snorted, but Trevor's icy-blue eyes glared at her.

"Life on the run hasn't treated you well," she continued, deliberately running her gaze up and down him, lingering on the handgun in his shoulder holster. "Scuffed work boots . . . jeans about to disintegrate . . . dirt ground deep into your hands. I don't think you lived the life of a millionaire. I'd guess you ended up as a ranch hand."

Trevor's barrel moved from Sandy to Mercy. Glancing at Art, she saw concern flash in his eyes. *Is Art not wholly committed to Trevor's plan?*

"It's not too late, Art," Mercy said. "Right now all you've done is point a weapon at me. I can't help you if you take it further." Her gaze went from his pistol to the rifle slung on his shoulder.

Two men. Four weapons.

Trevor laughed, and Mercy noticed his teeth were brown. *He was the charmer of the robbery bunch?*

"Oh, it's way too late for Art, Special Agent Kilpatrick. Waaaay too late." He laughed again.

313

Anger flickered across Art's face, and Mercy felt her heart sink. "What did you do, Art?" she whispered.

He said nothing, his face carefully blank.

Trevor looked from Art to Mercy. "Aren't you going to answer the special agent?" he prodded, his grin widening. "Tell her."

Mercy could barely breathe.

"I'm disappointed in you, Art," Trevor said with fake sorrow. He winked at Mercy. "Art here had a run-in with a reporter."

"Don't tell me you shot Tabitha Huff," she said softly, the dead woman's face fresh in her memory.

He looked away.

But Mercy knew.

"What did Trevor have on you, Art?" she asked. "What would push you to murder?"

"Shut up," said Trevor. He pointed his rifle back at Sandy. "This lady has also been telling you lies, Special Agent Kilpatrick. She knows exactly where the money is."

Every time he said Mercy's title, he slurred it like an expletive.

Mercy wasn't done with Art. "You were an FBI agent!" She hurled the words at him. "What was your price to betray your country? Thirty pieces of silver?"

Satisfaction filled her soul at his flinch.

Trevor sneered. "His price was two hundred grand."

Mercy contemplated Art with disgust. "For two hundred grand, you spent thirty years misleading a major investigation." She moved her gaze to Trevor. "What happened to your part of the money? You didn't spend it on clothes."

"Fuck you."

The rifle pointed her way again.

"Did Art come to you, Trevor? Did he track you down, and then you bought your way out?"

"Something like that. The feds were getting close. His wife had died, and he was drowning in medical bills. Once I discovered that, I knew I had him."

She turned a bitter gaze on Art. "Your sob story about your wife's cancer feels a little hollow now."

Art had kept his handgun pointed at the ground until now. He raised it, and a chill washed over Mercy as he pointed it directly at her head. "Do not talk about my wife." His voice was low, his words shrouded in pain.

Mercy didn't care. She turned her contempt to Trevor. "Did you shoot Ellis Mull?"

He sneered. "I didn't do it. It was that tiny little bitch."

He means Bree. She was the driver, not Sandy.

"Bull," Mercy said.

"No bull." Trevor flashed his brown teeth again. "She was vicious." He looked at Sandy. "Leah—Bree—told you where her money is. Spill it."

"Bree had money left? After thirty years? I doubt that," Mercy told him.

"Then why the fuck are you digging?"

"If I didn't, I'd always wonder if it existed, but I admit it was a long shot. Apparently your money didn't last long." She frowned. "Just how much did you end up with?"

Art's uncertain expression kept her peppering Trevor with questions. He wasn't completely on Trevor's side. She felt it and would press that advantage as long as she could.

No SWAT team is going to drop from the sky.

There is no other hope.

I know there is a decent man in there somewhere.

Trevor shrugged. "I took Ellis's portion along with my own. Leah and Nathan split with the rest of the money. Never saw her again until recently."

Bree shot Ellis, but you got his money? Right.

"What about Shane Gamble? He was just out of luck? No one held money for him in case he got out of prison?"

"Dunno. Ask Leah. She was his girlfriend."

Sandy gasped. "You're lying."

Trevor raised a brow at her. "They were hot and heavy. He brought her in at the last minute to drive for us but promised the money would still be split four ways."

Why am I surprised Gamble lied to me?

"It must have been a new relationship," Mercy murmured. "There's no record of a girlfriend." *Gamble protected Bree by telling the investigators the driver was "Jerry"?*

"Yeah." Trevor was done with the topic. "You. Redhead. Where's the money?"

Sandy was silent.

Trevor moved closer, his barrel inches from her face. "Where. Is. The. Money."

Lunge and shove the barrel up. Mercy saw it play out in her mind. *Could I get control of the rifle?* Trevor would still have a handgun. And there was Art to consider.

A faint tremor shot through Sandy.

"A minute ago you were my best friend," Trevor sneered. "Telling me you'd kept it secret from the feds. Now spill it!"

Sandy didn't speak.

Trevor hooked his rifle over his shoulder and stepped up, grabbing her ponytail in his fists, yanking her head to the left and down. Mercy took a step to grab his handgun.

"Mercy! Stop!"

She froze at Art's command. His handgun was pointed at her again, his eyes deadly serious this time. *He will shoot me.* She eyed the rifle over Trevor's shoulder. *Can I get that away from him?*

Trevor dragged Sandy toward the cliff. She fell to her knees as he hauled her by the hair, screaming and thrashing to get her hair out of his hands. Sandy was tall and strong, but surprise and terror had given him the advantage. Her piercing shrieks made the hair rise on Mercy's arms as she stood helplessly, watching her friend be dragged to a certain death.

Sandy flung herself on her stomach, using her entire body weight against him. Trevor continued to wrench her closer to the edge, swearing at the woman, pulling clumps of hair from her ponytail.

Shaking, Mercy looked at Art. He wasn't watching Trevor; he was watching her. "Try me," he stated.

"Where is the money?" Trevor shouted at Sandy. He had her at the rim, her head over the edge. He knelt on the center of her back as he seized her head and forced her to look down. "See those trees down there? Wanna join them?"

Mercy ached to cover her ears and drown out Sandy's cries. She screamed like a dying animal.

Trevor let go of the hair and pushed on Sandy's hip, shoving her body around to the edge.

He's going to roll her off.

"*Safety-deposit box!*" Sandy shrieked.

Trevor stopped. "Where?"

"Eagle's Nest." She started to sob, big gulping wet sobs.

Trevor hauled Sandy around until she was sitting upright with her back to the vista. "That's a good girl." He patted her head, and she jerked it away.

Sandy looked to Mercy, her eyes wet and full of fear. "Bree didn't want the FBI to know."

"You dragged me up here just to make me think you were helping?"

"She wanted the FBI to give up searching for the money. Believe it was gone."

"I knew it wasn't gone," Trevor crowed. He pointed enthusiastically at Art. "Told ya. I knew Leah would hold some of it for Shane."

"You think she held money for Shane Gamble for thirty years?" asked Mercy. "No woman is devoted to an absent guy for that long—especially a murderer." She swallowed. "Where's Nathan May and his money?"

"Don't care," said Trevor. "I found Leah, and that's enough for now." He threw back his head and laughed. "Could have knocked me senseless when I saw her face in the paper for some teaching award. I knew God was leading me to the money." He grinned. "Man, she was good at protecting her secret. It was worth two fingers to her."

Mercy lost her breath.

"You evil fuck," Sandy shouted from the ground, anger replacing her fear. "You tortured her for money you *hoped* existed? She might never be the same when she wakes up." Tears ran down her cheeks, and her hands curled into fists.

Mercy eyed Art. "What do you get out of this? I understand what you got back then, but now?" *Come on, Art.*

"I agreed I wouldn't rat his ass out," replied Trevor cheerfully. "No one will know about the money I gave him, how he lied at his job, or about the women he shot. Otherwise I'd tell—"

"'Women'?" Mercy cut in. Fury boiled under her skin.

"He's lucky the second woman is alive, since he thought she was *you*." Trevor savored the last word, his cocky gaze full of glee at the firework he'd just lit.

Mercy's focus settled on Art like a spotlight. Everything else was black.

"You almost killed my niece . . . because you thought it was me . . ."

Her legs wobbled. *I'm not going down.*

Art looked away.

318

"What happened to you, Art?"

Images of Kaylie bleeding, terrified out of her wits and asking if she was going to die, ricocheted in Mercy's mind. She longed to launch herself at the prick and pound his face until his blood ran like Kaylie's. But she was frozen.

"I trusted you," she whispered.

THIRTY-SEVEN

Truman and Samuel had found the narrow pass between two rocks and had been moving east for a good fifteen minutes. Truman was antsy, his gaze constantly darting around for the rock shaped like a horse head. Karl had said ten minutes from the pass, but it was an estimate.

There was no horse rock anywhere to be seen.

"Dammit," Samuel muttered.

"No shit."

"Was Karl wrong?"

"That narrow pass was definitely as he described," Truman stated, remembering how it'd threatened to trigger his anxiety when he couldn't see the way out. Now they were faced with a light spread of small pines and other trees. Karl hadn't mentioned those.

"He said the rock structure overlooked a valley. We haven't seen any cliffs yet, so let's keep going. Maybe it's on the other side of this grove," said Samuel, giving his horse a squeeze with his legs, his back straight and chin up. His hips naturally followed the movement of the horse, making it look as if he'd ridden all his life.

Truman urged his horse to follow Samuel. They'd cantered a good part of the way, feeling the pressure to get to Mercy and Sandy. When sweat had foamed on the horses' necks, they'd slowed to a walk, and now it seemed as if they were crawling.

After a minute Samuel pulled to a stop. "Truman," he said in a low voice as he pointed far ahead in the trees.

An ATV.

Truman immediately scanned their surroundings. Nothing. All quiet. "Let's move in a little closer."

"We need to go on foot," Samuel stated. "I don't think backup is coming soon," he added. "There's no way county can get here quickly."

"Mercy is our backup." *I hope.*

Samuel gave him a skeptical look but nodded.

Both men dismounted and wrapped their reins around a tree, giving the horses enough slack to graze, and then drew their weapons. They carefully moved to the ATV while constantly watching their surroundings. The ATV was old and beat-up, and Truman wondered how it'd made the journey from Bree's house carrying two men.

"I bet the ridge is directly east. They left the ATV here to go in quietly," Samuel said in a hushed voice.

"Let's go."

The two men moved cautiously through the grove of small trees. The ground was either rocks or packed dry dirt and was covered with old pine needles that continually cracked and snapped under their boots.

A piercing scream made Truman catch his breath.

"Sandy," said Samuel, looking pale.

Not Mercy.

Is that good or bad?

Male and female shouts sounded ahead, and Truman moved faster. As he got closer to the edge of the grove, he saw the back of a giant rock sitting on the edge of the ridge. Beyond the rock all he saw was blue sky; the ground dropped away. To the left, he made out three figures. *No, four. One is on the ground.* Spotting the red hair, he realized one of the men was struggling with Sandy. Relief swept through him as he spotted Mercy standing next to the rock.

He stared at the man with a weapon on her. *Holy shit. Art Juergen. How is Art involved in this?*

Money. Two million dollars went missing.

"Samuel," he whispered. "That's the FBI agent who assisted with the robbery case."

Shock crossed Samuel's features. "The retired one?"

"Yes." *The one Mercy trusted implicitly.*

"Mercy must be livid."

"I suspect that's putting it mildly."

How long has he lied to her?

"I don't recognize the other guy," said Truman. "Say . . . see that?" He pointed at a shovel leaning against the rock.

"Yeah. And the ground is all dug to hell." Samuel paused. "Holy crap. Were Sandy and Mercy digging for money?"

"That's my guess," Truman whispered, understanding why Mercy hadn't elaborated in her voice mail. Searching for buried treasure sounded ridiculous.

The screaming had stopped, and Sandy sat on the ground, her head down and her shoulders sagging. Truman couldn't hear the conversation, but the man by Sandy seemed quite pleased. Mercy's body language verified that she was furious.

"I'll go to the right of the rock," Samuel said softly.

"Left for me. I'll come in behind Juergen." Truman was still appalled at the sight of the former agent.

Money changes everyone.

Samuel moved right, pine needles crackling under his boots. Truman went left and spotted two tied horses that must belong to Sandy and Mercy. He moved until the horses blocked the people at the rock from seeing him.

Both horses lifted their heads and swiveled their ears toward him as their gazes locked on him in alert fascination.

Please no.

One gave a high-pitched whinny in his direction.

Mercy's center of balance was forward, and every muscle focused on Trevor's moves, waiting for his concentration to waver, aware she'd have a split second to make a decision. Being shot by Art was a risk she'd have to take.

At the whinny, Trevor turned toward the horses, and Mercy exploded into action, surging forward.

"Hey—" he started.

Mercy snatched the loosely held rifle from his left hand and swung the butt at his head like a bat, every ounce of her strength in the swing.

He ducked, but the rifle hit a glancing blow off his face. Mercy hurled the rifle over the cliff and had his handgun out of his holster before Trevor could see straight again. She pivoted behind him, snagged his neck in a chokehold, and pointed his weapon at Art.

At Mercy's lunge, Sandy scrambled and grabbed the shovel. She faced Art, her legs planted and slightly bent, the blade in front of her chest, ready to attack or defend.

"Behind me," Mercy ordered, panting for breath, every nerve throbbing with energy. Sandy obeyed, stepping sideways, her gaze never leaving Art.

Trevor thrashed, and Mercy tightened her arm. "Hold the fuck still," she said in his ear. His hands dug at her arm. She placed the tip of the barrel against Trevor's temple, her gaze locked on Art, and Trevor stilled.

Just try me.

Trevor wasn't the best shield, but he'd do.

I have no other options.

Art hadn't moved during the scramble. He stood in the same position, his weapon still trained on Mercy, his face blank.

Her gamble with Art's unwillingness to fire at her had paid off.

It could have gone so wrong.

"Damn you, Mercy. Don't make me do this." His voice cracked.

"You already did it when you shot my niece." She raised an eyebrow. "You don't want to try it again? What's one more murder?"

"Shoot her!" Trevor forced out, gasping for air.

His pulse thrummed in triple time against her arm.

"He's more likely to hit you," she muttered. She knew it, and Art knew it.

Does he care if he shoots Trevor?

My human shield is expendable. With Trevor dead, Art was free.

Art had to decide if he wanted another murder in his ledger. His weapon wavered, doubt in his eyes.

What will he do?

Her muscles were frozen to the point of pain, her brain scrambling through possible scenarios. None ended well.

At least I gave us a chance.

She shoved despair out of her thoughts. *I'm not giving up yet.*

I have to take a shot. She would have to move her weapon from Trevor's temple toward Art, and she suspected he'd shoot the moment her hand shifted. He wasn't going to give her a second chance. Odds were not in her favor.

It's my only choice.

Motion behind Art caught her eye. *Truman.*

She kept her expression stable, her gaze sharp on Art, as she mentally deflated in relief.

Don't give Truman away.

Apprehension halted her reprieve; Truman was in a bad position.

His weapon was aimed at Art's back, but if he missed Art, Mercy or Sandy could be hit.

I can't shoot at Art for the same reason. Truman could be hit.

The dilemma incensed her.

Art narrowed his eyes at her. "Who's behind me?" he hissed. He raised his voice and called out, "My finger is on the trigger. I'll put a bullet through both of them."

He's right. At this close distance, shooting Trevor means shooting me.

"Juergen," said Truman calmly. "Put your weapon down." Truman sidestepped slowly toward the cliff, trying to angle Mercy and Sandy out of his shot.

Art heard the crunch of Truman's steps and shifted, staying aligned between Mercy and Truman.

"Put it down, Art," Mercy asked. "This isn't worth it."

"And end up in prison for the rest of my life? I don't think so."

"You were a good agent, Art. I'm sorry this scum"—she squeezed Trevor's neck, making him squawk—"this scum blackmailed you." Trevor dug frantically at her arm, trying to loosen her hold, and she pressed the weapon into his head again. He froze.

It wasn't blackmail thirty years ago. It was Art's greed.

"I'll do my best to get you in one of those country club federal prisons," Mercy offered, knowing the murder of Tabitha Huff made it impossible.

Art laughed, a pathetic, suffocating laugh. "Quit trying to bullshit me, Mercy. I took the negotiation workshops too."

"I didn't," said Truman. "Put your fucking weapon down before I blow a hole in your skull like you did to Tabitha Huff, Juergen." He continued his slow steps, but Art kept perfect pace with him.

Art has eyes in the back of his head.

Truman's gaze darted beyond her and to her left. *He's not alone.* She imagined Truman's accomplice attempting to line up a shot from behind the horse's neck. It was nearly impossible.

Sandy kept a hand on Mercy's back for balance. Small tremors flowed through her fingers to Mercy's skin, and her rough breaths were loud in the tense air.

Art's bullet won't go through three of us. She's safe.

"Truman," said Sandy in a hoarse voice. "He shot Kaylie. He thought she was Mercy."

Mercy flinched but held her focus.

"You shot a child," Truman said flatly behind Art. "Tell me why I shouldn't shoot you in the back right now."

"You know as well as I do," Art stated. "You could accidentally kill your woman." He held Mercy's gaze. "I'm truly sorry for your niece, Mercy."

Mercy's knuckles turned white on Trevor's weapon. "Bullshit. You tried to kill *me.*" She concentrated to keep her arm steady. "You know what, Art? Remember how I told you I wanted to be friends after our one date? That was bullshit too. I refused because you were *too old for me!*"

Rage flashed on his face.

I pushed too hard.

She braced for his shot.

But the rage vanished, and his features sagged, turning him into an old man.

His transformation staggered her. The confident FBI agent was no more.

"I'm sorry, Mercy." He lowered the weapon, and Sandy noisily exhaled behind her.

He looks ready to fall apart. His weapon rose a few degrees and turned toward his head.

"Art! Don't!" she ordered. He met her gaze, and she silently pleaded with him. His hand halted, but his face filled with regret.

Mercy didn't relax and kept her eyes locked on him. "It's going to be okay, Art. You don't need to do that. Everything will be fine," she said automatically.

He knows it will never be fine again.

"Toss your gun back here," Truman commanded. "And then remove the rifle."

Art stretched out his arms and let the pistol dangle from one finger. He raised his chin, his eye contact staying with Mercy, looking ready for a crucifixion.

"Thank you, Art," she said, exhaling some of her tension.

He has a long road ahead of him.

He slowly rotated ninety degrees to his left, stopping to look out over the endless view.

"Your gun," Truman reminded him.

Art didn't move.

Mercy backed out of Truman's line of fire, dragging Trevor with her.

If Art fires at Truman, I won't hold back.

Art tossed the gun aside toward Truman, his arms still outstretched. He removed the rifle and flung it in the same direction.

Thank God.

Art looked back at Mercy, remorse in his gaze.

She said nothing. It was over. Art would never be a free man again.

He sacrificed—

Art darted two steps and leaped off the cliff.

Mercy couldn't breathe. Screams sounded in her head.

He didn't.

Art . . .

Truman lunged toward the ridge, his desperate act too late. He stumbled, landed on his chest, and slid partway over the edge. His head and arms dangled off the cliff, as he looked straight down hundreds of feet. Sandy shrieked and grabbed Mercy's shoulder, nearly knocking her over.

"Truman!" Mercy started to release Trevor to grab Truman, but loud thumps made her spin to her left. Samuel sprinted toward Truman. He grabbed the man's boots and hauled him back.

Truman rolled onto his back, staring at the sky, his chest heaving. "Holy fuck."

"No shit," answered Samuel. The officer took a tentative step to look over the edge and stepped back immediately.

"I didn't see him," said Samuel in a stunned voice. "No way he survived that."

"No," Truman agreed, still lying on his back. He turned his head and met Mercy's gaze.

Did that just happen?

Art is dead.

She couldn't speak. Her knees shook.

Art is dead. The phrase echoed in her mind.

Samuel took Trevor from her chokehold, and her arm's muscles protested as she straightened it. Samuel rapidly searched and cuffed Trevor.

"Oh my God," Sandy said, covering her face with her hands. "I'm going to see that for the rest of my life."

"Me too," Mercy said hoarsely. "Are you okay?"

"My scalp is burning, but I'm fine." Sandy dropped to the dirt and sat cross-legged, her shoulders slumping. "I just need to sit down."

Mercy did too. Truman sat up as she walked over. She took one of his hands and lowered herself heavily beside him. "I don't think anyone's legs feel very strong at the moment." She breathed hard as she looked off in the distance. The stunning vista felt tainted.

Could I have stopped him?

Truman awkwardly pulled her into his lap. "I need a moment," he said, burying his face in her neck.

She held her lips to his temple. "You're not the only one."

"I can't believe—"

"Don't talk about it right now," she ordered. The sight of Art leaping off the ridge would haunt her forever. It flashed on constant replay in her head.

328

They were silent for several seconds, each simply breathing and taking strength from the other.

"I love you," he stated.

She pressed her face harder into his rough stubble. "I love you more."

Samuel cleared his throat. "It's getting late. Can we take this asshole back to the station?"

Trevor glared at him.

Mercy didn't unwrap her arms from Truman's shoulders. "That's Trevor Whipple," she said. "He admitted torturing Bree to get her to tell him the location of the money left over from the robbery."

Truman started under her tight grip. "He's one of the original thieves?" He looked at the man. "Where the hell have you been for thirty years?"

Trevor was silent.

"We were right about Bree. She was the driver for the robbery." Mercy turned to Sandy, who still sat on the ground, the shovel across her lap. "Sandy . . . is the money really in a safety-deposit box?"

She slowly shook her head. "I lied," she whispered.

I knew it.

"I thought if they believed the money was in a bank, they would drag us back to town and not shoot us right here." Sandy's face crinkled, and tears threatened. "I'm sorry . . . I don't know anything about the money. Bree never told me. I was stupid to think she might have hid it up here."

"I guess we'll have to ask Bree when she wakes," stated Truman.

If she wakes.

Truman jerked in her arms. "Rose is in labor," he blurted. "I forgot to tell you."

Joy radiated through Mercy. *A month early . . . that's not too bad.* "We were a little busy, so I'll let it go this time." She kissed Truman's rough cheek but then frowned at the concern on his face. "What is it?"

"The baby is breech, and Rose is dehydrated from the flu. Everyone was rushing to the hospital when we left."

Worry for her sister made her crawl out of Truman's lap, her anxiety spiking. "We need to go." *Babies are breech all the time.*

But this is my sister.

"Your dad nearly went to the hospital instead of coming with us."

"My dad? He's here?" Surprise made Mercy search the area.

"He's not here, but he brought us his horses and provided directions to get here." He met Mercy's eyes. "He had to choose between going to Rose or helping you. He chose you."

He chose me.

Her head swam, and she felt as if she were peering over the cliff again.

THIRTY-EIGHT

The sky was just starting to darken as the group headed home. Knowing Rose was in labor made Mercy want to gallop her horse back.

But she stayed with the group.

They agreed to ride back to Bree's farm. Her barn had room for the two extra horses until Karl could come get them. Truman drove the ATV with Trevor cuffed behind him, and Samuel led Truman's horse. Trevor mouthed off several times. Truman finally threatened to tie him over a horse on his stomach, and he stayed quiet after that.

Mercy checked for cell phone reception two dozen times.

They were nearly to Bree's when she finally reached Pearl on the phone. She pelted her sister with a dozen questions.

"Slow down," Pearl ordered. "I can't answer everything at once. Kaylie's resting comfortably. The doctors are breathing a little easier because it's been twenty-four hours without a sign of infection."

Relief swamped Mercy.

"She's complaining that she can't see Rose even though they're in the same hospital," said Pearl.

Mercy couldn't help but smile. *That's my girl.* A good sign that Kaylie was on the mend.

"And Rose?" Mercy held her breath.

"She had a C-section. They couldn't turn the baby. The doctor preferred the surgery instead of attempting a vaginal birth, and Rose didn't have strength left for any kind of birth. The flu was really hard on her."

"Is the baby at risk from the flu?" Mercy whispered.

"They talked about separating Rose from the baby—"

"Oh no," Mercy gasped.

"But Rose's fever has been under control, and her lungs are clear. They don't believe she's contagious any longer, just wiped out and dehydrated, so they'll let the baby be with her if she wears a mask and washes her hands nonstop."

"When can we see her?"

"She's in recovery right now. Nick said she'll be in her room in about an hour."

"What did she have?" Mercy blurted.

Pearl laughed. "I wondered when you would ask. She had a boy, but I'll let Rose tell you the name when you see her."

"Ohhh. Darn you! That's going to drive me nuts."

"Dad said Truman was worried you were in some sort of danger," Pearl stated with a question in her tone.

"It's all good," Mercy said, too tired to tell the story. "We'll be at the hospital in a few hours. Tell Rose we're coming."

"She asked about you several times while she was in labor."

Guilt punched her in the chest. "I promised her I'd be there," Mercy said. "I told her she could count on me if no one else was available, and I let her down."

Pearl snorted. "Well, everyone was available except for you. I'd say you're off the hook."

"I wanted to be there," she said softly.

"We've been sitting in a waiting room for hours. No one was allowed in the surgery but Nick. You haven't missed anything."

The words didn't comfort her.

◆ ◆ ◆

It was midnight when Mercy and Truman finally reached the hospital.

Truman sent a text to Nick, who replied that they were currently awake, and then met them at the nurses' station to okay their visit. The tall man looked exhausted but ecstatic. Even though Nick had spent hours at the hospital and probably been sanitized from head to toe, Mercy smelled his usual scent of fresh-cut lumber. She and Truman followed him through security doors and down a hallway. Outside Rose's door, he pointed at the hand sanitizer on the wall, and both cleaned their hands. The lights were low as they entered Rose's room, and she turned her face toward Mercy.

A God-size punch hit Mercy in the chest at the sight of Rose sitting in bed holding her baby.

She's beautiful.

The few lights illuminated the head of Rose's bed, giving her a Madonna-like presence.

"Mercy?" she asked, her voice muffled behind her mask.

"Yes." Mercy was at her side in a split second, all eyes for the baby. The round head was so tiny, the nose and lips perfectly shaped, the closed eyelids nearly translucent. "Oh, Rose. He's lovely."

"I can't stop touching his hair." Rose softly stroked the dark fluff. "I can't believe he's really here."

"Pearl wouldn't tell me his name."

"Henry Levi."

Tears burned in Mercy's eyes. Her brothers. One who had died at birth and another who had died the previous year. She couldn't speak.

"Would you like to hold him?" Rose lifted him away from her chest.

Mercy took the tiny bundle, amazed at how light he was. Dulce weighed more. "Is . . . is he healthy?"

"Yes. Even though he's a month early the doctor is pleased with his development. We shouldn't be in the hospital any longer than normal."

"I'm so sorry I wasn't here, Rose. I know I promised—"

Rose waved a hand, dismissing her words. "Besides Nick, five different people offered to take me to the hospital. Everything was fine. Dad said you were on a job without cell service."

That is true. "Yes."

"He sounded worried." Her tone was inquisitive.

Dad . . . worried about me? "Everything turned out fine. I'll tell you the whole story tomorrow." Mercy changed the subject. "How are you feeling?"

"Very floaty. I don't know if it's the medication or Henry." Her voice took on a dreamy tone. "Mercy . . . It's like . . . a brand-new piece of my heart suddenly woke up. A huge section brimming with energy and soul-deep love. I can't explain it."

Truman came beside her. "Nice job, Rose." He gently touched a tiny clenched fist and looked at Mercy with a passionate fierceness she felt to her bones. The tiny boy had stirred something inside him.

He held her gaze for a long moment, keeping her speechless, before turning to Nick.

"Congratulations, Nick." Truman shook the tall man's hand and slapped him on the shoulder.

"The wedding is next," Nick stated.

Rose laughed. "He wanted to get married tomorrow, but Mom and I insist on a real wedding."

Nick looked abashed. "I'm willing to wait two months. Deborah claims she and Pearl can pull a wedding together by then."

"I'll help," Mercy said, her gaze back on the tiny human in her arms.

"How about you two?" Nick asked. "You pick a date yet?"

She exchanged a glance with Truman. They'd purposefully not announced a date, wanting to know Rose and Nick's plans first. "We decided on December."

"Definitely," added Truman, meeting her eyes.

He's still looking at me as if I'm his dinner . . . or dessert.

She handed the baby back to Rose. Without him, her arms felt weightless. *How did such a small bundle do that?* "We'll be back tomorrow, Rose." She kissed the top of her sister's head and gave Nick a hug. His smile had stretched from ear to ear their entire visit.

She wasn't sure who was luckier. He or Rose.

Outside Rose's door, Mercy nearly sat on the floor as exhaustion slammed into her.

"Home?" asked Truman.

"Kaylie."

"A short visit. Then home. You can see Bree tomorrow."

"I plan on it."

The next day brought two surprises for Mercy.

First she received word that Bree was conscious and talking.

Surprise number two was in her office when she arrived later that morning. Eddie was there, his arm in a sling to keep his shoulder still. She hugged him and stepped back, studying him from head to toe. "You look good, Peterson."

"I feel pretty good . . . thanks to you."

"You'd do the same for me."

"Yeah, but I wouldn't have been as prepared as you. I'd have to stuff your wound with moss or leaves. I don't think the doctors would approve." He sat and pointed at the chair behind her desk. "Tell me what happened yesterday."

Mercy set her bag in a drawer and lowered herself into her chair. "I'm still processing it all."

Eddie was silent as she relayed the story of hunting for treasure and Art's suicide.

He sat quietly for several moments, staring out the window. "Do you believe Sandy didn't know about the money?"

"I do. Trevor told us Bree's real name is Leah Devries. A woman with that name and of the right age in Northern California went off the radar thirty years ago. No one reported her missing. No family to speak of."

"She built a new life," said Eddie. "A good one. According to all reports, she's an amazing teacher."

"Ironically that's what brought her down. Trevor saw the coverage of her teacher of the year award and came after her."

"But he walked away with his portion and Ellis's. Greedy son of a bitch."

"And blew it all somehow. He's very vague about it, but I suspect a gambling problem."

"How does someone spend a million dollars and have nothing to show for it?" Eddie shook his head in wonder, and then his eyes lit up as he leaned forward. "You remember Larry Tyler, the guy who told us that Victor Diehl flashed a stack of cash all those years ago?" Eddie was brimming with excitement.

"Of course. I still need—"

"I went to Larry's house this morning while you were lazily sleeping in."

Mercy stopped. "You did?" She'd planned to visit him.

"I've been wondering who told Victor Diehl that the FBI was coming for his guns and land. Since Larry was the one who pointed us in Diehl's direction, I decided to start there. It took a while, but he finally admitted that he was paid five hundred dollars to tell a story to the FBI."

"Who paid him?" Mercy whispered. *I think I know.*

"Trevor. I showed Larry pictures of Art and Trevor, and he positively identified Trevor."

"I assume Trevor then called Victor to convince him he was about to be raided. He must have known how unstable Victor was. Trevor wanted us to walk into an ambush." Images of that violent day exploded in her head, and she shuddered. "We could have all been killed . . . even Art. Trevor was trying to derail the investigation."

"Larry is sitting in the county jail. He'll be charged."

"Good," answered Mercy. "One more detail to cross off my list. Thank you."

"We're still missing the fourth thief," Eddie pointed out.

"Nathan May." Mercy sighed, tapping her fingers. "I have some thoughts on that, but I want to hear what Bree has to say about him first."

Eddie stood up. "Let's go talk to her."

◆ ◆ ◆

It was hard not to stare at Bree's face.

Three days had passed since the attack, and she seemed puffier and more bruised than before. One eye was still swollen shut. Mercy asked Lucas and Sandy to leave while she and Eddie talked to Bree. She had total recall of her attack.

"Trevor walked right in my house." Bree inhaled deeply. "I didn't recognize him at first. He pulled a gun on me and then tied me to the chair." A shudder racked her body. "He was the one leaving me notes, threatening to harm Lucas if I didn't give him money. When the first note was left on my windshield, I spent the next two days at home, cowering in a ball in bed. *I knew* it had to be from either Trevor or Nathan May." She looked at Mercy with her one good eye. "But I didn't have any money. All I could think about was that Lucas would be attacked next because the money was gone."

"The money is gone?" Eddie asked.

Bree nodded. "Nathan and I each got a half million. It's trickled away year after year while maintaining the ranch. Facilities and health care for horses isn't cheap. When I realized Shane would never get out, I gave some of it to charities. Mostly kids' charities . . . some to the school district." She gave Eddie and Mercy a pleading look. "It was dirty money. I understood that, so I tried to do something good with it. When I gave Sandy some for her B&B, it was nearly gone." Bree shifted in her bed, moving her heavily bandaged hand to her stomach. "Trevor, Nathan, Ellis, and I spent a few days in that cabin, waiting for things to cool down. We didn't know what had happened to Shane after we left him behind. We knew he'd been shot but didn't know if he was dead or just injured."

Mercy listened in fascination. This woman had been part of one of the most notorious heists in modern history. And patiently tutored Ollie twice a week.

Who would have guessed?

"There was no radio reception at the cabin," Bree continued, "and as we waited, everyone's paranoia grew. At first we were amazed that we'd succeeded, but the possibility that Shane had died was a black cloud over us; the robbery was his master plan."

"You were dating him?" Mercy asked.

"Yes. For two weeks."

"And he convinced you to rob an armored truck?" Eddie was flabbergasted.

Even through her swelling and bruises, Mercy could see Bree's embarrassment. "I was only eighteen. He was very convincing. He has this way of talking . . ."

The interviews with Shane Gamble spun through Mercy's head. *I can see it. Especially on a young, impressionable teenager.*

"I had nothing," Bree said quietly. "My family had split up. No one cared if I lived or died. Shane cared and painted an amazing future for the two of us."

"You'd been dating two weeks." Eddie still couldn't wrap his head around the concept.

"Believe me, I know how ridiculous it sounds. But when you first fall for someone . . ." Bree's words slowed. "There's this high . . . Everything is shiny and new. And anything feels possible."

Eddie didn't look convinced.

"Shane protected you," Mercy said. "He told the investigators you were male. For decades, he stuck to the story."

Is that romantic or creepy?

Bree looked away from Mercy's gaze. "I know. He'd told me while we were dating that he'd take care of me until he died."

Creepy. Definitely creepy.

"Did you communicate with him?"

Pain flashed as Bree's cracked lips stretched into a grimace. "Yes. We'd made a promise that if we were separated after the robbery, we'd communicate through the personals in the *Midnight Voice*. Back then the magazine printed personal ads."

"Isn't that from a movie?" Eddie's forehead wrinkled.

"Yes. One of Madonna's."

"What did you tell each other through the ads?" Mercy asked, making a plan to find old issues. *An awkward way to communicate.*

Bree shrugged. "The usual. 'Love until death.' I said I'd wait for him, but when he was convicted of killing another inmate, I knew he'd never get out of prison until we both were old." She snorted. "I thought age fifty was over the hill back then." Her sigh filled the room. "I stopped responding and reading the ads after his conviction. It was one of the hardest things I ever did."

"What did you think when Tabitha Huff said she had a message for you?"

339

Her hand quivered as she gently touched a bruise on her cheek. "I was terrified. Even though her message said to be careful, and she wouldn't tell me who it was from, I assumed it was from Trevor. I was already getting notes from him. I thought he'd discovered how Shane and I used to communicate and sent her to scare me."

"But she talked to Sandy too," Mercy mentioned.

"That confused me. Sandy had nothing to do with the robbery or my past."

"Tabitha was investigating the robbery, and since both of you were targeted with graffiti, she thought that Sandy might be involved too." Mercy's heart ached at the sadness in Bree's single opened eye. "Tabitha figured out the driver was female. Shane must have accidentally implied it . . . although I find that hard to believe," Mercy said thoughtfully. "He doesn't say anything without a purpose."

Part of her first interview with Gamble rose in her mind. "When I first told him we'd found a body we believed was associated with the robbery, he was extremely tense and desperate for information. But after a minute he suddenly relaxed." Mercy thought hard, trying to remember the conversation. "I must have referred to the remains as 'he,' which told him the remains weren't yours. He was only concerned that you had died."

Bree didn't say anything.

"But instead you married, had a wonderful son, and helped hundreds of children." Mercy tipped her head the slightest bit as she held Bree's gaze. "You never felt the need to come forward?"

Bree visibly crumpled. "I was terrified, and the longer I waited, the deeper I dug my own hole. It's no excuse, but I was barely an adult. I didn't want to go to prison, and I worried the police would hound me about the other thieves. I knew nothing. I didn't have the guts to turn myself in." She coughed and flinched with pain. "I've lived with that guilt for nearly thirty years. I'd decide to confess and then chicken out.

340

Over and over. No one was supposed to die," she said earnestly, looking at both agents.

"What happened in the cabin when people started to get paranoid?" Mercy asked.

"Trevor and Ellis argued nonstop. Ellis wanted to leave; Trevor fought to stay, stating the entire United States was probably looking for us."

"And then?"

"We'd already divided the money into four portions. I got Shane's to hold until he got out of prison." She took a huge breath. "Ellis said he was leaving. He packed up his things . . . Trevor shot him and claimed Ellis's money. Terrified we were next, Nathan and I told Trevor he'd done the right thing by stopping Ellis." She looked at Mercy. "We snuck out that night."

"Trevor says you shot Ellis."

Bree's mouth dropped open. "He's lying. He and Ellis constantly fought."

"I thought they were best friends."

"Maybe before the robbery. Shane was the glue that held the four of them together. Without Shane, the dynamic changed. They turned on each other."

"Where's Nathan May?" Mercy asked softly.

Bree looked away. "I don't know. We split up once we got out. I never saw him again."

Oh, Bree. I'd hoped you'd be completely honest with me.

"Are you going to arrest me?" she asked, bringing her gaze back to Mercy.

"Yes."

Bree slumped in the hospital bed.

"But I believe the DA will make you a generous deal in exchange for testifying against Trevor for the murder of Ellis Mull. You've helped children for thirty years. I'm sure that will be taken into account."

"I understand."

Am I surprised this woman turned out to be an infamous bank robber? Mercy paused, searching her own feelings.

Surprised, yes. Angry or disgusted at her crime? Not so much.

She was a child conned into driving a car by a fast-talking man.

It's still a crime, and she is guilty.

Outside Bree's door, Eddie stopped Mercy, a serious look in his eyes. "Do you think she's telling the truth about Ellis Mull?"

"Yes."

"Do you need to talk to Shane Gamble again?"

Mercy thought. "I don't think so . . . He won't ever leave that prison. If the DA wants to talk to him, she's welcome to it."

"Do you think Bree will contact him?"

"I think she knows better. She's not eighteen anymore. She sees him for what he is." Mercy checked the time. "Truman is meeting me in a few minutes at Kaylie's room. Can you come with me? I need you to help me with something first. I have a hunch to follow up on."

"Sure. Let's go." Eddie started down the hall.

"Hey, Eddie."

He turned to look at her. He'd lost weight since he'd been shot, and his face was very thin. But he was still Eddie.

"I'm glad you're back." The words were too casual for how she really felt. Grateful. Very grateful.

He pushed his thick glasses up his nose in a familiar gesture that warmed her heart.

"Yeah. Me too."

Kaylie had visitors when Mercy and Eddie arrived. Cade sat on Kaylie's bed, gesturing animatedly while Kaylie hung on every word. Cade's father, Glenn, leaned against the wall, smiling at the two of them.

Mercy caught Glenn's eye and indicated that she wanted him to meet her in the hall. He stepped out of the room with her and Eddie.

"She looks good," the tall man told her. "I'm stunned at how fast she's recovered."

"That makes two of us." She liked Glenn. Cade was a hardworking, good kid because of Glenn's influence. "Think they'll last longer this time?"

Glenn snorted and grinned. "Why waste time thinking about it? They'll be off again next week . . . and then on again."

"Exactly." She studied his kind face, so reminiscent of his son's. "Say, Glenn . . . do you have a minute?" Out of the corner of her eye, she saw Eddie frown.

"You bet."

He followed her and Eddie down the hall. Eddie gave her a side-eye as they walked. She held his gaze.

I was right.

Eddie's eyebrows lowered in concentration, a gentle scowl on his face. When they reached a quiet alcove, Eddie took a long look at Glenn, and his face blanked.

I knew Eddie would see it.

As Mercy stood at Glenn's twelve o'clock position, Eddie subtly stepped to the four o'clock, ready if she needed him. *Always dependable.*

Glenn looked expectantly at her.

Mercy drew in a deep breath. "I know you're Nathan May."

Neither he nor Eddie flinched.

"I don't know what you're talking about."

She removed several folded-up pieces of paper from her bag and flipped through them until she found "Fat Nathan." She handed it to him. "This one has been driving me nuts. Several people said it looked familiar, and I realized this morning it looks like Cade. His face is similar to yours but much rounder." She dug out the old high school photo of a lean Nathan May. "In this photo, your hair is totally different and takes away the resemblance, but if I cover it . . ." She placed her hand over the hair. "It's a thin Cade."

Glenn stared at the picture for a long moment and then met her gaze. He was still expressionless. "That was a long time ago."

"Have you talked with Bree?"

"We've seen each other several times over the years. Neither of us ever said a word to the other. We both were living our own lives. Good lives with our families."

Mercy sighed.

No wonder Bree was reluctant to turn him in.

"What are you going to do?" he asked quietly.

"Who shot Ellis in that cabin?"

"Trevor," he said firmly. "Leah—Bree—and I were convinced we were next."

I believe him.

Mercy took the image from him and tucked all of them back in her bag. She met Eddie's gaze and nodded.

"Put your hands behind your back," Eddie said quietly, placing a hand on Glenn's upper arm. Glenn silently obeyed, but his face drooped, and his shoulders sagged. Mercy cuffed him as Eddie did a rapid one-handed search.

This situation isn't any easier for me than Bree's.

"I'll escort you outside," Eddie told him. "Then we're going to the county jail."

Glenn straightened and looked at Mercy. "Just tell Cade I had to leave, okay?" His tone was stoic as his eyes pleaded for her understanding. "Don't tell him about this. I'll tell him later . . . in my own way."

He's been expecting this moment for years. Poor Cade.

"I'll give him your message."

"Thank you for handling it this way." Glenn looked at Eddie. "I'm ready."

Mercy watched them walk away and disappear around a corner. Her heart was empty, her mind numb.

There's no winner in this case.

"Hey," said her favorite rumbly voice from behind her. Warm hands slid around her waist, and she melted back against Truman's chest. Her heart sped up, and her melancholy floated away. He turned her to face him and gave her a long kiss that made her toes curl. Their love was open and simple, easy and relaxed. A glaring contrast to the events of the last few days.

Everything is better when he's near.

He pulled back and looked into her eyes, his brows narrowing as he studied her face. "Is Kaylie okay?"

"Yes. Everything is going to be okay."

I know it will.

THIRTY-NINE

Ollie trudged through the grove of pines, keeping one eye on Shep, who stopped at every tree and sniffed.

He'd left a note for Truman early that morning stating that he was hiking and not to expect him back until dinner. Today's hike was in new territory for him, and it was the first time he'd been in the wilderness since Shep had found Ellis Mull's femur two weeks ago. He'd kept Shep close this trip, afraid the dog would wander off and return with another surprise.

The day was perfect to clear his head with a hike. Kaylie was out of the hospital and healing. Rose, Nick, and baby Henry were adjusting to life as a family.

I've never had so many people in my life.

He liked it. Although sometimes he needed silence and to be alone. Like today.

Bree was improving, but her future was uncertain. A court would make that decision.

Cade's family had pulled together. Their future was also in the hands of the court.

Ollie still struggled with the arrests in his community. That part he didn't like. But it wasn't for him to worry about.

The grove of pines opened up, and Ollie caught his breath at the endless vista. Shep darted to the edge of the cliff, and Ollie immediately called him back. Ollie took his time walking from the pines to the cliff's edge as he admired the giant horse head beside him. Tall, massive, eternal. Once he reached the rim, he ran his gaze from the north to the south. Ranch lands and fields as far as he could see. A few dark-green clumps of trees. One winding river.

He looked down, unable to estimate how high he towered over the trees and rocks at the foot of the sheer cliff. *Ten stories? Twenty?*

Art Juergen's body had been retrieved. No one would talk about it. Ollie didn't blame them.

He turned back to the horse. The ground was still choppy where Sandy and Mercy had dug, and it was too easy to picture the deadly standoff.

Truman and Mercy might not have survived.

But they had, and Ollie was thankful.

Counting my blessings today.

The rock horse watched him from its left eye. Ollie smiled and moved closer until he stood at the cheek and looked directly up at the rock that formed the eye. *Amazing.*

He turned and, with his back to the cheek, counted off twenty-two small steps in a straight line. When he stopped, he was on dirt. He slung off his backpack, pulled out a collapsible shovel, and began to dig. After fifteen minutes, he was sweating profusely, and his hole was only a foot deep. The small shovel was lame, and Shep was no help. At first the dog had nosed the hole with great interest, but now he lay in the shade a few yards away, panting and watching.

What if I'm wrong?

He thrust the shovel again and it clanked. Something black was in the ground. His pulse racing, Ollie dug, uncovering a rectangular shape.

Levering it out of the packed ground with his shovel, he realized it was wrapped in a black garbage bag. He peeled away the plastic, exposing a box decorated with snowmen and Christmas trees. The type of metal box used for holiday treats and gifts.

Ollie carried the box to Shep's shade under a pine and sat by his dog. "Look what I found, boy."

Shep sniffed the box and wagged his tail.

"Right?" said Ollie. "It's like a Christmas present."

He studied the box for another second, held his breath, and then pried off the lid.

Stacks of money in ziplock bags.

Ollie touched a bag, his heart pounding in his ears. "We've hit the jackpot, Shep."

He removed all the bags, unzipped one, and started to count.

It took many minutes. A little more than $100,000 had been hidden in the tin box.

Ollie put the money away, carefully sealing each bag and setting them all back in the tin.

He'd overheard Mercy talking to Truman about Bree's money. She had uncovered over $300,000 in donation receipts.

Shep put his head in Ollie's lap, his brown doggy eyes staring into Ollie's soul. "I know. We'll head home soon." Ollie scooted until his back was against a pine trunk and tucked his hands behind his head, gazing at one of the best views in the state and wondering how nature had created a horse's head in stone. It was an amazing location.

But bad shit went down here.

His mind wandered, remembering how Kaylie had collapsed in the parking lot, terror on her face. How he'd found Bree in her home, her severed fingers on the table beside her.

Money makes people do bad things.

He knew it and Bree knew it.

Does she remember she told me?

He'd been at her bedside five days ago when she'd opened her eyes from a sound sleep and met his gaze. "Left eye. Twenty-two steps. It's for Lucas. Save it for Lucas," she whispered. Her eyes fell shut, and she didn't open them again that evening. The words had rattled around in Ollie's head for days until he'd seen photos of where Art Juergen committed suicide. In one photo the horse's left eye stared directly at him.

I had to look. Otherwise I would have always wondered.

Ollie pushed to his feet and carried the box back to the hole. He set it down and scooped dirt onto its lid with his shovel. Moments later he stomped on the dirt, packing it solid. He ran a branch over the dry dirt and scattered pine needles about. The cursed treasure was hidden again.

Will I tell Lucas?

That's Bree's secret to share.

"Some secrets are better left buried," he told Shep.

The dog wagged his tail, and they started home.

Acknowledgments

Authors don't sit around waiting for their muse to show up and inspire them. We write. Even when our brains are completely blank (which happens a lot more than we let on), we sit down and force words through the keyboard. I know authors who wrote through family deaths, divorce, and illness. To get through the tough times, we surround ourselves with other writers who understand how isolated our chosen profession can be. We encourage each other during the dry spells, celebrate the amazing times, and joke our way through the numerous mundane and tedious days. This book was written during a dark time for me, and I wouldn't have succeeded without my tribe. Melinda, Toni, Amy, Selena, and Leanne always step up when I need a push. The amazing people at Montlake—Anh, Colleen, Jessica, Galen, and Gabby—go out of their way to support my work. My agent, Meg Ruley, is my enthusiastic head cheerleader and creates amazing opportunities for me. Of course, Charlotte Herscher is the person I rely on to kindly tell me when changes need to be made in my books. I can never see the forest for all the fat trees in my way.

To my readers, thank you for enjoying my Mercy books and returning for more. Your kind letters and messages make my day.

About the Author

Photo © 2016 Rebekah Jule Photography

Kendra Elliot has landed on the *Wall Street Journal* bestseller list multiple times and is the award-winning author of the Bone Secrets and Callahan & McLane series as well as the Mercy Kilpatrick novels: *A Merciful Death*, *A Merciful Truth*, *A Merciful Secret*, *A Merciful Silence*, and *A Merciful Fate*. Kendra is a three-time winner of the Daphne du Maurier Award, an International Thriller Writers finalist, and an RT Award finalist. She has always been a voracious reader, cutting her teeth on classic female heroines such as Nancy Drew, Trixie Belden, and Laura Ingalls. She was born and raised, and still lives, in the rainy Pacific Northwest with her family, but she looks forward to the day she can live in flip-flops. Visit her at www.kendraelliot.com.